Bernard Cornwell was born in London and raised in Essex, and now mainly lives in the USA, with his wife.

www.bernardcornwell.net

Also by Bernard Cornwell

The SHARPE series

The Grail Quest

HARLEQUIN
VAGABOND

STONEHENGE

The STARBUCK Chronicles

REBEL
COPPERHEAD
BATTLEFLAG
THE BLOODY GROUND

The WARLORD Chronicles

THE WINTER KING
THE ENEMY OF GOD
EXCALIBUR

GALLOWS THIEF

BERNARD CORNWELL

HarperCollins*Publishers*

HarperCollins*Publishers*
77–85 Fulham Palace Road,
Hammersmith, London W6 8JB

www.**fire**and**water**.com

This paperback edition 2002

9 8

First published in Great Britain by
HarperCollins*Publishers* 2001

This novel is entirely a work of fiction. The names,
characters and incidents portrayed in it are the work
of the author's imagination. Any resemblance to actual
persons, living or dead, events or localities
is entirely coincidental.

A catalogue record for this book
is available from the British Library

ISBN 0 00 712716 2

Set in PostScript Linotype Meridien with
Photina and Castellar display by
Rowland Phototypesetting Limited,
Bury St Edmunds, Suffolk

Printed and bound in Great Britain by
Clays Ltd, St Ives plc

For Antonia and Jef

GALLOWS
THIEF

Prologue

Sir Henry Forrest, banker and alderman of the City of London, almost gagged when he entered the Press Yard for the smell was terrible, worse than the reek of the sewer outflows where the Fleet Ditch oozed into the Thames. It was a stink from the cesspits of hell, an eye-watering stench that took a man's breath away and made Sir Henry take an involuntary step backwards, clap a handkerchief to his nose and hold his breath for fear that he was about to vomit.

Sir Henry's guide chuckled. 'I don't notice the smell no more, sir,' he said, 'but I suppose it's mortal bad in its way, mortal bad. Mind the steps here, sir, do mind 'em.'

Sir Henry gingerly took the handkerchief away and forced himself to speak. 'Why is it called the Press Yard?'

'In days gone by, sir, this is where the prisoners was pressed. They was squashed, sir. Weighed down by stones, sir, to persuade them to tell the truth. We don't do it any longer, sir, more's the pity, and as a consequence they lies like India rugs, sir, like India rugs.' The guide, one of the prison's turnkeys, was a fat man with

1

leather breeches, a stained coat, and a stout billy club. He laughed. 'There ain't a guilty man or woman in here, sir, not if you asks them!'

Sir Henry tried to keep his breathing shallow so he would not have to inhale the noxious miasma of ordure, sweat and rot. 'There is sanitation here?' he asked.

'Very up to date, Sir Henry, very up to date. Proper drains in Newgate, sir. We spoils them, we do, but they're filthy animals, sir, filthy. They fouls their own nest, sir, that's what they do, they fouls their own nest.' The turnkey closed and bolted the barred gate by which they had entered the yard. 'The condemned have the freedom of the Press Yard, sir, during daylight,' he said, 'except on high days and holidays like today.' He grinned, letting Sir Henry know that this was a jest. 'They has to wait till we're done, sir, and if you turn to your left you can join Mister Brown and the other gentlemen in the Association Room.'

'The Association Room?' Sir Henry enquired.

'Where the condemned associate, sir, during the daylight hours, sir,' the turnkey explained, 'except on high days and holidays like this one is today, sir, and those windows to your left, sir, those are the salt boxes.'

Sir Henry saw at the end of the yard, which was very narrow and long, fifteen barred windows. The windows were small, dark-shadowed and on three floors, and the cells behind those windows were called the salt boxes. He had no idea why they were called that and he did not like to ask in case he encouraged more of the turn-key's coarse humour, but Sir Henry knew that the fifteen salt boxes were also known as the devil's waiting rooms and the antechambers of hell. They were Newgate's condemned cells. A doomed man, his eyes a mere glitter behind the thick bars, stared back at Sir Henry who turned away as the turnkey hauled open the heavy door of the Association Room. 'Obliged to you, Sir Henry, obliged, I'm sure,' the turnkey knuckled his forehead as Sir Henry offered him a shilling in thanks for his guidance through the prison's labyrinthine passages.

Sir Henry stepped into the Association Room where he was greeted by the Keeper, William Brown, a lugubrious man with a bald head and heavy jowls. A stout priest wearing an old-fashioned wig, a cassock, stained surplice and Geneva bands stood smiling unctuously beside the Keeper. 'Pray allow me to name the Ordinary,' the Keeper said, 'the Reverend Doctor Horace Cotton. Sir Henry Forrest.'

Sir Henry took off his hat. 'Your servant, Doctor Cotton.'

'At your service, Sir Henry,' Doctor Cotton responded fulsomely, after offering Sir Henry a deep bow. The Ordinary's old-fashioned wig was three plump billows of white fleece that framed his whey-coloured face. There was a weeping boil on his left cheek while, as a specific against the prison's smell, a nosegay was tied around his neck, just above the Geneva bands.

'Sir Henry,' the Keeper confided to the prison chaplain, 'is here on official duty.'

'Ah!' Doctor Cotton's eyes opened wide, suggesting Sir Henry was in for a rare treat. 'And is this your first such visit?'

3

'My first,' Sir Henry admitted.

'I am persuaded you will find it edifying, Sir Henry,' the priest said.

'Edifying!' The choice of word struck Sir Henry as inappropriate.

'Souls have been won for Christ by this experience,' Doctor Cotton said sternly, 'won for Christ, indeed!' He smiled, then bowed obsequiously as the Keeper ushered Sir Henry away to meet the other six guests who had come for the traditional Newgate breakfast. The last of the guests was called Matthew Logan and he needed no introduction, for he and Sir Henry were old friends and, because both were city aldermen, they were considered very distinguished visitors this morning for the Court of Aldermen were the official governors of Newgate Prison. The Keeper and the Ordinary, whose salaries were fixed by the aldermen, pressed coffee on the two men, but both declined and Logan took Sir Henry's arm and led him to the hearth where they could talk privately beside the smouldering embers and smoking ashes.

'You're sure you want to see this through?' Logan asked his friend solicitously. 'You look damned pale.'

Sir Henry was a good-looking man, lean, tall and straight-backed with a clever and fastidious face. He was a banker, rich and successful. His hair, prematurely silver for he was only a few days past his fiftieth birthday, gave him a distinguished appearance, yet at that moment, standing in front of the prisoners' fireplace in the Association Room, he looked old, frail, emaciated and sickly. 'It's the early morning, Logan,' he explained,

4

'and I'm never at my shining best this close to dawn.'

'Quite,' Logan said, pretending to believe his friend's explanation, 'but this ain't an experience for everyone, though I must say the breakfast afterwards is very good. Devilled kidneys. This is probably my tenth or eleventh visit, and the breakfast has yet to disappoint me. How is Lady Forrest?'

'Florence keeps well, thank you for asking.'

'And your daughter?'

'Eleanor will doubtless survive her troubles,' Sir Henry said drily. 'A broken heart has yet to prove fatal.'

'Except in poets?'

'Damn poets, Logan,' Sir Henry said with a smile. He held his hands towards the remnants of the fire that was waiting to be blown back into life. The prisoners had left their cooking pots and cauldrons stacked about its edges and a pile of blackened potato peelings was curled in the ashes. 'Poor Eleanor,' Sir Henry said, 'if it was up to me, Logan, I'd let her marry, but Florence won't hear of it and I suppose she's right.'

'Mothers usually know best about such things,' Logan said airily, and then the room's low murmur of conversation died as the guests turned towards a barred door that had opened with a sudden and harsh squeal. For a heartbeat no one appeared in the doorway and it seemed all the guests held their breath, but then, to an audible gasp, a man carrying a stout leather bag stumped into sight. There was nothing about his appearance to explain the gasp. He was burly, red-faced and dressed in brown gaiters, black breeches and a black coat that was buttoned too tightly over his protuberant

5

belly. He respectfully pulled off a shabby brown hat when he saw the waiting gentry, but he offered no greeting and no one in the Association Room acknowledged his arrival.

'That,' Logan told Sir Henry under his breath, 'is Mister James Botting, more familiarly known as Jemmy.'

'The petitioner?' Sir Henry asked softly.

'The very same.'

Sir Henry suppressed a shudder and reminded himself that men should not be judged by their outward appearance, though it was hard not to disapprove of a being as ugly as James Botting, whose raw-beef slab of a face was disfigured by warts, wens and scars. His bald pate was surrounded by a fringe of lank brown hair that fell over his frayed collar and, when he grimaced, which he did every few seconds in a nervous habit, he displayed yellow teeth and shrunken gums. He had big hands which heaved a bench away from a table onto which he slung his leather bag. He unbuckled the bag and, conscious of being watched by the silent visitors, brought out eight coils of thin white cord. He placed the coils on the table where he fussily arranged them so that they were in a neat row and equidistant from each other. Next, and with the air of a conjuror, he took out four white cotton sacks, each about a foot square, that he placed by the coiled lines and last of all, after glancing up to make sure he was still being observed, he produced four heavy ropes made of three-stranded hemp. Each rope looked to be about ten or twelve feet long and each had a noose tied into one

6

end and an eye spliced in the other. James Botting laid the ropes on the table and then stepped back. 'Good morning, gentlemen,' he said smartly.

'Oh, Botting!' William Brown, the Keeper, spoke in a tone which suggested he had only just noticed Botting's presence. 'A very good morning to you.'

'And a nice one it is too, sir,' Botting said. 'I feared it might rain, there was such a pain in my elbow joints, but there ain't a cloud in sight, sir. Still just the four customers today, sir?'

'Just the four, Botting.'

'They've drawn a good crowd, sir, they have, a very good crowd.'

'Good, very good,' the Keeper said vaguely, then returned to his conversation with one of the breakfast guests. Sir Henry looked back to his friend Logan. 'Does Botting know why we're here?'

'I do hope not.' Logan, a banker like Sir Henry, grimaced. 'He might botch things if he did.'

'Botch things?'

'How better to prove he needs an assistant?' Logan suggested with a smile.

'Remind me what we pay him.'

'Ten shillings and sixpence a week, but there are emoluments. The hand of glory for one, and also the clothes and the ropes.'

'Emoluments?' Sir Henry was puzzled.

Logan smiled. 'We watch the proceedings up to a point, Sir Henry, but then we retire for devilled kidneys and as soon as we're gone Mister Botting will invite folk onto the scaffold for a touch of the dead man's hand. It's supposed to cure warts and I believe he charges one shilling and sixpence for each treatment. And as for the prisoners' clothes and the killing ropes? He sells the clothes to Madame Tussaud if she wants them, and if not then the clothes are sold as keepsakes and the rope is cut into fragments that are usually hawked about the streets. Believe me, Mister Botting does not suffer from penury. I've often thought we ought to offer the job of hangman to the highest bidder instead of paying the wretch a salary.'

Sir Henry turned to look at Botting's ravaged face. 'The hand of glory doesn't seem to work on the hangman though, does it?'

'Not a pretty sight, is he?' Logan agreed with a smile, then he held up his hand. 'Hear it?'

Sir Henry could hear a clanking sound. The room had fallen silent again and he felt a kind of chill dread. He also despised himself for the prurience that had persuaded him to come to this breakfast, then he shuddered as the door from the Press Yard opened.

Another turnkey came into the room. He knuckled his forehead to the Keeper, then stood beside a low slab of timber that squatted on the floor. The turnkey held a stout hammer and Sir Henry wondered what its purpose was, but he did not like to ask, and then the guests closest to the door hauled off their hats because the Sheriff and Under-Sheriff had appeared in the doorway and were ushering the prisoners into the Association Room. There were four of them, three men and a young woman. The latter was scarce more than a girl and had a pinched, pale and frightened face.

'Brandy, sir?' One of the Keeper's servants appeared beside Matthew Logan and Sir Henry.

'Thank you,' Logan said, and took two of the beakers. He handed one to Sir Henry. 'It's bad brandy,' he said under his breath, 'but a good precaution. Settles the stomach, eh?'

The prison bell suddenly began to toll. The girl twitched at the sound, then the turnkey with the hammer ordered her to put a foot onto the wooden anvil so her leg irons could be struck off. Sir Henry, who had long ceased to notice the prison's stench, sipped the brandy and feared it would not stay down. His head felt light, unreal. The turnkey hammered the rivets from the first manacle and Sir Henry saw that the girl's ankle was a welt of sores.

'Other foot, girl,' the turnkey said.

The bell tolled on and it would not stop now until all four bodies were cut down. Sir Henry was aware that his hand was shaking. 'I hear corn was fetching sixty-three shillings a quarter in Norwich last week,' he said, his voice too loud.

Logan was gazing at the quivering girl. 'She stole her mistress's necklace.'

'She did?'

'Pearls. She must have sold it, for the necklace was never found. Then the tall fellow next in line is a highwayman. Pity he isn't Hood, eh? Still, we'll see Hood swing one day. The other two murdered a grocer in Southwark. Sixty-three a quarter, eh? It's a wonder anyone can eat.'

The girl, moving awkwardly because she was

9

unaccustomed to walking without leg irons, shuffled away from the makeshift anvil. She began crying and Sir Henry turned his back on her. 'Devilled kidneys, you say?'

'The Keeper always serves devilled kidneys on hanging days,' Logan said, 'it's a tradition.'

The hammer struck at the highwayman's leg irons, the bell tolled and James Botting snapped at the girl to come to him. 'Stand still, girl,' he said, 'drink that if you want it. Drink it all.' He pointed to a beaker of brandy that had been placed on the table next to the neatly coiled ropes. The girl spilt some because her hands were shaking, but she gulped the rest down and then dropped the tin mug, which clattered on the flagstones. She began to apologise for her clumsiness, but Botting interrupted her. 'Arms by your side, girl,' he ordered her, 'arms by your side.'

'I didn't steal anything!' she wailed.

'Quiet, my child, quiet.' The Reverend Cotton had moved to her side and put a hand on her shoulder. 'God is our refuge and strength, child, and you must put your faith in him.' He kneaded her shoulder. She was wearing a pale-blue cotton dress with a drooping neckline and the priest's fingers pressed and caressed her exposed white flesh. 'The Lord is a very present help in times of trouble,' the Ordinary said, his fingers leaving pinkish marks on her white skin, 'and he will be thy comfort and guide. Do you repent your foul sins, child?'

'I stole nothing!'

Sir Henry forced himself to draw long breaths. 'Did

you escape those Brazilian loans?' he asked Logan.

'Sold them on to Drummonds,' Logan said, 'so I'm damned grateful to you, Henry, damned grateful.'

'It's Eleanor you must thank,' Sir Henry said. 'She saw a report in a Paris newspaper and drew the right conclusions. Clever girl, my daughter.'

'Such a pity about the engagement,' Logan said. He was watching the doomed girl who cried aloud as Botting pinioned her elbows with a length of cord. He fastened them behind her back, drawing the line so tight that she gasped with pain. Botting grinned at her cry, then yanked the cord even tighter, forcing the girl to throw her breasts forward so that they strained against the thin material of her cheap dress. The Reverend Cotton leant close so that his breath was warm on her face. 'You must repent, child, you must repent.'

'I didn't do it!' Her breath was coming in gasps and tears were streaming down her distorted face.

'Hands in front, girl!' Botting snapped and, when she awkwardly lifted her hands, he seized one wrist, encircling it with a second length of cord which he then looped about her other wrist. Her elbows were secured behind her body, her wrists in front, and because Botting had pulled her elbows so tightly together he could not join her wrists with the cord, but had to be content with linking them.

'You're hurting me,' she wailed.

'Botting?' the Keeper intervened.

'Shouldn't be my job to do the pinioning,' Botting snarled, but he loosened some of the tension from the cord holding her elbows and the girl nodded in pathetic thanks.

'She'd be a pretty thing,' Logan said, 'if she was cleaned up.'

Sir Henry was counting the pots in the hearth. Everything seemed unreal. God help me, he thought, God help me.

'Jemmy!' The highwayman, his leg irons struck off, greeted the hangman with a sneer.

'Come here, lad,' Botting ignored the familiarity. 'Drink that. Then put your arms by your side.'

The highwayman put a coin on the table beside the brandy beaker. 'For you, Jemmy.'

'Good lad,' the hangman said quietly. The coin would ensure that the highwayman's arms would not be pinioned too tightly, and that his death would be as swift as Botting could make it.

'Eleanor tells me she's recovered from the engagement,' Sir Henry said, his back still to the prisoners, 'but I don't believe her. She's very unhappy. I can tell. Mind you, I sometimes wonder if she's being perverse.'

'Perverse?'

'It occurs to me, Logan, that her attraction to Sandman has only increased since the engagement was broken.'

'He was a very decent young man,' Logan said.

'He is a very decent young man,' Sir Henry agreed.

'But scrupulous,' Logan said, 'to a fault.'

'To a fault indeed,' Sir Henry said. He was staring down at the floor now, trying to ignore the girl's soft sobbing. 'Young Sandman is a good man, a very good

12

man, but quite without prospects now. Utterly without prospects! And Eleanor cannot marry into a disgraced family.'

'Indeed she cannot,' Logan agreed.

'She says she can, but then, Eleanor would,' Sir Henry said, then shook his head. 'And none of it is Rider Sandman's fault, but he's penniless now. Quite penniless.'

Logan frowned. 'He's on half-pay, surely?'

Sir Henry shook his head. 'He sold his commission, gave the money towards the keep of his mother and sister.'

'He keeps his mother? That dreadful woman? Poor Sandman.' Logan laughed softly. 'But Eleanor, surely, is not without suitors?'

'Far from it,' Sir Henry sounded gloomy. 'They queue up in the street, Logan, but Eleanor finds fault.'

'She's good at that,' Logan said softly, though without malice for he was fond of his friend's daughter, though he thought her over-indulged. It was true that Eleanor was clever and too well read, but that was no reason to spare her the bridle, whip and spur. 'Still,' he said, 'doubtless she'll marry soon?'

'Doubtless she will,' Sir Henry said drily, for his daughter was not only attractive but it was also well known that Sir Henry would settle a generous income on her future husband. Which was why Sir Henry was sometimes tempted to let her marry Rider Sandman, but her mother would not hear of it. Florence wanted Eleanor to have a title, and Rider Sandman had none and now he had no fortune either, and so the marriage

13

between Captain Sandman and Miss Forrest would not now take place – Sir Henry's thoughts about his daughters prospects were driven away by a shriek from the doomed girl, a wailing shriek so pitiful that Sir Henry turned in shocked enquiry to see that James Botting had hung one of the heavy noosed ropes about her shoulders and the girl was shrinking from its touch as though the Bridport hemp was soaked in acid.

'Quiet, my dear,' the Reverend Cotton said, then he opened his prayer book and took a step back from the four prisoners who were all now pinioned.

'This was never the hangman's job,' James Botting complained before the Ordinary could begin reading the service for the burial of the dead. 'The irons was struck and the pinioning was done in the yard – in the yard – by the Yeoman of the Halter! By the Yeoman of the Halter. It was never the hangman's job to do the pinioning!'

'He means it was done by his assistant,' Logan muttered.

'So he does know why we're here?' Sir Henry commented as the Sheriff and Under-Sheriff, both in floor-length robes and wearing chains of office and both carrying silver-tipped staves, and both evidently satisfied that the prisoners were properly prepared, went to the Keeper who formally bowed to them before presenting the Sheriff with a sheet of paper.

'"I am the resurrection and the life,"' the Reverend Cotton intoned in a loud voice, '"he that believeth in me, though he were dead, yet shall he live."'

The Sheriff glanced at the paper, nodded in satisfaction and thrust it into a pocket of his fur-trimmed robe. Until now the four prisoners had been in the care of the Keeper of Newgate, but now they belonged to the Sheriff of the City of London who, formalities over, crossed to Sir Henry with an outstretched hand and a welcoming smile. 'You've come for the breakfast, Sir Henry?'

'I've come as a matter of duty,' Sir Henry said sternly, 'but it's very good to see you, Rothwell.'

'You must certainly stay for the breakfast,' the Sheriff said, as the Ordinary recited the prayers for the burial of the dead. 'They're very good devilled kidneys.'

'I could get a good breakfast at home,' Sir Henry said. 'No, I came because Botting has petitioned for an assistant and we thought, before justifying the expenditure, that we should judge for ourselves whether or not one was needed. You know Mister Logan?'

'The alderman and I are old acquaintances,' the Sheriff said, shaking Logan's hand. 'The advantage of giving the man an assistant,' he added to Sir Henry in a low voice, 'is that his replacement is already trained. And if there is trouble on the scaffold, well, two men are better than one. It's good to see you, Sir Henry, and you, Mister Logan.' He composed his face and turned to Botting. 'Are you ready, Botting?'

'Quite ready, sir, quite ready,' Botting said, scooping up the four white bags and thrusting them into a pocket.

'We can talk at breakfast,' the Sheriff said to Sir Henry. 'Devilled kidneys! I smelt them cooking as I came through.' He hauled a turnip watch from a fob pocket and clicked open its lid. 'Time to go, I think, time to go.'

The Sheriff led the procession out of the Association Room and across the narrow Press Yard. The Reverend Cotton had a hand on the girl's neck, guiding her as he read the burial service aloud, the same service that he had intoned to the condemned prisoners in the chapel the day before. The four prisoners had been in the famous Black Pew, grouped about the coffin on the table, and the Ordinary had read them their burial service and then preached that they were being punished for their sin as God had decreed men and women should be punished. He had described the waiting flames of hell, told them of the devilish torments that were even then being prepared for them, and he had reduced the girl and one of the two murderers to tears. The chapel's gallery had been filled with folk who had paid one shilling and sixpence apiece to witness the four doomed souls at their last church service.

The prisoners in the cells overlooking the Press Yard shouted protests and farewells as the procession passed. Sir Henry was alarmed by the noise and surprised to hear a woman's voice calling insults. 'Surely men and women don't share the cells?' he asked.

'Not any longer,' Logan said, then saw where his friend was looking, 'and I assume she's no prisoner, but a lady of the night, Sir Henry. They pay what's called "bad money" to the turnkeys so they can come and earn their living here.'

'Bad money? Good Lord!' Sir Henry looked pained. 'And we allow that?'

16

'We ignore it,' Logan said quietly, 'on the understanding that it's better to have whores in the prison
than prisoners rioting.' The Sheriff had led the procession down a flight of stone stairs into a tunnel that
ran beneath the main prison to emerge at the Lodge,
and the gloomy passage passed an empty cell with an
open door. 'That's where they spent their last night,'
Logan pointed into the cell. The doomed girl was swaying and a turnkey took her elbow and hurried her along.

' "We brought nothing into this world," ' the Reverend Cotton's voice echoed from the tunnel's damp granite walls, ' "and it is certain we can carry nothing out.
The Lord gave, and the Lord hath taken away, blessed
be the Name of the Lord." '

'I didn't steal anything!' the girl suddenly screamed.

'Quiet, lass, quiet,' the Keeper growled. All the men
were nervous. They wanted the prisoners to cooperate
and the girl was very close to hysteria.

' "Lord, let me know mine end," ' the Ordinary
prayed, ' "and the number of my days." '

'Please!' the girl wailed. 'No, no! Please.' A second
turnkey closed on her in case she collapsed and had to
be carried the rest of the way, but she stumbled on.

'If they struggle too much,' Logan told Sir Henry,
'then they're tied to a chair and hung that way, but I
confess I haven't seen that happen in many many years,
though I do remember that Langley had to do it once.'

'Langley?'

'Botting's predecessor.'

'You've seen a number of these things?' Sir Henry
asked.

17

'A good few,' Logan admitted. 'And you?'

'Never. I just conceived today as a duty.' Sir Henry watched the prisoners climb the steps at the end of the tunnel and wished he had not come. He had never seen a violent death. Rider Sandman, who was to have been his son-in-law, had seen much violent death because he had been a soldier and Sir Henry rather wished the younger man was here. He had always liked Sandman. Such a shame about his family.

At the top of the stairs was the Lodge, a cavernous entrance chamber that gave access to the street called the Old Bailey. The door that led to the street was the Debtor's Door and it stood open, but no daylight showed for the scaffold had been built directly outside. The noise of the crowd was loud now and the prison bell was muffled, but the bell of Saint Sepulchre's on the far side of Newgate Street was also tolling for the imminent deaths.

'Gentlemen?' The Sheriff, who was now in charge of the morning's proceedings, turned to the breakfast guests. 'If you'll climb the steps to the scaffold, gentlemen, you'll find chairs to right and left. Just leave two at the front for us, if you'd be so kind?'

Sir Henry, as he passed through the towering arch of the high Debtor's Door, saw in front of him the dark hollow underside of the scaffold and he thought how it was like being behind and underneath a stage supported by raw wooden beams. Black baize shrouded the planks at the front and side of the stage which meant that the only light came from the chinks between the timbers that formed the scaffold's elevated platform.

18

Wooden stairs climbed to Sir Henry's right, going up into the shadows before turning sharply left to emerge in a roofed pavilion that stood at the scaffold's rear. The stairs and the platform all looked very substantial and it was hard to remember that the scaffold was only erected the day before an execution and dismantled immediately after. The roofed pavilion was there to keep the honoured guests dry in inclement weather, but today the morning sun shone on Old Bailey and was bright enough to make Sir Henry blink as he turned the corner of the stairs and emerged into the pavilion.

A huge cheer greeted the guests' arrival. No one cared who they were, but their appearance presaged the coming of the prisoners. Old Bailey was crowded. Every window that overlooked the street was crammed and there were even folk on the rooftops.

'Ten shillings,' Logan said.

'Ten shillings?' Sir Henry was bemused again.

'To rent a window,' Logan explained, 'unless it's a celebrated crime being punished in which case the price goes up to two or even three guineas.' He pointed at a tavern that stood directly opposite the scaffold. 'The Magpie and Stump has the most expensive windows because you can see right down into the pit where they drop.' He chuckled. 'You can rent a telescope from the landlord and watch 'em die. But we, of course, get the best view.'

Sir Henry wanted to sit in the shadows at the back of the pavilion, but Logan had already taken one of the front chairs and Sir Henry just sat. His head was ringing with the terrible noise that came from the street. It was, he decided, just like being on a theatre's stage. He was overwhelmed and dazzled. So many people! Everywhere faces looking up at the black-draped platform. The scaffold proper, in front of the roofed pavilion, was thirty feet long and fifteen feet wide and topped by a great beam that ran from the pavilion's roof to the platform's end. Black iron butcher's hooks were screwed into the beam's underside and a ladder was propped against it.

A second ironic cheer greeted the sheriffs in their fur-trimmed robes. Sir Henry was sitting on a hard wooden chair that was slightly too small and desperately uncomfortable. 'It'll be the girl first,' Logan said.

'Why?'

'She's the one they've come to see,' Logan said. He was evidently enjoying himself and Sir Henry was surprised by that. How little we know our friends, he thought, then he again wished that Rider Sandman was here because he suspected that the soldier would not approve of death made this easy. Or had Sandman been hardened to violence?

'I should let him marry her,' he said.

'What?' Logan had to raise his voice because the crowd was shouting for the prisoners to be brought on.

'Nothing,' Sir Henry said.

'"I will keep my mouth as it were with a bridle,"' the Reverend Cotton's voice grew louder as he climbed the stairs behind the girl, '"while the ungodly is in my sight."'

A turnkey came first, then the girl, and she was awkward on the steps because her legs were still not used to being without irons and the turnkey had to steady her when she half tripped on the top step.

Then the crowd saw her. 'Hats off! Hats off!' The shout began at the front and echoed back. It was not respect that caused the cry, but rather because the taller hats of the folk in front obscured the view for those behind. The roar of the crowd was massive, crushing, and then the people surged forward so that the City Marshal and his men who protected the scaffold raised their staves and spears. Sir Henry felt besieged by noise and by the thousands of people with open mouths, shouting. There were as many women as men in the crowd. Sir Henry saw a respectable-looking matron stooping to a telescope in one of the windows of the Magpie and Stump. Beside her a man was eating bread and fried egg. Another woman had opera glasses. A pie-seller had set up his wares in a doorway. Pigeons, red kites and sparrows circled the sky in panic because of the noise. Sir Henry, his mind swimming, suddenly noticed the four open coffins that lay on the scaffold's edge. They were made of rough pine and were unplaned and resinous. The girl's mouth was open and her face, which had been pale, was now red and distorted. Tears ran down her cheeks as Botting took her by a pinioned elbow and led her onto the planks at the platform's centre. That centre was a trapdoor and it creaked under their weight. The girl was shaking and gasping as Botting positioned her under the beam at the platform's far end. Once she was in place Botting took a cotton bag from his pocket and pulled it over her hair so that it looked like a hat. She screamed at his touch and tried

21

to twist away from him, but the Reverend Cotton put a hand on her arm as the hangman took the rope from her shoulders and clambered up the ladder. He was heavy and the rungs creaked alarmingly. He slotted the small spliced eye over one of the big black butcher's hooks, then climbed awkwardly back down, red-faced and breathing hard. 'I need an assistant, don't I?' he grumbled. 'Ain't fair. Man always has an assistant. Don't fidget, missy! Go like a Christian!' He looked the girl in the eyes as he pulled the noose down around her head. He tightened the slip knot under her left ear, then gave the rope a small jerk as if to satisfy himself that it would take her weight. She gasped at the jerk, then screamed because Botting had his hands on her hair. 'Keep still, girl!' he snarled, then pulled down the white cotton bag so that it covered her face.

She screamed. 'I want to see!'

Sir Henry closed his eyes.

' "For a thousand years in thy sight are but as yester-day." ' The Ordinary had raised his voice so he could be heard above the crowd's seething din. The second prisoner, the highwayman, was on the scaffold now and Botting stood him beside the girl, crammed the bag on his head and climbed the ladder to fix the rope. ' "O teach us to number our days," ' the Reverend Cotton read in a singsong voice, ' "that we may apply our hearts unto wisdom." '

'Amen,' Sir Henry said fervently, too fervently.

'Here,' Logan nudged Sir Henry, whose eyes were still closed, and held out a flask. 'Good brandy. Smuggled.'

The highwayman had flowers in his buttonhole. He bowed to the crowd that cheered him, but his bravado was forced for Sir Henry could see the man's leg trembling and his bound hands twitching. 'Head up, darling,' he told the girl beside him.

Children were in the crowd. One girl, she could not have been a day over six years of age, sat on her father's shoulders and sucked her thumb. The crowd cheered each arriving prisoner. A group of sailors with long tarred pigtails shouted at Botting to pull down the girl's dress. 'Show us her bubbies, Jemmy! Go on, flop 'em out!'

'Be over soon,' the highwayman told the girl, 'you and I'll be with the angels, girl.'

'I didn't steal anything!' the girl wailed.

'Admit your guilt! Confess your sins!' the Reverend Cotton urged the four prisoners, who were all now lined up on the trapdoor. The girl was furthest from Sir Henry and she was shaking. All four had cotton bags over their faces and all had nooses about their necks. 'Go to God with a clean breast!' the Ordinary urged them. 'Cleanse your conscience, abase yourselves before God!'

'Go on, Jemmy!' a sailor called. 'Strip the frow's frock off!'

The crowd shouted for silence, hoping there would be some final words.

'I did nothing!' the girl screamed.

'Go to hell, you fat bastard,' one of the murderers snarled at the Ordinary.

'See you in hell, Cotton!' the highwayman called to the priest.

'Now, Botting!' The Sheriff wanted it done quickly and Botting scuttled to the back of the scaffold where he stooped and hauled a wooden bolt the size of a rolling pin from a plank. Sir Henry tensed himself, but nothing happened.

'The bolt,' Logan explained softly, 'is merely a locking device. He has to go below to release the trap.'

Sir Henry said nothing. He shrank aside as Botting brushed past him to go down the stairs at the back of the pavilion. Only the four condemned and the Ordinary were now out in the sunlight. The Reverend Cotton stood between the coffins, well clear of the trapdoor. '"For when thou art angry all our days are gone,"' he chanted, '"we bring our years to an end, as it were a tale that is told."'

'Fat bastard, Cotton!' the highwayman shouted. The girl was swaying and under the thin cotton that hid her face Sir Henry could see her mouth was opening and closing. The hangman had vanished under the platform and was clambering through the beams that supported the scaffold to reach a rope that pulled out the baulk of timber that supported the trapdoor.

'"Turn thee again, O Lord!"' The Reverend Cotton had raised one hand to the heavens and his voice to the skies. '"At the last and be gracious unto thy servants."'

Botting jerked the rope and the timber shifted, but did not slide all the way. Sir Henry, unaware that he was holding his breath, saw the trapdoor twitch. The girl sobbed and her legs gave way so that she collapsed on the still-closed trapdoor. The crowd uttered a collective yelp that died away when they realised the bodies

24

had not dropped, then Botting gave the rope an almighty heave and the timber shifted and the trapdoor swung down to let the four bodies fall. It was a short drop, only five or six feet, and it killed none of them. 'It was quicker when they used the cart at Tyburn,' Logan said, leaning forward, 'but we get more Morris this way.'

Sir Henry did not need to ask what Logan meant. The four were twitching, jerking and twisting. They were doing the Morris dance of the scaffold, the hempen measure, the dying capers that came from the stifling, killing, throttling struggles of the doomed. Botting, hidden down in the scaffold's well, leapt aside as the girl's bowels released themselves. Sir Henry saw none of it for his eyes were closed, and he did not even open them when the crowd cheered itself hoarse because Botting, using the highwayman's pinioned elbows as a stirrup, climbed up to squat like a black toad on the man's shoulders to hasten his dying. The highwayman had paid Botting so he would die more quickly and Botting was keeping faith with the bribe.

' "Behold, I show you a mystery." ' The Ordinary ignored the grinning Botting, who clung like a monstrous hump on the dying man's back. ' "We shall not all sleep," ' Cotton intoned, ' "but we shall all be changed in a moment, in the twinkling of an eye." '

'There's the first one gone,' Logan said, as Botting clambered down from the corpse's back, 'and I've got a mortal appetite now, by God, I have an appetite!'

Three of the four still danced, but ever more feebly. The dead highwayman swung with canted head as

Botting hauled on the girl's ankles. Sir Henry smelt dung, human dung, and he could suddenly take no more of the spectacle and so he stumbled down the scaffold steps into the cool, dark stone shelter of the Lodge. He vomited there, then gasped for breath and waited, listening to the crowd and to the creak of the scaffold's timbers, until it was time to go for breakfast.

For devilled kidneys. It was a tradition.

1

Rider Sandman was up late that Monday morning because he had been paid seven guineas to play for Sir John Hart's eleven against a Sussex team, the winners to share a bonus of a hundred guineas, and Sandman had scored sixty-three runs in the first innings and thirty-two in the second, and those were respectable scores by any standards, but Sir John's eleven had still lost. That had been on the Saturday and Sandman, watching the other batsmen swing wildly at ill-bowled balls, had realised that the game was being thrown. The bookmakers were being fleeced because Sir John's team had been expected to win handily, not least because the famed Rider Sandman was playing for it, but someone must have bet heavily on the Sussex eleven which, in the event, won the game by an innings and forty-eight runs. Rumour said that Sir John himself had bet against his own side and Sir John would not meet Sandman's eyes, which made the rumour believable.

So Captain Rider Sandman walked back to London. He walked because he refused to share a carriage with men who had accepted bribes to lose a match. He loved cricket, he was good at it, he had once, famously, scored a hundred and fourteen runs for an England eleven playing against the Marquess of Canfield's picked men and lovers of the game would travel many miles to see Captain Rider Sandman, late of His Majesty's 52nd Regiment of Foot, perform at the batting crease. But he hated bribery and he detested corruption and he possessed a temper, and that was why he fell into a furious argument with his treacherous team-mates and, when they slept that night in Sir John's comfortable house and rode back to London in comfort next morning, Sandman did neither. He was too proud.

Proud and poor. He could not afford the stagecoach fare, nor even a common carrier's fare, because in his anger he had thrown his match fee back into Sir John Hart's face and that, Sandman conceded, had been a stupid thing to do for he had earnt that money honestly, yet even so it had felt dirty. So he walked home, spending the Saturday night in a hayrick somewhere near Hickstead and trudging all that Sunday until the right sole was almost clean off his boot. He reached Drury Lane very late that night and he dropped his cricket gear on the floor of his rented attic room and stripped himself naked and fell into the narrow bed and slept. Just slept. And was still sleeping when the trapdoor dropped in Old Bailey and the crowd's cheer sent a thousand wings startling up into the smoky London sky. Sandman was still dreaming at half past eight. He was dreaming, twitching and sweating. He called out in incoherent alarm, his ears filled with the thump of hooves and the crash of muskets and cannon, his eyes astonished by the hook of sabres and slashes of straight-bladed swords, and this time the dream was going to end with the cavalry smashing through the thin red-coated ranks, but then the rattle of hooves melded into a rush of feet on the stairs and a sketchy knock on his flimsy attic door. He opened his eyes, realised he was no longer a soldier, and then, before he could call out any response, Sally Hood was in the room. For a second Sandman thought the flurry of bright eyes, calico dress and golden hair was a dream, then Sally laughed. 'I bleeding woke you. Gawd, I'm sorry!' She turned to go.

'It's all right, Miss Hood.' Sandman fumbled for his watch. He was sweating. 'What's the time?'

'Saint Giles just struck half after eight,' she told him.

'Oh, my Lord!' Sandman could not believe he had slept so late. He had nothing to get up for, but the habit of waking early had long taken hold. He sat up in bed, remembered he was naked and snatched the thin blanket up to his chest. 'There's a gown hanging on the door, Miss Hood, would you be so kind?'

Sally found the dressing gown. 'It's just that I'm late,' she explained her sudden appearance in his room, 'and my brother's brushed off and I've got work, and the dress has to be hooked up, see?' She turned her back, showing a length of bare spine. 'I'd have asked Mrs Gunn to do it,' Sally went on, 'only there's a hanging today so she's off watching. Gawd knows what she can see considering she's half blind and all drunk, but she does like a good hanging and she ain't got many pleasures left at her age. It's all right, you can get up now, I've got me peepers shut.'

Sandman climbed out of bed warily for there was only a limited area in his tiny attic room where he could stand without banging his head on the beams. He was a tall man, an inch over six foot, with pale-gold hair, blue eyes and a long, raw-boned face. He was not conventionally handsome, his face was too rugged for that, but there was a capability and a kindness in his expression that made him memorable. He pulled on the dressing gown and tied its belt. 'You say you've got work?' he asked Sally. 'A good job, I hope?'

'Ain't what I wanted,' Sally said, 'because it ain't on deck.'

'Deck?'

'Stage, Captain,' she said. She called herself an actress and perhaps she was, though Sandman had seen little evidence that the stage had much use for Sally who, like Sandman, clung to the very edge of respect-ability and was held there, it seemed, by her brother, a very mysterious young man who worked strange hours. 'But it ain't bad work,' she went on, 'and it is respectable.'

'I'm sure it is,' Sandman said, sensing that Sally did not really want to talk about it, and he wondered why she sounded so defensive about a respectable job and Sally wondered why Sandman, who was pal-pably a gentleman, was renting an attic room in the Wheatsheaf Tavern in London's Drury Lane. Down on his luck, that was for sure, but even so, the Wheat-sheaf? Perhaps he knew no better. The Wheatsheaf was famously a flash tavern, a home for every kind of thief from pickpockets to petermen, from burglars to shop-breakers, and it seemed to Sally that Captain Rider Sandman was as straight as a ramrod. But he was a nice man, Sally thought. He treated her like a lady, and though she had only spoken to him a couple of times as they edged past each other in the inn's corridors, she had detected a kindness in him. Enough kindness to let her presume on his privacy this Monday morning. 'And what about you, Captain?' she asked. 'You working?'

'I'm looking for employment, Miss Hood,' Sandman said, and that was true, but he was not finding any. He was too old to be an apprentice clerk, not qualified to work in the law or with money, and too squeamish to accept a job driving slaves in the sugar islands.

'I heard you was a cricketer,' Sally said.

'I am, yes.'

'A famous one, my brother says.'

'I'm not sure about that,' Sandman said modestly.

'But you can earn money at that, can't you?'

'Not as much as I need,' Sandman said, and then only in summer and if he was willing to endure the bribes and corruption of the game, 'and I have a small problem here. Some of the hooks are missing.'

'That's 'cos I never get round to mending them,' Sally said, 'so just do what you can.' She was staring at his mantel on which was a pile of letters, their edges frayed suggesting they had all been sent a long time in the past. She swayed forward slightly and managed to see that the topmost envelope was addressed to a Miss someone or other, she could not make out the name, but the one word revealed that Captain Sandman had been jilted and had his letters returned. Poor Captain Sandman, Sally thought.

'And sometimes,' Sandman went on, 'where there are hooks there are no eyes.'

'Which is why I brought this,' Sally said, dangling a frayed silk handkerchief over her shoulder. 'Thread it through the gaps, Captain. Make me decent.'

'So today I shall call on some acquaintances,' Sandman reverted to her earlier question, 'and see if they can offer me employment and then, this afternoon, I shall yield to temptation.'

'Ooh!' Sally smiled over her shoulder, all blue eyes and sparkle. 'Temptation?'

'I shall watch some cricket at the Artillery Ground.'

'Wouldn't tempt me,' Sally said, 'and by the by, Captain, if you're going down to breakfast then do it quick 'cos you won't get a bite after nine o'clock.'

'I won't?' Sandman asked, though in truth he had no intention of paying the tavern for a breakfast he could not afford.

'The 'sheaf''s always crowded when there's a hanging at Newgate,' Sally explained, ''cos the folk want their breakfasts on their way back, see? Makes 'em hungry. That's where my brother went. He always goes down Old Bailey when there's a scragging. They like him to be there.'

'Who does?'

'His friends. He usually knows one of the poor bastards being twisted, see?'

'Twisted?'

'Hanged, Captain. Hanged, twisted, crapped, nub-

32

bed, scragged or Jack Ketched. Doing the Newgate Morris, dancing on Jemmy Botting's stage, rope gargling. You'll have to learn the flash language if you live here, Captain.'

'I can see I will,' Sandman said, and had just begun to thread the handkerchief through the dress's gaping back when Dodds, the inn's errand boy, pushed through the half-open door and grinned to discover Sally Hood in Captain Sandman's room and Captain Sandman doing up her frock and him with tousled hair and dressed in nothing but a frayed old dressing gown.

'You'll catch flies if you don't close your bloody gob,' Sally told Dodds, 'and he ain't my boman, you spoony little bastard. He's just hooking me up 'cos my brother and Mother Gunn have gone to the crap. Which is where you'll end up if there's any bleeding justice.'

Dodds ignored this tirade and held a sealed paper towards Sandman. 'Letter for you, Captain.'

'You're very kind,' Sandman said, and stooped to his folded clothes to find a penny. 'Wait a moment,' he told the boy who, in truth, had shown no inclination to leave until he was tipped.

'Don't you bug him nothing!' Sally protested. She pushed Sandman's hand away and snatched the letter from Dodds. 'The little toe-rag forgot it, didn't he? No bleeding letter arrived this morning! How long's it been?'

Dodds looked at her sullenly. 'Came on Friday,' he finally admitted.

'If a bleeding letter comes on Friday then you bleeding deliver it on Friday! Now, on your trotters and fake away off!' She slammed the door on the boy. 'Lazy little bleeder. They should take him down bleeding Newgate and make him do the scaffold hornpipe. That would stretch his lazy bloody neck.'

Sandman finished threading the silk handkerchief through the gaps in the dress's fastenings, then stepped back and nodded. 'You look very fetching, Miss Hood.'

'You think so?'

'I do indeed,' Sandman said. The dress was pale green, printed with cornflowers, and the colours suited Sally's honey-coloured skin and curly hair that was as gold as Sandman's own. She was a pretty girl with clear blue eyes, a skin unscarred by pox and a contagious smile. 'The dress really does become you,' he said.

'It's the only half good one I've got,' she said, 'so it had better suit. Thank you.' She held out his letter. 'Close your eyes, turn round three times, then say your loved one's name aloud before you open it.'

Sandman smiled. 'And what will that achieve?'

'It will mean good news, Captain,' she said earnestly, 'good news.' She smiled and was gone.

Sandman listened to her footsteps on the stairs, then looked at the letter. Perhaps it was an answer to one of his enquiries about a job? It was certainly a very high class of paper and the handwriting was educated and stylish. He put a finger under the flap, ready to break the seal, then paused. He felt like a fool, but he closed his eyes, turned three times then spoke his loved one's name aloud: 'Eleanor Forrest,' he said, then opened his eyes, tore off the letter's red wax seal and unfolded the paper. He read the letter, read it again and tried to work out whether or not it really was good news.

The Right Honourable the Viscount Sidmouth presented his compliments to Captain Rider Sandman and requested the honour of a call at Captain Sandman's earliest convenience, preferably in the forenoon at Lord Sidmouth's office. A prompt reply to Lord Sidmouth's private secretary, Mister Sebastian Witherspoon, would be appreciated.

Sandman's first instinct was that the letter must be bad news, that his father had dunned the Viscount Sidmouth as he had dunned so many others and that his lordship was writing to make a claim on the pathetic shreds of the Sandman estate. Yet that was nonsense. His father, so far as Rider Sandman knew, had never encountered Lord Sidmouth and he would surely have boasted if he had for Sandman's father had liked the company of important men. And there were few men more important than the Right Honourable Henry Addington, first Viscount Sidmouth, erstwhile Prime Minister of Great Britain and now His Majesty's Principal Secretary of State in the Home Department.

So why did the Home Secretary want to see Rider Sandman?

There was only one way to find out.

So Sandman put on his cleanest shirt, buffed his fraying boots with his dirtiest shirt, brushed his coat and, thus belying his poverty by dressing as the gentleman he was, went to see Lord Sidmouth.

*　　*　　*

The Viscount Sidmouth was a thin man. He was thin-lipped and thin-haired, had a thin nose and a thin jaw that narrowed to a weasel-thin chin and his eyes had all the warmth of thinly knapped flint and his thin voice was precise, dry and unfriendly. His nickname was 'the Doctor', a nickname without warmth or affection, but apt, for he was clinical, disapproving and cold. He had made Sandman wait for two and a quarter hours, though as Sandman had come to the office without an appointment he could scarce blame the Home Secretary for that. Now, as a bluebottle buzzed against one of the high windows, Lord Sidmouth frowned across the desk at his visitor. 'You were recommended by Sir John Colborne.'

Sandman bowed his head in acknowledgement, but said nothing. There was nothing to say. A grandfather clock ticked loud in a corner of the office.

'You were in Sir John's battalion at Waterloo,' Sidmouth said, 'is that not so?'

'I was, my lord, yes.'

Sidmouth grunted as though he did not entirely approve of men who had been at Waterloo and that, Sandman reflected, might well have been the case for Britain now seemed divided between those who had fought against the French and those who had stayed at home. The latter, Sandman suspected, were jealous and liked to suggest, oh so delicately, that they had sacrificed an opportunity to gallivant abroad because of the need to keep Britain prosperous. The wars against Napoleon were two years in the past now, yet still the divide remained, though Sir John Colborne must possess some influence with the government if his recommendation had brought Sandman to this office. 'Sir John tells me you seek employment?' the Home Secretary asked.

'I must, my lord.'

'Must?' Sidmouth pounced on the word. 'Must? But you are on half pay, surely? And half pay is not an ungenerous emolument, I would have thought?' The question was asked very sourly, as though his lordship utterly disapproved of paying pensions to men who were capable of earning their own livings.

'I'm not eligible for half pay, my lord,' Sandman said. He had sold his commission and, because it was peacetime, he had received less than he had hoped, though it had been enough to secure a lease on a house for his mother.

'You have no income?' Sebastian Witherspoon, the Home Secretary's private secretary, asked from his chair beside his master's desk.

'Some,' Sandman said, and decided it was probably best not to say that the small income came from playing cricket. The Viscount Sidmouth did not look like a man who would approve of such a thing. 'Not enough,' Sandman amended his answer, 'and much of what I do earn goes towards settling my father's smaller debts. The tradesmen's debts,' he added, in case the Home Secretary thought he was trying to pay off the massive sums owing to the wealthy investors.

Witherspoon frowned. 'In law, Sandman,' he said, 'you are not responsible for any of your father's debts.'

'I am responsible for my family's good name,' Sandman responded.

Lord Sidmouth gave a snort of derision that could have been in mockery of Sandman's good name or an ironic response to his evident scruples or, more likely, was a comment on Sandman's father who, faced with the threat of imprisonment or exile because of his massive debts, had taken his own life and thus left his name disgraced and his wife and family ruined. The Home Secretary gave Sandman a long, sour inspection, then turned to look at the bluebottle thumping against the window. The grandfather clock ticked hollow. The room was hot and Sandman was uncomfortably aware of the sweat soaking his shirt. The silence stretched and Sandman suspected the Home Secretary was weighing the wisdom of offering employment to Ludovic Sandman's son. Wagons rumbled in the street beneath the windows. Hooves sounded sharp, and then, at last, Lord Sidmouth made up his mind. 'I need a man to undertake a job,' he said, still gazing at the window, 'though I should warn you that it is not a permanent position. In no way is it permanent.'

'It is anything but permanent,' Witherspoon put in.

Sidmouth scowled at his secretary's contribution. 'The position is entirely temporary,' he said, then gestured towards a great basket that stood waist high on the carpeted floor and was crammed with papers. Some were scrolls, some were folded and sealed with wax while a few showed legal pretensions by being wrapped in scraps of red ribbon. 'Those, Captain,' he said, 'are petitions.' Lord Sidmouth's tone made it plain that he loathed petitions. 'A condemned felon may petition the King in Council for clemency or, indeed, for a full pardon. That is their prerogative, Captain, and all such petitions from England and Wales come to this office. We receive close to two thousand a year! It seems that every person condemned to death manages to have a petition sent on their behalf, and they must all be read. Are they not all read, Witherspoon?'

Sidmouth's secretary, a young man with plump cheeks, sharp eyes and elegant manners, nodded. 'They are certainly examined, my lord. It would be remiss of us to ignore such pleas.'

'Remiss indeed,' Sidmouth said piously, 'and if the crime is not too heinous, Captain, and if persons of quality are willing to speak for the condemned, then we might show clemency. We might commute a sentence of death to, say, one of transportation?'

'You, my lord?' Sandman asked, struck by Sidmouth's use of the word 'we'.

'The petitions are addressed to the King,' the Home Secretary explained, 'but the responsibility for deciding on the response is properly left to this office and my decisions are then ratified by the Privy Council and I can assure you, Captain, that I mean ratified. They are not questioned.'

'Indeed not!' Witherspoon sounded amused.

'I decide,' Sidmouth declared truculently. 'It is one of the responsibilities of this high office, Captain, to decide which felons will hang and which will be spared. There are hundreds of souls in Australia, Captain, who owe their lives to this office.'

'And I am certain, my lord,' Witherspoon put in smoothly, 'that their gratitude is unbounded.'

Sidmouth ignored his secretary. Instead he tossed a scrolled and ribboned petition to Sandman. 'And once in a while,' he went on, 'once in a very rare while, a petition will persuade us to investigate the facts of the matter. On those rare occasions, Captain, we appoint an Investigator, but it is not something we like to do.' He paused, obviously inviting Sandman to enquire why the Home Office was so reluctant to appoint an Investigator, but Sandman seemed oblivious to the question as he slid the ribbon from the scroll. 'A person condemned to death,' the Home Secretary offered the explanation anyway, 'has already been tried. He or she has been judged and found guilty by a court of law, and it is not the business of His Majesty's government to revisit facts that have been considered by the proper courts. It is not our policy, Captain, to undermine the judiciary, but once in a while, very infrequently, we do investigate. That petition is just such a rare case.'

Sandman unrolled the petition, which was written in brownish ink on cheap yellow paper. 'As God is my wittness,' he read, 'hee is a good boy and could never have killd the Lady Avebury as God knows hee could not hert even a flie.' There was much more in the same manner, but Sandman could not read on because the Home Secretary had started to talk again.

'The matter,' Lord Sidmouth explained, 'concerns Charles Corday. That is not his real name. The petition, as you can see for yourself, comes from Corday's mother, who subscribes herself as Cruttwell, but the boy seems to have adopted a French name. God knows

40

why. He stands convicted of murdering the Countess of Avebury. You doubtless recollect the case?'

'I fear not, my lord,' Sandman said. He had never taken much interest in crime, had never bought the Newgate Calendars nor read the broadsheets that celebrated notorious felons and their savage deeds.

'There's no mystery about it,' the Home Secretary said. 'The wretched man raped and stabbed the Countess of Avebury and he thoroughly deserves to hang. He is due on the scaffold when?' He turned to Witherspoon.

'A week from today, my lord,' Witherspoon said.

'If there's no mystery, my lord,' Sandman said, 'then why investigate the facts?'

'Because the petitioner, Maisie Cruttwell,' Sidmouth spoke the name as though it tasted sour on his tongue, 'is a seamstress to Her Majesty, Queen Charlotte, and Her Majesty has graciously taken an interest.' Lord Sidmouth's voice made it plain that he could have gladly strangled King George III's wife for being so gracious. 'It is my responsibility, Captain, and my loyal duty to reassure Her Majesty that every possible enquiry has been made and that there is not the slightest doubt about the wretched man's guilt. I have therefore written to Her Majesty to inform her that I am appointing an Investigator who will examine the facts and thus offer an assurance that justice is indeed being done.' Sidmouth had explained all this in a bored voice, but now pointed a bony forefinger at Sandman. 'I am asking whether you will be that Investigator, Captain, and whether you comprehend what is needed.'

Sandman nodded. 'You wish to reassure the Queen,

my lord, and to do that you must be entirely satisfied of the prisoner's guilt.'

'No!' Sidmouth snapped, and sounded genuinely angry. 'I am already entirely satisfied of the man's guilt. Corday, or whatever he chooses to call himself, was convicted after the due process of the law. It is the Queen who needs reassurance.'

'I understand,' Sandman said.

Witherspoon leant forward. 'Forgive the question, Captain, but you're not of a radical disposition?'

'Radical?'

'You do not have objections to the gallows?'

'For a man who rapes and kills?' Sandman sounded indignant. 'Of course not.' The answer was honest enough, though in truth Sandman had not thought much about the gallows. It was not something he had ever seen, though he knew there was a scaffold at Newgate, a second south of the river at the Horse-monger Lane prison, and another in every assize town of England and Wales. Once in a while he would hear an argument that the scaffold was being used too widely or that it was a nonsense to hang a hungry villager for stealing a five-shilling lamb, but few folk wanted to do away with the noose altogether. The scaffold was a deterrent, a punishment and an example. It was a necessity. It was civilisation's machine and it protected all law-abiding citizens from their predators.

Witherspoon, satisfied with Sandman's indignant answer, smiled. 'I did not think you were a radical,' he said emolliently, 'but one must be sure.'

'So,' Lord Sidmouth glanced at the grandfather

clock, 'will you undertake to be our Investigator?' He
expected an immediate answer, but Sandman hesitated.
That hesitation was not because he did not want the
job, but because he doubted he possessed the qualifica-
tions to be an investigator of crime, but then, he wondered, who did? Lord Sidmouth mistook the hesitation
for reluctance. 'The job will hardly tax you, Captain,'
he said testily, 'the wretch is plainly guilty and one
merely wishes to satisfy the Queen's womanly concerns. A month's pay for a day's work?' He paused and
sneered. 'Or do you fear the appointment will interfere
with your cricket?'

Sandman needed a month's pay and so he ignored
the insults. 'Of course I shall do it, my lord,' he said, 'I
shall be honoured.'

Witherspoon stood, the signal that the audience was
over, and the Home Secretary nodded his farewell.
'Witherspoon will provide you with a letter of authorisation,' he said, 'and I shall look forward to receiving
your report. Good day to you, sir.'

'Your servant, my lord,' Sandman bowed, but
the Home Secretary was already attending to other
business.

Sandman followed the secretary into an ante-room
where a clerk was busy at a table. 'It will take a moment
to seal your letter,' Witherspoon said, 'so, please, sit.'

Sandman had brought the Corday petition with him
and now read it all the way through, though he gleaned
little more information from the ill-written words. The
condemned man's mother, who had signed the petition
with a cross, had merely dictated an incoherent plea for

43

mercy. Her son was a good boy, she claimed, a harmless soul and a Christian, but beneath her pleas were two damning comments. 'Preposterous,' the first read, 'he is guilty of a heinous crime,' while the second comment, in a crabbed handwriting, stated: 'Let the Law take its course.' Sandman showed the petition to Witherspoon. 'Who wrote the comments?'

'The second is the Home Secretary's decision,' Witherspoon said, 'and was written before we knew Her Majesty was involved. And the first? That's from the judge who passed sentence. It is customary to refer all petitions to the relevant judge before a decision is made. In this case it was Sir John Silvester. You know him?'

'I fear not.'

'He's the Recorder of London and, as you may deduce from that, a most experienced judge. Certainly not a man to allow a gross miscarriage of justice in his courtroom.' He handed a letter to the clerk. 'Your name must be on the letter of authorisation, of course. Are there any pitfalls in its spelling?'

'No,' Sandman said and then, as the clerk wrote his name on the letter, he read the petition again, but it presented no arguments against the facts of the case. Maisie Cruttwell claimed her son was innocent, but could adduce no proof of that assertion. Instead she was appealing to the King for mercy. 'Why did you ask me?' Sandman asked Witherspoon. 'I mean you must have used someone else as an Investigator in the past? Were they unsatisfactory?'

'Mister Talbot was entirely satisfactory,' Witherspoon said. He was now searching for the seal that would authenticate the letter, 'but he died.'

'Ah.'

'A seizure,' Witherspoon said, 'very tragic. And why you? Because, as the Home Secretary informed you, you were recommended.' He was scrabbling through the contents of a drawer, looking for the seal. 'I had a cousin at Waterloo,' he went on, 'a Captain Witherspoon, a Hussar. He was on the Duke's staff. Did you know him?'

'No, alas.'

'He died.'

'I am sorry to hear it.'

'It was perhaps for the best,' Witherspoon said. He had at last found the seal. 'He always said that he feared the war's ending. What excitement, he wondered, could peace bring?'

'It was a common enough fear in the army,' Sandman said.

'This letter,' the secretary was now heating a stick of wax over a candle flame, 'confirms that you are making enquiries on behalf of the Home Office and it requests all persons to offer you their cooperation, though it does not require them to do so. Note that distinction, Captain, note it well. We have no legal right to demand cooperation,' he said as he dripped the wax onto the letter, then carefully pushed the seal into the scarlet blob, 'so we can only request it. I would be grateful if you would return this letter to me upon the conclusion of your enquiries, and as to the nature of those enquiries, Captain? I suggest they need not be laborious.

There is no doubt of the man's guilt. Corday is a rapist, a murderer and a liar, and all we need of him is a confession. You will find him in Newgate and if you are sufficiently forceful then I have no doubt he will confess to his brutal crime and your work will then be done.' He held out the letter. 'I expect to hear from you very soon. We shall require a written report, but please keep it brief.' He suddenly withheld the letter to give his next words an added force. 'What we do not want, Captain, is to complicate matters. Provide us with a succinct report that will allow my master to reassure the Queen that there are no possible grounds for a pardon and then let us forget the wretched matter.'

'Suppose he doesn't confess?' Sandman asked.

'Make him,' Witherspoon said forcefully. 'He will hang anyway, Captain, whether you have submitted your report or not. It would simply be more convenient if we could reassure Her Majesty of the man's guilt before the wretch is executed.'

'And if he's innocent?' Sandman asked.

Witherspoon looked appalled at the suggestion. 'How can he be? He's already been found guilty!'

'Of course he has,' Sandman said, then took the letter and slipped it into the tail pocket of his coat. 'His Lordship,' he spoke awkwardly, 'mentioned an emolument.' He hated talking of money, it was so ungentlemanly, but so was his poverty.

'Indeed he did,' Witherspoon said. 'We usually paid twenty guineas to Mister Talbot, but I would find it hard to recommend the same fee in this case. It really is too trivial a matter so I shall authorise a draft for fifteen guineas. I shall send it to you, where?' He glanced down at his notebook, then looked shocked. 'Really? The Wheatsheaf? In Drury Lane?'

'Indeed,' Sandman said stiffly. He knew Witherspoon deserved an explanation for the Wheatsheaf was notorious as a haunt of criminals, but Sandman had not known of that reputation when he asked for a room and he did not think he needed to justify himself to Witherspoon.

'I'm sure you know best,' Witherspoon said dubiously.

Sandman hesitated. He was no coward, indeed he had the reputation of being a brave man, but that reputation had been earnt in the smoke of battle and what he did now took all his courage. 'You mentioned a draft, Mister Witherspoon,' he said, 'and I wondered whether I might persuade you to cash? There will be inevitable expenses . . .' His voice tailed away because, for the life of him, he could not think what those expenses might be.

Both Witherspoon and the clerk stared at Sandman as though he had just dropped his breeches. 'Cash?' Witherspoon asked in a small voice.

Sandman knew he was blushing. 'You want the matter resolved swiftly,' he said, 'and there could be contingencies that will require expenditure. I cannot foresee the nature of those contingencies, but . . .' He shrugged and again his voice tailed away.

'Prendergast,' Witherspoon looked at Sandman even as he spoke to the clerk, 'pray go to Mister Hodge's office, present him with my compliments and ask him

47

to advance us fifteen guineas,' he paused, still looking at Sandman, 'in cash.'

The money was found, it was given and Sandman left the Home Office with pockets heavy with gold. Damn poverty, he thought, but the rent was due at the Wheatsheaf and it had been three days since he had eaten a proper meal.

But fifteen guineas! He could afford a meal now. A meal, some wine and an afternoon of cricket. It was a tempting vision, but Sandman was not a man to shirk duty. The job of being the Home Office's Investigator might be temporary, but if he finished this first enquiry swiftly then he might look for other and more lucrative assignments from Lord Sidmouth, and that was an outcome devoutly to be wished and so he would forgo the meal, forget the wine and postpone the cricket.

For there was a murderer to see and a confession to obtain.

And Sandman went to fetch it.

In Old Bailey, a funnel-shaped thoroughfare that narrowed as it ran from Newgate Street to Ludgate Hill, the scaffold was being taken down. The black baize that had draped the platform was already folded onto a small cart and two men were now handing down the heavy beam from which the four victims had been hanged. The first broadsheets describing the executions and the crimes that had caused them were being hawked for a penny apiece to the vestiges of the morning's crowd who had waited to see Jemmy Botting haul the four dead bodies up from the hanging pit, sit them on the edge of the drop while he removed the nooses and then heave them into their coffins. Then a handful of spectators had climbed to the scaffold to have one of the dead men's hands touched to their warts, boils or tumours.

The coffins had at last been carried into the prison, but some folk still lingered just to watch the scaffold's dismemberment. Two hawkers were selling what they claimed were portions of the fatal ropes. Bewigged and black-robed lawyers hurried between the Lamb Inn, the Magpie and Stump and the courts of the Session House that had been built next to the prison. Traffic had been allowed back into the street so Sandman had to dodge between wagons, carriages and carts to reach the prison gate where he expected warders and locks, but instead he found a uniformed porter at the top of the steps and dozens of folk coming and going. Women were carrying parcels of food, babies and bottles of gin, beer or rum. Children ran and screamed, while two aproned tapmen from the Magpie and Stump across the street delivered cooked meals on wooden trays to prisoners who could afford their services.

'Your honour is looking for someone?' The porter, seeing Sandman's confusion, had pushed through the crowd to intercept him.

'I am looking for Charles Corday,' Sandman said, and when the porter looked bemused, added that he had come from the Home Office. 'My name is Sandman,' he explained, 'Captain Sandman, and I'm

Lord Sidmouth's official Investigator.' He drew out the letter with its impressive Home Office seal.

'Ah!' The porter was quite uninterested in the letter. 'You've replaced Mister Talbot, God rest his soul. A proper gentleman he was, sir.'

Sandman put the letter away. 'I should, perhaps, pay my respects to the Governor?' he suggested.

'The Keeper, sir, Mister Brown is the Keeper, sir, and he won't thank you for any respects, sir, on account that they ain't needful. You just goes in, sir, and sees the prisoner. Mister Talbot, now, God rest him, he took them to one of the empty salt boxes and had a little chat.' The porter grinned and mimed a punching action. 'A great one for the truth was Mister Talbot. A big man, he was, but so are you. What was your fellow called?'

'Corday.'

'He's condemned, is he? Then you'll find him in the Press Yard, your honour. Are you carrying a stick, sir?'

'A stick?'

'A pistol, sir. No? Some gentlemen do, but weapons ain't advisable, sir, on account that the bastards might overpower you. And a word of advice, Captain?' The porter, his breath reeking of rum, turned and took hold of Sandman's lapel to add emphasis to his next words. 'He'll tell you he didn't do it, sir. There ain't a guilty man in here, not one! Not if you ask them. They'll all swear on their mothers' lives they didn't do it, but they did. They all did.' He grinned and released his grip on Sandman's coat. 'Do you have a watch, sir? You do, sir? Best not take anything in that might be stolen. It'll be in the cupboard here, sir, under lock, key and my eye. Round that corner, sir, you'll find some stairs. Go down, sir, follow the tunnel and don't mind the smell. Mind your backs!' This last call was to all the folk in the lobby because four workmen, accompanied by three watchmen armed with truncheons, were carrying a plain wooden coffin out through the prison door. 'It's the girl what was stretched this morning, sir,' the porter confided in Sandman. 'She's going to the surgeons. The gentlemen do like a young lady to dissect, they do. Down the stairs, sir, and follow your nose.'

The smell of unwashed bodies reminded Sandman of Spanish billets crowded with tired redcoats and the stench became even more noxious as he followed the stone-flagged tunnel to where more stairs climbed to a guardroom beside a massive barred gate that led into the Press Yard. Two turnkeys, both armed with cudgels, guarded the gate. 'Charles Corday?' one responded when Sandman enquired where the prisoner might be found. 'You can't miss him. If he ain't in the yard then he'll be in the Association Room.' He pointed to an open door across the yard. 'He looks like a bleeding mort, that's why you can't mistake him.'

'A mort?'

The man unbolted the gate. 'He looks like a bloody girl, sir,' he said scornfully. 'Pal of his, are you?' The man grinned, then the grin faded as Sandman turned and stared at him. 'I don't see him in the yard, sir,' the turnkey had been a soldier and he instinctively straightened his back and became respectful under Sandman's

51

gaze, 'so he'll be in the Association Room, sir. That door over there, sir.'

The Press Yard was a narrow space compressed between high, dank buildings. What little light came into the yard arrived over a thicket of spikes that crowned the Newgate Street wall beside which a score of prisoners, easily identifiable because of their leg irons, sat with their visitors. Children played round an open drain. A blind man sat by the steps leading to the cells, muttering to himself and scratching at the open sores on his manacled ankles. A drunk, also in chains, lay sleeping while a woman, evidently his wife, wept silently beside him. She mistook Sandman for a wealthy man and held out a begging hand. 'Have pity on a poor woman, your honour, have pity.'

Sandman went into the Association Room which was a large space filled with tables and benches. A coal fire burnt in a big grate where stew pots hung from a crane. The pots were being stirred by two women who were evidently cooking for a dozen folk seated round one of the long tables. The only turnkey in the room, a youngish man armed with a truncheon, was also at the table, sharing a gin bottle and the laughter which died abruptly when Sandman appeared. Then the other tables fell silent as forty or fifty folk turned to look at the newcomer. Someone spat. Something about Sandman, maybe his height, spoke of authority and this was not a place where authority was welcome.

'Corday!' Sandman called, his voice taking on the familiar officer's tone. 'I'm looking for Charles Corday!' No one answered. 'Corday!' Sandman called again.

'Sir?' The answering voice was tremulous and came from the room's furthest and darkest corner. Sandman threaded his way through the tables to see a pathetic figure curled against the wall there. Charles Corday was very young, he looked scarce more than seventeen, and he was thin to the point of frailty with a deathly pale face framed by long fair hair that did, indeed, look girl-ish. He had long eyelashes, a trembling lip and a dark bruise on one cheek.

'You're Charles Corday?' Sandman felt an instinctive dislike of the young man, who looked too delicate and self-pitying.

'Yes, sir.' Corday's right arm was shaking.

'Stand up,' Sandman ordered. Corday blinked in sur-prise at the tone of command, but obeyed, flinching because the leg irons bit into his ankles. 'I've been sent by the Home Secretary,' Sandman said, 'and I need somewhere private where we can talk. We can use the cells, perhaps. Do we reach them from here? Or from the yard?'

'The yard, sir,' Corday said, though he scarcely seemed to have understood the rest of Sandman's words.

Sandman led Corday towards the door. 'Is he your boman, Charlie?' a man in leg shackles enquired. 'Come for a farewell cuddle, has he?' The other prisoners laughed, but Sandman had the experienced officer's ability to know when to ignore insubordination and he just kept walking, but then he heard Corday squeal and he turned to see that a greasy-haired and unshaven man was holding Corday's hair like a leash. 'I was talking to you, Charlie!' the man said. He yanked Corday's hair, making the boy squeal again. 'Give us a kiss, Charlie,' the man demanded, 'give us a kiss.' The women at the table by the fire laughed at Corday's predicament.

'Let him go,' Sandman said.

'You don't give orders here, culley,' the unshaven man growled. 'No one gives orders in here, there aren't any orders any more, not till Jemmy comes to fetch us away, so you can fake away off, culley, you can –' The man stopped suddenly, then gave a curious scream. 'No!' he shouted. 'No!'

Rider Sandman had ever suffered from a temper. He knew it and he fought against it. In his everyday life he adopted a tone of gentle deliberation, he used courtesy far beyond necessity, he elevated reason and he reinforced it with prayer, and he did all that because he feared his own temper, but not all the prayer and reason and courtesy had eliminated the foul moods. His soldiers had known there was a devil in Captain Sandman. It was a real devil and they knew he was not a man to cross because he had that temper as sudden and as fierce as a summer storm of lightning and thunder. And he was a tall and strong man, strong enough to lift the unshaven prisoner and slam him against the wall so hard that the man's head bounced off the stones. Then the man screamed because Sandman had driven a hard fist into his lower belly. 'I said let him go,' Sandman snapped. 'Did you not hear what I said? Are you deaf or are you just a bloody God-damned idiot?' He slapped the man once, twice, and his eyes were blazing and his voice was seething with a promise of even more terrible violence. 'Damn it! What kind of fool do you take me for?' He jerked the man. 'Answer me!'

'Sir?' the unshaven man managed to say.

'Answer me. God damn it!' Sandman's right hand was about the prisoner's throat and he was throttling the man, who was incapable of saying anything now. There was utter silence in the Association Room. The man, gazing into Sandman's pale eyes, was choking.

The turnkey, as appalled by the force of Sandman's anger as any of the prisoners, nervously crossed the room. 'Sir? You're throttling him, sir.'

'I'm damn well killing him,' Sandman snarled.

'Sir, please, sir.'

Sandman suddenly came to his senses, then let the prisoner go. 'If you cannot be courteous,' he told the half-choked man, 'then you should be silent.'

'He won't give you any more lip, sir,' the turnkey said anxiously, 'I warrant he won't, sir.'

'Come, Corday,' Sandman ordered, and stalked out of the room.

There was a sigh of relief when he left. 'Who the hell was that?' the bruised prisoner managed to ask through the pain in his throat.

'Never laid peepers on him.'

'Got no right to hit me,' the prisoner said, and his friends growled their assent though none cared to follow Sandman and debate the assertion.

Sandman led a terrified Corday across the Press Yard to the steps which led to the fifteen salt boxes. The five cells on the ground floor were all being used by prostitutes and Sandman, the temper still seething in him, did not apologise for interrupting them, but just slammed the doors then climbed the stairs to find an empty cell on the first floor. 'In there,' he told Corday, and the frightened youth scuttled past him. Sandman shuddered at the stink in this ancient part of the jail that had survived the fires of the Gordon Riots. The rest of the prison had burnt to ash during the riots, but these floors had merely been scorched and the salt boxes looked more like mediaeval dungeons than modern cells. A rope mat lay on the floor, evidently to serve as a mattress, blankets for five or six men were tossed in an untidy pile under the high-barred window while an unemptied night bucket stank in a corner.

'I'm Captain Rider Sandman,' he introduced himself again to Corday, 'and the Home Secretary has asked me to enquire into your case.'

'Why?' Corday, who had sunk onto the pile of blankets, nerved himself to ask.

'Your mother has connections,' Sandman said shortly, the temper still hot in him.

'The Queen has spoken for me?' Corday looked hopeful.

'Her Majesty has requested an assurance of your guilt,' Sandman said stuffily.

'But I'm not guilty,' Corday protested.

'You've already been condemned,' Sandman said, 'so your guilt is not at issue.' He knew he sounded unbearably pompous, but he wanted to get this distasteful meeting over so he could go to the cricket. It would, he thought, be the swiftest fifteen guineas he had ever earnt for he could not imagine this despicable creature resisting his demands for a confession. Corday looked pathetic, effeminate and close to tears. He was wearing dishevelled but fashionably elegant clothes; black breeches, white stockings, a frilled white shirt and a blue silk waistcoat, but he had neither cravat nor a topcoat. The clothes, Sandman suspected, were all a good deal more expensive than anything he himself possessed and they only increased his dislike of Corday, whose voice had a flat and nasal quality with an accent that betrayed social pretensions. A snivelling little upstart, was Sandman's instinctive judgement; a boy scarce grown and already aping the manners and fashion of his betters.

'I didn't do it!' Corday protested again, then began to cry. His thin shoulders heaved, his voice grizzled and the tears ran down his pale cheeks.

Sandman stood in the cell door-way. His predecessor had evidently beaten confessions out of prisoners, but Sandman could not imagine himself doing the same. It was not honourable and could not be done, which meant the wretched boy would have to be persuaded into telling the truth, but the first necessity was to stop him weeping. 'Why do you call yourself Corday,' he asked, hoping to distract him, 'when your mother's name is Cruttwell?'

Corday sniffed. 'There's no law against it.'

'Did I say there was?'

'I'm a portrait painter,' Corday said petulantly, as if he needed to reassure himself of that fact, 'and clients prefer their painters to have French names. Cruttwell doesn't sound distinguished. Would you have your portrait painted by Charlie Cruttwell when you could engage Monsieur Charles Corday?'

'You're a painter?' Sandman could not hide his surprise.

'Yes!' Corday, his eyes reddened from crying, looked belligerently at Sandman, then he collapsed into misery again. 'I was apprenticed to Sir George Phillips.'

'He's very successful,' Sandman said scornfully, 'despite possessing a prosaically English name. And Sir Thomas Lawrence doesn't sound very French to me.'

'I thought changing my name would help,' Corday said sulkily. 'Does it matter?'

'Your guilt matters,' Sandman said sternly, 'and, if nothing else, you might face the judgement of your Maker with a clear conscience if you were to confess it.'

Corday stared at Sandman as though his visitor were mad. 'You know what I'm guilty of?' he finally asked. 'I'm guilty of aspiring to be above my station. I'm guilty of being a decent painter. I'm guilty of being a much better damned painter than Sir George bloody Phillips, and I'm guilty, my God how I'm guilty, of being stupid, but I did not kill the Countess of Avebury! I did not!'

Sandman did not like the boy, but he felt in danger of being convinced by him and so he steeled himself by remembering the warning words of the porter at the prison gate. 'How old are you?' he asked.

'Eighteen,' Corday answered.

'Eighteen,' Sandman echoed. 'God will have pity on your youth,' he said. 'We all do stupid things when we're young, and you have done terrible things, but

God will weigh your soul and there is still hope. You aren't doomed to hell's fires, not if you confess and if you beg God for forgiveness.'

'Forgiveness for what?' Corday asked defiantly.

Sandman was so taken aback that he said nothing.

Corday, red-eyed and pale-faced, stared up at the tall Sandman. 'Look at me,' he said, 'do I look like a man who has the strength to rape and kill a woman, even if I wanted to? Do I look like that?' He did not. Sandman had to admit it, at least to himself, for Corday was a limp and unimpressive creature, weedy and thin, who now began to weep again. 'You're all the same,' he whined. 'No one listens! No one cares! So long as someone hangs, no one cares.'

'Stop crying, for God's sake!' Sandman snarled, and immediately chided himself for giving way to his temper. 'I'm sorry,' he muttered.

Those last two words made Corday frown in puzzlement. He stopped weeping, looked at Sandman and frowned. 'I didn't do it,' he said softly, 'I didn't do it.'

'So what happened?' Sandman asked, despising himself for having lost control of the interview.

'I was painting her,' Corday said. 'The Earl of Avebury wanted a portrait of his wife and he asked Sir George to do it.'

'He asked Sir George, yet you were painting her?' Sandman sounded sceptical. Corday, after all, was a mere eighteen years old while Sir George Phillips was celebrated as the only rival to Sir Thomas Lawrence.

Corday sighed as though Sandman was being deliberately obtuse. 'Sir George drinks,' he said scornfully.

'He starts on blackstrap at breakfast and bowzes till night, which means his hand shakes. So he drinks and I paint.'

Sandman backed into the corridor to escape the smell of the unemptied night bucket in the cell. He wondered if he was being naïve, for he found Corday curiously believable. 'You painted in Sir George's studio?' he asked, not because he cared, but because he wanted to fill the silence.

'No,' Corday said. 'Her husband wanted the portrait set in her bedroom, so I did it there. Have you any idea how much bother that is? You have to take an easel and canvas and chalk and oils and rags and pencils and dropcloths and mixing bowls and more rags. Still, the Earl of Avebury was paying for it.'

'How much?'

'Whatever Sir George could get away with. Eight hundred guineas? Nine? He offered me a hundred.' Corday sounded bitter at that fee, though it seemed like a fortune to Sandman.

'Is it usual to paint a portrait in a lady's bedroom?' Sandman asked in genuine puzzlement. He could imagine a woman wanting herself depicted in a drawing room or under a tree in a great sunlit garden, but the bedroom seemed a very perverse choice to him.

'It was to be a boudoir portrait,' Corday said, and though the term was new to Sandman he understood what it meant. 'They're very fashionable,' Corday went on, 'because these days all the women want to look like Canova's Pauline Bonaparte.'

Sandman frowned. 'You confuse me.'

Corday raised suppliant eyes to heaven in the face of such ignorance. 'The sculptor Canova,' he explained, 'did a likeness of the Emperor's sister that is much celebrated and every beauty in Europe wishes to be depicted in the same pose. The woman reclines on a chaise longue, an apple in her left hand and her head supported by her right.' Corday, rather to Sandman's embarrassment, demonstrated the pose. 'The salient feature,' the boy went on, 'is that the woman is naked from the waist up. And a good deal below the waist, too.'

'So the Countess was naked when you painted her?' Sandman asked.

'No,' Corday hesitated, then shrugged. 'She wasn't to know she was being painted naked, so she was in a morning gown and robe. We would have used a model in the studio to do the tits.'

'She didn't know?' Sandman was incredulous.

'Her husband wanted a portrait,' Corday said impatiently, 'and he wanted her naked, and she would have refused him, so he lied to her. She didn't mind doing a boudoir portrait, but she wasn't going to unpeel for anyone, so we were going to fake it and I was just doing the preliminary work, the drawing and tints. Charcoal on canvas with a few colours touched in; the colours of the bed covers, the wallpaper, her ladyship's skin and hair. Bitch that she was.'

Sandman felt a surge of hope, for the last four words had been malevolent, just as he expected a murderer would speak of his victim. 'You didn't like her?'

'Like her? I despised her!' Corday spat. 'She was a

61

trumped up demi-rep!' He meant she was a courtesan, a high-class whore. 'A buttock,' Corday downgraded her savagely, 'nothing else. But just because I didn't like her doesn't make me a rapist and murderer. Besides, do you really think a woman like the Countess of Avebury would allow a painter's apprentice to be alone with her? She was chaperoned by a maid all the time I was there. How could I have raped or murdered her?'

'There was a maid?' Sandman asked.

'Of course there was,' Corday insisted scornfully, 'an ugly bitch called Meg.'

Sandman was totally confused now. 'And, presumably, Meg spoke at your trial?'

'Meg has disappeared,' Corday said tiredly, 'which is why I am going to hang.' He glared at Sandman. 'You don't believe me, do you? You think I'm making it up. But there was a maid and her name was Meg and she was there and when it came to the trial she couldn't be found.' He had spoken defiantly, but his demeanour suddenly changed as he began to weep again. 'Does it hurt?' he asked. 'I know it does. It must!'

Sandman stared down at the flagstones. 'Where was the house?'

'Mount Street,' Corday was hunched and sobbing, 'it's just off . . .'

'I know where Mount Street is,' Sandman interrupted a little too sharply. He was embarrassed by Corday's tears, but persevered with questions that were now actuated by a genuine curiosity. 'And you admit to being in the Countess's house on the day she was murdered?'

'I was there just before she was murdered!' Corday

said. 'There were back stairs, servants' stairs, and there was a knock on the door there. A deliberate knock, a signal, and the Countess became agitated and insisted I leave at once. So Meg took me down the front stairs and showed me the door. I had to leave everything, the paints, canvas, everything, and that convinced the constables I was guilty. So within an hour they came and arrested me at Sir George's studio.'

'Who sent for the constables?'

Corday shrugged to suggest he did not know. 'Meg? Another of the servants?'

'And the constables found you at Sir George's studio. Which is where?'

'Sackville Street. Above Gray's, the jewellers.' Corday stared red-eyed at Sandman. 'Do you have a knife?'

'No.'

'Because if you do, then I beg you give it me. Give it me! I would rather cut my wrists than stay here! I did nothing, *nothing*! Yet I am beaten and abused all day, and in a week I hang. Why wait a week? I am already in hell. I am in hell!'

Sandman cleared his throat. 'Why not stay up here, in the cells? You'd be alone here.'

'Alone? I'd be alone for two minutes! It's safer downstairs where at least there are witnesses.' Corday wiped his eyes with his sleeve. 'What do you do now?'

'Now?' Sandman was nonplussed. He had expected to listen to a confession and then go back to the Wheatsheaf and write a respectful report. Instead he was confused.

'You said the Home Secretary wanted you to make enquiries. So will you?' Corday's gaze was challenging, then he crumpled. 'You don't care. No one cares!'

'I shall make enquiries,' Sandman said gruffly, and suddenly he could not take the stench and the tears and the misery any more and so he turned and ran down the stairs. He came into the fresher air of the Press Yard, then had a moment's panic that the turnkeys would not unbolt the gate that would let him into the tunnel, but of course they did.

The porter unlocked his cupboard and took out Sandman's watch, a gold-cased Breguet that had been a gift from Eleanor. Sandman had tried to return the watch with her letters, but she had refused to accept them. 'Find your man, sir?' the porter asked.

'I found him.'

'And he spun you a yarn, I've no doubt,' the porter chuckled. 'Spun you a yarn, eh? They can gammon you, sir, like a right patterer. But there's an easy way to know when a felon's telling lies, sir, an easy way.'

'I should be obliged to hear it,' Sandman said.

'They're speaking, sir, that's how you can tell they're telling lies, they're speaking.' The porter thought this a fine joke and wheezed with laughter as Sandman went down the steps into Old Bailey.

He stood on the pavement, oblivious of the crowd surging up and down. He felt soiled by the prison. He clicked open the Breguet's case and saw it was just after half past two in the afternoon; he wondered where his day had gone. *To Rider*, Eleanor's inscription inside the watch case read, *in aeternam*, and that palpably false

64

promise did not improve his mood. He clicked the lid shut just as a workman shouted at him to mind himself. The trapdoor, pavilion and stairs of the scaffold had all been dismantled and now the tongue-and-groove cladding that had screened the platform was being thrown down and the planks were falling perilously near Sandman. A carter hauling a vast wagon of bricks whipped blood from the flanks of his horses, even though the beasts could make no headway against the tangle of vehicles that blocked the street.

Sandman finally thrust the watch into his fob pocket and walked northwards. He was torn. Corday had been found guilty and yet, though Sandman could not find a scrap of liking for the young man, his story was believable. Doubtless the porter was right and every man in Newgate was convinced of his own innocence, yet Sandman was not entirely naïve. He had led a company of soldiers with consummate skill and he reckoned he could distinguish when a man was telling the truth. And if Corday was innocent then the fifteen guineas that weighed down Sandman's pockets would be neither swiftly nor easily earnt.

He decided he needed advice.

So he went to watch some cricket.

2

Sandman reached Bunhill Row just before the city clocks struck three, the jangling of the bells momentarily drowning the crack of bat on ball, the deep shouts and applause of the spectators. It sounded like a large crowd and, judging by the shouts, a good match. The gatekeeper waved him through. 'I ain't taking your sixpence, Captain.'

'You should, Joe.'

'Aye, and you should be playing, Captain.' Joe Mallock, gatekeeper at the Artillery Ground, had once bowled for the finest clubs in London before painful joints had laid him low, and he well remembered one of his last games when a young army officer, scarce out of school, had thrashed him all over the New Road outfield in Marylebone. 'Been too long since we seen you bat, Captain.'

'I'm past my prime, Joe.'

'Past your prime, boy? Past your prime! You aren't even thirty yet. Now go on in. Last I heard England was fifty-six runs up with only four in hand. They need you!'

A raucous jeer rewarded a passage of play as Sandman walked towards the boundary. The Marquess of Canfield's eleven were playing an England eleven and one of the Marquess's fielders had dropped an easy catch and now endured the crowd's scorn. 'Butterfingers!' they roared. 'Fetch him a bucket!'

Sandman glanced at the blackboard and saw that England, in their second innings, were only sixty runs ahead and still had four wickets in hand. Most of the crowd were cheering the England eleven and a roar greeted a smart hit that sent the ball scorching towards the field's far side. The Marquess's bowler, a bearded giant, spat on the grass then stared up at the blue sky as if he was deaf to the crowd's noise. Sandman watched the batsman, Budd it was, walk down the wicket and pat down an already smooth piece of turf.

Sandman strolled past the carriages parked by the boundary. The Marquess of Canfield, white-haired, white-bearded and ensconced with a telescope in a landau, offered Sandman a curt nod, then pointedly looked away. A year ago, before the disgrace of Sandman's father, the Marquess would have called out a greeting, insisted on sharing a few moments of gossip and begged Sandman to play for his team, but now the Sandman name was dirt and the Marquess had pointedly cut him. But then, from further about the boundary and as if in recompense, a hand waved vigorously from another open carriage and an eager voice shouted a greeting. 'Rider! Here! Rider!'

The hand and voice belonged to a tall, ragged young man who was painfully thin, very bony and lanky, dressed in shabby black and smoking a clay pipe that trickled a drift of ash down his waistcoat and jacket. His red hair was in need of a pair of scissors for it collapsed across his long-nosed face and flared above his wide and old-fashioned collar. 'Drop the carriage steps,' he instructed Sandman, 'come on in. You're monstrous late. Heydell scored thirty-four in the first innings and very well scored they were too. How are you, my dear fellow? Fowkes is bowling creditably well, but is a bit errant on the off side. Budd is carrying his bat, and the creature who has just come in is called Fellowes and I know nothing about him. You should be playing. You also look pale. Are you eating properly?'

'I eat,' Sandman said, 'and you?'

'God preserves me, in His effable wisdom He preserves me.' The Reverend Lord Alexander Pleydell settled back on his seat. 'I see my father ignored you?'

'He nodded to me.'

'He nodded? Ah! What graciousness. Is it true you played for Sir John Hart?'

'Played and lost,' Sandman said bitterly. 'They were bribed.'

'Dear Rider! I warned you of Sir John! Man's nothing but greed. He only wanted you to play so that everyone would assume his team was incorruptible and it worked, didn't it? I just hope he paid you well for he must have made a great deal of money from your gullibility. Would you like some tea? Of course you would. I shall have Hughes bring us tea and cake from Mrs Hillman's stall, I think, don't you? Budd looks good as ever, don't he? What a hitter he is! Have you ever lifted

68

his bat? It's a club, a cudgel! Oh, well done, sir! Well struck! Go hard, sir, go hard!' He was cheering on England and doing it in a very loud voice so that his father, whose team was playing against England, would hear him. 'Capital, sir, well done! Hughes, my dear fellow, where are you?'

Hughes, Lord Alexander's manservant, approached the side of the carriage. 'My lord?'

'Say hello to Captain Sandman, Hughes, and I think we might venture a pot of Mrs Hillman's tea, don't you? And perhaps some of her apricot cake?' His Lordship put money into his servant's hand. 'What are the bookies saying now, Hughes?'

'They strongly favour your father's eleven, my lord.'

Lord Alexander pressed two more coins on his servant. 'Captain Sandman and I will wager a guinea apiece on an England win.'

'I can't afford such a thing,' Sandman protested, 'and besides I detest gambling on cricket.'

'Don't be pompous,' Lord Alexander said, 'we're not bribing the players, merely risking cash on our appreciation of their skill. You truly do look pale, Rider, are you sickening? Cholera, perhaps? The plague? Consumption, maybe?'

'Prison fever.'

'My dear fellow!' Lord Alexander looked horrified. 'Prison fever? And for God's sake sit down.' The carriage swayed as Sandman sat opposite his friend. They had attended the same school where they had become inseparable friends and where Sandman, who had always excelled at games and was thus one of the school's heroes, had protected Lord Alexander from the bullies who believed his lordship's clubbed foot made him an object of ridicule. Sandman, on leaving school, had purchased a commission in the infantry while Lord Alexander, who was the Marquis of Canfield's second son, had gone to Oxford where, in the first year that such things were awarded, he had taken a double first. 'Don't tell me you've been imprisoned,' Lord Alexander now chided Sandman.

Sandman smiled and showed his friend the letter from the Home Office and then described his afternoon, though the telling of his tale was constantly interrupted by Lord Alexander's exclamations of praise or scorn for the cricket, many of them uttered through a mouthful of Mrs Hillman's apricot cake which his lordship reduced to a spattering of crumbs that joined the ashes on his waistcoat. Beside his chair he kept a bag filled with clay pipes and as soon as one became plugged he would take out another and strike flint on steel. The sparks chipped from the flint smouldered on his coat and on the carriage's leather seat where they were either beaten out or faded on their own as his lordship puffed more smoke. 'I must say,' he said when he had considered Sandman's story, 'that I should deem it most unlikely that young Corday is guilty.'

'But he's been tried.'

'My dear Rider! My dear, dear Rider! Rider, Rider, Rider. Rider! Have you ever been to the Old Bailey sessions? Of course you haven't, you've been far too busy smiting the French, you wretch. But I dare say that inside of a week those four judges get through a hundred cases. Five a day apiece? They often do more. These folk don't get trials, Rider, they get dragged through the tunnel from Newgate, come blinking into the Session House, are knocked down like bullocks and hustled off in manacles! It ain't justice!'

'They are defended, surely?'

Lord Alexander turned a shocked face on his friend. 'The sessions ain't your Courts Martial, Rider. This is England! What barrister will defend some penniless youth accused of sheep stealing?'

'Corday isn't penniless.'

'But I'll wager he isn't rich. Good Lord, Rider, the woman was found naked, smothered in blood, with his palette knife in her throat.'

Sandman, watching the batsmen steal a quick single after an inelegant poke had trickled the ball down to square leg, was amused that his friend knew the details of Corday's crime, suggesting that Lord Alexander, when he was not deep in volumes of philosophy, theology and literature, was dipping into the vulgar broadsheets that described England's more violent crimes. 'So you're suggesting Corday is guilty,' Sandman said.

'No, Rider, I am suggesting that he looks guilty. There is a difference. And in any respectable system of justice we would devise ways of distinguishing between the appearance and the reality of guilt. But not in Sir John Silvester's courtroom. The man's a brute, a conscienceless brute. Oh, well struck, Budd, well struck! Run, man, run! Don't dawdle!' His lordship took up a new pipe and began setting fire to himself. 'The whole system,' he said between puffs, 'is pernicious.

Pernicious! They'll sentence a hundred folk to hang, then only kill ten of them because the rest have commuted sentences. And how do you obtain a commutation? Why, by having the squire or the parson or his lordship sign the petition. But what if you don't know such elevated folk? Then you'll hang. Hang. You fool! You fool! Did you see that? Fellowes is bowled, by God! Middle stump! Closed his eyes and swung! He should be hanged. You see, Rider, what is happening? Society, that's the respectable folk, you and me, well you at least, have devised a way to keep the lower orders under our control. We make them depend upon our mercy and our loving kindness. We condemn them to the gallows, then spare them and they are supposed to be grateful. Grateful! It is pernicious.' Lord Alexander was thoroughly worked up now. His long hands were wringing together and his hair, already hopelessly tousled, was being shaken into a worse disorder. 'Those damned Tories;' he glared at Sandman, including him in this condemnation, 'utterly pernicious!' He frowned for a second, then a happy idea struck him. 'You and I, Rider, we shall go to a hanging!'

'No!'

'It's your duty, my dear fellow. Now that you are a functionary of this oppressive state you should understand just what brutality awaits these innocent souls. I shall write to the Keeper of Newgate and demand that you and I are given privileged access to the next execution. Oh, a change of bowler. This fellow's said to twist it very cannily. You will have supper with me tonight?'

'In Hampstead?'

'Of course in Hampstead,' Lord Alexander said, 'it is where I live and dine, Rider.'

'Then I won't.'

Lord Alexander sighed. He had tried hard to persuade Sandman to move into his house and Sandman had been tempted, for Lord Alexander's father, despite disagreeing with all his son's radical beliefs, lavished an allowance on him that permitted the radical to enjoy a carriage, stables, servants and a rare library, but Sandman had learnt that to spend more than a few hours in his friend's company was to end up arguing bitterly. It was better, far better, to be independent.

'I saw Eleanor last Saturday,' Lord Alexander said with his usual tactlessness.

'I trust she was well?'

'I'm sure she was, but I rather think I forgot to ask. But then, why should one ask? It seems so redundant. She was obviously not dying, she looked well, so why should I ask? You recall Paley's *Principles*?'

'Is that a book?' Sandman asked, and was rewarded with an incredulous look. 'I've not read it,' he added hastily.

'What have you been doing with your life?' Lord Alexander asked testily. 'I shall lend it to you, but only so that you can understand the vile arguments that are advanced on the scaffold's behalf. Do you know,' Lord Alexander emphasised his next point by stabbing Sandman with the mouthpiece of his pipe, 'that Paley actually condoned hanging the innocent on the specious grounds that capital punishment is a necessity, that errors cannot be avoided in an imperfect world and that the guiltless suffer, therefore, so that general society might be safer. The innocent who are executed thus form an inevitable, if regrettable, sacrifice. Can you credit such an argument? They should have hanged Paley for it!'

'He was a clergyman, I believe?' Sandman said, applauding a subtle snick that sent a fielder running towards the Chiswell Street boundary.

'Of course he was a clergyman, but what does that have to do with the matter? I am a clergyman, does that give my arguments divine force? You are absurd at times.' Lord Alexander had broken the stem of his pipe while prodding his friend and now needed to light another. 'I confess that Thomas Jefferson makes the exact same point, of course, but I find his reasoning more elegant than Paley's.'

'Meaning,' Sandman said, 'that Jefferson is a hero of yours and can do no wrong.'

'I hope I am more discerning than that,' Lord Alexander replied huffily, 'and even you must allow that Jefferson has political reasons for his beliefs.'

'Which makes them all the more reprehensible,' Sandman said, 'and you're on fire.'

'So I am,' Lord Alexander beat at his coat. 'Eleanor asked after you, as I recall.'

'She did?'

'Did I not just say so? And I said I had no doubt you were in fine fettle. Oh, well struck, sir, well struck. Budd hits almost as hard as you! She and I met at the Egyptian Hall. There was a lecture about,' he paused, frowning as he stared at the batsmen, 'bless me, I've quite forgotten why I went, but Eleanor was there with Doctor Vaux and his wife. My God, that man is a fool.'

'Vaux?'

'No, the new batsman! No point in waving the bat idly! Strike, man, strike, it's what the bat is for! Eleanor had a message for you.'

'She did?' Sandman's heart quickened. His engagement to Eleanor might be broken off, but he was still in love with her. 'What?'

'What, indeed?' Lord Alexander frowned. 'Slipped my mind, Rider, slipped it altogether. Dear me, but it can't have been important. Wasn't important at all. And as for the Countess of Avebury!' He shuddered, evidently unable to express any kind of opinion on the murdered woman.

'What of her ladyship?' Sandman asked, knowing it would be pointless to pursue Eleanor's forgotten message.

'Ladyship! Ha!' Lord Alexander's exclamation was loud enough to draw the gaze of a hundred spectators. 'That baggage,' he said, then remembered his calling. 'Poor woman, but translated to a warmer place, no doubt. If anyone wanted her dead I should think it would be her husband. The wretched man must be weighted down with horns!'

'You think the Earl killed her?' Sandman asked.

'They're estranged, Rider, is that not an indication?'

'Estranged?'

'You sound surprised. May one ask why? Half

England's husbands seem to be estranged from their wives. It is hardly an uncommon situation.'

Sandman was surprised because he could have sworn Corday had said the Earl had commissioned his wife's portrait, but why would he do that if they were estranged? 'Are you certain they're estranged?' he asked.

'I have it on the highest authority,' Lord Alexander said defensively. 'I am a friend of the Earl's son. Christopher, his name is, and he's a most cordial man. He was at Brasenose when I was at Trinity.'

'Cordial?' Sandman asked. It seemed an odd word.

'Oh, very!' Alexander said energetically. 'He took an extremely respectable degree, I remember, then went off to study with Lasalle at the Sorbonne. His field is etymology.'

'Bugs?'

'Words, Rider, words.' Lord Alexander rolled his eyes at Sandman's ignorance. 'The study of the origins of words. Not a serious field, I always think, but Christopher seemed to think there was work to be done there. The dead woman, of course, was his stepmother.'

'He talked to you of her?'

'We talked of serious things,' Alexander said reprovingly, 'but naturally, in the course of any acquaintanceship, one learns trivia. There was little love lost in that family, I can tell you. Father despising the son, father hating the wife, wife detesting the husband and the son bitterly disposed towards both. I must say the Earl and Countess of Avebury form an object lesson in the perils

76

of family life. Oh well struck! Well struck! Good man! Capital work! Scamper, scamper!'

Sandman applauded the batsman, then sipped the last of his tea. 'I'm surprised to learn that Earl and Countess were estranged,' he said, 'because Corday claimed that the Earl commissioned the portrait. Why would he do that if they're estranged?'

'You must ask him,' Lord Alexander said, 'though my guess, for what it is worth, is that Avebury, though jealous, was still enamoured of her. She was a noted beauty and he is a noted fool. Mind you, Rider, I make no accusations. I merely assert that if anyone wanted the lady dead then it could well have been her husband, though I doubt he would have struck the fatal blow himself. Even Avebury is sensible enough to hire someone else to do his dirty work. Besides which he is a martyr to gout. Oh, well hit! Well hit! Go hard, go hard!'

'Is the son still in Paris?'

'He came back. I see him from time to time, though we're not as close as when we were at Oxford. Look at that! Fiddling with the bat. It's no good poking at balls!'

'Could you introduce me?'

'To Avebury's son? I suppose so.'

The game ended at shortly past eight when the Marquess's side, needing only ninety-three runs to win, collapsed. Their defeat pleased Lord Alexander, but made Sandman suspect that bribery had once again ruined a game. He could not prove it, and Lord Alexander scoffed at the suspicion and would not hear of it when Sandman tried to refuse his gambling winnings. 'Of course you must take it,' Lord Alexander insisted.

'Are you still lodging in the Wheatsheaf? You do know it's a flash tavern?'

'I know now,' Sandman admitted.

'Why don't we have supper there? I can learn some demotic flash, but I suppose all flash is demotic. Hughes? Summon the carriage horses, and tell Williams we're going to Drury Lane.'

Flash was the slang name for London's criminal life and the label attached to its language. No one stole a purse, they filed a bit or boned the cole or clicked the ready bag. Prison was a sheep walk or the quod, Newgate was the King's Head Inn and its turnkeys were gaggers. A good man was flash scamp and his victim a mum scull. Lord Alexander was reckoned a mum scull, but a genial one. He learnt the flash vocabulary and paid for the words by buying ale and gin, and he did not leave till well past midnight and it was then that Sally Hood came home on her brother's arm, both of them worse for drink, and they passed Lord Alexander who was standing by his carriage, which he had been delighted to learn was really a rattler, while its lamps were a pair of glims. He was holding himself upright by gripping a wheel when Sally hurried past. He stared after her open-mouthed. 'I am in love, Rider,' he declared too loudly.

Sally glanced back over her shoulder and gave Sandman a dazzling smile. 'You are not in love, Alexander,' Sandman said firmly.

Lord Alexander kept staring after Sally until she had vanished through the Wheatsheaf's front door. 'I am in love,' Lord Alexander insisted. 'I have been smitten by Cupid's arrow. I am enamoured. I am fatally in love.'

'You're a very drunken clergyman, Alexander.'

'I am a very drunken clergyman in love. Do you know the lady? You can arrange an introduction?' He lurched after Sally, but his club foot slipped on the cobbles and he fell full length. 'I insist, Rider!' he said from the ground. 'I insist upon paying the lady my respects. I wish to marry her.' In truth he was so drunk he could not stand, but Sandman, Hughes and the coachman managed to get his lordship into his carriage and then, glims glimmering, it rattled north.

It was raining next morning and all London seemed in a bad mood. Sandman had a headache, a sore belly and the memory of Lord Alexander singing the gallows song that he had been taught in the taproom.

> And now I'm going to hell, going to hell,
> And wouldn't we do well, we do well,
> If you go there to dwell, there to dwell,
> Damn your eyes.

The tune was lodged in Sandman's mind and he could not rid himself of it as he shaved, then made tea over the back room fire where the tenants were allowed to boil their water. Sally hurried in, her hair in disarray, but with her dress already hooked up. She ladled herself a cup of water and lifted it in a mock toast. 'Breakfast,' she told Sandman, then grinned. 'I hear you was jolly last night?'

'Good morning, Miss Hood,' Sandman groaned.

She laughed. 'Who was that cripple cove you was with?'

'He is my particular friend,' Sandman said, 'the Reverend Lord Alexander Pleydell, MA, is second son of the Marquess and Marchioness of Canfield.'

Sally stared at Sandman. 'You're gammoning me.'

'I promise I am not.'

'He said he was in love with me.'

Sandman had hoped she had not heard. 'And doubtless this morning, Miss Hood,' he said, 'when he is sober, he will still be in love with you.'

Sally laughed at Sandman's tact. 'Is he really a reverend? He don't dress like one.'

'He took orders when he left Oxford,' Sandman explained, 'but I rather think he did it to annoy his father. Or perhaps, at the time, he wanted to become a fellow of his college? But he's never looked for a living. He doesn't need a parish or any other kind of job because he's rather rich. He claims he's writing a book, but I've seen no evidence of it.'

Sally drank her water, then grimaced at the taste. 'A reverend rich cripple?' She thought for a moment, then smiled mischievously. 'Is he married?'

'No,' Sandman said, and did not add that Alexander regularly fell in love with every pretty shopgirl he saw.

'Well, I could do a hell of a lot worse than a crocked parson, couldn't I?' Sally said, then gasped as a clock struck nine. 'Lord above, I'm late. This bugger I'm working for likes to start early.' She ran.

Sandman pulled on his greatcoat and set off for

Mount Street. Investigate, Alexander had urged him, so he would. He had six days to discover the truth, and he decided he would begin with the missing maid, Meg. If she existed, and on this wet morning Sandman was dubious of Corday's story, then she could end Sandman's confusion by confirming or denying the painter's tale. He hurried up New Bond Street, then realised with a start that he would have to walk past Eleanor's house in Davies Street and, because he did not want anyone there to think he was being importunate, he avoided it by taking the long way round and so was soaked to the skin by the time he reached the house in Mount Street where the murder had taken place.

It was easy enough to tell which was the Earl of Avebury's town house, for even in this weather and despite a paucity of pedestrians, a broadsheet seller was crouching beneath a tarpaulin in an effort to hawk her wares just outside the murder house. 'Tale of a murder, sir,' she greeted Sandman, 'just a penny. 'Orrible murder, sir.'

'Give me one.' Sandman waited as she extricated a sheet from her tarpaulin bag, then he climbed the steps and rapped on the front door. The windows of the house were shuttered, but that meant little. Many folk, stuck in London outside of the season, closed their shutters to suggest they had gone to the country, but it seemed the house really was empty for Sandman's knocking achieved nothing.

'There's no one home,' the woman selling the broadsheets said, 'not been anyone home since the murder, sir.' A crossing sweeper, attracted by Sandman's

81

hammering, had come to the house and he also confirmed that it was empty.

'But this is the Earl of Avebury's house?' Sandman asked.

'It is, sir, yes, sir,' the crossing sweeper, a boy of about ten, was hoping for a tip, 'and it's empty, your lordship.'

'There was a maid here,' Sandman said, 'called Meg. Did you know her?'

The crossing sweeper shook his head. 'Don't know no one, your honour.' Two more boys, both paid to sweep horse manure off the streets, had joined the crossing sweeper. 'Gorn away,' one of them commented.

A charlie, carrying his watchman's staff, came to gawp at Sandman, but did not interfere, and just then the front door of the next house along opened and a middle-aged woman in dowdy clothes appeared on the step. She shuddered at the rain, glanced nervously at the small crowd outside her neighbour's door, then put up an umbrella. 'Madam!' Sandman called. 'Madam!'

'Sir?' The woman's clothes suggested she was a servant, perhaps a housekeeper.

Sandman pushed past his small audience and took off his hat. 'Forgive me, madam, but Viscount Sidmouth has charged me with investigating the sad events that occurred here.' He paused and the woman just gaped at him as the rain dripped off the edges of her umbrella, though she seemed impressed by the mention of a viscount, which was why Sandman had introduced it. 'Is it true, ma'am,' Sandman went on, 'that there was a maid called Meg in the house?'

The woman looked back at her closed front door as if seeking an escape, but then nodded. 'There was, sir, there was.'

'Do you know where she is?'

'They've gone, sir, gone. All gone, sir.'

'But where?'

'They went to the country, sir, I think.' She dropped Sandman a curtsey, evidently hoping that would persuade him to go away.

'The country?'

'They went away, sir. And the Earl, sir, he has a house in the country, sir, near Marlborough, sir.'

She knew nothing more. Sandman pressed her, but the more he questioned her the less certain she was of what she had already told him. Indeed, she was sure of only one thing, that the Countess's cooks, footmen, coachmen and maids were all gone and she thought, she did not know, that they must have gone to the Earl's country house that lay close to Marlborough. 'That's what I told you,' one of the sweeping boys said, 'they've gorn.'

'Her ladyship's gorn,' the watchman said, then laughed, 'torn and gorn.'

'Read all about it,' the broadsheet seller called optimistically.

It seemed evident that there was little more to learn in Mount Street, so Sandman walked away. Meg existed? That confirmed part of Corday's tale, but only part, for the painter's apprentice could still have done the murder when the maid was out of the room. Sandman thought of the Newgate porter's assurance that all felons lied and he wondered if he was being unforgivably naïve in doubting Corday's guilt. The wretched boy had, after all, been tried and convicted, and though Lord Alexander might scorn British justice, Sandman found it hard to be so dismissive. He had spent most of the last decade fighting for his country against a tyranny that Lord Alexander celebrated. A portrait of Napoleon hung on his friend's wall, together with George Washington and Thomas Paine. Nothing English, it seemed to Sandman, ever pleased Lord Alexander, while anything foreign was preferable, and not all the blood that had dripped from the guillotine's blade would ever convince Lord Alexander that liberty and equality were incompatible, a point of view which seemed glaringly obvious to Sandman. Thus, it seemed, were they doomed to disagree. Lord Alexander Pleydell would fight for equality while Sandman believed in liberty, and it was unthinkable to Sandman that a freeborn Englishman would not get a fair trial, yet that was precisely what his appointment as Investigator was encouraging him to think. It was more comforting to believe Corday was a liar, yet Meg undoubtedly existed and her existence cast doubt on Sandman's stout belief in British justice.

He was walking east on Burlington Gardens, thinking these wild thoughts and only half aware of the rattle of carriages splashing through the rain, when he saw that the end of the street was plugged by a stonemason's wagons and scaffolding, so he turned down Sackville Street where he had to step into the gutter because a small crowd was standing under the awning of Gray's jewellery shop. They were mostly sheltering from the rain, but a few were admiring the rubies and sapphires of a magnificent necklace that was on display inside a gilded cage in the jeweller's window. Gray's. The name reminded Sandman of something, so that he stopped in the street and stared up past the awning.

'You tired of bleeding life?' a carter snarled at Sandman, and hauled on his reins. Sandman ignored the man. Corday had said that Sir George Phillips's studio was here, but Sandman could see nothing in the windows above the shop. He stepped back to the pavement to find a doorway to one side of the shop, plainly separate from the jewellery business, but no plate announced who lived or traded behind the door that was painted a shining green and furnished with a well-polished brass knocker. A one-legged beggar sat in the doorway, his face disfigured by ulcers. 'Spare a coin for an old soldier, sir?'

'Where did you serve?' Sandman asked.

'Portugal, sir, Spain, sir and Waterloo, sir.' The beggar patted his stump. 'Lost the gam at Waterloo, sir. Been through it all, sir, I have.'

'What regiment?'

'Artillery, sir. Gunner, sir.' He sounded more nervous now.

'Which battalion and company?'

'Eighth battalion, sir,' the beggar was now plainly uncomfortable and his answer was unconvincing.

'Company?' Sandman demanded. 'And company commander's name?'

85

'Why don't you brush off,' the man snarled.

'I wasn't long in Portugal,' Sandman told the man, 'but I did fight through Spain and I was at Waterloo.' He lifted the brass knocker and rapped it hard. 'We had some difficult times in Spain,' he went on, 'but Waterloo was by far the worst and I have great sympathy for all who fought there.' He knocked again. 'But I can get angry, bloody angry,' his temper was rising, 'with men who claim to have fought there and did not! It bloody annoys me!'

The beggar scrambled away from Sandman's temper and just then the green door opened and a black page-boy of thirteen or fourteen recoiled from Sandman's savage face. He must have thought the face meant trouble for he tried to close the door, but Sandman managed to put his boot in the way. Behind the boy was a short elegant hallway, then a narrow staircase. 'Is this Sir George Phillips's studio?' Sandman asked.

The pageboy, who was wearing a shabby livery and a wig in desperate need of powdering, heaved on the door, but could not prevail against Sandman's much greater strength. 'If you ain't got an appointment,' the boy said, 'then you ain't welcome.'

'I have got an appointment.'

'You have?' The surprised boy let go of the door, making Sandman stumble as it suddenly swung open. 'You have?' the boy asked again.

'I have an appointment,' Sandman said grandly, 'from Viscount Sidmouth.'

'Who is it, Sammy?' a voice boomed from upstairs.

'He says he's from Viscount Sidmouth.'

'Then let him up! Let him up! We are not too proud to paint politicians. We just charge the bastards more.'

'Take your coat, sir?' Sammy asked, giving Sandman a perfunctory bow.

'I'll keep it.' Sandman edged into the hallway which was tiny, but nevertheless decorated in a fashionable striped wallpaper and hung with a small chandelier. Sir George's rich patrons were to be welcomed by a liveried page and a carpeted entrance, but as Sandman climbed the stairs the elegance was tainted by the reek of turpentine and the room at the top, which was supposed to be as elegant as the hallway, had been conquered by untidiness. The room was a salon where Sir George could show his finished paintings and entice would-be subjects to pay for their portraits, but it had become a dumping place for half-finished work, for palettes of crusted paint, for an abandoned game pie that had mould on its pastry, for old brushes, rags and a pile of men's and women's clothes. A second flight of stairs went to the top floor and Sammy indicated that Sandman should go on up. 'You want coffee, sir?' he asked, going to a curtained doorway that evidently hid a kitchen. 'Or tea?'

'Tea would be kind.'

The ceiling had been knocked out of the top floor to open the long room to the rafters of the attic, then skylights had been put in the roof so that Sandman seemed to be climbing into the light. Rain pattered on the tiles and enough dripped through to need catchment buckets that had been placed all about the studio. A black pot-bellied stove dominated the room's centre, though now it did nothing except serve as a table for a bottle of wine and a glass. Next to the stove an easel supported a massive canvas while a naval officer posed with a sailor and a woman on a platform at the farther end. The woman screamed when Sandman appeared, then snatched up a drab cloth that covered a tea chest on which the naval officer was sitting.

It was Sally Hood. Sandman, his wet hat in his right hand, bowed to her. She was holding a trident and wearing a brass helmet and very little else. Actually, Sandman realised, she was wearing nothing else, though her hips and thighs were mostly screened by an oval wooden shield on which a union flag had been hastily drawn in charcoal. She was, Sandman realised, Britannia. 'You are feasting your eyes,' the man beside the easel said, 'on Miss Hood's tits. And why not? As tits go, they are splendid, quintessence of bubby.'

'Captain,' Sally acknowledged Sandman in a small voice.

'Your servant, Miss Hood,' Sandman said, bowing again.

'Good Lord Almighty!' the painter said. 'Have you come to see me or Sally?' He was an enormous man, fat as a hogshead, with great jowls, a bloated nose and a belly that distended a paint-smeared shirt decorated with ruffles. His white hair was bound by a tight cap of the kind that used to be worn beneath wigs.

'Sir George?' Sandman asked.

'At your service, sir.' Sir George attempted a bow, but was so fat he could only manage a slight bend at what passed for his waist, but he made a pretty gesture

88

with the brush in his hand, sweeping it as though it were a folded fan. 'You are welcome,' he said, 'so long as you seek a commission. I charge eight hundred guineas for a full length, six hundred from the waist up, and I don't do heads unless I'm starving and I ain't been starving since 'ninety-nine. Viscount Sidmouth sent you?'

'He doesn't wish to be painted, Sir George.'

'Then you can bugger off!' the painter said. Sandman ignored the suggestion, instead looking about the studio which was a riot of plaster statues, curtains, discarded rags and half-finished canvasses. 'Oh, make yourself at home here, do,' Sir George snarled, then shouted down the stairs. 'Sammy, you black bastard, where's the tea?'

'Brewing!' Sammy called back.

'Hurry it!' Sir George threw down his palette and brush. Two youths were flanking him, both painting waves on the canvas and Sandman guessed they were his apprentices. The canvas itself was vast, at least ten feet wide, and it showed a solitary rock in a sunlit sea on which a half-painted fleet was afloat. An admiral was seated on the rock's summit where he was flanked by a good-looking young man dressed as a sailor and by Sally Hood undressed as Britannia. Quite why the admiral, the sailor and the goddess should have been so marooned on their isolated rock was not clear and Sandman did not like to ask, but then he noticed that the officer who was posing as the admiral could not have been a day over eighteen yet he was wearing a gold-encrusted uniform on which shone two jewelled stars. That puzzled Sandman for a heartbeat, then he saw that the boy's empty right sleeve was pinned to his coat's breast. 'The real Nelson is dead,' Sir George had been following Sandman's eyes and thus deducing his train of thought, 'so we make do as best we can with young Master Corbett there, and do you know what is the tragedy of young Master Corbett's life? It is that his back is turned to Britannia, thus he must sit there for hours every day in the knowledge that one of the ripest pairs of naked tits in all London are just two feet behind his left ear and he can't see them. Ha! And for God's sake, Sally, stop hiding.'

'You ain't painting,' Sally said, 'so I can cover up.' She had dropped the grey cloth that turned the tea chest into a rock and was instead wearing her street coat.

Sir George picked up his brush. 'I'm painting now,' he snarled.

'I'm cold,' Sally complained.

'Too grand suddenly to show us your bubbies, are you?' Sir George snarled, then looked at Sandman. 'Has she told you about her lord? The one who's sweet on her? We'll soon all be bowing and scraping to her, won't we? Yes, your ladyship, show us your tits, your ladyship.' He laughed, and the apprentices all grinned.

'She hasn't lied to you,' Sandman said. 'His lordship exists, I know him, he is indeed enamoured of Miss Hood, and he is very rich. More than rich enough to commission a dozen portraits from you, Sir George.'

Sally gave him a look of pure gratitude while Sir George, discomfited, dabbed the brush into the paint on his palette. 'So who the devil are you?' he demanded of Sandman. 'Besides being an envoy of Sidmouth's?'

'My name is Captain Rider Sandman.'

'Navy, army, fencibles, yeomanry or is the captaincy a fiction? Most ranks are these days.'

'I was in the army,' Sandman said.

'You can uncover,' Sir George explained to Sally, 'because the captain was a soldier which means he's seen more tits than I have.'

'He ain't seen mine,' Sally said, clutching the coat to her bosom.

'How do you know her?' Sir George asked Sandman in a suspicious tone.

'We lodge in the same tavern, Sir George.'

Sir George snorted. 'Then either she lives higher in the world than she deserves, or you live lower. Drop the coat, you stupid bitch.'

'I'm embarrassed,' Sally confessed, reddening.

'He's seen worse than you naked,' Sir George commented sourly, then stepped back to survey his painting. ' "The Apotheosis of Lord Nelson", would you believe? And you are wondering, are you not, why I don't have the little bugger in an eyepatch? Are you not wondering that?'

'No,' Sandman said.

'Because he never wore an eyepatch, that's why. Never! I painted him twice from life. He sometimes wore a green eyeshade, but never a patch, so he won't have one in this masterpiece commissioned by their Lordships of the Admiralty. They couldn't stand the little bugger when he was alive, now they want him up on their wall. But what they really want to suspend on their panelling, Captain Sandman, is Sally Hood's tits. Sammy, you black bastard! What in God's name are you bloody doing down there? Growing the bloody tea leaves? Bring me some brandy!' He glared at Sandman. 'So what do you want of me, Captain?'

'To talk about Charles Corday.'

'Oh, Good Christ alive,' Sir George blasphemed, and stared belligerently at Sandman. 'Charles Corday?' He said the name very portentously. 'You mean grubby little Charlie Cruttwell?'

'Who now calls himself Corday, yes.'

'Doesn't bloody matter what he calls himself,' Sir George said, 'they're still going to stretch his skinny neck next Monday. I thought I might go and watch. It ain't every day a man sees one of his own apprentices hanged, more's the pity.' He cuffed one of the youths who was laboriously painting in the white-flecked waves, then scowled at his three models. 'Sally, for God's sake, your tits are my money. Now, pose as you're paid to!'

Sandman courteously turned his back as she dropped the coat. 'The Home Secretary,' he said, 'has asked me to investigate Corday's case.'

Sir George laughed. 'His mother's been bleating to the Queen, is that it?'

'Yes.'

'Lucky little Charlie that he has such a mother. You want to know whether he did it?'

'He tells me he didn't.'

'Of course he tells you that,' Sir George said scornfully. 'He's hardly likely to offer you a confession, is he? But oddly enough he's probably telling the truth. At least about the rape.'

'He didn't rape her?'

'He might have done,' Sir George was making delicate little dabs with the brush which were magically bringing Sally's face alive under the helmet. 'He might have done, but it would have been against his nature.' Sir George gave Sandman a sly glance. 'Our Monsieur Corday, Captain, is a sodomite.' He laughed at Sandman's expression. 'They'll hang you for being one of those, so it don't make much difference to Charlie whether he's guilty or innocent of murder, do it? He's certainly guilty of sodomy so he thoroughly deserves to hang. They all do. Nasty little buggers. I'd hang them all and not by the neck either.'

Sammy, minus his livery coat and wig, brought up a tray on which were some ill-assorted cups, a pot of tea and a bottle of brandy. The boy poured tea for Sir George and Sandman, but only Sir George received a glass of brandy. 'You'll get your tea in a minute,' Sir George told his three models, 'when I'm ready.'

'Are you sure?' Sandman asked him.

'About them getting their tea? Or about Charlie being a sodomite? Of course I'm bloody sure. You could unpeel Sally and a dozen like her right down to the raw and he wouldn't bother to look, but he was always trying to get his paws on young Sammy here, wasn't he, Sammy?'

'I told him to fake away off,' Sammy said.

'Good for you, Samuel!' Sir George said. He put

93

down his brush and gulped the brandy. 'And you are wondering, Captain, are you not, why I would allow a filthy sodomite into this temple of art? I shall tell you. Because Charlie was good. Oh, he was good.' He poured more brandy, drank half of it, then returned to the canvas. 'He drew beautifully, Captain, drew like the young Raphael. He was a joy to watch. He had the gift, which is more than I can say for this pair of butcher boys.' He cuffed the second apprentice. 'No, Charlie was good. He could paint as well as draw, which meant I could trust him with flesh, not just draperies. In another year or two he'd have been off on his own. The picture of the Countess? It's there if you want to see how good he was.' He gestured to some unframed canvasses that were stacked against a table that was littered with jars, paste, knives, pestles and oil flasks. 'Find it, Barney,' Sir George ordered one of his apprentices. 'It's all his work, Captain,' Sir George went on, 'because it ain't got to the point where it needs my talent.'

'He couldn't have finished it himself?' Sandman asked. He sipped the tea, which was an excellent blend of gunpowder and green.

Sir George laughed. 'What did he tell you, Captain? No, let me guess. Charlie told you that I wasn't up to it, didn't he? He said I was drunk, so he had to paint her ladyship. Is that what he told you?'

'Yes,' Sandman admitted.

Sir George was amused. 'The lying little bastard. He deserves to hang for that.'

'So why did you let him paint the Countess?'

'Think about it,' Sir George said. 'Sally, shoulders

94

back, head up, nipples out, that's my girl. You're Britannia, you rule the bleeding waves, you're not some bloody Brighton whore drooping on a boulder.'

'Why?' Sandman persisted.

'Because, Captain,' Sir George paused to make a stroke with the brush, 'because we were gammoning the lady. We were painting her in a frock, but once the canvas got back here we were going to make her naked. That's what the Earl wanted and that's what Charlie would have done. But when a man asks a painter to depict his wife naked, and a remarkable number do, then you can be certain that the resulting portrait will not be displayed. Does a man hang such a painting in his morning room for the titillation of his friends? He does not. Does he show it in his London house for the edification of society? He does not. He hangs it in his dressing room or in his study where none but himself can see it. And what use is that to me? If I paint a picture, Captain, I want all London gaping at it. I want them queueing up those stairs begging me to paint one just like it for themselves and that means there ain't no money in society tits. I paint the profitable pictures, Charlie was taking care of the boudoir portraits.' He stepped back and frowned at the young man posing as a sailor. 'You're holding that oar all wrong, Johnny. Maybe I should have you naked. As Neptune.' He turned and leered at Sandman. 'Why didn't I think of that before? You'd make a good Neptune, Captain. Fine figure you've got. You could oblige me by stripping naked and standing opposite Sally? We'll give you a triton shell to hold, erect. I've got a triton shell somewhere, I used it for the Apotheosis of the Earl St Vincent.'

'What do you pay?' Sandman asked.

'Five shillings a day.' Sir George had been surprised by the response.

'You don't pay me that!' Sally protested.

'Because you're a bloody woman!' Sir George snapped, then looked at Sandman. 'Well?'

'No,' Sandman said, then went very still. The apprentice had been turning over the canvasses and Sandman now stopped him. 'Let me see that one,' he said, pointing to a full-length portrait.

The apprentice pulled it from the stack and propped it on a chair so that the light from a skylight fell on the canvas, which showed a young woman sitting at a table with her head cocked in what was almost but not quite a belligerent fashion. Her right hand was resting on a pile of books while her left held an hourglass. Her red hair was piled high to reveal a long and slender neck that was circled by sapphires. She was wearing a dress of silver and blue with white lace at the neck and wrists. Her eyes stared boldly out of the canvas and added to the suggestion of belligerence, which was softened by the mere suspicion that she was about to smile.

'Now that,' Sir George said reverently, 'is a very clever young lady. And be careful with it, Barney, it's going for varnishing this afternoon. You like it, Captain?'

'It's –' Sandman paused, wanting a word that would flatter Sir George, 'it's wonderful,' he said lamely.

'It is indeed,' Sir George said enthusiastically, stepping away from Nelson's half-finished apotheosis to admire the young woman whose red hair was brushed away from a forehead that was high and broad, whose nose was straight and long and whose mouth was generous and wide, and who had been painted in a lavish sitting room beneath a wall of ancestral portraits which suggested she came from a family of great antiquity, though in truth her father was the son of an apothecary and her mother a parson's daughter who was considered to have married beneath herself. 'Miss Eleanor Forrest,' Sir George said. 'Her nose is too long, her chin too sharp, her eyes more widely spaced than convention would allow to be beautiful, her hair is lamentably red and her mouth is too lavish, yet the effect is extraordinary, is it not?'

'It is,' Sandman said fervently.

'Yet of all the young woman's attributes,' Sir George had entirely dropped his bantering manner and was speaking with real warmth, 'it is her intelligence I most admire. I fear she is to be wasted in marriage.'

'She is?' Sandman had to struggle to keep his voice from betraying his feelings.

'The last I heard,' Sir George returned to Nelson, 'she was spoken of as the future Lady Eagleton. Indeed I believe the portrait is a gift for him, yet Miss Eleanor is much too clever to be married to a fool like Eagleton.' Sir George snorted. 'Wasted.'

'Eagleton?' Sandman felt as though a cold hand had gripped his heart. Had that been the import of the message Lord Alexander had forgotten? That Eleanor was engaged to Lord Eagleton?

'Lord Eagleton, heir to the Earl of Bridport and a bore. A bore, Captain, a bore and I detest bores. Is Sally Hood really to be a lady? Good God incarnate, England has gone to the weasels. Stick 'em out, darling, they ain't noble yet and they're what the Admiralty is paying for. Barney, find the Countess.'

The apprentice hunted on through the canvasses. The wind gusted, making the rafters creak. Sammy emptied two of the buckets into which rain was leaking, chucking them out of the back window and provoking a roar of protest from below. Sandman stared out of the front windows, looking past the awning of Gray's jewellery shop into Sackville Street. Was Eleanor really to marry? He had not seen her in over six months and it was very possible. Her mother, at least, was in a hurry to have Eleanor walk to an altar, preferably an aristocratic altar, for Eleanor was twenty-five now and would soon be reckoned a shelved spinster. Damn it, Sandman thought, but forget her. 'This is it, sir.' Barney, the apprentice, interrupted his thoughts. He propped an unfinished portrait over Eleanor's picture. 'The Countess of Avebury, sir.'

Another beauty, Sandman thought. The painting was hardly begun, yet it was strangely effective. The canvas had been sized, then a charcoal drawing made of a woman reclining on a bed that was surmounted by a tent of peaked material. Corday had then painted in patches of the wallpaper, the material of the bed's tent, the bedspread, the carpet, and the woman's face. He had lightly painted the hair, making it seem wild as though the Countess was in a country wind rather than her London bedroom, and though the rest of the canvas was hardly touched by any other colour, yet somehow it was still breathtaking and full of life.

'Oh, he could paint, our Charlie, he could paint.' Sir George, wiping his hands with a rag, had come to look at the picture. His voice was reverent and his eyes betrayed a mixture of admiration and jealousy. 'He's a clever little devil, ain't he?'

'Is it a good likeness?'

'Oh, yes,' Sir George nodded, 'indeed yes. She was a beauty, Captain, a woman who could make heads turn, but that's all she was. She was out of the gutter, Captain. She was what our Sally is. She was an opera dancer.'

'I'm an actress,' Sally insisted hotly.

'An actress, an opera dancer, a whore, they're all the same,' Sir George growled, 'and Avebury was a fool to have married her. He should have kept her as his mistress, but never married her.'

'This tea's bloody cold,' Sally complained. She had left the dais and discarded her helmet.

'Go and have some dinner, child,' Sir George said grandly, 'but be back here by two of the clock. Have you finished, Captain?'

Sandman nodded. He was staring at the Countess's picture. Her dress had been very lightly sketched, presumably because it was doomed to be obliterated, but her face, as striking as it was alluring, was almost completed. 'You said, did you not,' he asked, 'that the Earl of Avebury commissioned the portrait?'

'I did say so,' Sir George agreed, 'and he did.'

'Yet I heard that he and his wife were estranged?'
Sandman said.

'So I understand,' Sir George said airily, then gave a
wicked laugh. 'He was certainly cuckolded. Her ladyship
had a reputation, Captain, and it didn't involve feeding
the poor and comforting the afflicted.' He was pulling
on an old-fashioned coat, all wide cuffs, broad collars
and gilt buttons. 'Sammy,' he shouted down the stairs,
'I'll eat the game pie up here! And some of that salmagundi if it ain't mouldy. And you can open another
of the 'nine clarets.' He lumbered to the window and
scowled at the rain fighting against the smoke of a thousand chimneys.

'Why would a man estranged from his wife spend
a fortune on her portrait?' Sandman asked.

'The ways of the world, Captain,' Sir George said
portentously, 'are a mystery even unto me. How the
hell would I know?' Sir George turned from the
window. 'You'd have to ask his cuckolded lordship. I
believe he lives near Marlborough, though he's reputed
to be a recluse so I suspect you'd be wasting your journey. On the other hand, perhaps it isn't a mystery.
Maybe he wanted revenge on her? Hanging her naked
tits on his wall would be a kind of revenge, would it
not?'

'Would it?'

Sir George chuckled. 'There is none so conscious of
their high estate as an ennobled whore, Captain, so why
not remind the bitch of what brought her the title? Tits,
sir, tits. If it had not been for her good tits and long legs
she'd still be charging ten shillings a night. But did little

100

Charlie the sodomite kill her? I doubt it, Captain, I doubt it very much, but nor do I care very much. Little Charlie was getting too big for his boots, so I won't mourn to see him twitching at the end of a rope. Ah!' He rubbed his hands as his servant climbed the stairs with a heavy tray. 'Dinner! Good day to you, Captain, I trust I have been of service.'

Sandman was not sure Sir George had been of any service, unless increasing Sandman's confusion was of use, but Sir George was done with him now and Sandman was dismissed.

So he left. And the rain fell harder.

'That fat bastard never offers us dinner!' Sally Hood complained. She was sitting opposite Sandman in a tavern on Piccadilly where, inspired by Sir George Phillips's dinner, they shared a bowl of salmagundi: a cold mixture of cooked meats, anchovies, hard-boiled eggs and onions. 'He guzzles himself, he does,' Sally went on, 'and we're supposed to bleeding starve.' She tore a piece of bread from the loaf, poured more oil into the bowl then smiled shyly at Sandman. 'I was so embarrassed when you walked in.'

'No need to be,' Sandman said. On his way out of Sir George's studio he had invited Sally to join him and they had run through the rain and taken shelter in the Three Ships where he had paid for the salmagundi and a big jug of ale with some of the money advanced to him by the Home Office.

Sally shook salt into the bowl, then stirred the

mixture vigorously. 'You won't tell anyone?' she asked very earnestly.

'Of course not.'

'I know it ain't actressing,' she said, 'and I don't like that fat bastard staring at me all day, but it's rhino, isn't it?'

'Rhino?'

'Money.'

'It's rhino,' Sandman agreed.

'And I shouldn't have said anything about your friend,' Sally said, 'because I felt such a fool.'

'You mean Lord Alexander?'

'I am a fool, aren't I?' She grinned at him.

'Of course not.'

'I am,' she said fervently, 'but I don't want to be doing this forever. I'm twenty-two now and I'll have to find something soon, won't I? And I wouldn't mind meeting a real lord.'

'You want to marry?'

She nodded, shrugged, then speared half a boiled egg. 'I don't know,' she admitted. 'I mean when life's good, it's very good. Two years ago I never seemed not to be working. I was a witch's servant girl in a play about some Scottish king,' she wrinkled her face trying to think of the name, then shook her head, 'bastard, he was, then I was a dancing girl in a pageant about some black king what got himself killed in India and he was another bastard, but these last two or three months? Nothing! There's not even work at Vauxhall Gardens!'

'What did you do there?'

Sally closed her eyes as she thought. 'Tabbel,' she said, 'tabbler?'

'*Tableaux vivants*?'

'That's it! I was a goddess for three months last summer. I was up a tree, playing a harp and the rhino wasn't bad. Then I got a turn in Astley's with the dancing horses and that kept me through the winter, but there's nothing now, not even down the Strand!' She meant the newer theatres that offered more music and dancing than the two older theatres in Drury Lane and Covent Garden. 'But I've got a private show coming up,' she added, sniffing at the prospect.

'Private?' Sandman asked.

'A rich cove wants his girl to be an actress, see? So he hires the theatre when it's out of season and he pays us to sing and dance and he pays an audience to cheer and he pays the scribblers to write her up in the papers as the next Vestris. You want to come? It's Thursday night at Covent Garden, and it's only the one night so it ain't going to pay any bills, is it?'

'If I can I'll come,' Sandman promised.

'What I need,' Sally said, 'is to join a company, and I could if I was willing to be a frow. You know what that is? Of course you do. And that fat bastard,' she jerked her head, meaning Sir George Phillips, 'he thinks I'm a frow, but I'm not!'

'I never supposed you were.'

'Then you're the only bloody man who didn't.' She grinned at him. 'Well, you and my brother. Jack would kill anyone who said I was a frow.'

'Good for Jack,' Sandman said. 'I rather like your brother.'

'Everyone likes Jack,' Sally said.

'Not that I really know him, of course,' Sandman said, 'but he seems friendly.' Sally's brother, on the few occasions Sandman had encountered him, had seemed a confident, easy-mannered man. He was popular, presiding over a generous table in the Wheatsheaf's taproom and he was strikingly handsome, attracting a succession of young women. He was also mysterious for no one in the tavern would say exactly what he did for a living, though undoubtedly the living was reasonably good for he and Sally rented two large rooms on the Wheatsheaf's first floor. 'What does your brother do?' Sandman asked Sally now and, in return, received a very strange look. 'No, really,' he said, 'what does he do? It's just that he keeps odd hours.'

'You don't know who he is?' Sally asked.

'Should I?'

'He's Robin Hood,' Sally said, then laughed when she saw Sandman's face. 'That's my Jack, Captain,' she said, 'Robin Hood.'

'Good Lord,' Sandman said. Robin Hood was the nickname of a highwayman who was wanted by every magistrate in London. The reward for him was well over a hundred pounds and it was constantly rising.

Sally shrugged. 'He's a daft one, really. I keep telling him he'll end up doing Jemmy Botting's hornpipe, but he won't listen. And he looks after me. Well up to a point, he does, but it's always feast or famine with Jack and when he's in cash he gives it to his ladies. But he's good to me, he is, and he wouldn't let no one touch me.' She frowned. 'You won't tell anyone?'

'Of course I won't!'

'I mean everyone in the 'sheaf knows who he is, but none of them would tell on him.'

'Nor would I,' Sandman assured her.

'Of course you wouldn't,' Sally said, then grinned. 'So what about you? What do you want out of life?'

Sandman, surprised to be asked, thought for a moment. 'I suppose I want my old life back.'

'War? Being a soldier?' She sounded disapproving.

'No. Just the luxury of not worrying about where the next shilling comes from.'

Sally laughed. 'We all want that.' She poured more oil and vinegar into the bowl and stirred it. 'So you had money, did you?'

'My father did. He was a very rich man, but then he made some bad investments, he borrowed too much money, he gambled and he failed. So he forged some notes and presented them at the Bank of . . .'

'Notes?' Sally did not understand.

'Instructions to pay money,' Sandman explained, 'and of course it was a stupid thing to do, but I suppose he was desperate. He wanted to raise some money then flee to France, but the forgeries were detected and he faced arrest. They would have hanged him, except that he blew his brains out before the constables arrived.'

'Gawd,' Sally said, staring at him.

'So my mother lost everything. She now lives in Winchester with my younger sister and I try to keep them alive. I pay the rent, look after the bills, that sort of thing.' He shrugged.

'Why don't they work?' Sally asked truculently.

'They're not used to the idea,' Sandman said, and Sally echoed the words, though not quite aloud. She just mouthed it and Sandman laughed. 'This all happened just over a year ago,' he went on, 'and I'd already left the army by then. I was going to get married. We'd chosen a house in Oxfordshire, but of course she couldn't marry me when I became penniless.'

'Why not?' Sally demanded.

'Because her mother wouldn't let her marry a pauper.'

'Because she was poor as well?' Sally asked.

'On the contrary,' Sandman said, 'her father had promised to settle six thousand a year on her. My father had promised me more, but once he went bankrupt, of course . . .' Sandman shrugged, not bothering to finish the sentence.

Sally was staring at him wide-eyed. 'Six thousand?' she asked. 'Pounds?' She merely breathed the last word, unable to comprehend such wealth.

'Pounds,' Sandman confirmed.

'Bloody hell!' It was sufficient to persuade her to stop eating for a while, then she remembered her hunger and dug in again. 'Go on,' she encouraged him.

'So I stayed with my mother and sister for a while, but that really wasn't practicable. There was no work for me in Winchester, so I came to London last month.'

Sally thought this was amusing. 'Never really worked in your life before, eh?'

'I was a good soldier,' Sandman said mildly.

'I suppose that is work,' Sally allowed grudgingly, 'of a sort.' She chased a chicken leg round the bowl. 'But what do you want to do?'

Sandman gazed up at the smoke-stained ceiling. 'Just work,' he said vaguely. 'I'm not trained for anything. I'm not a lawyer, not a priest. I taught in Winchester College for two terms,' he paused, shuddering at the memory, 'so I thought I'd try the London merchants. They hire men to supervise estates, you see. Tobacco estates and sugar plantations.'

'Abroad?' Sally asked.

'Yes,' Sandman said gently, and he had indeed been offered such work on a sugar estate in Barbados, but the knowledge that the appointment would necessitate the supervision of slaves had forced him to refuse. His mother had scoffed at his refusal, calling him weak-willed, but Sandman was content with his choice.

'But you don't need to go abroad now,' Sally said, 'not if you're working for the Home Secretary.'

'I fear it is very temporary employment.'

'Thieving people off the gallows? That ain't temporary! Full bloody time if you ask me.' She stripped the meat from the chicken bone with her teeth. 'But are you going to get Charlie out of the King's Head Inn?'

'Do you know him?'

'Met him once,' she said, her mouth full of chicken, 'and fat Sir George is right. He's a pixie.'

'A pixie? Never mind, I think I know. And you think he's innocent?'

'Of course he's bloody innocent,' she said forcefully.

'He was found guilty,' Sandman pointed out gently.

'In the Old Bailey sessions? Who was the judge?'

'Sir John Silvester,' Sandman said.

'Bloody hell! Black Jack?' Sally was scathing. 'He's a bastard. I tell you, Captain, there are dozens of innocent souls in their graves because of Black Jack. And Charlie is innocent. Has to be. He's a pixie, isn't he? He wouldn't know what to do with a woman, let alone rape one! And whoever killed her gave her a right walloping and Charlie ain't got the meat on his bones to do that kind of damage. Well, you've seen him, ain't you? Does he look like he could have slit her throat? What does it say there?' She pointed to the penny broadsheet that Sandman had taken from his pocket and smoothed on the table. At the top of the sheet was an ill-printed picture of a hanging which purported to be the imminent execution of Charles Corday and showed a hooded man standing in a cart beneath the gallows. 'They always use that picture,' Sally said, 'I wish they'd find a new one. They don't even use a cart any more. Fake off, culley!' The last three words were snapped at a well-dressed man who had approached her, bowed and was about to speak. He backed away with alarm on his face. 'I know what he wants,' Sally explained to Sandman.

Sandman had looked alarmed at her outburst, but now laughed and then looked back at the broadsheet. 'According to this,' he said, 'the Countess was naked when she was found. Naked and bloody.'

'She were stabbed, weren't she?'

'It says Corday's knife was in her throat.'

'He couldn't have stabbed her with that,' Sally said dismissively, 'it ain't sharp. It's a, I don't know, what do you call it? It's for mixing paint up, it ain't for chivving.'

'Chivving?'

'Cutting.'

'So it's a palette knife,' Sandman said, 'but it says here she was stabbed twelve times in the . . .' He hesitated.

'In the tits,' Sally said. 'They always say that if it's a woman. Never get stabbed anywhere else. Always in the bubbies.' She shook her head. 'That don't sound like a pixie to me. Why would he strip her, let alone kill her? You want any more of this?' She pushed the bowl towards him.

'No, please. You have it.'

'I could eat a bloody horse.' She pushed her plate aside and simply put the bowl in front of her. 'No,' she said after a moment's reflection, 'he didn't do it, did he?' She stopped again, frowning, and Sandman sensed she was debating whether to tell him something and he had the sense to keep quiet. She looked up at him, as if judging whether she really liked him or not, then she shrugged. 'He bleeding lied to you,' she said quietly.

'Corday?'

'No! Sir George! He lied. I heard him tell you the Earl wanted the painting, but he didn't.'

'He didn't?'

'They was talking about it yesterday,' Sally said earnestly, 'him and a friend, only he thinks I don't listen. I just stand there catching cold and he talks like I wasn't anything except a pair of tits.' She poured herself more ale. 'It wasn't the Earl who ordered the painting. Sir George told his friend, he did, then he looked at me and he said, "You're not hearing this, Sally Hood." He actually said that!'

'Did he say who did commission the painting?'

Sally nodded. 'It was a club what ordered the painting, only he'd be mad if he knew I'd told you 'cos he's scared to death of the bastards.'

'A club commissioned it?'

'Like a gentlemen's club. Like Boodle's or White's, only it ain't them, it's got a funny name. The Semaphore Club? No, that ain't right. Sema? Serra? I don't know. Something to do with angels.'

'Angels?'

'Angels,' Sally confirmed. 'Semaphore? Something like that.'

'Seraphim?'

'That's it!' She was hugely impressed that Sandman had found the name. 'The Seraphim Club.'

'I've never heard of it.'

'It's meant to be real private,' Sally said, 'I mean really private! It ain't far. In St James's Square, so they've got to have money. Too rich for me, though.'

'You know about it?'

'Not much,' she said, 'but I was asked to go there once, only I wouldn't 'cos I'm not that sort of actress.'

'But why would the Seraphim Club want the Countess's portrait?' Sandman asked.

'God knows,' Sally said.

'I shall have to ask them.'

She looked alarmed. 'Don't tell them I told you!

110

Sir George will kill me! And I need the work, don't I?'

'I won't say you told me,' he promised her, 'and anyway, I don't suppose they killed her.'

'So how do you find out who did?' Sally asked.

It was a good question, Sandman thought, and he gave it an honest answer. 'I don't know,' he admitted ruefully. 'I thought when the Home Secretary asked me to investigate that all I had to do was go to Newgate and ask some questions. Rather like questioning one of my soldiers. But it isn't like that. I have to find the truth and I'm not even sure where to begin. I've never done anything like it before. In fact I don't know anyone who has. So I suppose I ask questions, don't I? I talk to everyone, ask them whatever I can think of, and hope I can find the servant girl.'

'What servant girl?'

So Sandman told her about Meg and how he had gone to the house on Mount Street and been told that all the servants had been discharged. 'They might have gone to the Earl's house in the country,' he said, 'or maybe they were just discharged.'

'Ask the servants,' Sally said. 'Ask the other servants in the street and all the other streets nearby. One of them will know. Servants' gossip tells you everything. Oh my gawd, is that the time?' A clock in the tavern had just chimed twice. Sally snatched up her coat, grabbed the last of the bread and ran.

And Sandman sat and read the broadsheet again. It told him very little, but it gave him time to think.

And time to wonder why a private club, a very

private club with an angelic name, wanted a lady painted naked.

It was time, he thought, to find out. It was time to visit the seraphim.

3

It had stopped raining, though the air felt greasy and the stones of St James's Street glistened as though they had been given a coat of varnish. Smoke from countless chimneys gusted low on the chill wind, whirling smuts and ash like dark snow. Two smart carriages rattled up the hill past a third that had lost a wheel. A score of men were offering advice about the canted vehicle while the horses, a lively team of matching bays, were walked up and down by a coachman. Two drunks, fashionably dressed, supported each other as they bowed to a woman who, as elegantly dressed as her admirers, sauntered down the pavement with a furled parasol. She ignored the drunks, just as she took no note of the obscene suggestions shouted at her from the windows of the gentlemen's clubs. She was no lady, Sandman guessed, for no respectable woman would ever walk in St James's Street. She gave him a bold stare as he neared her and Sandman politely touched a hand to his hat, but gave her the wall and walked on. 'Too hot for you, is she?' a man shouted at Sandman from a window.

Sandman ignored the jibe. Think straight, he told

himself, think straight, and to help himself do that he stopped on the corner of King Street and gazed towards St James's Palace as though its ancient bricks could give him inspiration.

Why, he asked himself, was he going to the Seraphim Club? Because, if Sally was right, they had commissioned the portrait of the murdered countess, but so what? Sandman was beginning to suspect that the painting had nothing whatever to do with the murder. If Corday was telling the truth then the murderer was almost certainly the person who had interrupted the painter when they knocked on the door from the back stairs, but who that had been Sandman had not the slightest idea. So why was he going to the Seraphim Club? Because, he decided, the mysterious club had evidently known the dead woman and they had lavished money on a portrait of her, and the portrait, unknown to her ladyship, was to show her naked, which suggested that a member of the club had either been her lover or that she had refused to be his lover, and love, like rejection, was a route to hatred and hatred led to murder and that chain of thought spurred Sandman to wonder whether the painting was connected with the murder after all. It was all confusing, so very confusing, and he was getting nowhere by trying to think straight about it and so he began walking again.

Nothing marked the Seraphim Club's premises, but a crossing sweeper pointed Sandman to a house with shuttered windows on the square's eastern side. Sandman walked across the square and, as he came close, saw a carriage drawn by four horses standing at the kerb outside the club. The carriage was painted dark blue and on its doors were red shields blazoned with golden-robed angels in full flight. The carriage had evidently just collected a passenger for it pulled away as Sandman went to the door that was painted a glossy blue and bore no brass plate. A gilded chain hung in the shallow porch and when it was pulled a bell sounded deep within the building. Sandman was about to tug the chain a second time when he noticed a wink of light in the door's centre and he saw that a spyhole had been drilled through the blue-painted timber. Someone, he reckoned, was peering at him and so he stared back until he heard a bolt being drawn. A second bolt scraped, then a lock turned and at last the door was reluctantly swung open by a servant dressed in a waspish livery of black and yellow. The servant inspected Sandman. 'Are you sure, sir,' he asked after a pause, 'that you have the right house?' The 'sir' had no respect in it, but was a mere formality.

'This is the Seraphim Club?'

The servant hesitated. He was a tall man, probably within a year or two of Sandman's own age, and had a face darkened by the sun, scarred by violence and hardened by experience. A brutal but good-looking man, Sandman thought, with an air of competence. 'This is a private house, sir,' the servant said firmly.

'Belonging, I believe, to the Seraphim Club,' Sandman said brusquely, 'with whom I have business.' He waved the Home Secretary's letter. 'Government business,' he added and, without waiting for any answer, he stepped past the servant into a hall that was

115

high, elegant and expensive. The floor was a chess board of gleaming black and white marble squares, and more marble framed the hearth, in which a small fire burnt and above which an overmantel was framed with a gilded riot of cherubs, flower sprays and acanthus leaves. A chandelier hung in the well of a staircase and its branches must have held at least a hundred unlit candles. Dark paintings hung on white walls. A cursory glance showed Sandman they were landscapes and sea-scapes with not a single naked lady in view.

'The government, sir, has no business here, no business at all,' the tall servant said. He seemed surprised that Sandman had dared to walk past him and, as if in reproof, was pointedly holding the front door open as an invitation for Sandman to leave. Two more servants, both big and both in the same black and yellow livery, had come from a side room to encourage the unwanted visitor's departure.

Sandman looked from the two newcomers to the taller servant holding the door and he noticed the man's good looks were marred by tiny black scars on his right cheek. Most people would hardly have noticed the scars, which were little more than dark flecks under the skin, but Sandman had acquired the habit of looking for the powder burns. 'Which regiment?' he asked the man.

The servant's face twitched in a half-smile. 'First Foot Guards, sir.'

'I fought beside you at Waterloo,' Sandman said. He pushed the letter into his jacket pocket, then stripped off his wet greatcoat which, with his hat, he tossed onto a gilded chair. 'You're probably right,' he told the man, 'the government almost certainly doesn't have any business here, but I suspect I need to be told that by an officer of the club. There is a secretary? A presiding officer? A committee?' Sandman shrugged. 'I apologise, but the government is like French dragoons. If you don't beat the hell out of them the first time then they only come back twice as strong the next.'

The tall servant was trapped between his duty to the club and his fellow-feeling for another soldier, but his loyalty to the Seraphim won. He let go of the front door and flexed his hands as if readying for a fight. 'I'm sorry, sir,' he insisted, 'but they'll only tell you to make an appointment.'

'Then I'll wait here till they do tell me that,' Sandman said. He went to the small fire and stretched his hands towards its warmth. 'My name's Sandman, by the way, and I'm here on behalf of Lord Sidmouth.'

'Sir, they don't permit waiting,' the servant said, 'but if you'd like to leave a card, sir, in the bowl on the table?'

'Don't have a card,' Sandman said cheerfully.

'Time to go,' the servant said, and this time he did not call Sandman 'sir', but instead approached the visitor with a chilling confidence.

'It's all right, Sergeant Berrigan,' a smooth voice cut in from behind Sandman, 'Mister Sandman will be tolerated.'

'Captain Sandman,' Sandman said, turning.

An exquisite, a fop, a beau faced him. He was a tall and extraordinarily handsome young man in a brass-buttoned black coat, white breeches so tight that they could have been shrunk onto his thighs, and glistening black top boots. A stiff white cravat billowed from a plain white shirt which was framed by his coat collar that stood so high that it half covered the man's ears. His hair was black and cut very short, framing a pale face that had been shaved so close that the white skin seemed to gleam. It was an amused and clever face, and the man was carrying a quizzing-glass, a slender gold wand supporting a single lens through which he gave Sandman a brief inspection before offering a slight and courteous bow. 'Captain Sandman,' he said, putting a gentle stress on the first word, 'I do apologise. And I should have recognised you. I saw you knock fifty runs off Martingale and Bennett last year. Such a pity that your prowess has not entertained us at any London ground this season. My name, by the way, is Skavadale, Lord Skavadale. Do come into the library, please,' he gestured to the room behind him. 'Sergeant, would you be so kind as to hang up the Captain's coat? By the porter's fire, I think, don't you? And what would you like as a warming collation, Captain? Coffee? Tea? Mulled wine? Smuggled brandy?'

'Coffee,' Sandman said. He smelt lavender water as he went past Lord Skavadale.

'It's a perfectly horrid day, is it not?' Skavadale asked as he followed Sandman into the library. 'And yesterday was so very fine. I ordered fires, as you can see, not so much for warmth as to drive out the damp.' The library was a large, well-proportioned room where a generous fire burnt in a wide hearth between the high book-shelves. A dozen armchairs were scattered across the floor, but Skavadale and Sandman were the only occupants. 'Most of the members are in the country at this time of year,' Skavadale explained the room's emptiness, 'but I had to drive up to town on business. Rather dull business, I fear.' He smiled. 'And what is your business, Captain?'

'An odd name,' Sandman ignored the question, 'the Seraphim Club?' He looked about the library, but there was nothing untoward about it. The only painting was a life-size, full-length portrait that hung above the mantel. It showed a thin man with a rakish good-looking face and lavishly curled hair that hung past his shoulders. He was wearing a tight-waisted coat made of floral silk with lace at its cuffs and neck, while across his chest was a broad sash from which hung a basket-hilted sword.

'John Wilmot, second Earl of Rochester,' Lord Skavadale identified the man. 'You know his work?'

'I know he was a poet,' Sandman said, 'and a libertine.'

'Lucky man to be either,' Skavadale said with a smile. 'He was indeed a poet, a poet of the highest wit and rarest talent, and we think of him, Captain, as our exemplar. The seraphim are higher beings, the highest, indeed, of all the angels. It is a small conceit of ours.'

'Higher than mere mortals like the rest of us?' Sandman asked sourly. Lord Skavadale was so courteous, so perfect and so poised that it annoyed Sandman.

'We merely try to excel,' Skavadale said pleasantly, 'as I am sure you do, Captain, in cricket and whatever else it is that you do, and I am being remiss in not giving you an opportunity to tell me what that might be.'

That opportunity had to wait a few moments, for a servant came with a silver tray on which were porcelain cups and a silver pot of coffee. Neither Lord Skavadale nor Sandman spoke as the coffee was poured and, in the silence, Sandman heard a strange intermittent squeaking that sounded from a nearby room. Then he detected the clash of metal and realised that men were fencing and the squeaks were the sound of their shoes on a chalked floor. 'Sit, please,' Skavadale said when the servant had fed the fire and gone from the room, 'and tell me what you think of our coffee.'

'Charles Corday,' Sandman said, taking a chair.

Lord Skavadale looked bemused, then smiled. 'You had me confused for a second, Captain. Charles Corday, of course, the young man convicted of the Countess of Avebury's murder. You are indeed a man of mystery. Please do tell me why you raise his name?'

Sandman sipped the coffee. The saucer was blazoned with a badge showing a golden angel flying on a red shield. It was just like the escutcheon Sandman had seen painted on the carriage door, except that this angel was quite naked. 'The Home Secretary,' Sandman said, 'has charged me with investigating the facts of Corday's conviction.'

Skavadale raised an eyebrow. 'Why?'

'Because there are doubts about his guilt,' Sandman said, careful not to say that the Home Secretary did not share those doubts.

'It is reassuring to know that our government goes

to such lengths to protect its subjects,' Skavadale said piously, 'but why would that bring you to our door, Captain?'

'Because we know that the portrait of the Countess of Avebury was commissioned by the Seraphim Club,' Sandman said.

'Was it, now?' Skavadale asked mildly. 'I do find that remarkable.' He lowered himself to perch on the leather-topped fender, taking exquisite care not to crease his coat or breeches. 'The coffee comes from Java,' he said, 'and is, we think, rather good. Don't you?'

'What makes the matter more interesting,' Sandman went on, 'is that the commission for the portrait demanded that the lady be depicted naked.'

Skavadale half smiled. 'That sounds very sporting of the Countess, don't you think?'

'Though she was not to know,' Sandman said.

'Well, I never,' Skavadale mouthed the vulgarity with careful articulation, but despite the mockery his dark eyes were very shrewd and he did not look surprised at all. He laid the quizzing-glass down on a table, then sipped his coffee. 'Might I ask, Captain, how you learnt all these remarkable facts?'

'A man facing the gallows can be very forthcoming,' Sandman said, evading the question.

'You're informing me that Corday told you this?'

'I saw him yesterday.'

'Let us hope that the imminence of death makes him truthful,' Skavadale said. He smiled. 'I confess I know nothing of this. It is possible that one of our

121

members commissioned the portrait, but alas, they did not confide in me. But, I am forced to wonder, does it matter? How does it affect the young man's guilt?'

'You speak for the Seraphim Club, do you?' Sandman asked, again evading the question. 'Are you the secretary? Or an officer?'

'We have nothing so vulgar as officers, Captain. We members are few in number and count ourselves as friends. We do employ a man to keep the books, but he makes no decisions. Those are made by all of us together, as friends and as equals.'

'So if the Seraphim Club were to commission a portrait,' Sandman persisted, 'then you would know.'

'I would indeed,' Skavadale said forcefully, 'and no such portrait was commissioned by the club. But, as I say, it is possible that one of the members commissioned it privately.'

'Is the Earl of Avebury a member?' Sandman asked.

Skavadale hesitated. 'I really cannot divulge who our members are, Captain. This is a private club. But I think it is safe for me to tell you that we do not have the honour of the Earl's company.'

'Did you know the Countess?' Sandman asked.

Skavadale smiled. 'Indeed I did, Captain. Many of us worshipped at her shrine for she was a lady of divine beauty and we regret her death exceedingly. Exceedingly.' He put his half-drunk coffee on a table and stood up. 'I fear your visit to us has been wasted, Captain. The Seraphim Club, I do assure you, commissioned no portraits and Mister Corday, I fear, has misinformed you. Can I see you to the front door?'

122

Sandman stood. He had learnt nothing and been made to feel foolish, but just then a door crashed open behind him and he turned to see that one of the book-cases had a false front of leather spines glued to a door, and a young man in breeches and shirt was standing there with a fencing foil in his hand and an antagonistic expression on his face. 'I thought you'd seen the culley off, Johnny,' he said to Skavadale, 'but you ain't.'

Skavadale, smooth as honey, smiled. 'Allow me to name Captain Sandman, the celebrated cricketer. This is Lord Robin Holloway.'

'Cricketer?' Lord Robin Holloway was momentarily confused. 'I thought he was Sidmouth's lackey.'

'I'm that too,' Sandman said.

Lord Robin heard the belligerence in Sandman's voice and the foil in his hand twitched. He had none of Skavadale's courtesy. He was in his early twenties, Sandman judged, and was as tall and handsome as his friend, but where Skavadale was dark, Holloway was golden. His hair was gold, there was gold on his fingers and a gold chain about his neck. He licked his lips and half raised the sword. 'So what does Sidmouth want of us?' he demanded.

'Captain Sandman was finished with us,' Skavadale said firmly.

'I came to ask about the Countess of Avebury,' Sandman said.

'In her grave, culley, in her grave,' Holloway said. A second man appeared behind him, also holding a foil, though Sandman suspected from the man's plain shirt and trousers that he was a club servant, perhaps their

123

master-at-arms. The room beyond the false door was a fencing room for it had racks of foils and sabres and a plain hardwood floor. 'What did you say your name was?' Holloway demanded of Sandman.

'I didn't,' Sandman said, 'but my name is Sandman, Rider Sandman.'

'Ludovic Sandman's son?'

Sandman inclined his head. 'I am.'

'Bloody man cheated me,' Lord Robin Holloway said. His eyes, slightly protuberant, challenged Sandman. 'Owes me money!'

'A matter for your lawyers, Robin,' Lord Skavadale was emollient.

'Six thousand bloody guineas,' Lord Robin Holloway said, 'and because your bloody father put a bullet between his eyes, we don't get payment! So what are you going to do about that, culley?'

'Captain Sandman is leaving,' Lord Skavadale said firmly, and took Sandman's elbow.

Sandman shook him off. 'I've undertaken to pay some of my father's debts,' he told Lord Robin. Sandman's temper was brewing, but it did not show on his face and his voice was still respectful. 'I am paying the debts to the tradesmen who were left embarrassed by my father's suicide. As to your debt?' He paused. 'I plan to do nothing whatsoever about it.'

'Damn you, culley,' Lord Robin said, and he drew back the foil as if to slash it across Sandman's cheek.

Lord Skavadale stepped between them. 'Enough! The Captain is going.'

'You should never have let him in,' Lord Robin said,

124

'he's nothing but a slimy little spy for bloody Sidmouth! Next time, Sandman, use the tradesman's entrance at the back. The front door is for gentlemen.' Sandman had been controlling his temper and was moving towards the front hall, but now, very suddenly, he turned and walked back past both Skavadale and Holloway. 'Where the devil are you going?' Holloway demanded.

'The back door, of course,' Sandman said, and then stopped by the master-at-arms and held out his hand. The man hesitated, glanced at Skavadale, then frowned as Sandman just snatched the foil from him. Sandman turned to Holloway again. 'I've changed my mind,' he said, 'I think I'll use the front door after all. I feel like a gentleman today. Or does your lordship have a mind to stop me?'

'Robin,' Lord Skavadale cautioned his friend.

'Damn you,' Holloway said, and he twitched up the foil, swatted Sandman's blade aside and lunged.

Sandman parried to drive Holloway's blade high and wide, then slashed his foil across his lordship's face. The blade's tip was buttoned so it could not pierce or slash, but it still left a red welt on Holloway's right cheek. Sandman's blade came back fast to mark the left cheek, then he stepped three paces back and lowered the sword. 'So what am I?' he asked. 'Tradesman or gentleman?'

'To hell with you!' Holloway was in a fury now and did not recognise that his opponent had also lost his temper, but Sandman's temper was cold and cruel while Holloway's was all heat and foolishness. Holloway slashed the foil like a sabre, hoping to open Sandman's face with the sheer force of the steel's whiplike strike, but Sandman swayed back, let the blade pass an inch from his nose and then stepped forward and lunged his weapon into Holloway's belly. The button stopped the blade from piercing cloth or skin, and the weapon bent like a bow and Sandman used the spring of the blade to throw himself backwards as Lord Robin Holloway slashed again. Sandman stepped another pace back, Holloway mistook the move for nervousness and lunged his blade at Sandman's neck.

'Puppy,' Sandman said, and there was an utter disdain in his voice. 'You feeble little puppy,' he said, and began to fight, only now his rage was released – an incandescent and killing rage, an anger that he fought against, that he hated, that he prayed would leave him – and he was no longer fencing, but trying to kill. He stamped forward, his blade a hissing terror, and the button raked Lord Holloway's face, almost taking an eye, then the blade slashed across Lord Holloway's nose, opening it so that blood ran and the steel whipped back, fast as a snake's strike, and Lord Holloway cringed away from the pain and then, suddenly, a pair of very strong arms was wrapped about Sandman's chest. Sergeant Berrigan was holding him and the master-at-arms was standing in front of Lord Robin Holloway while Lord Skavadale wrenched the foil from his friend's hand.

'Enough!' Skavadale said. 'Enough!' He threw Holloway's foil to the far end of the room, then took Sandman's blade and tossed it after the first. 'You will leave, Captain,' he insisted, 'you will leave now!'

Sandman shook Berrigan's arms away. He could see the fear in Lord Robin's eyes. 'I was fighting real men,' he told Lord Robin, 'when you were pissing your childhood breeches.'

'Go!' Skavadale snapped.

'Sir?' Berrigan, as tall as Sandman, jerked his head towards the front hall. 'I think it's best if you go, Captain.'

'If you discover the person who commissioned the portrait,' Sandman spoke to Skavadale, 'then I would be grateful if you would inform me.' He had no realistic hope that Lord Skavadale would do any such thing, but asking the question allowed him to leave with a measure of dignity. 'A message can be left for me at the Wheatsheaf in Drury Lane.'

'Good day, Captain,' Skavadale said coldly. Lord Robin glared at Sandman, but said nothing. He had been whipped and he knew it. The master-at-arms looked respectful, but he understood swordsmanship.

Sandman's hat and greatcoat, both of them half dried and wholly brushed clean, were brought to him in the hallway where Sergeant Berrigan opened the front door. The Sergeant nodded bleakly at Sandman, who stepped past him onto the front step. 'Best not to come back, sir,' Berrigan said quietly, then slammed the door.

It started to rain again.

Sandman walked slowly northwards.

He was truly nervous now, so nervous that he

127

wondered whether he had gone to the Seraphim Club merely to delay this next duty.

Was it a duty? He told himself it was, though he suspected it was an indulgence and was certain it was foolishness. Yet Sally had been right. Find the girl Meg, find her and so discover the truth, and the best way of finding a servant was to ask other servants which was why he was walking to Davies Street, a place he had assiduously avoided for the last six months.

Yet when he knocked on the door it all seemed so familiar and Hammond, the butler, did not even blink an eyelid. 'Captain Rider,' he said, 'what a pleasure, sir, may I take your coat? You should carry an umbrella, sir.'

'You know the Duke never approved of umbrellas, Hammond.'

'The Duke of Wellington might order the fashion of soldiers, sir, but his Grace has no authority over London pedestrians. Might I enquire how your mother is, sir?'

'She doesn't change, Hammond. The world suits her ill.'

'I am sorry to hear it, sir.' Hammond hung Sandman's coat and hat on a rack that was already heavy with other garments. 'Have you an invitation card?' He asked.

'Lady Forrest is giving a musical entertainment? I'm afraid I wasn't invited. I was hoping Sir Henry was at home, but if not I can leave a note.'

'He is home, sir, and I am sure he will want to receive you. Why don't you wait in the small parlour?'

The small parlour was the twice the size of the drawing room in the house Sandman rented for his mother and sister in Winchester, a fact his mother mentioned frequently but which did not bear thinking of now, and so he gazed at a painting of sheep in a meadow and listened to a tenor singing a flamboyant piece beyond the double doors that led to the larger rooms at the back of the house. The man finished with a flourish, there was a patter of applause and then the door from the hall opened and Sir Henry Forrest came in. 'My dear Rider!'

'Sir Henry.'

'A new French tenor,' Sir Henry said dolefully, 'who should have been stopped at Dover.' Sir Henry had never much appreciated his wife's musical entertainments and usually took good care to avoid them. 'I forgot there was an entertainment this afternoon,' he explained, 'otherwise I might have stayed at the bank.' He gave Sandman a sly smile. 'How are you, Rider?'

'I'm well, thank you. And you, sir?'

'Keeping busy, Rider, keeping busy. The Court of Aldermen demands time and Europe needs money and we supply it, or at least we scrape up the business that Rothschild and Baring don't want. Have you seen the price of corn? Sixty-three shillings a quarter in Norwich last week. Can you credit it?' Sir Henry had given Sandman's clothes a swift inspection to determine if his fortunes had improved and decided they had not. 'How is your mother?'

'Querulous,' Sandman said.

Sir Henry grimaced. 'Querulous, yes. Poor woman.' He shuddered. 'Still has the dogs, does she?'

'I fear so, sir.' Sandman's mother lavished affection on two lap dogs; noisy, ill-mannered and smelly.

Sir Henry opened the drawer of a sideboard and took out two cigars. 'Can't smoke in the conservatory today,' he said, 'so we might as well be hanged for fumigating the parlour, eh?' He paused to light a tinder box, then the cigar. His height, slight stoop, silver hair and doleful face had always reminded Sandman of Don Quixote, yet the resemblance was misleading as dozens of business rivals had discovered too late. Sir Henry, son of an apothecary, had an instinctive understanding of money; how to make it, how to use it and how to multiply it. Those skills had helped build the ships and feed the armies and cast the guns that had defeated Napoleon and they had brought Henry Forrest his knighthood, for which his wife was more than grateful. He was, in brief, a man of talent, though hesitant in dealing with people. 'It's good to see you, Rider,' he said now and he meant it, for Sandman was one of the few people Sir Henry felt comfortable with. 'It's been too long.'

'It has, Sir Henry.'

'So what are you doing these days?'

'A rather unusual job, sir, which has persuaded me to seek a favour from you.'

'A favour, eh?' Sir Henry still sounded friendly, but there was caution in his eyes.

'I really need to ask it of Hammond, sir.'

'Of Hammond, eh?' Sir Henry peered at Sandman as if he was unsure whether he had heard correctly. 'My butler?'

'I should explain,' Sandman said.

'I imagine you should,' Sir Henry said and then, still frowning in perplexity, went back to the sideboard where he poured two brandies. 'You will have a glass with me, won't you? It still seems odd to see you out of uniform. So what is it you want of Hammond?'

But before Sandman could explain, the double doors to the drawing room opened and Eleanor was standing there and the light from the large drawing room was behind her so that it seemed as if her hair was a red halo about her face. She looked at Sandman, then took a very long breath before smiling at her father. 'Mother was concerned that you would miss the duet, Papa.'

'The duet, eh?'

'The Pearman sisters, Papa, have been practising for weeks,' Eleanor explained, then looked back again to Sandman. 'Rider,' she said softly.

'Miss Eleanor,' he said very formally, then bowed.

She gazed at him. Behind her, in the drawing room, a score of guests were perched on gilt chairs that faced the open doors of the conservatory where two young women were seating themselves on the piano bench. Eleanor glanced at them, then firmly closed the doors. 'I think the Pearman sisters can manage without me. How are you, Rider?'

'I am well, thank you, well.' He had thought for a second that he would not be able to speak for the breath had caught in his throat and he could feel tears in his eyes. Eleanor was wearing a dress of pale-green silk with yellow lace at the breast and cuffs. She had a necklace of gold and amber that Sandman had not seen before, and he felt a strange jealousy of the life she had led in the last six months. She was, he remembered, engaged to be married and that cut deep, though he took care to betray nothing. 'I am well,' he said again, 'and you?'

'I am distraught that you are well,' Eleanor said with mock severity. 'To think you can be well without me? This is misery, Rider.'

'Eleanor,' her father chided her.

'I tease, Papa, it is permitted, and so few things are.' She turned on Sandman. 'Have you just come to town for the day?'

'I live here,' Sandman said.

'I didn't know.' Her grey eyes seemed huge. What had Sir George Phillips said of her? That her nose was too long, her chin too sharp, her eyes too far apart, her hair too red and her mouth too lavish, and it was all true, yet just by looking at her Sandman felt almost light-headed, as though he had drunk a whole bottle of brandy and not just two sips. He stared at her and she stared back and neither spoke.

'Here in London?' Sir Henry broke the silence.

'Sir?' Sandman forced himself to look at Sir Henry.

'You live here, Rider? In London?'

'In Drury Lane, sir.'

Sir Henry frowned. 'That's a trifle –' he paused, 'dangerous?'

'It's a tavern,' Sandman explained, 'that was recommended to me by a Rifle officer in Winchester and I was settled in before I discovered it was, perhaps, a less than desirable address. But it suits me.'

'Have you been here long?' Eleanor asked.

'Three weeks,' he admitted, 'a little over.'

She looked, Sandman thought, as though he had struck her in the face. 'And you didn't call?' she protested.

Sandman felt himself reddening. 'I was not sure,' he said, 'to what end I should call. I thought you would appreciate it if I did not.'

'If you thought at all,' Eleanor said tartly. Her eyes were grey, almost smoky, with flecks of green in them.

Sir Henry gestured feebly towards the doors. 'You're missing the duet, my dear,' he said, 'and Rider came here to see Hammond, of all people. Isn't that right, Rider? It's not really a social call at all.'

'Hammond, yes,' Sandman confirmed.

'What on earth do you want with Hammond?' Eleanor asked, her eyes suddenly bright with inquisitiveness.

'I'm sure that's for the two of them to discuss,' Sir Henry said stiffly, 'and me, of course,' he added hastily.

Eleanor ignored her father. 'What?' she demanded of Sandman.

'Rather a long story, I fear,' Sandman said apologetically.

'Better that than listening to the Pearman sisters murder their music teacher's setting of Mozart,' Eleanor said, then took a chair and put on an expectant face.

'My dear,' her father began, and was immediately interrupted.

133

'Papa,' Eleanor said sternly, 'I am sure that nothing Rider wants with Hammond is unsuitable for a young woman's ears, and that is more than I can say for the effusions of the Pearman girls. Rider?'

Sandman suppressed a smile and told his tale, and that gave rise to astonishment for neither Eleanor nor her father had connected Charles Corday with Sir George Phillips. It was bad enough that the Countess of Avebury had been murdered in the next street, now it seemed that the convicted murderer had spent time in Eleanor's company. 'I'm sure it's the same young man,' Eleanor said, 'though I only ever heard him referred to as Charlie. But he seemed to do a great deal of the work.'

'That probably was him,' Sandman said.

'Best not to tell your mother,' Sir Henry observed gently.

'She'll think I came within an inch of being murdered,' Eleanor said.

'I doubt he is a murderer,' Sandman put in.

'And besides, you were chaperoned, surely?' her father enquired of Eleanor.

'Of course I was chaperoned, Papa. This is,' she looked at Sandman and raised an eyebrow, 'a respectable family.'

'The Countess was also chaperoned,' Sandman said, and he explained about the missing girl, Meg, and how he needed servants to retail the local gossip about the fate of the staff from Avebury's house. He apologised profusely for even thinking of involving Hammond. 'Servants' tittle-tattle isn't something

134

I'd encourage, sir,' he said, and was interrupted by Eleanor.

'Don't be so stuffy, Rider,' she said, 'it doesn't require encouraging or discouraging, it just happens.'

'But the truth is,' Sandman went on, 'that the servants all talk to each other and if Hammond can ask the maids what they've heard . . .'

'Then you'll learn nothing,' Eleanor interrupted again.

'My dear,' her father protested.

'Nothing!' Eleanor reiterated firmly. 'Hammond is a very good butler and an admirable Christian, indeed I've often thought he would make a quite outstanding bishop, but the maid servants are all quite terrified of him. No, the person to ask is my maid Lizzie.'

'You can't involve Lizzie!' Sir Henry objected.

'Why ever not?'

'Because you can't,' her father said, unable to find a cogent reason. 'It simply isn't right.'

'It isn't right that Corday should hang! Not if he's innocent. And you, Papa, should know that! I've never seen you so shocked!'

Sandman looked enquiringly at Sir Henry, who shrugged. 'Duty took me to Newgate,' he admitted. 'We City aldermen, I discovered, are the legal employers of the hangman and the wretch has petitioned us for an assistant. One never likes to disburse funds unnecessarily, so two of us undertook to discover the demands of his work.'

'And have you made a decision yet?' Eleanor asked.

'We're taking the Sheriff's advice,' Sir Henry said. 'My own inclination was to refuse the request, but I confess that might have been mere prejudice against the hangman. He struck me as a vile wretch, vile!'

'Not an employment that would attract persons of quality,' Eleanor remarked drily.

'Botting, he's called, James Botting.' Sir Henry shuddered. 'Hanging's not a pretty thing, Rider, have you ever seen one?'

'I've seen men after they've been hanged,' Sandman said, thinking of Badajoz with its ditch steaming with blood and its streets filled with screams. The British army, breaking into the Spanish city despite a grim French defence, had inflicted a terrible revenge on the inhabitants and Wellington had ordered the hangmen to cool the redcoats' anger. 'We used to hang plunderers,' he explained to Sir Henry.

'I suppose you had to,' Sir Henry said. 'It's a terrible death, terrible. But necessary, of course, no one disputes that . . .'

'They do,' his daughter put in.

'No one of sound mind disputes it,' her father amended his statement firmly, 'but I trust I shall never have to witness another.'

'I should like to see one,' Eleanor said.

'Don't be ridiculous,' her father snapped.

'I should!' Eleanor insisted. 'We are constantly told that the purpose of execution is twofold; to punish the guilty and to deter others from crime, to which intent it is presented as a public spectacle, so my immortal

136

soul would undoubtedly be safer if I was to witness a hanging and thus be prejudiced against whatever crime I might one day be tempted to commit.' She looked from her bemused father to Sandman, then back to her father again. 'You're thinking I'm an unlikely felon, Papa? That's kind of you, but I'm sure the girl who was hanged last Monday was an unlikely felon.'

Sandman looked at Sir Henry, who nodded unwilling confirmation. 'They hanged a girl, I'm afraid,' he said, then stared at the rug, 'and only a young thing, Rider. Only a young thing.'

'Perhaps,' Eleanor persisted, 'if her father had taken her to witness a hanging then she would have been deterred from her crime. You could even say, Papa, that you are failing in your Christian and paternal duty if you do not take me to Newgate.'

Sir Henry stared at her, not certain that she was talking in jest, then he looked at Sandman and shrugged as if to suggest that his daughter was not to be taken seriously. 'So you think, Rider, that my servants might have heard of this girl Meg's fate?'

'I was hoping so, sir. Or that they could ask questions of the servants who live in Mount Street. The Avebury house isn't a stone's throw away and I'm sure all the servants in the area know each other.'

'I'm sure Lizzie knows everyone,' Eleanor said pointedly.

'My dear,' her father spoke sternly, 'these are delicate matters, not a game.'

Eleanor gave her father an exasperated look. 'It is

servants' gossip, Papa, and Hammond is above such things. Lizzie, on the other hand, thrives on it.'

Sir Henry shifted uncomfortably. 'There's no danger, is there?' he asked Sandman.

'I can't think so, sir. As Eleanor says, we only want to know where the girl Meg went, and that's merely gossip.'

'Lizzie can explain her interest by saying one of our coachmen was sweet on her,' Eleanor said enthusiastically. Her father was unhappy at the thought of involving Eleanor, but he was almost incapable of refusing his daughter. She was his only child and such was his affection for her that he might even have permitted her to marry Sandman despite Sandman's poverty and despite the disgrace attendant on his family, but Lady Forrest had other ideas. Eleanor's mother had always seen Rider Sandman as second best. It was true that when the original engagement took place Sandman had the prospect of considerable wealth, enough to have persuaded Lady Forrest that he would just about make an acceptable son-in-law, but he did not have the one thing Lady Forrest wanted above all else for her daughter. He had no title and Lady Forrest dreamt that Eleanor would one day be a duchess, a marchioness, a countess or, at the very least, a lady. Sandman's impoverishment had given Lady Forrest the excuse to pounce and her husband, for all his indulgence of Eleanor, could not prevail against his wife's determination that her child should be the titled mistress of marble stairways, vast acres and ballrooms large enough to manoeuvre whole brigades.

So though Eleanor might not marry where she wanted, she would be allowed to ask her maidservant to delve the gossip from Mount Street. 'I shall write to you,' Eleanor said to Sandman, 'if you tell me where?'

'Care of the Wheatsheaf,' Sandman told her, 'in Drury Lane.'

Eleanor stood and, rising onto tiptoe, kissed her father's cheek. 'Thank you, Papa,' she said.

'Whatever for?'

'For letting me do something useful, even if it is only encouraging Lizzie's propensity for gossip, and thank you, Rider.' She took his hand. 'I'm proud of you.'

'I hope you always were.'

'Of course I was, but this is a good thing you're doing.' She held onto his hand as the door opened.

Lady Forrest came in. She had the same red hair and the same beauty and the same force of character as her daughter, though Eleanor's grey eyes and intelligence had come from her father. Lady Forrest's eyes widened when she saw her daughter holding Sandman by the hand, but she forced a smile. 'Captain Sandman,' she greeted him in a voice that could have cut glass, 'this is a surprise.'

'Lady Forrest,' Sandman managed a bow, despite his trapped hand.

'Just what are you doing, Eleanor?' Lady Forrest's voice was now only a few degrees above freezing.

'Reading Rider's palm, Mama.'

'Ah!' Lady Forrest was immediately intrigued. She feared her daughter's unsuitable attachment to a pauper, but was thoroughly attracted to the idea of supernatural forces. 'She will never read mine, Captain,' Lady Forrest said, 'she refuses. So what do you see there?'

Eleanor pretended to scrutinise Sandman's palm. 'I scry,' she said portentously, 'a journey.'

'Somewhere pleasant, I hope?' Lady Forrest said.

'To Scotland,' Eleanor said.

'It can be very pleasant at this time of year,' Lady Forrest remarked.

Sir Henry, wiser than his wife, saw a reference to Gretna Green looming. 'Enough, Eleanor,' he said quietly.

'Yes, Papa.' Eleanor let go of Sandman's hand and dropped her father a curtsey.

'So what brings you here, Rid –' Lady Forrest almost forgot herself, but managed a timely correction. 'Captain?'

'Rider very kindly brought me news of a rumour that the Portuguese might be defaulting on their short-term loans,' Sir Henry answered for Sandman, 'which doesn't surprise me, I must say. We advised against the conversion, as you'll remember, my dear.'

'You did, dear, I'm sure.' Lady Forrest was not sure at all, but she was nevertheless satisfied with the explanation. 'Now, come, Eleanor,' she said, 'tea is being served and you are ignoring our guests. We have Lord Eagleton here,' she told Sandman proudly.

Lord Eagleton was the man whom Eleanor was supposed to be marrying and Sandman flinched. 'I'm not acquainted with his Lordship,' he said stiffly.

'Hardly surprising,' Lady Forrest said, 'for he only moves in the best of circles. Henry, must you smoke in here?'

'Yes,' Sir Henry said, 'I must.'

'I do hope you enjoy your visit to Scotland, Captain,' Lady Forrest said, then led her daughter away and closed the door on the cigar smoke.

'Scotland,' Sir Henry said gloomily, then shook his head. 'They don't hang nearly as many in Scotland as we do in England and Wales. Yet, I believe, the murder rate is no higher.' He stared at Sandman. 'Strange that, wouldn't you say?'

'Very strange, sir.'

'Still, I suppose the Home Office knows its business.' He turned and gazed moodily into the hearth. 'It isn't a quick death, Rider, not quick at all, yet the Keeper was inordinately proud of the whole process. Wanted our approbation and insisted on showing us the rest of the prison.' Sir Henry fell silent, frowning. 'You know,' he went on after a while, 'there's a corridor from the prison to the Sessions House? So the prisoners don't need to walk in the street when they go to trial. Birdcage Walk, they call it, and it's where they bury the hanged men. And women, I suppose, though the girl I saw hanged was taken to the surgeons for dissection.' He had been looking into the empty fireplace as he spoke, but now looked up at Sandman. 'The flagstones of Birdcage Walk were wobbling, Rider, wobbling. That's because the graves are always settling underneath them. They had casks of lime there to hasten the decomposition. It was vile. Indescribably vile.'

141

'I'm sorry you had to experience it,' Sandman said.

'I thought it my duty,' Sir Henry replied with a shudder. 'I was with a friend and he took an indecent delight in it all. The gallows is a necessary thing, of course it is, but not to be enjoyed, surely? Or am I being too scrupulous?'

'You're being very helpful, Sir Henry, and I'm grateful.'

Sir Henry nodded. 'It'll be a day or two before you get your answer, I'm sure, but let's hope it helps. Are you going? You must come again. Rider, you must come again.' He took Sandman through to the hall and helped him with his coat.

And Sandman walked away, not even noticing whether it was raining or not.

He was thinking of Lord Eagleton. Eleanor had not behaved as though she were in love with his lordship, indeed she had made a face expressing distaste when his lordship's name was mentioned, and that gave Sandman hope. But then, he asked himself, what did love have to do with marriage? Marriage was about money and land and respectability. About staying above financial ruin. About reputation.

And love? God damn it, Sandman thought, but he was in love.

It was not raining now, indeed it was a beautiful late afternoon with a rare clear sky above London. Everything looked clean-cut, newly washed, pristine. The rain clouds had flown westwards and fashionable London was spilling onto the streets. Open carriages, pulled by matching teams with polished coats and ribboned manes, clipped smartly towards Hyde Park for the daily parade. Street bands vied with each other, trumpets shrilling, drums banging and collectors shaking their money boxes. Sandman was oblivious.

He was thinking of Eleanor and when he could no longer wring any clue as to her intentions from every remembered glance and nuance, he wondered what he had achieved in the day. He had learnt, he thought, that Corday had mostly told him the truth and he had confirmed to himself that bored young aristocrats were among the least courteous of all men, and he had usefully started Eleanor's maid on her search for gossip, but in truth, he had not learnt much. He could not report anything to Viscount Sidmouth. So what to do?

He thought about that when he returned to the Wheatsheaf and took his laundry down to the woman who charged a penny for each shirt, and he had to stand talking for twenty minutes or else she took offence. Then he stitched up his boots, using a sailmaker's needle and palm leather which he borrowed from the landlord and when his boots were crudely mended he brushed his coat, trying to get a stain out of the tail. He reflected that of all the inconveniences of poverty, the lack of a servant to keep clothes clean was the most time-consuming. Time. It was what he needed most, and he tried to decide what he should do next. Go to Wiltshire, he told himself. He did not want to go because it was far, it would be expensive and he had no assurance that he would find the girl Meg if he went, but if he waited to hear from Eleanor then it might already be too late. There was a chance, even a good chance, that the servants from the London house had all been taken down to the Earl's country estate. So go there, he told himself. Catch the mail coach in the morning and he would be there by early afternoon and he could catch the mail coach back in the next day's dawn, but he cringed at the expense. He thought of using a stage coach and guessed that would cost no more than a pound each way, but the stage coach would not get him to Wiltshire before the evening, it would probably take him at least two or three hours to find the Earl of Avebury's house, and so he was unlikely to reach it before dark, and that meant he would have to wait until next morning to approach the household, while if he used the mail coach he would be at the Earl's estate by mid-afternoon at the latest. It would cost him at least twice as much, but Corday only had five days left and Sandman counted his change and wished he had not been so generous as to buy Sally Hood her dinner, then chided himself for that ungallant thought and walked down to the mail office on Charing Cross where he paid two pounds and seven shillings for the last of the four seats on the next morning's mail to Marlborough.

He went back to the Wheatsheaf where, in the inn's back room among the beer barrels and the broken furniture waiting for repair, he blacked and polished his newly mended boots. It was a dark and malodorous space, haunted by rats and by Dodds, the inn's errand boy and Sandman, seated on a barrel in a dark corner, heard Dodds's tuneless whistle and was about to call out a greeting when he heard a stranger's voice. 'Sandman ain't upstairs.'

'I saw him come in,' Dodds said in his usual truculent manner.

Sandman, very quietly, pulled on his boots. The stranger's voice had been harsh, not one inviting Sandman to call out and identify himself, but rather to persuade him to look for a weapon – the only thing to hand was a barrel stave. It was not much, but he held it like a sword as he edged towards the door.

'You find anything?' the stranger asked.

'This tail and a cricket bat,' another man answered and Sandman, still in the shadows, swayed forward and saw a young man holding his bat and his army sword. The two men must have gone upstairs and found Sandman absent, so the one had come down to look for him while the other had stayed to search his room and found the only two things of any value. Sandman could ill afford to lose either and his task now was to retrieve the bat and sword, and to discover who the two men were.

'I'll look in the taproom,' the first man said.

'Bring him back here,' the second said, and so delivered himself into Sandman's mercy.

Because all Sandman needed to do was wait. The first man followed Dodds through the service door and left the second man in the passage, where he half drew Sandman's sword and peered at the inscription on the blade. He was still peering when Sandman stepped from the back room and rammed the stave like a truncheon into the man's kidneys. The wood splintered with the impact and the man lurched forward, gasping, and Sandman let go of the stave, seized the man's hair and pulled him backwards. The man flailed for balance, but Sandman tripped him so that he crashed back onto the floor, where Sandman stamped hard on his groin. The man shrieked and curled around his agony.

Sandman retrieved the bat and sword that had fallen in the passageway. The fight had not taken more than a few seconds and the man was moaning and twitching, incapacitated by sheer pain, but that did not mean he would not recover quickly. Sandman feared he might be carrying a pistol, so he used the sword scabbard to tweak the man's coat aside.

And saw yellow and black livery. 'You're from the Seraphim Club?' Sandman asked, and the man gasped through his pain, but the answer was not informative and Sandman was not minded to obey the injunction. He stooped by the man, felt in his coat pockets and found a pistol which he tugged out, though in his haste he ripped the pocket's lining with the pistol's doghead. 'Is it loaded?' he asked.

The man repeated his injunction, so Sandman put the barrel by his head and cocked the gun. 'I'll ask again,' he said, 'is it loaded?'

'Yes!'

'So why are you here?'

'They wanted you fetched back to the club.'

'Why?'

'I don't know! They just sent us.'

It made sense that the man knew little more than that, so Sandman stepped back. 'Just get out,' he said. 'Collect your friend in the taproom and tell him that if he wants to make trouble for a soldier then he should bring an army.'

The man twisted on the floor and looked up incredulously. 'I can go?'

'Get out,' Sandman said, and he watched the man climb to his feet and limp out of the passage. So why, he wondered, would the Seraphim Club want him? And why send two bullies to fetch him? Why not just send an invitation?

He followed the limping man into the taproom where a score of customers were seated at the tables. A blind fiddler was tuning his instrument in the chimney corner and he looked up sharply, white eyes blank, as Sally Hood uttered a squeak of alarm. She was staring at the gun in Sandman's hand. He raised it, pointing the blackened muzzle at the ceiling, and the two men took the hint and fled. Sandman carefully lowered the flint and pushed the weapon into his belt as Sally ran across the room. 'What's happening?' she asked, and in her anxiety she clutched Sandman's arm.

'It's all right, Sally,' Sandman said.

'Oh bleeding hell, it's not,' she said, and now she was looking past him, her eyes huge, and Sandman heard the sound of a gun being cocked.

He eased his arm from Sally's grip and turned to see a long-barrelled pistol pointing between his eyes. The Seraphim Club had not sent two men to fetch him, but three, and the third, Sandman suspected, was the most

147

dangerous of all, for it was Sergeant Berrigan, once of His Majesty's First Foot Guards. He was sitting in a booth, grinning, and Sally took hold of Sandman's arm again and uttered a small moan of fear.

'It's like French dragoons, Captain,' Sergeant Berrigan said. 'If you don't see the bastards off properly the first time, then sure as eggs they'll be back to trap you.'

And Sandman was trapped.

4

Sergeant Berrigan kept the pistol pointed at Sandman for a heartbeat, then he lowered the flint, put the weapon on the table and nodded at the bench opposite. 'You just won me a pound, Captain.'

'You bastard!' Sally spat at Berrigan.

'Sally! Sally!' Sandman calmed her.

'He's got no bleeding right to point a stick at you,' she protested, then turned on Berrigan. 'Who do you bleeding think you are?'

Sandman eased her onto the bench, then sat beside her. 'Allow me to name Sergeant Berrigan,' he told her, 'once of His Majesty's First Foot Guards. This is Miss Sally Hood.'

'Sam Berrigan,' the Sergeant said, plainly amused by Sally's fury, 'and I'm honoured, miss.'

'I'm bleeding not honoured.' She glared at him.

'A pound?' Sandman asked Berrigan.

'I said those two dozy bastards wouldn't take you, sir. Not Captain Sandman of the 52nd.'

Sandman half smiled. 'Lord Skavadale seemed to know me as a cricketer, not as a soldier.'

'I was the one what knew the regiment you served in,' Berrigan said, then snapped his fingers and one of the serving girls came running. Sandman was not particularly impressed that Berrigan knew his old regiment, but he was very impressed by a stranger who could command such instant service in the Wheatsheaf. There was something very competent about Sam Berrigan. 'I'll have an ale, miss,' the Sergeant told the girl, then he looked at Sally. 'Your pleasure, Miss Hood?'

Sally debated with herself for a second, deciding whether her pleasure was to reject Sam Berrigan's offer, then she decided life was too short to turn down a drink. 'I'll have a gin punch, Molly,' she said sulkily.

'Ale,' Sandman said.

Berrigan put a coin in Molly's palm, folded her fingers over it and then held on to her hand. 'A jug of ale, Molly,' he said, 'and make sure the gin punch is as fine as any we'd get at Limmer's.'

Molly, entranced by the Sergeant, dropped a curtsey to him. 'Mister Jenks, sir,' she whispered, 'he don't like sticks on his tables.'

Berrigan smiled, let go of her hand and put the pistol in a deep pocket of his jacket. He looked at Sandman. 'Lord Robin Holloway sent those two,' he said dismissively, 'and the Marquess sent me.'

'Marquess?'

'Skavadale, Captain. He didn't want you to come to any harm.'

'His lordship is very generous suddenly.'

'No, sir,' Berrigan said. 'The Marquess doesn't want

150

to stir up trouble, but Lord Robin? He don't care. He's a halfwit is what he is. He sent those two to persuade you back to the club where he planned to challenge you.'

'To a duel?' Sandman was amused.

'Pistols, I imagine,' Berrigan was equally amused. 'I can't see him wanting to take you on with a blade again. But I told the Marquess those two would never force you. You were too good a soldier.'

Sandman smiled. 'How do you know what kind of a soldier I was, Sergeant?'

'I know exactly what sort of swoddy you was,' Berrigan said. He had a good face, Sandman thought, broad, tough and with confident eyes.

Sandman shrugged. 'I don't believe I had any particular reputation.'

Berrigan looked at Sally. 'It was the end of the day at Waterloo, miss, and we was beaten. I knew it. I've been in enough fights to know when you're beaten, and we was just standing there and dying. We hadn't given in, don't get me wrong, miss, but the bloody Crapauds had us beat. There was simply too many of the bastards. We'd been killing them all day and still they kept coming and it was day's end and the last of them was coming up the hill and there were four times as many of them as there were of us. I watched him,' he jerked his head at Sandman, 'and he was walking up and down in front of the line like he didn't have a care in the world. You'd lost your hat, hadn't you, sir?'

Sandman laughed at that memory. 'I had, you're right.' His bicorne hat had been blasted off by a French musket ball and it had vanished. He had immediately searched the fire-blackened ground where he was standing, but the hat had gone. He never did find it.

'It was his fair hair,' Berrigan explained to Sally. 'Stood out in a dark day. Up and down he walked and the Crapauds had a swarm of skirmishers not fifty paces off and they was all shooting at him and he didn't blink an eyelid. Just walked.'

Sandman was embarrassed. 'I was only doing my duty, Sergeant, like you were, and I was terrified, I can tell you.'

'But you're the one we noticed doing the duty,' Berrigan said, then looked back to Sally who was listening open-mouthed. 'He's walking up and down and the Emperor's own guard are coming up the hill at us, and I thought to myself, that's it! That's it, Sam. A short life and a shallow grave, 'cos there were precious few of us left, but the Captain here, he was still strolling like it was Sunday in Hyde Park and then he stopped walking and he watched the Frenchies as cool as you like, and then he laughed.'

'I don't remember that,' Sandman said.

'You did,' Berrigan insisted. 'There's death in blue-coats coming up the hill and you were laughing!'

'I had a Colour Sergeant who made very bad jokes at inappropriate moments,' Sandman said, 'so I imagine he said something rather indecent.'

'Then I watched him take his men round the flank of the bastards,' Berrigan continued telling Sally his story, 'and he beat them into hell.'

'That wasn't me,' Sandman said reprovingly. 'It was

152

Johnny Colborne who marched us round the flank. It was his regiment.'

'But you led them,' Berrigan insisted. 'You led.'

'No, no, no,' Sandman countered. 'I was just closest to you, Sergeant, and we certainly didn't beat the French guards alone. As I recall your regiment was in the thick of it?'

'We was good that day,' Berrigan allowed, 'we was very good and we bloody well had to be 'cos the Crapauds were fierce as buggery.' He poured two pots of ale, then raised his own tankard. 'Your very good health, Captain.'

'I'll drink to that,' Sandman said, 'though I doubt your employers would share the sentiment?'

'Lord Robin don't like you,' Berrigan said, 'on account that you made him look a bloody idiot, but that ain't difficult seeing as he is a bloody idiot.'

'Maybe they don't like me,' Sandman observed, 'because they don't want the Countess's murder investigated?'

'Don't suppose they care one way or another,' Berrigan said.

'I hear they commissioned the portrait, and the Marquess admitted knowing the dead woman.' Sandman tallied the points that counted against Berrigan's employers. 'And they refuse to answer questions. I suspect them.'

Berrigan drank from his tankard, then refilled it from the jug. He stared at Sandman for a few seconds, then shrugged. 'They're the Seraphim Club, Captain, so yes, they've done murder, and they've thieved, they've

153

bribed, they've even tried highway robbery. They call them pranks. But killing the Countess? I've heard nothing.'

'Would you have heard?' Sandman asked.

'Maybe not,' Berrigan allowed. 'But we servants know most of what they do because we clean up after them.'

'Because they're being flash?' Sally sounded indignant. It was one thing for her friends at the Wheatsheaf to be criminals, but they had been born poor. 'Why the hell do they want to be flash?' she asked. 'They're rich already, ain't they?'

Berrigan looked at her, evidently liking what he saw. 'That's exactly why they do it, miss, because they are rich,' he said. 'Rich, titled and privileged, and on account of that they reckon they're better than the rest of us. And they're bored. What they want, they take and what gets in their way, they destroy.'

'Or get you to destroy it?' Sandman guessed.

Berrigan gave Sandman a very level look. 'There are thirty-eight Seraphims,' he said, 'and twenty servants, and that don't count the kitchens or the girls. And it takes all twenty of us to clean up their messes. They're rich enough so they don't have to care,' his tone suggested he was warning Sandman, 'and they're bastards, Captain, real bastards.'

'Yet you work for them,' Sandman spoke very gently.

'I'm no saint, Captain,' Berrigan said, 'and they pay me well.'

'Because they need your silence?' Sandman guessed

154

and, when there was no reply, he pushed a little harder. 'What do they need your silence about?'

Berrigan glanced at Sally, then looked back to Sandman. 'You don't want to know,' he growled.

Sandman understood the implications of that quick glance at Sally. 'Rape?' he asked.

Berrigan nodded, but said nothing.

'Is that the purpose of the club?' Sandman asked.

'The purpose,' Berrigan said, 'is for them to do whatever they want. They're all lords or baronets or rich as hell and the rest of the world are peasants, and they reckon they have the right to do whatever they fancy. There's not a man there who shouldn't be hanged.'

'You included?' Sandman asked and, when the Sergeant did not answer, he asked another question. 'Why are you telling me all this?'

'Lord Robin Holloway,' Berrigan said, 'wants you dead because you humiliated him, but I won't stand for it, Captain, not after Waterloo. That was a – ' he paused, frowning as he tried and failed to find the right word – 'I didn't think I'd live through it,' he confessed instead, 'and nothing's been the same since. We went to the gates of hell, miss,' he looked at Sally, 'and we got deep scorched, but we marched out again.' The Sergeant's voice had been hoarse with emotion and Sandman understood that. He had met many soldiers who could begin crying just thinking about their years of service, about the battles they had endured and the friends they had lost. Sam Berrigan looked as hard as a cobble-stone, and undoubtedly he was, but he was also a very sentimental man. 'There's been hardly a day that I haven't seen you in my mind,' Berrigan went on, 'out on that ridge in that bloody smoke. It's what I remember about the battle, just that, and I don't know why. So I don't want you harmed by some spavined halfwit like Lord Robin Holloway.'

Sandman smiled. 'I think you're here, Sergeant, because you want to leave the Seraphim Club.'

Berrigan leant back and contemplated Sandman and then, more appreciatively, Sally. She blushed under his scrutiny, and he took a cigar from his inside pocket and struck a light with a tinder box. 'I don't intend to be any man's servant for long,' he said when the cigar was drawing, 'but when I leave, Captain, I'll set up in business.'

'Doing what?' Sandman asked.

'These,' Berrigan tapped the cigar. 'A lot of gentlemen acquired a taste for these in the Spanish war, but they're curious hard to come by. I find them for the club members and I make almost as much tin that way as I do from wages. You understand me, Captain?'

'I'm not sure I do.'

'I don't need your advice, I don't need your preaching and I don't need your help. Sam Berrigan can look after himself. I just came to warn you, nothing else. Get out of town, Captain.'

'Joy shall be in heaven,' Sandman said, 'over one sinner that repenteth.'

'Oh no. No, no, no,' Berrigan shook his head. 'I just done you a favour, Captain, and that's it!' He stood up, 'And that's all I came to do.'

Sandman smiled. 'I could do with some help, Sergeant, so when you decide to leave the club, come and find me. I'm leaving London tomorrow, but I'll be back here on Thursday afternoon.'

'You'd better bloody be,' Sally put in.

Sandman, amused, raised an eyebrow.

'It's that private performance,' Sally explained. 'You're coming to Covent Garden to cheer me, aren't you? It's Aladdin.'

'Aladdin, eh?'

'A half bloody rehearsed Aladdin. Got to be in there tomorrow morning to learn the steps. You are coming, aren't you, Captain?'

'Of course I am,' Sandman said, and looked back to Berrigan. 'So I'll be back here on Thursday and thank you for the ale, and when you decide to help me, then you know where to find me.'

Berrigan stared at him for a heartbeat, said nothing, then nodded at Sally and walked away after putting a handful of coins on the table. Sandman watched him leave. 'A very troubled young man, Sally,' he said.

'Don't look troubled to me. Good-looking though, ain't he?'

'Is he?'

'Course he is!' Sally said forcefully.

'But he's still troubled,' Sandman said. 'He wants to be good and finds it easy to be bad.'

'Welcome to life,' Sally said.

'So we're going to have to help make him good, aren't we?'

'We?' She sounded alarmed.

'I've decided I can't put the world to rights all on my own,' Sandman said. 'I need allies, my dear, and you're elected. So far there's you, someone I saw this afternoon, maybe Sergeant Berrigan and . . .' Sandman turned as a newcomer to the taproom knocked down a chair, apologised profusely, fumbled his walking stick and then struck his head on a beam. The Reverend Lord Alexander Pleydell had arrived. '. . . and your admirer makes four,' Sandman finished.

And maybe five, for Lord Alexander had a young man with him, a young man with an open face and a troubled expression. 'You're Captain Sandman?' The young man did not wait for an introduction, but just hurried across the room and held out his hand.

'At your service,' Sandman said cautiously.

'Thank God I've found you!' the young man said. 'My name is Carne, Christopher Carne.'

'I'm pleased to meet you,' Sandman said politely, though the name meant nothing to him and the young man's face was quite unfamiliar.

'The Countess of Avebury was my stepmother,' Carne explained. 'I am my father's only son, only child indeed, and thus heir to the earldom.'

'Ah,' Sandman said.

'We must talk,' Carne said. 'Please, we must talk.'

Lord Alexander was bowing to Sally and, at the same time, blushing deep scarlet. Sandman knew his friend would be content for a while, so he led Carne to the back of the taproom where a booth offered some privacy.

'We must talk,' Carne said again. 'Dear God, Sandman, you can prevent a great injustice and God knows you must.'

So they talked.

He was, of course, the Lord Christopher Carne. 'Call me Kit,' he said, 'please.'

Sandman was no radical. He had never shared Lord Alexander's passion to pull down a society based on wealth and privilege, but nor did he like calling men 'my lord' unless he truly found them or their office worthy of respect. He had no doubt that the Marquess of Skavadale had noted that reluctance, just as Sandman had noted that the Marquess was gentleman enough not to remark on it. But though Sandman was unwilling to address Lord Christopher Carne as my lord, he was equally unwilling to call him Kit, so it was better to call him nothing.

Sandman just listened. Lord Christopher Carne was a nervous, hesitant young man with thick-lensed spectacles. He was very short, had thin hair and the faintest suggestion of a stammer. In all he was not a prepossessing man, though he did possess an intensity of manner that compensated for his apparent weakness. 'My father,' he told Sandman, 'is a dreadful man, just d-dreadful.'

'Dreadful?'

'It is as though the ten commandments, Sandman, were quite d-deliberately compiled as a challenge to him. Especially the seventh!'

'Adultery?'

'Of course. He ignores it, Sandman, ignores it!' Behind the magnifying lenses of his glasses Lord Christopher's eyes widened as though the very thought of adultery was horrid, then his lordship blushed as if to mention it was shameful. He was dressed, Sandman noted, respectably enough in a well-cut coat and a fine shirt, but the cuffs of both were stained with ink, betraying a bookish disposition. 'My p-point,' Lord Christopher seemed uncomfortable under Sandman's scrutiny, 'is that like many habitual sinners, my father takes umbrage when he is sinned against.'

'I don't understand.'

Lord Christopher blinked several times. 'He has sinned with many men's wives, Captain Sandman,' he said uncomfortably, 'but he was furious when his own wife was unfaithful.'

'Your stepmother?'

'Just so. He threatened to kill her! I heard him.'

'To threaten to kill someone,' Sandman observed, 'is not the same as killing them.'

'I am apprised of the difference,' Lord Christopher answered with a surprising asperity, 'but I have talked with Alexander and he tells me you have a duty to the painter, Cordell?'

'Corday.'

'Just so, and I cannot believe, cannot believe he did it! What cause did he have? But my father, Sandman, my father had cause.' Lord Christopher spoke with a savage vehemence, even leaning forward and gripping Sandman's wrist as he made the accusation. Then, realising what he had done, he blushed and let go. 'You will perhaps understand,' he went on more mildly, 'if I tell you a little of my father's story.'

The tale was briefly told. The Earl's first wife, Lord Christopher's mother, had been the daughter of a noble family and, Lord Christopher averred, a living saint. 'He treated her wretchedly, Sandman,' he said, 'shaming her, abusing her and insulting her, but she endured it with a Christian forbearance until she died. That was in 'nine. God rest her dear soul.'

'Amen,' Sandman said piously.

'He hardly mourned her,' Lord Christopher said indignantly, 'but just went on taking women to his bed and among them was Celia Collett. She was scarce a child, Sandman, a mere third his age! But he was besotted.'

'Celia Collett?'

'My stepmother, and she was clever, Sandman, she was clever.' The savagery was back in his voice. 'She was an opera dancer at the Sans Pareil. Do you know it?'

'I know of it,' Sandman said mildly. The Sans Pareil on the Strand was one of the new unlicensed theatres that put on entertainments that were lavish with dance and song and if Celia, Countess of Avebury, had graced its stage then she must have been beautiful.

'She refused his advances,' Lord Christopher took up his tale again. 'She turned him down flat! Kept him from her b-bed till he married her, and then she led him a dance, Sandman, a dance! I won't say he didn't deserve it, for he did, but she took what money she could and used it to buy horns for his head.'

161

'You obviously didn't like her?' Sandman observed.

Lord Christopher blushed again. 'I hardly knew her,' he said uncomfortably, 'but what was there to like? The woman had no religion, few manners and scarce any education.'

'Did your father – does your father,' Sandman amended himself, 'care for such things as religion, manners or education?'

Lord Christopher frowned as though he did not understand the question, then nodded. 'You have understood him precisely,' he said. 'My father cares nothing for God, for letters or for courtesy. He hates me, Sandman, and do you know why? Because the estate is entailed onto me. His own father did that, his very own father!' Lord Christopher tapped the table to emphasise his point. Sandman said nothing, but he understood that an entailed estate implied a great insult to the present Earl of Avebury for it meant that his father, Lord Christopher's grandfather, had so mistrusted his own son that he had made certain he could not inherit the family fortune. Instead it was placed in the hands of trustees and, though the present earl could live off the estate's income, the capital and the land and investments would all be held in trust until he died, when they would pass to Lord Christopher. 'He hates me,' Lord Christopher went on, 'not only because of the entail, but because I have expressed a wish to take holy orders.'

'A wish?' Sandman asked.

'It is not a step to b-be taken lightly,' Lord Christopher said sternly.

'Indeed not,' Sandman said.

'And my father knows that when he dies and the family fortune passes to me that it will be used in God's service. That annoys him.'

The conversation, Sandman thought, had passed a long way from Lord Christopher's assertion that his father had committed the murder. 'It is, I understand,' he said carefully, 'a considerable fortune?'

'Very considerable,' Lord Christopher said evenly.

Sandman leant back. Gales of laughter gusted about the taproom which was crowded now, though folk instinctively avoided the booth where Sandman and Lord Christopher talked so earnestly. Lord Alexander was staring with doglike devotion at Sally, oblivious of the other men trying to catch her attention. Sandman looked back to the diminutive Lord Christopher. 'Your stepmother,' he said, 'had a considerable household in Mount Street. What happened to those servants?'

Lord Christopher blinked rapidly as if the question surprised him. 'I have no conception.'

'Would they have gone to your father's estate?'

'They might.' Lord Christopher sounded dubious. 'Why do you ask?'

Sandman shrugged, as if the questions he was asking were of no great importance, though the truth was that he disliked Lord Christopher and he also knew that dislike was as irrational and unfair as his distaste for Charles Corday. Lord Christopher, like Corday, lacked what, for want of a better word, Sandman thought of as manliness. He doubted that Lord Christopher was a

163

pixie, as Sally would put it, indeed the glances he kept throwing towards Sally suggested the opposite, but there was a petulant weakness in him. Sandman could imagine this small, learned man as a clergyman obsessed with his congregation's pettiest sins, and his distaste for Lord Christopher meant he had no wish to prolong this conversation so instead of admitting to Meg's existence he just said that he would like to discover from the servants what had happened on the day of the Countess's murder.

'If they're loyal to my father,' Lord Christopher said, 'they will tell you nothing.'

'Why should that loyalty make them dumb?'

'Because he killed her!' Lord Christopher cried too loudly, and immediately blushed when he saw he had attracted the attention of folk at other tables. 'Or at least he c-caused her to be killed. He has gout, he no longer walks far, but he has men who are loyal to him, men who do his bidding, evil men.' He shuddered. 'You must tell the Home Secretary that Corday is innocent.'

'I doubt it will make any difference if I do,' Sandman said.

'No? Why? In God's name, why?'

'Lord Sidmouth takes the view that Corday has already been found guilty,' Sandman explained, 'so to change that verdict I need either to produce the true murderer, with a confession, or else adduce proof of Corday's innocence that is incontrovertible. Opinion, alas, does not suffice.'

Lord Christopher gazed at Sandman in silence for a few heartbeats. 'You must?'

'Of course I must.'

'Dear God!' Lord Christopher seemed astonished and leant back, looking faint. 'So you have five days to find the real killer?'

'Indeed.'

'So the boy is doomed, is he not?'

Sandman feared Corday was doomed, but he would not admit it. Not yet. For there were still five days left to find the truth and thus to steal a soul from Newgate's scaffold.

At half past four in the morning a pair of lamps glimmered feebly from the windows of the yard of the George Inn. Dawn was touching the roofs with a wan gleam. A caped coachman yawned hugely, then flicked his whip at a snarling terrier that slunk out of the way of the massive coachhouse doors that were dragged open to reveal a gleaming dark-blue mail coach. The vehicle, bright with new varnish and with its doors, windows, harness pole and splinter bar picked out in scarlet, was manhandled onto the yard's cobbles where a boy lit its two oil lanterns and a half-dozen men heaved the mail bags into its boot. The eight horses, high-stepping and frisky, their breath misting the night air, were led from the stables. The two coachmen, both in the Royal Mail's blue and red livery and both armed with blunderbusses and pistols, locked the boot and then watched as the team was harnessed. 'One minute!' a voice shouted, and Sandman drank the scalding coffee that the inn had provided for the mail's passengers. The lead coachman yawned again, then clambered up to the box. 'All aboard!'

There were four passengers. Sandman and a middle-aged clergyman took the front seat with their backs to the horses, while an elderly couple sat opposite them and so close that their knees could not help touching Sandman's. Mail coaches were light and cramped, but twice as fast as the larger stage coaches. There was a squeal of hinges as the inn yard's gates were dragged open, then the carriage swayed as the coachmen whipped the team out into Tothill Street. The sound of the thirty-two hooves echoed sharp from houses and the wheels cracked and rumbled as the coach gathered speed, but Sandman was fast asleep again by the time it reached Knightsbridge.

He woke at about six o'clock to find the coach was rattling along at a fine pace, swaying and lurching through a landscape of small fields and scattered coverts. The clergyman had a notebook on his lap, half-moon spectacles on his nose and a watch in his hand. He was peering though the windows on either side, searching for milestones, and saw that Sandman had woken.

'A fraction over nine miles an hour!' he exclaimed.

'Really?'

'Indeed!' Another milestone passed and the clergyman began working out sums on the page of his notebook. 'Ten and carry three, that's half again, minus sixteen, carry two. Well, I never! Certainly nine and a quarter! I once travelled at an average velocity of eleven miles an hour, but that was in eighteen-o-four and it was a very dry summer. Very dry, and the roads were smooth–' the coach hit a rut and lurched violently, throwing the clergyman against Sandman's shoulder – 'very smooth indeed,' he said, then peered through the window again. The elderly man clutched a valise to his chest and looked terrified, as though Sandman or the clergyman might prove to be a thief, though in truth highwaymen like Sally's brother were a much greater danger. Not this morning, though, for Sandman saw that two robin redbreasts were riding escort. The redbreasts were the Horse Patrol, all retired cavalrymen who, uniformed in blue coats over red waistcoats and armed with pistols and sabres, guarded the roads close to London. The two patrolmen kept the coach company until it clattered through a village and there the pair peeled away towards a tavern where, despite the early hour, a couple of men in long smocks were already sitting in the porch and drinking ale.

Sandman gazed fixedly out of the window, revelling in being out of London. The air seemed so remarkably clean. There was no pervading stench of coal smoke and horse dung, just the morning sunlight on summer leaves and the sparkle of a stream twisting beneath willows and alders beside a field of grazing cattle who looked up as the coachman sounded the horn. They were still close to London and the landscape was flat, but well drained. Good hunting country, Sandman thought, and imagined pursuing a fox beside this road. He felt his dream horse gather itself and leap a hedge, heard the huntsman's horn and the hounds giving tongue.

'Going far?' The clergyman interrupted his reverie.

'Marlborough.'

'Fine town, fine town.' The clergyman, an arch-deacon, had abandoned his computations about the coach's speed and now rambled on about visiting his sister in Hungerford. Sandman made polite responses, but still kept looking out of the window. The fields were near harvest and the heads of rye, barley and wheat were heavy. The land was becoming hillier now, but the rattling, swaying and jolting coach kept up its fine pace and spewed a tail of dust that whitened the hedgerows. The horn warned folk of its approach and children waved as the eight horses thundered past. A blacksmith, leather apron blackened by fire, stood in his doorway. A woman shook her fist when her flock of geese scattered from the coach's noise, a child whirled a rattle in a vain attempt to drive predatory jays from rows of pea plants, then the sound of the trace chains and hooves and clattering wheels was echoing back from the seemingly endless wall of a great estate.

The Earl of Avebury, Sandman decided, would probably live in just such a walled estate, a great swathe of aristocratic country cut off by bricks, gamekeepers and watchmen. Suppose the Earl refused to see him? His lordship was said to be a recluse and the further west Sandman went the more he feared he would be summarily ejected from the estate, but that was a risk he would have to take. He forgot his fears as the coach lurched into a street of modern brick houses, the horn sounded urgently and Sandman realised they had come to the village of Reading where

168

the coach swung into an inn yard to find the new horses waiting.

'Less than two minutes, gentlemen!' The two coachmen swung down from their box and, because the day was getting warmer, took off their triple-caped coats. 'Less than two minutes and we don't wait for laggards, milords.'

Sandman and the archdeacon had a companionable piss in the corner of the inn yard, then they each gulped down a cup of lukewarm tea as the new horses were harnessed and the old team, white with sweat, were led to the water trough. A sack of mail had been pulled from the boot and another took its place before the two coachmen scrambled up to their leather-cushioned perch. 'Time, gentlemen! Time!'

'One minute and forty-five seconds!' a man called from the inn door. 'Well done, Josh! Well done, Tim!'

The horn sounded, the fresh horses pricked back their ears and Sandman slammed the coach door and was thrown into the rear seat as the vehicle lurched forward. The elderly couple had left the coach, their place taken by a middle-aged woman who, within a mile, was vomiting from the offside window. 'You must forgive me,' she gasped.

'It is a motion mighty like a ship, ma'am,' the archdeacon observed, and took a silver flask from his pocket. 'Brandy might help?'

'Oh, Lord above!' the woman wailed in horrified refusal, then craned and retched through the window again.

'The springs are soft,' the archdeacon pointed out.

'And the road's very bumpy,' Sandman added.

'Especially at eight and a half miles an hour.' The archdeacon was busy with watch and pencil again, struggling gainfully to make legible figures despite the jolting. 'It always takes time to settle a new team and speed, which we lack, smooths a road.'

Sandman's spirits rose as each mile passed. He was happy, he suddenly realised, but quite why, he was not sure. Perhaps, he thought, it was because his life had purpose again, a serious purpose, or perhaps it was because he had seen Eleanor and nothing about her demeanour, he had decided, betrayed an imminent marriage to Lord Eagleton.

Lord Alexander Pleydell had hinted as much the previous evening, most of which he had spent worshipping at Sally Hood's shrine, though Sally herself had seemed distracted by her memories of Sergeant Berrigan. Not that Lord Alexander had noticed. He, like Lord Christopher Carne, was struck dumb by Sally, so dumb that for most of the evening the two aristocrats had merely gaped at her, sometimes stammering a commonplace until at last Sandman had taken Lord Alexander into the back parlour. 'I want to talk to you,' he had said.

'I want to continue my conversation with Miss Hood,' Lord Alexander had complained pettishly, worried that his friend Kit was being given untrammelled access to Sally.

'And so you shall,' Sandman assured him, 'but talk to me first. What do you know about the Marquess of Skavadale?'

'Heir to the Dukedom of Ripon,' Lord Alexander had said immediately, 'from one of the old Catholic families of England. Not a clever man, and it's rumoured the family has monetary troubles. They were once very rich, exceedingly so, with estates in Cumberland, Yorkshire, Cheshire, Hertfordshire, Kent and Sussex, but father and son are both gamblers so the rumours may well be true. He was a reasonable bat at Eton, but can't bowl. Why do you ask?'

'Lord Robin Holloway?'

'Youngest son of the Marquess of Bleasby and a thoroughly nasty boy who takes after his father. Has plenty of money, no brains and he killed a man in a duel last year. No cricketer, I fear.'

'Did he fight the duel with swords or pistols?'

'Swords, as it happened. It was fought in France. Are you going to make enquiries about the whole of the aristocracy?'

'Lord Eagleton?'

'A fop, but a useful left hand batsman who sometimes plays for Viscount Barchester's team, but is otherwise utterly undistinguished. A bore indeed, despite being a passable cricketer.'

'The sort of man who might appeal to Eleanor?'

Alexander stared at Sandman in astonishment. 'Don't be absurd, Rider,' he said, lighting another pipe. 'She wouldn't stand him for two minutes!' He frowned as if trying to remember something, but whatever it was did not come to mind.

'Your friend Lord Christopher,' Sandman had said, 'is convinced his father committed the murder.'

'Or had someone else commit it,' Alexander said. 'It seems likely. Kit sought me out when he heard you were investigating the matter and I applaud him for doing so. He, like me, is avid that no injustice should occur next Monday. Now, do you think I might go back to my conversation with Miss Hood?'

'Tell me what you know about the Seraphim Club first.'

'I have never heard of it, but it sounds like an association of high-minded clergymen.'

'It isn't, believe me. Is there any significance in the word seraphim?'

Lord Alexander had sighed. 'The seraphim, Rider, are reckoned to be the highest order of angels. The credulous believe there to be nine such orders; seraphim, cherubim, thrones, dominions, virtues, powers, principalities, archangels and, at the very bottom, mere common angels. This is not, I hasten to assure you, the creed of the Church of England. The word seraphim is thought to derive from a Hebrew word meaning serpent, the association is obscure yet suggestive. In the singular it is a seraph, a glorious creature that has a bite like fire. It is also believed that the seraphim are the patrons of love. Why they should be such I have no idea, but so it is said, just as it is claimed that the cherubim are patrons of knowledge. I momentarily forget what the other orders do. Have I satisfied your curiosity or do you wish this lecture to continue?'

'The seraphim are angels of love and poison?'

'A crude, but apt summary,' Lord Alexander had said grandly, then insisted they go back to the taproom

172

where he had again been struck dumb by Sally's presence. He stayed till past midnight, became drunk and verbose, then left with Lord Christopher, who had drunk little and had to support his friend, who staggered from the Wheatsheaf declaring his undying love for Sally in a voice slurred by brandy.

Sally had frowned as Lord Alexander's coach had left. 'Why did he call me stupid?'

'He didn't,' Sandman had said, 'he just said you were the *stupor mundi*, the wonder of the world.'

'Bloody hell, what's the matter with him?'

'He's frightened of your beauty,' Sandman had said, and she had liked that and Sandman had gone to bed wondering how he would ever wake in time to catch the mail coach, yet here he was, rattling through as glorious a summer's day as any a man could dream of.

The road ran alongside a canal and Sandman admired the narrow painted barges that were hauled by great horses with ribboned manes and brass-hung harnesses. A child bowled a hoop along the towpath, ducks paddled, God was in His heaven and it took a keen eye to see that all was not quite as well as it looked. The thatch of many roofs was threadbare and in every village there were two or three cottages that had collapsed and were now overgrown with bindweed. There were too many tramps on the roads, too many beggars by the churchyards, and Sandman knew a good number of them had been redcoats, riflemen or sailors. There was hardship here, hardship among plenty, the hardship of rising prices and too few jobs, and hidden behind the cottages and the ancient churches and the heavy elm trees were parish workhouses that were filled with refugees from the bread riots that had flared in England's bigger cities, yet still it was all so heartbreakingly beautiful. The foxgloves made thickets of scarlet beneath the pink roses in the hedgerows. Sandman could not take his eyes from the view. He had not been in London a full month, yet already it seemed too long.

At noon the coach swung across a stone bridge and clattered up a brief hill into the great wide main street of Marlborough, with its twin churches and capacious inns. A small crowd was waiting for the mail and Sandman pushed through the folk and out under the tavern's arch. A carrier's cart was plodding eastwards and Sandman asked the man where he might find the Earl of Avebury's estate. Carne Manor was not far, the carrier said, just over the river and up the hill and on the edge of Savernake. A half-hour's walk, he thought, and Sandman, hunger gnawing at his belly, walked south towards the deep trees of Savernake Forest.

He was hot. He had been carrying his coat, a garment that was not needed on this warm day though he had been grateful for it when he left the Wheatsheaf at dawn. He asked for more directions in a hamlet and was sent down a long lane that twisted between beech woods until he came to Carne Manor's great brick wall, which he followed until he reached a lodge and a pair of cast iron gates hung from stone pillars surmounted with carved griffins. A gravel drive, thick with weeds, led from the locked gates. A bell hung by the lodge, but though Sandman tolled it a dozen times no one answered. Nor could he see anyone inside the estate.

174

Either side of the drive was parkland, a sward of grass dotted by fine elms, beeches and oaks, but no cattle or deer grazed the grass that grew lank and was thick with cornflowers and poppies. Sandman gave the bell a last forlorn tug and, when its sound had faded into the warm afternoon, he stepped back and looked at the spikes on top of the gates. They looked formidable, so he went back up the lane until he came to a place where an elm, growing too close to the wall, had buckled the bricks. The tree's proximity to the wall made it easy to climb. He paused a second on the mortared coping, then dropped down into the park. The grass was long enough to conceal a spring trap set against poachers and so he moved carefully until he reached the gravel drive and then turned towards the house that was hidden beyond some woods growing along the crest of a low hill.

He walked slowly, half expecting a gamekeeper or some other servant to intercept him, but he saw no one as he followed the drive through a fine stand of beeches in the centre of which was an overgrown glade surrounding a mossy statue of a naked woman hoisting a biblical water jar onto her shoulder. Sandman walked on and, from the far side of the beeches, he could at last see Carne Manor a half-mile away. It was a fine stone building with a façade of three high gables on which ivy grew about mullioned windows. Stables, coach houses and a brick-walled kitchen garden lay to the west, while behind the house were terraced lawns dropping to a placid stream. He walked on down the long drive. It suddenly seemed a futile expedition, futile and expensive, for the Earl's reputation as a recluse suggested that Sandman would most likely be greeted with a horsewhip.

The sound of his steps seemed extraordinarily loud as he crossed the great sweep of gravel where carriages could turn in front of the house, though the weeds, grass and moss growing so thick among the stones suggested that few coaches ever did. Sandman climbed the entrance steps. Two glazed lanterns were mounted either side of the porch, though one had a glass pane missing and a bird's nest was smothering its candle holder. He hauled on the bell chain and, when he heard no sound, pulled again and waited. The wooden door had gone grey with age and was stained with rust that had leaked from its decorative metal studs. Bees drifted into the shallow porch. A young cuckoo, looking uncannily like a hawk, flew across the drive. The afternoon was warm and Sandman wished he could abandon this search for a reclusive earl and just go down by the stream and sleep in the shade of some great tree.

Then a harsh banging to his right made Sandman step back to see that a man was trying to open a leaded window in the room closest to the porch. The window was evidently jammed, for the man struck it so hard that Sandman was certain the leaded lights would smash, but then it jarred open and the man leant out. He was in late middle age, had a very pale face and unkempt hair, which suggested he had just woken from a deep sleep. 'The house,' he said testily, 'is not open to visitors.'

'I hadn't supposed it was,' Sandman said, though it had occurred to him to ask the housekeeper, if such a person had answered the door, for a view of the public rooms. Most great houses allowed such visits, but plainly the Earl of Avebury did not extend the courtesy. 'Are you his lordship?' he asked.

'Do I look like him?' the man answered in an irritated tone.

'I have business with his lordship,' Sandman explained.

'Business? Business?' The man spoke as though he had never heard of such a thing, and then a look of alarm crossed his pale features. 'Are you a lawyer?'

'It is delicate business,' Sandman said emphatically, suggesting it was none of the servant's, 'and my name,' he added, 'is Captain Sandman.' It was a mere courtesy to provide his name and a reproof because he had not been asked for it.

The man gazed at him for a heartbeat, then retreated inside. Sandman waited. The bees buzzed by the ivy and house martins swerved above the weed-strewn gravel, but the servant did not return and Sandman, piqued, hauled on the bell-pull again.

A window on the other side of the porch was forced open and the same servant appeared there. 'A captain of what?' he demanded peremptorily.

'The 52nd Foot,' Sandman answered, and the servant vanished for a second time.

'His lordship wishes to know,' the servant reappeared at the first window, 'whether you were with the 52nd at Waterloo.'

'I was,' Sandman said.

The servant went back inside, there was another

pause and then Sandman heard bolts being shot on the far side of the door, which eventually creaked open, and the servant offered a sketchy bow. 'We don't get visitors,' he said. 'Your coat and hat, sir? Sandman, you said?'

'Captain Sandman.'

'Of the 52nd Foot indeed, sir, this way, sir.'

The front door opened onto a hall panelled in a dark wood where a fine white-painted stairway twisted upwards beneath portraits of heavily jowled men in ruffs. The servant led Sandman down a passageway into a long gallery lined by tall velvet-curtained windows on one side and great paintings on the other. Sandman had expected the house to be as dirty as the grounds were unkempt, but it was all swept and the rooms smelt of wax polish. The paintings, so far as he could see in the curtained gloom, were exceptionally fine. Italian, he thought, and showing gods and goddesses disporting in vineyards and on dizzying mountainsides. Satyrs pursued naked nymphs and it took Sandman a moment or two to realise that all the paintings showed nudes: a gallery of feminine, abundant and generous flesh. He had a sudden memory of some of his soldiers gaping at just such a painting that had been captured from the French at the battle of Vitoria. The canvas, cut from its frame, had been purloined by a Spanish muleteer to use as a waterproof tarpaulin and the redcoats had bought it from him for tuppence, hoping to use it as a groundsheet. Sandman had purchased it from its new owners for a pound and sent it to headquarters, where it was identified as one of the many masterpieces looted from the Escorial, the King of Spain's palace.

'This way, sir,' the servant interrupted his reverie. The man opened a door and announced Sandman who was suddenly dazzled, for the room into which he had been ushered was vast and its windows that faced south and west were uncurtained and the sun was streaming in to illuminate a huge table. For a few seconds Sandman could not understand the table for it was green and lumpy and smothered in scraps that he thought at first were flowers or petals, then his eyes adjusted to the sunlight and he saw that the coloured scraps were model soldiers. They were thousands of toy soldiers on a table covered in green baize that had been draped across some kind of blocks so that it resembled the valley in which the battle of Waterloo had been fought. He gaped at it, astonished by the size of the model which was at least thirty feet long and twenty deep. Two girls sat at a side table with brushes and paint, which they applied to lead soldiers. Then a squeaking noise made him look into the dazzle by a south window, where he saw the Earl.

His lordship was in a wheeled chair like those Sandman's mother had liked to use in Bath when she was feeling particularly poorly, and the squeak had been the sound of the ungreased axles turning as a servant pushed the Earl towards his visitor.

The Earl was dressed in the old fashion that had prevailed before men had adopted sober black or dark blue. His coat was of flowered silk, red and blue, with enormously wide cuffs and a lavish collar over which

179

fell a cascade of lace. He wore a full-bottomed wig that framed an ancient, lined face that was incongruously powdered, rouged and decorated with a velvet beauty spot on one sunken cheek. He had not been properly shaved, and patches of white stubble showed in the folds of his skin. 'You are wondering,' he addressed Sandman in a shrill voice, 'how the models are inserted onto the centre of the table, are you not?'

The question had not even occurred to Sandman, but now he did find it puzzling, for the table was far too big for its centre to be reached from the sides, and if a person were to walk across the model then they would inevitably crush the little trees that were made from sponge or else they would disarrange the serried ranks of painted soldiers. 'How is it done, my lord?' Sandman asked. He did not mind calling the Earl 'my lord' for he was an old man and it was a mere courtesy that youth owed to age.

'Betty, dearest, show him,' the earl commanded, and one of the two girls dropped her paintbrush and disappeared beneath the table. There was a scuffling sound, then a whole section of the valley rose into the air to become a wide hat for the grinning Betty. 'It is a model of Waterloo,' the Earl said proudly.

'So I see, my lord.'

'Maddox tells me you were in the 52nd. Show me where they were positioned.'

Sandman walked about the table's edge and pointed to one of the red-coated battalions on the ridge above the Chateau of Hougoumont. 'We were there, my lord,' he said. The model really was extraordinary. It showed the two armies at the beginning of the fight, before the ranks had been bloodied and thinned and before Hougoumont had burnt to a black shell. Sandman could even make out his own company on the 52nd's flank, and assumed that the little mounted figure just ahead of the painted ranks was meant to be himself. That was an odd thought.

'Why are you smiling?' the Earl demanded.

'No reason, my lord,' Sandman looked at the model again, 'except that I wasn't on horseback that day.'

'Which company?'

'Grenadier.'

The Earl nodded. 'I shall replace you with a foot soldier,' he said. His chair squealed as he pursued Sandman about the table. His lordship had blue-gartered silk stockings, though one of his feet was heavily bandaged. 'So tell me,' the Earl demanded, 'did Bonaparte lose the battle by delaying the start?'

'No,' Sandman said curtly.

The Earl signalled the servant to stop pushing the chair. He was close to Sandman now and could stare up at him with red-rimmed eyes that were dark and bitter. The Earl was much older than Sandman had expected. Sandman knew the Countess had still been young when she died, and she had been beautiful enough to be painted naked, yet her husband looked ancient despite the wig, the cosmetics and the lace frills. He stank, too; a reek of stale powder, unwashed clothes and sweat. 'Who the devil are you?' the Earl growled.

'I have come from Viscount Sidmouth, my lord, and . . .'

'Sidmouth?' the Earl interrupted. 'I don't know a Viscount Sidmouth. Who the devil is the Viscount Sidmouth?'

'The Home Secretary, my lord.' That information prompted no reaction at all, so Sandman explained further. 'He was Henry Addington, my lord, and was once the Prime Minister? Now he is Home Secretary.'

'Not a real lord then, eh?' the Earl declared. 'Not an aristocrat! Have you noticed how the damned politicians make themselves into peers? Like turning a toilet into a fountain, ha! Viscount Sidmouth? He's no gentleman. A bloody politician is all he is! A trumped up liar! A cheat! I assume he is first viscount?'

'I am sure he is, my lord,' Sandman said.

'Ha! A back-alley aristo, eh? A piece of God-damn slime! A well-dressed thief! I'm the sixteenth earl.'

'Your family amazes us all, my lord,' Sandman said, with an irony that was utterly wasted on the Earl, 'but however new his ennoblement, I still come with the viscount's authority.' He produced the Home Secretary's letter, which was waved away. 'I have heard, my lord,' Sandman went on, 'that the servants from your town house in Mount Row are now here?' He had heard nothing of the sort, but perhaps the bald statement would elicit agreement from the Earl. 'If that's so, my lord, then I would like to talk with one of them.'

The Earl shifted in the chair. 'Are you suggesting,' he asked in a dangerous voice, 'that Blucher might have come sooner had Bonaparte attacked earlier?'

'No, my lord.'

'Then if he'd attacked earlier he'd have won!' the Earl insisted.

Sandman looked at the model. It was impressive, comprehensive and all wrong. It was too clean for a start. Even in the morning, before the French attacked, everyone was filthy because, on the previous day, most of the army had slogged back from Quatre Bras through quagmires of mud and then they had spent the night in the open under successive cloudbursts. Sandman remembered the thunder and the lightning whiplashing the far ridge and the terror when some cavalry horses broke free in the night and galloped among the sodden troops.

'So why did Bonaparte lose?' the Earl demanded querulously.

'Because he allowed his cavalry to fight unsupported by foot or artillery,' Sandman said shortly. 'And might I ask your lordship what happened to the servants from the house in Mount Street?'

'So why did he commit his cavalry when he did, eh? Tell me that?'

'It was a mistake, my lord, even the best generals make them. Did the servants come back here?'

The Earl petulantly slapped the wicker arms of his chair. 'Bonaparte didn't make futile mistakes! The man might be scum, but he's clever scum. So why?'

Sandman sighed. 'Our line had been thinned, we were on the reverse slope of the hill and it must have seemed, from their side of the valley, that we were beaten.'

'Beaten?' The Earl leapt on that word.

'I doubt we were even visible,' Sandman said. 'The Duke had ordered the men to lie down so, from the French viewpoint, it must have looked as if we just vanished. The French saw an empty ridge, they doubtless saw our wounded retreating into the forest behind, and they must have thought we were all retreating, so they charged. My lord, tell me what happened to your wife's servants.'

'Wife? I don't have a wife. Maddox!'

'My lord?' The servant who had let Sandman into the house stepped forward.

'The cold chicken, I think, and some champagne,' the Earl demanded, then scowled at Sandman. 'Were you wounded?'

'No, my lord.'

'So you were there when the Imperial Guard attacked?'

'I was there, my lord, from the guns that signalled the first French assault to the very last shot of the day.'

The Earl seemed to shudder. 'I hate the French,' he said suddenly. 'I detest them. A race of dancing-masters, and we brought glory on ourselves at Waterloo, Captain, glory!'

Sandman wondered what glory came from defeating dancing-masters, but said nothing. He had met other men like the Earl, men who were obsessed by Waterloo and who wanted to know every remembered minute of the battle, men who could not hear enough tales from that awful day, and all of those men, Sandman knew, had one thing in common: none had been there. Yet they revered that day, thinking it the supreme moment of their lives and of Britain's history. Indeed, for some it seemed as though history itself had come to its end on June 18th, 1815, and that the world would never again see a rivalry to match that of Britain and France. That rivalry had given meaning to a whole generation, it had burnt the globe, matching fleets and armies in Asia, America and Europe, and now it was all gone and there was only dullness in its place and, for the Earl of Avebury, as for so many others, that dullness could only be driven away by reliving the rivalry. 'So tell me,' the Earl said, 'how many times the French cavalry charged.'

'Did you bring the servants from Mount Street to this house?' Sandman asked.

'Servants? Mount Street? You're drivelling. Were you at the battle?'

'All day, my lord. And all I wish to know from you, my lord, is whether a maid called Meg came here from London.'

'How the devil would I know what happened to that bitch's servants, eh? And why would you ask?'

'A man is in prison, my lord, awaiting execution for the murder of your wife, and there is good reason to believe him innocent. That is why I am here.'

The Earl gazed up at Sandman, then began to laugh. The laugh came from deep in his narrow chest and it racked him, dredged up phlegm that half choked him, brought tears to his eyes and left him gasping. He fumbled a handkerchief from his lace-frilled sleeve and wiped his eyes, then spat into it. 'She wronged a man at the very end, did she?' he asked in a hoarse voice.

'Oh, she was good, my Celia, she was so very good at being bad.' He hawked another gobbet of spittle into the handkerchief, then glowered at Sandman. 'So, how many battalions of Napoleon's Guard climbed the hill?'

'Not enough, my lord. What happened to your wife's servants?'

The Earl ignored Sandman because the cold chicken and champagne had been placed on the edge of the model table. He summoned Betty to cut up the chicken and, as she did so, he put an arm round her waist. She seemed to shudder slightly as he first touched her, but then tolerated the caresses.

The Earl, a length of spittle hanging from his wattled jaw, turned his red, rheumy eyes on Sandman. 'I have always liked women young,' he said, 'young and tender. You!' This was to the other girl. 'Pour the champagne, child.' The girl stood on his other side and the Earl put a hand under her skirt while she poured the champagne. He still stared defiantly at Sandman. 'Young flesh,' he growled, 'young and soft.' His servants gazed at the panelled walls and Sandman turned away to look out of the window at two men scything the lawn while a third raked up the clippings. Two herons flew above the distant stream.

The Earl released his grip on the two girls, then gobbled his chicken and slurped his champagne. 'I was told,' he dismissed the two girls back to their painting by slapping their rumps, 'that the French cavalry charged at least twenty times. Was that so?'

'I didn't count,' Sandman said, still looking out of the window.

'Perhaps you were not there after all?' the Earl suggested.

Sandman did not rise to the bait. He was still looking through the window, but instead of seeing the long scythes hiss through the grass, he was staring down a smoky slope in Belgium. He was seeing his recurring dream, watching the French cavalry surge up the slope, their horses labouring in the damp earth. The air on the British-held ridge had seemed heated, as though the door of hell's great oven had been left ajar, and in that heat and smoke the French horsemen had never stopped coming. Sandman had not counted their charges for there were too many, a succession of cavalrymen thumping about the British squares, their horses bleeding and limping, the smoke of the muskets and cannon drifting over the British standards, the ground underfoot a matted tangle of trampled rye stalks, thick as a woven rush mat, but damp and rotten from the rain. The Frenchmen had been grimacing, their eyes red from the smoke and their mouths open as they shouted for their doomed emperor. 'All I remember clearly, my lord,' Sandman said, turning from the window, 'was feeling grateful to the French.'

'Grateful, why?'

'Because so long as their horsemen milled so thick about our squares then their artillery could not fire on us.'

'But how many charges did they make? Someone must know!' The Earl was petulant.

'Ten?' Sandman suggested. 'Twenty? They just kept coming. And they were hard to count because of the smoke. And I remember being very thirsty. And we didn't just stand and watch them coming, we were looking backwards, too.'

'Backwards? Why?'

'Because once a charge had gone through the squares, my lord, they had to come back again.'

'So they were attacking from both sides?'

'From every side,' Sandman said, remembering the swirl of horsemen, the mud and straw kicking up from the hooves and the screams of the dying horses.

'How many cavalry?' the Earl wanted to know.

'I didn't count, my lord. How many servants did your wife have in Mount Street?'

The Earl grinned, then turned from Sandman. 'Bring me a horseman, Betty,' he ordered and the girl dutifully brought him a model French dragoon in his greencoat. 'Very pretty, my dear,' the Earl said, then put the dragoon on the table and hauled Betty onto his lap. 'I am an old man, Captain,' he said, 'and if you want something of me then you must oblige me. Betty knows that, don't you, child?'

The girl nodded. She flinched as the Earl dug a skeletal hand into her dress to cradle one of her breasts. She was perhaps fifteen or sixteen, a country girl, curly-haired, freckled and with a round healthy face.

'How must I oblige you, my lord?' Sandman asked.

'Not as Betty does! No, no!' The Earl leered at Sandman. 'You will tell me all I want to know, Captain, and perhaps, when you are done, I shall tell you a little of what you want to know. Rank has its privileges!'

Outside, in the hall, a clock struck six and the sound

seemed melancholy in the great empty house. Sandman felt the despair of wasted time. He needed to discover if Meg was here and he needed to return to London, and he sensed that the Earl would play with him all evening and at the end send him away with his questions unanswered. The Earl, sensing and enjoying Sandman's disapproval, pulled the girl's breasts out of her dress. 'Let us begin at the beginning, Captain,' he said, lowering his face to nuzzle the warm flesh, 'let us begin at dawn, eh? It had been raining, yes?'

Sandman walked round the table until he was behind the Earl, where he stooped so his face was close to the stiff hairs of the wig. 'Why not talk about the battle's end, my lord?' Sandman asked in a low voice. 'Why not talk about the attack of the Imperial Guard? Because I was there when we wheeled out of line and took the bastards in the flank.' He crouched even lower. He could smell his lordship's reek and see a louse crawling along the wig's edge. He lowered his voice to a hoarse whisper. 'They'd won the battle, my lord, it was all over except the pursuit, but we changed history in an eyeblink. We marched out of line and we gave them volley fire, my lord, and then we fixed bayonets and I can tell you exactly how it happened. I can tell you how we won, my lord.' Sandman's temper was rising now and there was a bitterness in his voice. 'We won! But you'll never hear that story, my lord, never, because I'll make damn sure that not one officer of the 52nd will ever talk to you! You understand that? Not one officer will ever talk to you. Good day, my lord. Perhaps your servant will be kind enough to show me out?' He walked towards the door. He would ask the servant if Meg had come here and if not, which he suspected would prove the case, then this whole journey would have been a waste of time and money.

'Captain!' The Earl had tipped the girl off his lap. 'Wait!' His rouged face twitched. There was malevolence in it; an old, bitter, hard-hearted malevolence, but he so badly wanted to know exactly how Bonaparte's vaunted Guard had been beaten off, so he snarled at the two girls and the servants to leave the room. 'I'll be alone with the Captain,' he said.

It still took time to draw the tale from him. Time and a bottle of smuggled French brandy, but eventually the Earl spewed the bitter tale of his marriage, confirming what Lord Christopher had already told Sandman. Celia, second wife to the sixteenth earl of Avebury, had been on stage when the Earl first saw her. 'Legs,' the Earl said dreamily, 'such legs, Captain, such legs. That was the first thing about her I saw.'

'At the Sans Pareil?' Sandman asked.

The Earl shot Sandman a very shrewd glance. 'Who've you been talking to?' he demanded. 'Who?'

'People talk in town,' Sandman said.

'My son?' the Earl guessed, then laughed. 'That little fool? That pasty little weakling? Good God, Captain, I should have culled that one when he was an infant. His mother was a holy damned fool and swiving her was like rogering a prayerful mouse, and the bloody fool thinks he's taken after her, but he hasn't. There's me in him. He might be forever on his knees, Captain, but he's always thinking of tits and bum, legs and tits again. He might fool himself, but he don't fool me. Says he wants to be a priest! But he won't. What he wants, Captain, is for me to be dead and then the estate is his, all of it! It's entailed onto him, did he tell you that? And he'll spend it all on tits, legs and bums, just as I would have done, only the difference between that stammering little fool and me is that I was never ashamed. I enjoyed it, Captain, I still do, and he suffers from guilt. Guilt!' The Earl spat the word, whirling a length of spittle across the room. 'So what did the pallid little halfwit tell you? That I killed Celia? Perhaps I did, Captain, or perhaps Maddox went up to town and did it for me, but how will you prove it, eh?' The Earl waited for an answer, but Sandman did not speak. 'Did you know, Captain,' the Earl asked, 'that they hang an aristocrat with a silken rope?'

'I did not, my lord.'

'So they say,' the Earl declared, 'so they do say. The common folk get turned off with a yard or two of common hemp, but we lords get a rope of silk and I'd gladly wear a silk rope in exchange for that bitch's death. Lord, but she robbed me blind. Never knew a woman to spend money like it! Then when I came to my senses I tried to cut off her allowance. I denied her debts and told the estate's trustees to turn her out of the house, but the bastards left her there. Maybe she was swiving one of them? That's how she made her money, Captain, by diligent swiving.'

'You're saying she was a whore, my lord?'

'Not a common whore,' the Earl said, 'she was no mere buttock, I'll say that for her. She called herself a

191

cantatrice, an actress, a dancer, but in truth she was a clever bitch and I was a fool to exchange a marriage for a season of her swiving, however good she was.' He grinned at himself, then turned his rheumy eyes on Sandman. 'Celia used blackmail, Captain. She'd take a young man about town as a lover, commit the poor fool to write a letter or two begging her favours, and then when he engaged to marry an heiress she threatened to reveal the letters. Made a pretty penny, she did! She told me as much! Told me to my face. Told me she didn't need my cash, had her own.'

'Do you know what men she treated thus, my lord?'

The Earl shook his head. He stared at the model battle, unwilling to meet Sandman's eyes. 'I didn't want to know names,' he said softly and, for the first time, Sandman felt some pity for the old man.

'And the servants, my lord? The servants from your London house. What happened to them?'

'How the devil would I know? They ain't here.' He scowled at Sandman. 'And why would I want that bitch's servants here? I told Faulkner to get rid of them, just to get rid of them.'

'Faulkner?'

'A lawyer, one of the trustees, and like all lawyers he's a belly-crawling piece of shit.' The Earl looked up at Sandman. 'I don't know what happened to Celia's damned servants,' he said, 'and I don't care. Now, go to the door and find Maddox and tell him you and I will sup on beef, and then, damn you, tell me what happened when the Emperor's Guard attacked.'

So Sandman did.

He had come to Wiltshire, he had not found Meg, but he had learnt something.

Though whether it was enough, he did not know. And in the morning he went back to London.

5

Sandman got back to London late on Thursday afternoon. He had taken the mail coach from Marlborough, justifying the expense by the time he was saving, but just outside Thatcham one of the horses had thrown a shoe and then, near the village of Hammersmith, a haywain with a broken axle was blocking a bridge and Sandman reckoned it would have been far quicker to have walked the last few miles rather than wait while the road was cleared, but he was tired after sleeping fitfully on a pile of straw in the yard of the King's Head in Marlborough and so he stayed with the coach. He was also irritated, for he reckoned his journey to Wiltshire had been largely wasted. He doubted the Earl of Avebury had either killed or arranged the killing of his wife, but he had never thought the man guilty in the first place. The only advantage Sandman had gained was to learn that the dead Countess had kept herself by blackmailing her lovers, but that did not help him to discover who those lovers had been.

He used the side door of the Wheatsheaf that opened into the tavern's stableyard where he pumped water into the tin cup chained to the handle. He drank it down, pumped again, then turned as the click of hooves sounded in the stable entrance where he saw Jack Hood heaving a saddle onto a tall and handsome black horse. The highwayman nodded a curt acknowledgement of Sandman's presence, then stooped to buckle the girth. Like his horse, Jack Hood was tall and dark. He wore black boots, black breeches and a narrow waisted black coat, and he wore his black hair long and tied with a ribbon of black silk at the nape of his neck. He straightened and gave Sandman a crooked grin. 'You look tired, Captain.'

'Tired, poor, hungry and thirsty,' Sandman said, and pumped a third cup of water.

'That's what the square life does for you,' Hood said cheerfully. He slid two long-barrelled pistols into their saddle holsters. 'You should be on the cross like me.'

Sandman drank down the water and let the cup drop. 'And what will you do, Mister Hood,' he asked, 'when they catch you?'

Hood led the horse into the waning evening sunlight. The beast was fine bred and nervous, high-stepping and skittish; a horse, Sandman suspected, that could fly like the night wind when escape was needed. 'When I'm caught?' Hood asked. 'I'll come to you for help, Captain. Sally says you're a crap prig.'

'A gallows thief.' Sandman had learnt enough flash to be able to translate the phrase. 'But I haven't stolen one man from the scaffold yet.'

'And I doubt you ever will,' Hood said grimly, 'because that ain't the way the world works. They don't care how many they hang, Captain, so long as the rest of us take note that they do hang.'

'They care,' Sandman insisted, 'why else did they appoint me?'

Hood offered Sandman a sceptical look, then put his left foot into the stirrup and hauled himself into the saddle. 'And are you telling me, Captain,' he asked as he fiddled his right foot into its stirrup, 'that they appointed you out of the goodness of their hearts? Did the Home Secretary discover a sudden doubt about the quality of justice in Black Jack's court?'

'No,' Sandman allowed.

'They appointed you, Captain, because someone with influence wanted Corday's case examined. Someone with influence, am I right?'

Sandman nodded. 'Exactly right.'

'A cove can be as innocent as a fresh-born babe,' Hood said sourly, 'but if he don't have a friend with influence then he'll hang high. Ain't that so?' Jack Hood flicked his coat tails out over his horse's rump, then gathered the reins. 'And as like as not I'll finish my days on Jem Botting's dancing floor and I don't lose sleep nor tears over it. The gallows is there, Captain, and we live with it till we die on it, and we won't change it because the bastards don't want it changed. It's their world, not ours, and they fight to keep it the way they want. They kill us, they send us to Australia or else they break us on the treadmill, and you know why? Because they fear us. They fear we'll become like the French mob. They fear a guillotine in Whitehall and to keep it from happening they build a scaffold in Newgate. They might let you save one man, Captain, but don't think you'll change anything.' He pulled on thin black leather gloves. 'There are some coves to see you in the back slum, Captain,' he said, meaning that there were some men waiting for Sandman in the back parlour. 'But before you talk with them,' Hood went on, 'you should know I took my dinner at the Dog and Duck.'

'In St George's Fields?' Sandman asked, puzzled by the apparently irrelevant statement.

'A lot of the high toby live and dine there,' Hood said, 'on account that it's convenient for the western roads.' He meant that a number of highwaymen patronised the tavern. 'And I heard a whisper there, Captain. Your life, fifty quid.' He raised an eyebrow. 'You've upset someone, Captain. I've spread word in the 'sheaf that no one's to touch you because you've been kind to my Sal and I look after those that look after her, but I can't control every flash bowzing house in London.'

Sandman felt a lurch of his heart. Fifty guineas for his life? Was that a compliment or an insult? 'You would not know, I suppose,' he asked, 'who has staked the money?'

'I asked, but no one knew. But it's firm cash, Captain, so watch yourself. I'm obliged to you.' These last four words were because Sandman had hauled open the yard gate.

Sandman looked up at the horseman. 'You're not going to see Sally on stage tonight?'

Hood shook his head. 'Seen her often enough,' he said curtly, 'and I've business of my own that she won't

197

be watching.' He touched his spurs to his horse's flanks and, without a word of farewell, rode northwards behind a wagon loaded with newly baked bricks.

Sandman closed the gate. Viscount Sidmouth, when he had given Sandman this job, had hinted it would be easy, a month's pay for a day's work, but it was suddenly a life for a month's pay. Sandman turned and gazed at the dirty windows of the back parlour, but he could not see beyond the gloss of the evening light on the small panes. Whoever waited there could see him, but he could not see them and so he did not go directly to the parlour, but instead cut through the barrel room to the passage where there was a serving hatch. He nudged the hatch open, careful not to make a noise, then stooped to peer through the crack.

He heard the footsteps behind him, but before he could turn a pistol barrel was cold by his ear. 'A good soldier always makes a reconnaissance, eh Captain?' Sergeant Berrigan said. 'I thought you'd come here first.'

Sandman straightened and turned to see that the Sergeant was grinning, pleased because he had outmanoeuvred Sandman. 'So what are you going to do, Sergeant?' he asked. 'Shoot me?'

'Just making sure you ain't got any sticks on you, Captain,' Berrigan said, then used his pistol barrel to push open the flaps of Sandman's jacket and, satisfied that the Captain was not armed, he jerked his head towards the parlour door. 'After you, Captain.'

'Sergeant,' Sandman began, planning to appeal to Berrigan's better nature, but that nature was nowhere to be seen, for the Sergeant just cocked the pistol and aimed it at Sandman's chest. Sandman thought about knocking the barrel aside and bringing his knee up into Berrigan's groin, but the Sergeant gave him a half-smile and an almost imperceptible shake of his head as though inviting Sandman to try. 'Through the door, eh?' Sandman asked and, when Berrigan nodded, he turned the knob and went into the back parlour.

The Marquess of Skavadale and Lord Robin Holloway were on the settle at the far side of the long table. Both were exquisitely dressed in superbly cut black coats, blossoming cravats and skin-tight breeches. Holloway scowled to see Sandman, but Skavadale courteously stood and offered a smile. 'My dear Captain Sandman, how very kind of you to join us.'

'Been waiting long?' Sandman asked truculently.

'A half-hour,' Skavadale replied pleasantly. 'We did expect to find you here already, but the wait has not been unduly tedious. Please, sit.'

Sandman sat reluctantly, first glancing at Berrigan who came into the parlour, closed the door and lowered the pistol's flint, though he did not put the weapon away. Instead the Sergeant stood beside the door and watched Sandman. The Marquess of Skavadale took the cork from some wine and poured out a glassful. 'A rather raw claret, Captain, but probably welcome after your journey? But how could we have expected the finest wine here, eh? This is the Wheatsheaf, flash, but not flush, eh? That's rather good, don't you think, Robin? Flash, but not flush?'

Lord Robin Holloway neither smiled nor spoke, but

just stared at Sandman. There were still two raw scars across his cheeks and nose where Sandman had whipped him with the fencing foil. Skavadale pushed the glass of wine across the table, then looked pained when Sandman shook his head in refusal. 'Oh come, Captain,' Skavadale said with a frown, 'we're here to be friendly.'

'And I'm here because I was threatened with a pistol.'

'Put it away, Sergeant,' Skavadale ordered, then he toasted Sandman. 'I've learnt a little about you in the last couple of days, Captain. I already knew you were a formidable cricketer, of course, but you have another reputation besides.'

'For what?' Sandman asked bleakly.

'You were a good soldier,' Skavadale said.

'So?'

'But unfortunate in your father,' Skavadale said gently. 'Now, as I understand things, Captain, you are supporting your mother and sister. Am I right?' He waited for a reply, but Sandman neither spoke nor moved. 'It's sad,' Skavadale went on, 'when folk of refinement are condemned to poverty. If it were not for you, Captain, your mother would long have been reduced to accepting charity and your sister would be what? A governess? A paid companion? Yet with a small dowry she could still marry perfectly well, could she not?'

Sandman still kept silent, yet Lord Skavadale had spoken nothing but the truth. Belle, Sandman's sister, was nineteen years old and had only one hope of escaping poverty which was to marry well, yet without a dowry she could not hope to find a respectable husband. She would be lucky to find a tradesman willing to marry her, and even if she did then Sandman knew his sister would not accept such a husband for, like her mother, she had an exaggerated sense of her own high standing in society. A year ago, before her father's death, Belle might have expected a dowry of several thousand pounds, enough to attract an aristocrat and provide a healthy income, and she still yearned for those prospects and, in some obscure way, she blamed Sandman for their loss. That was why Sandman was in London, because he could no longer bear the reproaches of his mother and sister, who expected him to replace his father as a provider of endless luxuries.

'Now,' Skavadale said, 'your father's gambling has reduced the family to penury. Is that not right, Captain? Yet you are trying to pay off some of his debts. You've chosen a difficult path and it's very honourable of you, very honourable. Ain't that honourable, Robin?'

Lord Robin Holloway said nothing. He just shrugged, keeping his cold eyes on Sandman.

'So what will you do, Captain?' Skavadale asked.

'Do?'

'A mother and a sister to keep, debts to pay, and no employment other than an occasional game of cricket?' Skavadale asked, raising his eyebrows in mock surprise. 'And, as I understand it, the Home Secretary's demands upon you are very temporary and are hardly likely to lead to a permanent fortune. So what will you do?'

'What will you do?' Sandman asked.

'I beg your pardon?'

'As I understand it,' Sandman said, remembering Lord Alexander's description of the Marquess of Skavadale, 'you are not unlike me. Your family once possessed a great fortune, but it also possessed gamblers.'

The Marquess looked irritated for a second, but let the insult pass. 'I shall marry well,' he said lightly, 'meaning I shall marry wealth. And you?'

'Maybe I shall marry well, too,' Sandman retorted.

'Really?' Skavadale raised a sceptical eyebrow. 'I shall succeed to a dukedom, Sandman, and that's a great lure to a girl. What's your attraction? Skill at cricket? Fascinating memories of Waterloo?' His lordship's voice was still polite, but the scorn was obvious. 'Girls who possess money,' Skavadale went on, 'either marry more money or else they seek rank, because money and rank, Captain, are the only two things that matter in this world.'

'Truth?' Sandman suggested. 'Honour?'

'Money,' Skavadale repeated flatly, 'and rank. My family may be close to bankruptcy, but we have rank. By God, we have rank, and that will restore our fortune.'

'Money and rank,' Sandman said reflectively. 'So how do you console a man like Sergeant Berrigan whose rank is lowly and whose fortune, I surmise, is paltry?'

Skavadale gave the Sergeant a lazy glance. 'I advise him, Captain, to attach himself to a man of rank and fortune. That is the way of the world. He serves, I reward, and together we prosper.'

'And where do I fit into this divinely ordained scheme?' Sandman enquired.

Skavadale gave a ghost of a smile. 'You are a gentleman, Captain, so you possess rank, but you have been denied your share of wealth. If you will allow us,' he gestured to include the sallow Lord Robin Holloway, 'and by us I mean the whole membership of the Seraphim Club, we should like to remedy that lack.' He took a piece of paper from his pocket, placed it on the table and slid it towards Sandman.

'Remedy?' Sandman asked bleakly, but Skavadale said nothing, just pointed at the paper that Sandman picked up, opened and saw, first, Lord Robin Holloway's extravagantly scrawled signature and then he saw the figure. He stared at it, then looked up at Lord Skavadale, who smiled. Sandman looked at the paper again. It was a money draft, payable to Rider Sandman, drawn on the account of Lord Robin Holloway at Coutts Bank, to the value of twenty thousand guineas.

Twenty thousand. His hands shook slightly and he forced himself to take a deep breath.

It solved everything. Everything.

Twenty thousand guineas could pay off his father's small debts, buy his mother and sister a fine house and there would still be enough left over to yield an income of six or seven hundred pounds a year, which was small compared to the money Sandman's mother had once been used to, but six hundred pounds a year could keep a woman and her daughter in country gentility. It was respectable. They might not be able to afford a carriage and horses, but they could keep a maid and a cook, they could put a gold coin in the collection plate each Sunday and they could receive their neighbours in sufficient style. They could stop complaining to Rider Sandman of their poverty.

There was a great clatter of hooves and chains as a dray arrived in the yard, but Sandman was oblivious of the noise. He was being tempted by the thought that he was not responsible for his father's debts, and if he ignored the tradesmen who had been taken close to ruin by Ludovic Sandman's suicide then he could get his mother an income of perhaps eight hundred a year. Best of all, though, and most tempting of all, was the knowledge that twenty thousand guineas would be a fortune sufficient to overcome Lady Forrest's objections to his marrying Eleanor. He stared at the money draft. It made all things possible. Eleanor, he thought, Eleanor, and he thought of the money Eleanor would bring him and he knew he would be wealthy again and he would have horses in his stables and he could play cricket all summer and hunt all winter. He would be a proper gentleman again. He would no longer need to scratch for pennies or spend time worrying about the laundry.

He looked up into Lord Robin Holloway's eyes. The young man was a fool who had wanted to challenge Sandman to a duel, now he was giving him a fortune? Lord Robin ignored Sandman's gaze, staring off at a cobweb high on the parlour's panelling. Lord Skavadale smiled at Sandman. It was the smile of a man enjoying another's good fortune, yet it filled Sandman with shame. Shame because he had been tempted, truly tempted. 'You think we are trying to bribe you?' Lord Skavadale had seen Sandman's change of expression and asked the question anxiously.

'I did not expect such kindness from Lord Robin,' Sandman said drily.

'Every member of the Seraphim contributed,' the Marquess said, 'and my friend Robin collated the funds. It is, of course, a gift, not a bribe.'

'A gift?' Sandman repeated the words bitterly. 'Not a bribe?'

'Of course it's not a bribe,' Skavadale said sternly, 'indeed not.' He stood and went to the window where he watched the beer-barrels being rolled down planks from the dray's bed, then he turned and smiled. 'I am offended, Captain Sandman, when I see a gentleman reduced to penury. Such a thing goes against the natural order, wouldn't you say? And when that gentleman is an officer who has fought gallantly for his country, then the offence is all the greater. I told you that the Seraphim Club is composed of men who attempt to excel, who celebrate the higher achievements. What else are angels but beings that do good? So we should like to see you and your family restored to your proper place in society. That is all.' He shrugged as though the gesture was really very small.

Sandman wanted to believe him. Lord Skavadale had sounded so reasonable and calm, as though this transaction was something very ordinary. Yet Sandman knew better. 'You're offering me charity,' he said.

Lord Skavadale shook his head. 'Merely a correction of blind fate, Captain.'

'And if I allow my fate to be corrected,' Sandman asked, 'what would you want in return?'

Lord Skavadale looked offended, as though it had not even occurred to him that Sandman might perform some small service in return for being given a small fortune. 'I should only expect, Captain,' he spoke stiffly, 'that you would behave like a gentleman.'

Sandman glanced at Lord Robin Holloway, who had not spoken. 'I trust,' Sandman said frostily, 'that I always behave thus.'

'Then you will know, Captain,' Skavadale said pointedly, 'that gentlemen do not perform paid employment.'

Sandman said nothing.

Lord Skavadale bridled slightly at Sandman's silence. 'So naturally, Captain, in return for accepting that draft, you will resign any paid offices that you might enjoy.'

Sandman looked down at the small fortune. 'So I write to the Home Secretary and resign as his Investigator?'

'It would surely be the gentlemanly thing to do,' Skavadale observed.

'How gentlemanly is it,' Sandman asked, 'to let an innocent man hang?'

'Is he innocent?' Lord Skavadale enquired. 'You told the Sergeant you would bring proof from the countryside, and did you?' He waited, but it was plain from Sandman's face that there was no proof. Lord Skavadale shrugged as if to suggest that Sandman might just as well abandon a hopeless hunt and accept the money.

And Sandman was tempted, he was so very tempted,

but he was also ashamed of that temptation and so he nerved himself and then tore the draft into shreds. He saw Lord Skavadale blink with surprise when he made the first rip, and then his lordship looked furious and Sandman felt a pulse of fear. It was not fear of Lord Skavadale's anger, but for his own future and for the enormity of the fortune he was rejecting.

He scattered the scraps on the table. The Marquess of Skavadale and Lord Robin Holloway stood. Neither spoke. They looked at Sergeant Berrigan and it seemed that some kind of unspoken message was delivered before, without even glancing at Sandman, they went. Their footsteps receded down the passage as cold metal touched the back of Sandman's neck and he knew it was the pistol. Sandman tensed, planning to throw himself backwards in hope of unbalancing Berrigan, but the Sergeant ground the cold barrel hard into Sandman's neck. 'You had your chance, Captain.'

'You still have one, Sergeant,' Sandman said.

'But I ain't a fool,' Berrigan went on, 'and I ain't killing you here. Not here and now. Too many folk in the inn. I kill you here, Captain, and I'm dancing in Newgate.' The pistol's pressure vanished, then the Sergeant leant close to Sandman's ear. 'Watch yourself, Captain, watch yourself.' It was the exact same advice that Jack Hood had given.

Sandman heard the door open and shut, and the Sergeant's footsteps fade.

Twenty thousand guineas, he thought. Gone.

*　　*　　*

The Reverend Lord Alexander Pleydell had secured one of the Covent Garden Theatre's stage boxes for the performance. 'I cannot say I am expecting great artistry,' he declared as he followed Sandman through the crowds, 'except from Miss Hood. I am sure she will be more than dazzling.' His lordship, like Sandman, was clutching his pockets for theatre crowds were famous hunting grounds for cly-fakers, knucklers, divers, dummy hunters and buzz-coves, all of them, to Lord Alexander's delight, different names for pickpockets. 'Do you realise,' he said in his shrill voice, 'that there is a whole hierarchy of cly-fakers?'

'I was listening to the conversation, Alexander,' Sandman said. Lord Alexander, before they left the Wheatsheaf, had insisted on another tutorial in the flash language, this one from the landlord, Jenks, who rather liked having a reverend lord as a customer. The Reverend Lord had taken notes, delighted to discover that the lowest rank of cly-faker was the clouter, a child who snitched handkerchiefs, while the lords of the buzzing trade were the thimble-coves who stole watches. It was not just the practitioners of the trade who had names, the pockets themselves were all differentiated. 'Garret,' Lord Alexander chanted, 'hoxter, kickseys, pit, rough-fammy, salt box cly and slip. Did I miss one?'

'I wasn't paying attention.' Sandman edged closer to the brightly lit awning of the theatre.

'Garret, hoxter, kickseys, pit, rough-fammy, salt box cly and slip,' Lord Alexander announced again to the bemusement of the crowd. The garret was the fob pocket of a waistcoat while the lower pockets were rough-fammies, the kicksies were pockets in breeches, the hoxter was a coat's inside pocket, an unflapped chest pocket was a pit, an outside coat pocket protected by a flap was a salt box cly while a tail pocket, the easiest of all to pick, was a slip. 'Do you think,' Lord Alexander shouted over the noise of the crowd, 'that Miss Hood will join us for supper after the performance?'

'I'm sure she'll be more than happy to bask in the admiration of one of her admirers.'

'One of?' Lord Alexander asked anxiously. 'You're not thinking of Kit Carne, are you?'

Sandman was not thinking of Lord Christopher Carne, but he shrugged as though the Earl of Avebury's heir was indeed a rival for Sally's hand. Lord Alexander looked very disapproving. 'Kit is not a serious man, Rider.'

'I thought he was very serious.'

'I have decided he is weak,' Lord Alexander said loftily.

'Weak?'

'The other night,' Lord Alexander said, 'he just stared at Miss Hood with a vacant look on his face! Ridiculous behaviour. I was talking to her and he was just gaping! Lord knows what she thought of him.'

'I can't imagine,' Sandman said.

'He was gaping like a fish!' Lord Alexander said, then turned in alarm as a child squealed. The child's pain was met by a roar of laughter. 'What happened?' Lord Alexander asked anxiously.

'Someone lined their pockets with fish-hooks,' Sandman guessed, 'and a clouter just got torn fingers?' It was a common precaution against pickpockets.

'A lesson the child will not forget,' Lord Alexander said piously. 'But I mustn't be hard on Kit. He has little experience of women and I fear he has no defences against their charms.'

'That,' Sandman said, 'from a man who is eager to watch Sally Hood dance, is rich.'

Lord Alexander grinned. 'Even I am not perfect. Kit wanted to come tonight, but I told him to buy his own ticket. Good Lord, he might even have wanted to come to supper with Miss Hood afterwards! Do you think she might like to visit Newgate with us?'

'Visit Newgate?'

'For a hanging! I told you I was requesting a privileged seat from the prison authorities, so I wrote to them. No answer yet, but I'm sure they'll consent.'

'And I'm sure I don't want to go,' Sandman shouted over the crowd's noise, and just then the throng gave an inexplicable lurch and Sandman was able to make a lunge for the doorway. If it was a paid crowd causing the crush, he thought, then it was costing Mister Spofforth a rare fortune. Mister Spofforth was the man who had taken the theatre for the evening on behalf of his protégée, a Miss Sacharissa Lasorda, who was billed as the new Vestris. The old Vestris was only twenty years old and a dazzling Italian actress who was reputed to add three hundred pounds a night to a theatre's takings merely by baring her legs, and Mister Spofforth was now trying to launch Miss Lasorda on a career of similar profitability.

'Do you know Spofforth?' Sandman asked his friend. They were inside the theatre now and an old woman was leading them up musty stairs to their box.

'Of course I know William Spofforth,' Lord Alexander's club foot banged against the risers as he struggled manfully up the dark stairs, 'he was at Marlborough. He's a rather foolish young man whose father made a fortune in sugar. Young Spofforth, our host tonight, kept wicket, but had no idea how to place fielders.'

'I always think the captain or bowler should do that,' Sandman observed mildly.

'An absurd statement,' Lord Alexander snapped. 'Cricket will cease to be cricket when the Keeper abandons his duties of field setting. He sees as the batsman does, so who else is better placed to set a field? Truly, Rider, I am second to none in my admiration of your batting, but when it comes to a theoretical understanding of the game then you really are a child.' It was an old argument, and one that happily engaged them as they took their places above the stage's apron. Lord Alexander had his bag of pipes and lit his first of the evening, the smoke wreathing past a large sign that prohibited smoking. The house was full, over three thousand spectators, and it was rowdy because a good number of the audience were already drunk, suggesting that Mister Spofforth's servants must have dredged the taverns to find his supporters. A group of newspaper writers was being plied with champagne, brandy and

211

oysters in a box opposite Lord Alexander's plush eyrie. Mister Spofforth, an aloof beau with a collar rising past his ears, was in the neighbouring box from where he kept an anxious eye on the journalists who were costing him so much and whose verdict could make or break his lover, but one critic was already asleep, another was fondling a woman while the remaining two were loudly haranguing the box's attendant for more champagne. A dozen musicians filed into the pit and began tuning their instruments.

'I'm putting together a gentlemen's eleven to play against Hampshire at the end of the month,' Lord Alexander said, 'and I rather hoped you'd want to play.'

'I'd like that, yes. Would the game be in Hampshire?' Sandman asked the question anxiously, for he did not particularly want to go near Winchester and his mother's querulous demands.

'Here, in London,' Lord Alexander said, 'at Thomas Lord's ground.'

Sandman grimaced. 'That wretched hillside?'

'It's a perfectly good ground,' Lord Alexander said huffily, 'a slight slope, maybe? And I've already wagered fifty guineas on the game, which is why I'd like you to play. I shall go higher if you're in my team.'

Sandman groaned. 'Money's ruining the game, Alexander.'

'Which is why those of us who oppose corruption must be energetic in our patronage of the game,' Lord Alexander insisted. 'So will you play?'

'I'm very out of practice,' Sandman warned his friend.

'Then get into practice,' Lord Alexander said testily, lighting another pipe. He frowned at Sandman. 'You look depressingly glum. Don't you enjoy the theatre?'

'Very much.'

'Then look as if you do!' Lord Alexander polished the lens of his opera glasses on the tails of his coat. 'Do you think Miss Hood would enjoy cricket?'

'I can't imagine her playing it, somehow.'

'Don't be so grotesquely absurd, Rider, I mean as a spectator.'

'You must ask her, Alexander,' Sandman said. He leant over the edge of the box to look down into the stalls, where a claque from the Wheatsheaf were readying themselves to cheer Sally. A pair of whores were working their way around the edge of the pit and one of them, seeing him peer down, mimed that she would come up to the box. Sandman hastily shook his head and pulled back out of sight. 'Suppose she's dead,' he asked suddenly.

'Miss Hood? Dead? Why should she be?' Lord Alexander looked very worried. 'Was she ill? You should have told me!'

'I'm talking about the maidservant. Meg.'

'Oh, her,' Lord Alexander said absently, then frowned at his pipe. 'Do you recall those Spanish cigars that were all the rage when you were fighting against the forces of enlightenment in Spain?'

'Of course I do.'

'You can't get them anywhere, and I did like them.'

'Try Pettigrews in Old Bond Street,' Sandman said,

sounding annoyed that his friend had ignored his concerns about Meg.

'I've tried. They have none. And I did like them.'

'I know someone who's thinking of importing them,' Sandman said, remembering Sergeant Berrigan.

'Let me know if they do,' Lord Alexander blew smoke towards the gilded cherubs on the ceiling. 'Are your friends in the Seraphim Club aware that you are pursuing Meg?'

'No.'

'So they have no cause to find and kill her. And if they had wished to kill her at the time of the Countess's murder, supposing that they did, indeed, perform that wicked deed, then they would have left her body with her mistress's corpse so that Corday could be convicted of both murders. Which suggests, does it not, that the girl is alive? It occurs to me, Rider, that your duties as an Investigator demand a great deal of logical deduction, which is why you are such a poor choice for the post. Still, you may always consult me.'

'You're very kind, Alexander.'

'I try to be, dear boy.' Lord Alexander, pleased with himself, beamed. 'I do try to be.'

A cheer sounded as boys went round the theatre extinguishing the lamps. The musicians gave a last tentative squeak, then waited for the conductor's baton to fall. Some of the audience in the pit began to whistle as a demand for the curtains to part. Most of the scene-shifting was done by sailors, men accustomed to ropes and heights, and, just as at sea, some of the signals were given by whistles and the audience's whistling betrayed

214

their impatience, but the curtain stayed obstinately shut. More lamps were extinguished, then the big reflective lanterns at the edges of the stage were unmasked, the drummer gave a portentous roll and a player in a swathing cloak leapt from between the curtains to recite the prologue on the stage's wide apron:

> 'In Africa, so far from home,
> A little lad was wont to roam.
> Aladdin was our hero's name . . .'

He got no further before the audience drowned him in a cacophony of shouting, hissing and whistling. 'Show us the girl's pins!' a man yelled from the box next to Sandman. 'Show us her gams!'

'I think Vestris's supporters are here!' Lord Alexander shouted in Sandman's ear.

Mister Spofforth was looking ever more anxious. The newspaper writers were beginning to pay attention now that the crowd was in full cry, but the musicians, who had heard it all before, began to play and that slightly calmed the audience, who gave a cheer as the prologue was abandoned and the heavy scarlet curtains parted to reveal a glade in Africa. Oak trees and yellow roses framed an idol that guarded the entrance to a cave where a dozen white-skinned natives were sleeping. Sally was one of the natives, who were inexplicably dressed in white stockings, black velvet jackets and very short tartan skirts. Lord Alexander bellowed a cheer as the twelve girls got to their feet and began dancing. The Wheatsheaf's customers in the pit also cheered loudly and Vestris's supporters, assuming that the cheers came from Spofforth's paid claque, began to jeer. 'Bring on the girl!' the man in the next box demanded. A plum arced onto the stage to splatter against the idol, which looked suspiciously like a Red Indian's totem pole. Mister Spofforth was making helpless gestures to calm an audience that was determined to make mayhem, or at least the half who had been rented by Vestris's supporters were, while the other half, paid by Mister Spofforth, were too cowed to fight back. Some of the crowd had rattles that filled the high gilded hall with a crackling and echoing din. 'It's going to be very nasty!' Lord Alexander said with relish. 'Oh, this is splendid!'

The theatre's management must have believed that the sight of Miss Sacharissa Lasorda would calm the tumult, for the girl was pushed prematurely onto the stage. Mister Spofforth stood and began to applaud as she staggered out of the wings and his claque took their cue and cheered so lustily that they actually drowned the catcalls for a while. Miss Lasorda, who played the Sultan of Africa's daughter, was dark-haired and certainly pretty, but whether her legs deserved to be as famous as Vestris's was still a mystery, for she was wearing a long skirt embroidered with crescent moons, camels and scimitars. She seemed momentarily alarmed to find herself on stage, but then bowed to her supporters before beginning to dance.

'Show us your gams!' the man in the next box shouted.

'Skirt off! Skirt off! Skirt off!' the crowd in the stalls began to chant, and a shower of plums and apples hurtled onto the stage. 'Skirt off! Skirt off! Skirt off!'

Mister Spofforth was still making calming gestures with his hands, but that only made him a target and he ducked as a well-aimed volley of fruit spattered his box.

Lord Alexander had tears of joy running down his cheeks. 'I do so like the theatre,' he said, 'dear sweet God, I do so love it. This must have cost that young fool two thousand pounds at the very least!'

Sandman did not hear what his friend had said and so leant towards him. 'What?' he asked.

He heard something smack into the wall at the back of the box and saw, in the shadows there, a puff of dust. It was only then that he realised a shot had been fired in the theatre and astonished, he gaped up to see a patch of smoke in the dim heights of an upper gallery box. A rifle, he thought. It had a different sound from a musket. He remembered the greenjackets at Waterloo, remembered the distinctive sound of their weapons, and then he realised someone had just shot at him and he was so shocked that he did not move for a few seconds. Instead he stared up at the spreading smoke and realised that the audience was going silent. Some had heard the shot over the raucous din of rattles, whistles and shouts, while others could smell the reeking powder smoke, then someone screamed in the upper gallery. Miss Lasorda stared upwards, mouth open.

Sandman snatched open the door to the box and saw two men running up the stairs with pistols in their hands. He slammed the door. 'Meet me in the Wheat-sheaf,' he told Lord Alexander, and he swung his legs over the box's balustrade, paused a second, then jumped. He landed heavily, turning his left ankle and

217

almost falling. The audience cheered, thinking Sandman's leap was part of the entertainment, but then some in the stalls began to scream for they could see the two men in Lord Alexander's box and they could see the pistols.

'Captain!' Sally shouted, and pointed to the wings.

Sandman stumbled. There was a pain in his ankle, a terrible pain that made him stagger towards the idol guarding the cave mouth. He turned to see the two men in the box, both pointing their pistols but neither dared fire onto the stage which was crowded with dancers. Then one of the men threw a leg over the box's gilded lip and Sandman limped into the wings where a man dressed as a harlequin and another with a blackened face, a tall crown and a magic lamp waited. Sandman pushed between them, staggered through a tangle of ropes, then down some stairs and, at the bottom, turned into a passage. He did not think his left ankle was broken, but he must have twisted it and every step was an agony. He stopped in the passage, his heart beating, and flattened himself against the wall. He heard the screams from the dancers on stage, then the pounding of feet down wooden stairs, and a second later a man came round the corner and Sandman tripped him, then stamped hard on the back of his neck. The man grunted and Sandman took the pistol out of his suddenly feeble hand. He turned the man over. 'Who are you?' he asked, but the man merely spat up at Sandman, who struck him with the pistol barrel, then fished in the man's pockets to find a handful of cartridges. He stood, wincing from the pain in his left leg, then limped down the passage to the stage door. More footsteps sounded behind him and he turned, pistol raised, but it was Sally running towards him with her street clothes bundled in a cloak.

'You all right?' she asked him.

'Twisted my ankle.'

'Bleeding ruckus back there,' Sally said, 'there's more fruit on the bloody deck than there is in the market.'

'Deck?' he asked.

'Stage,' she explained shortly, then pulled open the door.

'You should go back,' Sandman said.

'I should do a lot of bleeding things, but I don't,' Sally said, 'so come on.' She tugged him out into the street. A man whistled at the sight of her long legs in the white stockings and she snarled at him to fake away off, then draped the cloak about her shoulders. 'Lean on me,' she told Sandman, who was limping and grunting from pain. 'You're in a bad bleeding way, ain't you?'

'Sprained ankle,' Sandman said. 'I don't think it's broken.'

'How do you know?'

'Because it isn't grating with every step.'

'Bloody hell,' Sally said. 'What happened?'

'Someone shot at me; a rifle.'

'Who?'

'I don't know.' Sandman said. The Seraphim Club? That seemed most likely, especially after Sandman had turned down their vast bribe, but that did not explain

219

Jack Hood's assertion that there was a price on Sandman's head. Why would the Seraphim Club pay criminals to do what they or their servants were more than capable of doing? 'I really don't know,' he said, puzzled and frightened.

They had come from the rear of the theatre and now walked or, in Sandman's case, hobbled under the piazza of the Covent Garden market. The summer evening meant it was still light, though the shadows were long across the cobbles that were littered with the remnants of vegetables and squashed fruit. A rat slithered across Sandman's path. He constantly glanced behind, but he could see no obvious enemies. No sign of Sergeant Berrigan or anyone in a black and yellow livery. No sign of Lord Robin Holloway or the Marquess of Skavadale. 'They'll be expecting me to go back to the Wheatsheaf,' he told Sally.

'They won't know which bleeding door you're going in, though, will they?' Sally said, 'and once you're inside you're bleeding safe, Captain, because there ain't a man there who won't protect you.' She turned in sudden alarm as hurried footsteps sounded behind, but it was only a child running from an irate man accusing the boy of being a pickpocket. Flower sellers were arranging their baskets on the pavement, ready for the crowds to come from the two nearby theatres. Whistles and rattles sounded. 'Bleeding charlies on their way to the spell,' Sally said, meaning that the constables from Bow Street were converging on the Covent Garden Theatre. She frowned at the pistol in Sandman's hand. 'Hide that stick. Don't want a charlie scurfing you.'

Sandman pushed the gun into a pocket. 'Are you sure you shouldn't be at the theatre?'

'They ain't ever going to get that bleeding circus started again, not that it ever did get started, did it? Dead before it was born. No, Miss Sacharissa's little night of fame got the jump, didn't it? Mind you, her name ain't Sacharissa Lasorda.'

'I never thought it was.'

'Flossie, she's called, and she used to be the pal of a fire-eater at Astleys. Must be thirty if she's a day, and last I heard she was earning her bunce in an academy.'

'She was a schoolteacher?' Sandman asked, sounding surprised, for few women chose that profession and Miss Lasorda, or whatever she was called, did not look like a teacher.

Sally laughed so much she had to support herself by leaning on Sandman. 'Lord, I love you, Captain,' she said, still laughing. 'An academy ain't for learning. At least not letters. It's a brothel!'

'Oh,' Sandman said.

'Not far now,' Sally said as they approached the Drury Lane Theatre, from which a burst of applause sounded. 'How's your ankle?'

'I think I can walk,' Sandman said.

'Try,' Sally encouraged him, then watched as Sandman hobbled a few steps. 'You don't want to take that boot off tonight,' she said. 'Your ankle's going to swell something horrible if you do.' She walked on ahead and opened the Wheatsheaf's front door. Sandman half expected to see a man waiting there with a pistol, but the doorway was empty.

221

'We don't want to be looking over our shoulders all night,' Sandman said, 'so I'm going to see if the back parlour's free.' He led Sally across the crowded taproom where the landlord was holding court at a table. 'Is the back parlour free?' Sandman asked him.

Jenks nodded. 'The gentleman said you'd be back, Captain, and he kept it for you. And there's a letter for you as well, brought by a slavey.'

'A footman,' Sally translated for Sandman, 'and what gentleman reserved the back slum?'

'It must be Lord Alexander,' Sandman explained, 'because he wanted you and me to have dinner with him.' He took the letter from Mister Jenks and smiled at Sally. 'You don't mind Alexander's company?'

'Mind Lord Alexander? He'll just gawp at me like a Billingsgate cod, won't he?'

'How fickle your affection is, Miss Hood,' Sandman said, and received a blow on the shoulder as a reward.

'Well he does!' Sally said, and gave a cruelly accurate imitation of Lord Alexander's goggling devotion. 'Poor old cripple,' she said sympathetically, then glanced down at her short tartan skirt under the cloak. 'I'd better change into something decent or else his eyes will pop right out.'

Sandman pretended to be heart-broken. 'I rather like that Scottish skirt.'

'And I thought you was a gentleman, Captain,' Sally said, then laughed and ran up the stairs as Sandman shouldered open the back parlour door and, with great relief, sank into a chair. It was dark in the room because the shutters were closed and the candles extinguished, so he leant forward and pulled the nearest shutter open and saw that it was not Lord Alexander who had reserved the back parlour, but another gentleman altogether, though perhaps Sergeant Berrigan was not truly a gentleman.

The Sergeant was lounging on the settle, but now raised his pistol and aimed it at Sandman's forehead. 'They want you dead, Captain,' he said, 'they want you dead. So they sent me because when you want a dirty job done neatly, you send a soldier. Ain't that the truth? You send a soldier.'

So they had sent Sam Berrigan.

Sandman knew he should do something fast. Throw himself forward? But his ankle was throbbing and he knew he could never move quicker than Berrigan who was fit, tough and experienced. He thought of pulling out the pistol he had taken from his attacker in the theatre, but by the time he dragged it from his pocket Berrigan would already have fired, so instead Sandman decided he would just keep the Sergeant talking until Sally arrived and could raise the alarm. He lifted his left foot and rested it on a chair. 'I sprained it,' he told Berrigan, 'jumping onto the stage.'

'Stage?'

'At Miss Hood's performance. Someone tried to kill me.'

'Not us, Captain,' Berrigan said.

'Someone with a rifle.'

'Lot of those left from the wars,' Berrigan said. 'You

can pick up a used Baker for seven or eight shillings. So someone other than the Seraphim Club wants you dead, eh?'

Sandman stared at the Sergeant. 'Are you sure it wasn't the Seraphim Club?'

'They sent me, Captain, only me,' Berrigan said, 'and I wasn't at the theatre.'

Sandman stared at him, wondering who in God's name had put a price on his head. 'It must be a great relief being dishonest,' he said.

Berrigan grinned. 'Relief?'

'No one trying to kill you, no scruples about accepting thousands of guineas? I'd say it was a relief. My problem, Sergeant, is that I so feared being like my father that I set out to behave in an utterly dissimilar manner. I set out to be consciously virtuous. It was exceedingly tedious of me and it annoyed him hugely. I suppose that's why I did it.'

If Berrigan was surprised or discomfited by this strange admission, he did not show it. Instead he seemed interested. 'Your father was dishonest?'

Sandman nodded. 'If there was any justice in this world, Sergeant, then he would have been hanged at Newgate. He wasn't a felon like the folk who live here. He didn't rob stage coaches or pick pockets or burgle houses, instead he tied people's money into crooked schemes and he'd still be doing it if he hadn't met an even cleverer man who did it back to him. And there was me, claiming to be virtuous, but I still took his money all my life, didn't I?'

Sergeant Berrigan lowered the pistol's cock, then

224

put the weapon on the table. 'My father was honest.'

'He was? Not is?'

Berrigan used a tinder box to light two candles, then lifted a jug of ale that he had kept hidden on the floor. 'My father died a couple of years ago. He was a blacksmith in Putney, and he wanted me to learn the trade, but of course I wouldn't. I knew better, didn't I?' He sounded rueful. 'I wanted life to be easier than forever shoeing horses and banging up trace-chains.'

'So you joined the army to escape the smithy?'

Berrigan laughed. 'I joined the army to escape a hanging.' He poured the ale and pushed a tankard towards Sandman. 'I was peter hunting. Do you know what that is?'

'I live here, remember,' Sandman said. Peter hunting was the trade of cutting luggage off the backs of coaches and, if it was well done, the coachmen and passengers had no idea that their trunks had been slashed off the rack. To prevent it many coaches used steel chains to secure the baggage, but a good peter hunter carried a jemmy to prise the chain's anchoring staples from the coach's chassis.

'I got caught,' Berrigan said, 'and the beak said I could stand trial or join the army. And nine years later I was a sergeant.'

'A good one, eh?'

'I could keep order,' Berrigan said bleakly.

'So could I, oddly enough,' Sandman said, and it was not such a strange claim as it sounded. Many officers relied on their sergeants to keep order, but Sandman had possessed a natural and easy authority.

He had been a good officer and he knew it and, if he was honest with himself, he missed it. He missed the war, missed the certainties of the army, missed the excitements of campaigning and missed the companionship of his company. 'Spain was the best,' he said. 'We had such happy times in Spain. Some bloody awful times too, of course, but I don't remember those. You were in Spain?'

''twelve to 'fourteen,' Berrigan said.

'Those were mostly good times,' Sandman said, 'but I hated Waterloo.'

The Sergeant nodded. 'It was bad.'

'I've never been so damned frightened in my life,' Sandman said. He had been shaking when the Imperial Guard came up the hill. He remembered his right arm quivering and he had been ashamed to show such fear; it had not occurred to him until much later that most of the men on the ridge, and most of the men coming to attack them, were just as frightened and just as ashamed of their fears. 'The air was warm,' he said, 'like an oven door had been opened. Remember?'

'Warm,' Berrigan agreed, then frowned. 'A lot of folk want you dead, Captain.'

'It puzzles me,' Sandman admitted. 'When Skavadale offered me that money I was convinced that either he or Lord Robin had murdered the Countess, but now? Now there's someone else out there. Maybe they're the real murderer and the strange thing is I haven't a clue who it might be. Unless this has the answer?' He lifted the letter that the landlord had given him. 'Can you push a candle towards me?'

The letter was written on pale-green paper and was in a handwriting he knew only too well. It was from Eleanor, and he remembered how his heart would leap whenever her letters arrived in Spain or France. Now he slit her green wax seal and unfolded the thin paper. He had hoped the letter would reveal Meg's whereabouts, but instead Eleanor was asking Sandman to meet her next morning at Gunter's confectionery store in Berkeley Square. There was a postscript. *I think I might have news*, she had written, but nothing else.

'No,' he said, 'I don't have the truth yet, but I think I'll have it soon.' He laid the letter down. 'Aren't you supposed to shoot me?'

'In a tavern?' Berrigan shook his head. 'Cut your throat, more like. It's quieter. But I'm trying to decide whether Miss Hood will ever talk to me again if I do.'

'I doubt she ever will,' Sandman said with a smile.

'And the last time I was on your side,' Berrigan said, 'things looked rough, but we did win.'

'Against the Emperor's own guard, too,' Sandman agreed.

'So I reckon I'm on your side again, Captain,' the Sergeant said.

Sandman smiled and raised his tankard in a mock toast. 'But if you don't kill me, Sergeant, can you return to the Seraphim Club? Or will they regard your disobedience as cause for dismissal?'

'I can't go back,' Berrigan said, and gestured at a

heavy bag, a haversack and his old army knapsack that lay together on the floor.

Sandman showed neither pleasure nor surprise. He was pleased, but he was not surprised because from the very first he had sensed that Berrigan was looking for an escape from the Seraphim. 'Do you expect wages?' he asked the Sergeant.

'We'll split the reward, Captain.'

'There's a reward?'

'Forty pounds,' Berrigan said, 'is what the magistrates pay to anyone who brings in a proper felon. Forty.' He saw that the reward money was news to Sandman and shook his head in disbelief. 'How the hell else do you think the watchmen make a living?'

Sandman felt very foolish. 'I didn't know.'

Berrigan filled up both ale tankards. 'Twenty for you, Captain, and twenty for me.' He grinned. 'So what are we doing tomorrow?'

'Tomorrow,' Sandman said, 'we begin by going to Newgate. Then I am meeting a lady and you will, well, I don't know what you'll do, but we shall see, won't we?' He twisted in the chair as the door opened behind him.

'Bleeding hell,' Sally frowned when she saw the pistol on the table, then glared at Berrigan. 'What the hell are you doing here?'

'Come to have supper with you, of course,' Berrigan said.

Sally blushed, and Sandman looked out the window so as not to embarrass her and reflected that his allies now consisted of a club-footed reverend aristocrat of radical views, a sharp-tongued actress, a felonious sergeant and, he dared to hope, Eleanor.

And together they had just three days to catch a killer.

6

It was raining next morning when Sandman and Berrigan walked to Newgate Prison. Sandman was still limping badly, grimacing every time he put weight on his left foot. He had wrapped a bandage tight about the boot, but the ankle still felt like jellied fire. 'You shouldn't be walking,' Berrigan told him.

'I shouldn't have walked when I sprained the other ankle at Burgos,' Sandman said, 'but it was either that or get captured by the Frogs. So I walked back to Portugal.'

'You, an officer?' Berrigan was amused. 'No gee-gee?'

'I loaned my gee-gee,' Sandman said, 'to someone who was really injured.'

Berrigan walked in silence for a few paces. 'We had a lot of good officers, really,' he said after a while.

'And there I was,' Sandman said, 'thinking I was unique.'

'Because the bad officers didn't last too long,' Berrigan went on, 'especially when there was a fight. Wonderful what a bullet in the back will do.' The Sergeant had slept in the Wheatsheaf's back parlour after it became clear he was not to be invited to share Sally's bed, though Sandman, watching the two during the evening, had thought it a damn close-run thing. Lord Alexander, oblivious that he was losing Sally to a low born rival, had stared at her in dumb admiration until he nerved himself to tell her a joke, but as the jest depended for its humour on an understanding of the Latin gerund, it failed miserably. When Lord Alexander finally fell asleep the Sergeant carried him out to his carriage which took him home. 'He can drink, that cove,' Berrigan had said in admiration.

'He can't drink,' Sandman had said, 'and that's his problem.' Lord Alexander, he thought, was bored and boredom drove him to drink, while Sandman was anything but bored. He had lain awake half the night trying to work out who beyond the Seraphim Club might want him dead, and it had only been when the bell of St Paul's church rang two o'clock that the answer had come to him with a clarity and force that made him ashamed for not having thought of so obvious a solution before. He shared it with Berrigan as they walked down Holborn beneath clouds so low they seemed to touch the belching chimneys.

'I know who's paying to have me killed.'

'It ain't the Seraphim Club,' Berrigan insisted. 'They'd have told me just to make sure I didn't get in the way of some other cove.'

'It isn't the club,' Sandman agreed, 'because they decided to buy me off, but the only member with sufficient funds immediately available was Lord Robin Holloway, and he detests me.'

'He does,' Berrigan agreed, 'but they all contributed.'

'No they didn't,' Sandman said. 'Most of the members are in the country and there won't have been time to solicit them. Skavadale doesn't have the funds. Maybe one or two members in London donated, but I'll wager the largest part of the twenty thousand came from Lord Robin Holloway, and he only did it because Skavadale begged him or ordered him or persuaded him, and I think he probably agreed to pay me, but privately arranged to have me killed before I could accept or, God forbid, cash his note.'

Berrigan thought about it, then reluctantly nodded. 'He's capable of that. Nasty piece of work, he is.'

'But maybe he'll call off his dogs,' Sandman said, 'now that he knows I'm not taking his money?'

'Except if he killed the Countess,' Berrigan suggested, 'he might still want you nubbed. What the hell's happening here?' His question was caused because the only thing moving on Newgate Hill was a trickle of dirty water in the gutter. The carts and carriages in the roadway were motionless, all held up by a wagon that had shed its load of pear saplings at the corner of Old Bailey and Newgate Street. Men shouted, whips cracked, horses buried their faces in nosebags and nothing moved. Berrigan shook his head. 'Who'd want half a ton of bloody pear trees?'

'Someone who likes pears?'

'Someone who needs their bloody brains reamed out,' the Sergeant grumbled, then stopped to gaze at the granite façade of Newgate Prison. It squatted grim and gaunt, sparsely supplied with windows, solid and forbidding. The rain was falling harder, but the Sergeant still stared in apparent fascination. 'Is this where they hang them?'

'Right outside the Debtor's Door, whichever one that is.'

'I've never been to a hanging here,' Berrigan admitted.

'Nor have I.'

'Been to one at Horsemonger Lane prison, but they hang them up on the roof of the gateway there and you don't see a lot from the street. Bit of jerking, that's all. My mum used to like going to Tyburn.'

'Your mother did?'

'It was a day out for her,' Berrigan had heard the surprise in Sandman's voice and sounded defensive. 'She likes a day out, my mum does, but she says the Old Bailey's too far – one day I'll hire a coach and bring her up.' He grinned as he climbed the prison steps. 'I always reckoned I'd end up in here.'

A turnkey accompanied them through the tunnel to the Press Yard and pointed out the large cell where those to be hanged spent their last night. 'If you want to see a hanging,' he confided to Sandman, 'then you come on Monday, 'cos we'll be ridding England of two of the bastards, but there won't be a crowd. Not a big one, anyway, on account that neither of 'em is what you'd call notorious. You want a big crowd? Hang someone notorious, sir, someone notorious, or else string up a woman. The Magpie and Stump got through a fortnight's supply of ale last Monday, and that was only 'cos we scragged a woman. Folks do like to see a woman strangling. Did you hear how that one ended?'

'Ended?' Sandman asked, puzzled by the question. 'I assume she died.'

'Died and went to the anatomists, sir, what do like a young 'un to slice apart, but she was hanged for the theft of a pearl necklace and I do hear how the owner found the necklace last week.' The man chuckled. 'Fallen down the back of a sofa! Might be rumour, of course, might just be rumour.' He shook his head in wonderment at fate's arbitrary ways. 'But it's a strange business, life, isn't it?'

'Death is,' Sandman said bitterly.

The turnkey fumbled with the Press Yard's pad-locked gate, unaware that his callousness had provoked Sandman's anger. Berrigan saw it and tried to divert the Captain. 'So why are we seeing this Corday?' he asked.

Sandman hesitated. He had not yet told the Sergeant about the missing maid, Meg, and it had crossed his mind that perhaps Berrigan had not really changed sides at all. Had the Seraphim Club sent him as a spy? Yet that seemed unlikely, and the Sergeant's change of heart appeared to be sincere, even if it was prompted more by an attraction to Sally than any sincere repentance. 'There was a witness,' he told Berrigan, 'and I need to know more about her. And if I find her . . .' He left that thought unfinished.

'And if you find her?'

'Then someone will hang,' Sandman said, 'but not Corday.' He nodded a curt acknowledgement to the turnkey who had unlocked the gate, then led Berrigan across the stinking yard and into the Association Room. It was crowded because the rain had driven the prisoners and their visitors indoors and they stared resentfully at Sandman and his companion as the two threaded their way through the tables to the shadowed back of the room where Sandman expected to find Corday. The artist was evidently a changed man for, instead of cowering from his persecutors, he was now holding court at the table closest to the fire where, with a thick pile of paper and a stick of charcoal, he was drawing a portrait of a prisoner's woman. A small crowd surrounded him, admiring his skill, and they parted reluctantly to let Sandman through. Corday gave a small start of recognition when he saw his visitors, then quickly looked away. 'I need a word with you,' Sandman said.

'He'll talk to you when he's finished,' a huge man, black-haired, long-bearded and with a massive chest, growled from the bench beside Corday, 'and he won't be finished for a while, so wait, my culleys, wait.'

'And who are you?' Berrigan asked.

'I'm the cove telling you to wait,' the man said. He had a West Country accent, greasy clothes and a thick matted beard. He probed a finger into a capacious nostril as he stared belligerently at Berrigan, then withdrew it and gave the pickings a close inspection. He cleaned his nail by running it through his beard, then looked defiantly at Sandman. 'Charlie's time is valuable,' he explained, 'and there's not much left of it.'

'It's your life, Corday,' Sandman said.

'Don't listen to him, Charlie!' the big man said.

'You've got no friends in this wicked world except me and I know what's –' He stopped abruptly and uttered a gasping, mewing noise as his eyes widened in shock. Sergeant Berrigan had gone to stand behind him and now gave a jerk with his right hand that made the big man grunt in renewed pain.

'Sergeant!' Sandman remonstrated with mock concern.

'Just teaching the culley manners,' Berrigan said, and thumped the man in the kidneys a second time. 'When the Captain wants a word, you nose-picking piece of garbage, you jump to attention, you do, eyes front, mouth shut, heels together and back straight! You don't tell him to wait, that ain't polite.'

Corday looked anxiously at the bearded man. 'Are you all right?'

'He'll be fine,' Berrigan answered for his victim. 'You just talk to the Captain, boy, because he's trying to save your miserable bleeding life. You want to play games, culley?' The bearded man had stood and attempted to ram his elbow back into Berrigan's belly, but the Sergeant now thumped him across the ear, tripped him and, while he was still off balance, ran him hard and fast until he slammed into a table. Berrigan thumped the man's face down hard. 'You bleeding stay there, culley, till we're done.' He tapped the back of the man's head as an encouragement, then stalked back to Corday's table. 'Everyone on parade, Captain,' he reported, 'ready and willing.'

Sandman edged a woman aside so he could sit opposite Corday. 'I need to talk to you about the maid,' he

236

said softly, 'about Meg. I don't suppose you knew her surname? No? So what did Meg look like?'

'Your friend shouldn't have hit him!' Corday, still distracted by his companion's pain, complained to Sandman.

'What did she bloody look like, son?' Berrigan shouted in his best sergeant's manner, and Corday twitched with sudden terror, then set aside the half-finished portrait and, without a word, began to sketch on a clean sheet of paper. He worked fast, the charcoal making a small scratching noise in the silence of the big room.

'She's young,' Corday said, 'maybe twenty-four or -five? She has a pockmarked skin and mouse-coloured hair. Her eyes have a greenish tint and she has a mole here.' He flicked a mark on the girl's forehead. 'Her teeth aren't good. I've only drawn her face, but you should know she had broad hips and a narrow chest.'

'Small tits, you mean?' Berrigan growled.

Corday blushed. 'She was small above the waist,' he said, 'but big beneath it.' He finished the drawing, frowned at it for a moment, then nodded in satisfaction and handed the sheet to Sandman.

Sandman stared at the picture. The girl was ugly, and then he thought she was more than ugly. It was not just the pox-scarred skin, the narrow jaw, the scrawny hair and small eyes, but a suggestion of knowing hardness that sat strangely on such a young face. If the portrait was accurate then Meg was not just repulsive, but evil. 'Why would the Countess employ such a creature?' he asked.

'They worked together in the theatre,' Corday said.

'Worked together? Meg was an actress?' Sandman sounded astonished.

'No, she was a dresser.' Corday looked down at the portrait and seemed embarrassed. 'She was more than a dresser, I think.'

'More than?'

'A procuress,' Corday said, looking up at Sandman.

'How do you know?'

The painter shrugged. 'It's strange how people will talk when you're making their portrait. They forget you're even there. You just become part of the furniture. So the Countess and Meg talked, I listened.'

'Did you know,' Sandman asked, 'that the Earl didn't commission the portrait?'

'He didn't?' That was plainly news to Corday. 'Sir George said he did.'

Sandman shook his head. 'It was commissioned by the Seraphim Club. Have you heard of it?'

'I've heard of it,' Corday said, 'but I've never been there.'

'So you wouldn't know why they commissioned the portrait?'

'How would I know that?' Corday asked.

Berrigan had come to stand at Sandman's shoulder. He grimaced at the sight of Meg's portrait and Sandman turned the drawing so Berrigan could get an even better look. 'Did you ever see her?' he asked, wondering if the girl had ever been taken to the Seraphim Club, but Berrigan shook his head.

Sandman looked back to Corday. 'There is a chance,' he said, 'that we shall find her.'

'How great a chance?' Corday's eyes were glistening.

'I don't know,' Sandman said. He saw the hope fade in Corday's eyes. 'Do you have ink here?' he asked. 'A pen?'

Corday had both and Sandman tore one of the big pieces of drawing paper in half, dipped the steel nib in the ink, let it drain and began to write. 'Dear Witherspoon,' he began, 'the bearer of this letter, Sergeant Samuel Berrigan, is a companion of mine. He served in the First Foot Guards and I trust him absolutely.' Sandman was not certain those last four words were entirely true, but he had little choice now but to assume Berrigan was trustworthy. He dipped the nib into the ink again, conscious that Corday was reading the words from across the table. 'The regrettable possibility occurs that I might need to communicate with his lordship on Sunday next and, in the presumption that his lordship will not be at the Home Office on that day, I beg you to tell me where he might be found. I apologise for prevailing upon your time, and assure you I do it only because I may have matters of the gravest urgency to report.' Sandman read the letter over, subscribed it, and blew on the ink to dry it. 'He won't like that,' he said to no one in particular, then folded the letter and stood.

'Captain!' Corday, his eyes full of tears, appealed to Sandman.

Sandman knew what the boy wanted to hear, but he could not offer him any kind of assurance. 'I am doing my best,' he said lamely, 'but I can promise you nothing.'

'You're going to be all right, Charlie,' the bearded West Countryman consoled Corday and Sandman, who could add nothing more helpful, thrust the portrait inside his coat and led Berrigan back to the prison entrance.

The Sergeant shook his head in apparent wonder when they reached the Lodge. 'You didn't tell me he was a bloody pixie!'

'Does it matter?'

'It would be nice to think we was making an effort for a proper man,' Berrigan growled.

'He's a very good painter.'

'So's my brother.'

'He is?'

'He's a house-painter, Captain. Gutters, doors and windows. And he ain't a pixie like that little worm.'

Sandman opened the prison's outer door and shuddered at the sight of the pelting rain. 'I don't much like Corday either,' he confessed, 'but he's an innocent man, Sergeant, and he doesn't deserve the rope.'

'Most of those who hang don't.'

'Maybe. But Corday's ours, pixie or not.' He gave Berrigan the folded letter. 'Home Office. You ask to see a man called Sebastian Witherspoon, give him that, then meet me at Gunter's in Berkeley Square.'

'And all for a bloody pixie, eh?' Berrigan asked, then he thrust the letter into a pocket and, with a grimace at the rain, dashed out into the traffic. Sandman, limping painfully, followed more slowly.

He feared that the rain might have persuaded Eleanor and her mother to abandon their expedition, but he walked to Berkeley Square anyway and was soaked by the time he arrived at the door of Gunter's. A footman stood under the shelter of the shop's awning and looked askance at Sandman's shabby coat, then opened the door reluctantly as if to give Sandman time to reflect on whether he really wanted to go inside.

The front of the shop was made of two wide windows behind which were gilded counters, spindly chairs, tall mirrors and spreading chandeliers that had been lit because the day was so gloomy. A dozen women were shopping for Gunter's famous confections; chocolates, meringue sculptures and delicacies of spun-sugar, marzipan and crystallised fruit. The conversation stopped as Sandman entered and the women stared at him as he dripped on the tiled floor, then they began talking again as he made his way to the large room at the back where a score of tables were set beneath the wide skylights of stained glass. Eleanor was not at any of the half-dozen occupied tables, so Sandman hung his coat and hat on a bentwood stand and took a chair at the back of the room where he was half hidden by a pillar. He ordered coffee and a copy of the *Morning Chronicle*.

He idly read the newspaper. There had been more rick-burnings in Sussex, a bread riot in Newcastle, and three mills burnt and their machines broken in Derbyshire. The militia had been summoned to keep the peace in Manchester, where flour had been selling at four shillings and ninepence a stone. The magistrates in Lancashire were calling on the Home Secretary to suspend habeas corpus as a means of restoring order. Sandman looked at his watch and saw that Eleanor was already ten minutes late. He sipped the coffee and felt uncomfortable because the chair and table were too small, making him feel as though he were perched in a school room. He looked back to the newspaper. A river had flooded in Prussia and it was feared there were at least a hundred drowned. The whale ship *Lydia* out of Whitehaven was reported lost with all hands off the Grand Banks. The East Indiaman *Calliope* had arrived in the Pool of London with a cargo of porcelain, ginger, indigo and nutmegs. A riot at the Covent Garden Theatre had left heads and bones broken, but no serious casualties. Reports that a shot had been fired in the theatre were being denied by the managers. There was the click of footsteps, a wafting of perfume and a sudden shadow fell across his newspaper. 'You look gloomy, Rider,' Eleanor's voice said.

'There is no good news,' he said, standing. He looked at her and felt his heart miss a beat, so that he could scarcely speak. 'There is really no good news anywhere in all the world,' he managed to say.

'Then we must make some,' Eleanor said, 'you and I.' She handed an umbrella and her damp coat to one of the waitresses, then stepped close to Sandman and planted a kiss on his cheek. 'I think I am yet angry with you,' she said softly, still standing close.

'With me?'

'For coming to London and not telling me.'

'Our engagement is broken, remember?'

'Oh, I had quite forgotten,' she said acidly, then glanced at the other tables. 'I'm causing scandal, Rider, by being seen alone with a damp man.' She kissed him again, then stood back so he could pull out a chair for her. 'So let them have their scandal, and I shall have one of Gunter's vanilla ices with the powdered chocolate and crushed almonds. So will you.'

'I'm content with coffee.'

'Nonsense, you will have what is put in front of you. You look too thin.' She sat and peeled off her gloves. Her red hair was drawn up into a small black hat decorated with tiny jet beads and a modest plume. Her dress was a muted dark brown with a barely distinguishable flower pattern worked in black threads and was high-collared, modest, almost plain, and decorated with only one small jet brooch, yet somehow she looked more alluring than the scantily clad dancing girls who had scattered when Sandman leapt down onto the stage the night before. 'Mother is being measured for a new corset,' Eleanor said, pretending to be oblivious of his inspection, 'so she will be at least two hours. She believes I am at Massingberds, choosing a hat. My maid Lizzie is chaperoning me, but I've bribed her with two shillings and she's gone to see the pig-headed woman at the Lyceum.'

'Pig-headed? As in obstinate?'

'Don't be silly, Rider, I trust all women are obstinate. This one is pig-headed as in ugly. She snuffles her food from a trough, we're told, and has stiff pink whiskers. It sounds a very unlikely beast, but Lizzie was enchanted

243

at the prospect and I was quite tempted to go myself, but I'm here instead. Did I see you limping?'

'I sprained an ankle yesterday,' he said, then had to tell the whole story which, of course, enchanted Eleanor.

'I'm jealous,' she said when he had finished. 'My life is so dull! I don't jump onto stages pursued by foot-pads! I am exceedingly jealous.'

'But you have news?' Sandman asked.

'I think so. Yes, definitely.' Eleanor turned to the waitress and ordered tea, the vanilla confection with the chocolate and almonds and, as an afterthought, brandy snaps. 'They have an ice house out the back,' she told Sandman when the girl had gone, 'and I asked to see it a few weeks ago. It's like a cellar with a dome and every winter they bring the ice down from Scotland packed in sawdust and it stays solid all summer. There was a frozen rat between two of the blocks and they were very embarrassed about it.'

'I should think they would be.' Sandman was suddenly acutely aware of his own shabbiness, of the frayed cuffs of his coat and the broken stitching at the top of his boots. They had been good boots, too, from Kennets of Silver Street, but even the best boots needed care. Merely staying respectably dressed needed at least an hour a day, and Sandman did not have that hour.

'I tried to persuade father to build an ice house,' Eleanor said, 'but he just went grumpy and complained about the expense. He's having one of his economy drives at the moment, so I told him I'd save him the cost of a society wedding.'

244

Sandman gazed into her grey-green eyes, wondering what message was being sent by her apparent glibness. 'Was he pleased?'

'He just muttered to me how prudence was one of the virtues. He was embarrassed by the offer, I think.'

'How would you save him the expense? By remaining a spinster?'

'By eloping,' Eleanor said, her gaze very steady.

'With Lord Eagleton?'

Eleanor's laugh filled the big space of Gunter's back room, causing a momentary hush at the other tables. 'Eagleton's such a bore!' Eleanor said much too loudly. 'Mama was very keen I should marry him, because then, in due course, I would be her ladyship and Mama would be unbearable. Don't tell me you thought I was betrothed to him?'

'I heard that you were. I was told your portrait was a gift for him.'

'Mother said we should give it to him, but father wants it for himself. Mother just wants me to marry a title, she doesn't mind what or who it is, and Lord Eagleton wants to marry me, which is tedious because I can't abide him. He sniffs before he talks.' She gave a small sniff. 'Dear Eleanor, sniff, how charming you look, sniff. I can see the moon reflected in your eyes, sniff.'

Sandman kept a straight face. 'I never told you I saw the moon reflected in your eyes. I fear that was remiss of me.'

They looked at each other and burst out laughing. They had always been able to laugh since the very first day they had met, when Sandman was newly home

245

after being wounded at Salamanca and Eleanor was just twenty and determined not to be impressed by a soldier, but the soldier had made her laugh and still could, just as she could amuse him.

'I think,' Eleanor said, 'that Eagleton spent a week rehearsing the words about the moon, but he spoilt it by sniffing. Really, Rider, talking to Eagleton is like conversing with an asthmatic lap dog. Mama and he seem to believe that if they wish it long enough then I will surrender to his sniffs, and I gathered a rumour of our betrothal had been bruited about so I deliberately told Alexander to inform you I was not going to marry the noble sniffer. Now I find Alexander never told you?'

'I fear not.'

'But I told him distinctly!' Eleanor said indignantly. 'I met him at the Egyptian Hall.'

'He told me that much,' Sandman said, 'but he quite forgot any message you might have sent. He'd even forgotten why he had gone to the Egyptian Hall.'

'For a lecture by a man called Professor Popkin on the newly discovered location of the Garden of Eden. He wants us to believe that paradise is to be found at the confluence of the Ohio and the Mississippi Rivers. He informed us that he once ate a very fine apple there.'

'That sounds like proof positive,' Sandman said gravely, 'and did he become wise after eating the fruit?'

'He became erudite, learned, sagacious and clever,' Eleanor said, and Sandman saw there were tears in her eyes. 'And,' she went on, 'he encouraged us to uproot ourselves and follow him to this new world of milk, honey and apples. Would you like to go there, Rider?'

'With you?'

'We could live naked by the rivers,' Eleanor said, as a tear escaped to trickle down her cheek, 'innocent as babes and avoiding serpents.' She could not go on and lowered her face so he could not see her tears. 'I'm so very sorry, Rider,' she said quietly.

'About what?'

'I should never have let Mama persuade me to break off the engagement. She said your family's disgrace was too absolute, but that's nonsense.'

'The disgrace is dire,' Sandman admitted.

'That was your father. Not you!'

'I sometimes think I am very like my father,' Sandman said.

'Then he was a better man than I realised,' Eleanor said fiercely, then dabbed at her eyes with a handkerchief. The waitress brought their ices and brandy snaps and, thinking that Eleanor had been upset by something Sandman had said, gave him a reproachful look. Eleanor waited for the girl to move away. 'I hate crying,' she said.

'You do it rarely,' Sandman said.

'I have been weeping like a fountain these six months,' Eleanor said, then looked up at him. 'Last night I told Mama I consider myself betrothed to you.'

'I'm honoured.'

'You're supposed to say it is mutual.'

Sandman half smiled. 'I would like it to be, truly.'

'Father won't mind,' Eleanor said, 'at least I don't think he will mind.'

'But your mother will?'

'She does! When I told her my feelings last night she insisted I ought to visit Doctor Harriman. Have you heard of him? Of course you haven't. He is an expert, Mama tells me, in feminine hysteria and it is considered a great honour to be examined by him. But I don't need him! I'm not hysterical, I am merely, inconveniently, in love with you, and if your damned father had not killed himself then you and I would be married by now. I do envy men.'

'Why?'

'They can swear and no one lifts an eyebrow.'

'Swear, my dear,' Sandman said.

Eleanor did, then laughed. 'That felt very good. Oh dear, one day we shall be married and I shall swear too much and you will get bored with me.' She sniffed, then sighed as she tasted the ice. 'That is real paradise,' she said, prodding the ice with the long silver spoon, 'and I swear nothing at the confluence of the Ohio and Mississippi Rivers can rival it. Poor Rider. You shouldn't even think of marrying me. You should tip your hat at Caroline Standish.'

'Caroline Standish? I've not heard of her.' He tasted the ice and it was, as Eleanor had said, pure paradise.

'Caroline Standish is perhaps the richest heiress in England, Rider, and a very pretty girl she is too, but you should be warned that she is a Methodist. Golden hair, damn her, a truly lovely face and probably thirty thousand a year? But the drawback is that you cannot drink ardent spirits in her presence, neither smoke, nor blaspheme, nor take snuff, nor really enjoy yourself in any way. Her father made his money in the potteries, but they now live in London and worship at that vulgar little chapel in Spring Gardens. I'm sure you could attract her eye.'

'I'm sure I could,' Sandman said with a smile.

'And I'm confident she will approve of cricket,' Eleanor said, 'so long as you don't play it on the Sabbath. Do you still indulge in cricket, Rider?'

'Not as often as Alexander would like.'

'They say that Lord Frederick Beauclerk earns six hundred a year gambling on cricket. Could you do that?'

'I'm a better batsman than him,' Sandman said truthfully enough. Lord Frederick, a friend of Lord Alexander's and, like him, an aristocrat in holy orders, was the secretary of the Marylebone Cricket Club that played at Thomas Lord's ground. 'But I'm a worse gambler,' Sandman went on. 'Besides, Beauclerk wagers money he can afford to lose, and I don't have such funds.'

'Then marry the pious Miss Standish,' Eleanor said. 'Mind you, there is the small inconvenience that she is already betrothed, but there are rumours that she's not altogether persuaded that the future Duke of Ripon is nearly as godly as he pretends. He goes to the Spring Gardens chapel, but only, one suspects, so that he can pluck her golden feathers once he has married her.'

'The future Duke of Ripon?' Sandman asked.

'He has his own title, of course, but I can't remember it. Mother would know it.'

Sandman went very still. 'Ripon?'

'A cathedral city in Yorkshire, Rider.'

249

'The Marquess of Skavadale,' Sandman said, 'is the title carried by the heir to the Dukedom of Ripon.'

'That's him! Well done!' Eleanor frowned at him. 'Have I said something wrong?'

'Skavadale isn't godly at all,' Sandman said, and he remembered the Earl of Avebury describing how his wife had blackmailed young men about town. Had Skavadale been blackmailed by the Countess? Skavadale was famously short of money and his father's estates were evidently mortgaged to the hilt, yet Skavadale had managed to become betrothed to the wealthiest heiress in England and if he had been ploughing the Countess of Avebury's furrow she would surely have found him a ripe target for blackmail. His family might have lost most of its fortune, but there would be some funds left and there would be porcelain, silver and paintings that could be sold; more than enough to keep the Countess content.

'You're mystifying me,' Eleanor complained.

'I think the Marquess of Skavadale is my murderer,' Sandman said, 'either him or one of his friends.' If Sandman had been forced to put money on the murderer's identity he would have chosen Lord Robin Holloway rather than the Marquess, but he was quite certain it was one of them.

'So you don't need to know what Lizzie discovered?' Eleanor asked, disappointed.

'Your maid? Of course I want to know. I need to know.'

'Meg wasn't very popular with the other servants. They thought she was a witch.'

'She looks like one,' Sandman said.

'You've already found her?' Eleanor asked, excited.

'No, I saw a portrait.'

'Everyone seems to sit these days,' Eleanor said.

'This portrait.' Sandman pulled the drawing from inside his coat and showed it to Eleanor.

'Rider, you don't think she's the pig-faced woman, do you?' Eleanor asked. 'No, she can't be, she has no whiskers.' She sighed. 'Poor girl, to be so ugly.' She stared at the drawing for a long while, then rolled it up and pushed it back to Sandman. 'What was I saying? Oh yes, Lizzie discovered that Meg was carried away from the Countess's town house by a carriage, a very smart carriage that was either black or dark blue, and with a strange coat-of-arms painted on its door. It wasn't a complete coat-of-arms, just a shield showing a red field decorated with a golden angel.' Eleanor crumbled a brandy snap. 'I asked Hammond if he knew of that shield and he became very refined. "A field gules, Miss Forrest," he insisted to me, "with an angel or", but astonishingly he didn't know who it belonged to and consequently he was most upset.'

Sandman smiled at the thought of Sir Henry Forrest's butler being unable to identify a coat-of-arms. 'He shouldn't feel upset,' Sandman said, 'because I doubt the College of Arms issued that device. It's the badge of the Seraphim Club.'

Eleanor grimaced, remembering what Sandman had told her and her father earlier in the week, though in truth Sandman had not revealed all he knew about the

251

Seraphim. 'And the Marquess of Skavadale,' she said quietly, 'is a member of the Seraphim Club?'

'He is,' Sandman confirmed.

She frowned. 'So he's your murderer? It's that easy?'

'The members of the Seraphim Club,' Sandman said, 'consider themselves beyond the law. They believe their rank, their money and their privilege will keep them safe. And quite possibly they're right, unless I can find Meg.'

'If Meg lives,' Eleanor said quietly.

'If Meg lives,' Sandman agreed.

Eleanor stared at Sandman and her eyes seemed bright and big. 'I feel rather selfish now,' she said.

'Why?'

'Worrying about my small problems when you have a murderer to find.'

'Your problems are small?' Sandman asked with a smile.

Eleanor did not return the smile. 'I am not willing, Rider,' she said, 'to give you up. I tried.'

He knew how much effort it had taken for her to say those words and so he reached for her hand and kissed her fingers. 'I have never given you up,' he said, 'and next week I shall talk to your father again.'

'And if he says no?' She clutched his fingers.

'Then we shall go to Scotland,' Sandman said. 'We shall go to Scotland.'

Eleanor held tight to his hand. She smiled. 'Rider? My prudent, well-behaved, honourable Rider? You would elope?'

He returned the smile. 'Of late, my dear,' he said, 'I

have been thinking about that afternoon and evening I spent on the ridge at Waterloo and I remember making a decision there, and it's a decision I am constantly in danger of forgetting. If I survived that day, I promised myself, then I would not die with regrets. I would not die with wishes, dreams and desires unfulfilled. So yes, if your father refuses to let us marry, then I shall take you to Scotland and let the devil take the hindmost.'

'Because I am your wish, dream and desire?' Eleanor asked with tears in her eyes and a smile on her face.

'Because you are all of those things,' Sandman said, 'and I love you besides.'

And Sergeant Berrigan, dripping with rainwater and grinning with delight at discovering Sandman at so delicate a moment, was suddenly standing beside them.

The Sergeant began to whistle 'Spanish Ladies' as they climbed Hay Hill towards Old Bond Street. It was a cheerful whistle, one that proclaimed that he was not at all interested in what he had just seen, and a well-judged whistle that, in the army, would have been recognised as entirely insubordinate, but quite unpunishable. Sandman, still limping, laughed. 'I was once engaged to Miss Forrest, Sergeant.'

'German coach there, Captain, see it? Heavy bloody thing.' Berrigan still pretended to be uninterested, pointing instead at a massive carriage that was sliding dangerously on the hill's rain-slicked cobbles. The coachman was hauling on the brake, the horses were skittering nervously, but then the wheels struck the kerb and steadied the vehicle. 'Shouldn't be allowed,' Berrigan said, 'foreign bloody coaches cracking up our roads. They should tax the buggers blind or else send them back across the bloody Channel where they belong.'

'And Miss Forrest broke off the engagement because her parents did not want her to marry a pauper,' Sandman said, 'so now, Sergeant, you know all.'

'Didn't look much like a broken bloody engagement to me, sir. Staring into your eyes like the sun, moon and sparkles were trapped there.'

'Yes, well. Life is complicated.'

'I hadn't noticed,' Berrigan said sarcastically. He grimaced at the weather, though the rain was now spitting rather than cascading. 'And talking of complications,' he went on, 'Mister Sebastian Witherspoon was not a happy man. Not a happy man at all. In fact, if I was to be accurate, he was bloody annoyed.'

'Ah! He has adduced that I am not behaving as he expected?'

'He wanted to know what you were bloody up to, Captain, so I said I didn't know.'

'He surely refused to accept that assurance?'

'He could do what he bloody liked, Captain, but I told him yes sir, no sir, I don't know a blessed thing sir, up your back alley, sir, and go to hell, sir, but all of it in a deeply respectful manner.'

'You behaved, in other words, like a sergeant?' Sandman asked, and laughed again. He remembered that subservient insolence from his own sergeants; an apparent cooperation masking a deep intransigence.

'But did he tell you where the Home Secretary will be on Sunday?'

'His lordship won't be at his home, Captain, on account that the builders are putting in a new staircase in his house which they promised to have finished last May and which they ain't even painted yet, so his lordship is borrowing a house in Great George Street. Mister Witherspoon said he hopes he don't see you any day soon and, anyway, his lordship won't thank you for disturbing him on Sunday on account that his lordship is of the Godly persuasion, and anyway Mister Witherspoon, like his holy lordship, trusts that the bloody pixie is hanged by his bloody neck till he's bloody well dead like what he bloody deserves to be.'

'I'm sure he didn't say the last.'

'Not quite,' Berrigan admitted cheerfully, 'but I did, and Mister Witherspoon began to think well of me. Another few minutes and he'd have given you the butt end and made me the Investigator instead.'

'God help Corday then, eh?'

'The little bugger would go to the gallows so bleeding fast that his twinkle toes wouldn't touch the ground,' Berrigan said happily. 'So where are we going now?'

'We're going to see Sir George Phillips, because I want to know if he can tell me exactly who commissioned the Countess's portrait. Know that man's name, Sergeant, and we have our murderer.'

'You hope,' Berrigan said dubiously.

'Miss Hood is also at Sir George's studio. She models for him.'

'Ah!' Berrigan cheered up.

'And even if Sir George won't tell us, then I've also learnt that my one witness was carried away in the Seraphim Club's carriage.'

'One of their carriages,' Berrigan corrected him, 'they have two.'

'So I assume one of the club's coachmen can tell us where they took her.'

'I imagine they might,' Berrigan said, 'though they might need some persuading.'

'A pleasing prospect,' Sandman said, arriving at the door beside the jeweller's shop. He knocked and, as before, the door was answered by Sammy, the black page, who immediately tried to shut it. Sandman bulled his way through. 'Tell Sir George,' he said imperiously, 'that Captain Rider Sandman and Sergeant Samuel Berrigan have come to talk to him.'

'He don't want to talk to you,' Sammy said.

'Go and tell him, child!' Sandman insisted.

Instead Sammy made an ill-judged attempt to dodge past Sandman into the street, only to be caught by Sergeant Berrigan, who lifted the lad and slammed him against the door post. 'Where were you going, boy?' Berrigan demanded.

'Why don't you fake off?' Sammy said defiantly, then yelped. 'I wasn't going anywhere!' Berrigan drew back his fist again. 'He told me if you was to come again,' Sammy said hastily, 'I was to go and fetch help.'

'From the Seraphim Club?' Sandman guessed, and the boy nodded. 'Hold onto him, Sergeant,' Sandman said, then began climbing the stairs. 'Fee, fi, fo, fum!' he chanted at the top of his voice, 'I smell the blood of an Englishman!' He was making the noise to warn Sally so that Sergeant Berrigan would not see her naked. Sandman had no doubt that Berrigan would be getting that treat very soon, but Sandman also had no doubt that Sally would want to decide when that would be. 'Sir George!' he bellowed. 'Are you there?'

'Who the devil is it?' Sir George shouted. 'Sammy?'

'Sammy's a prisoner,' Sandman shouted.

'God's bollocks! It's you?' Sir George, for a fat man, moved with remarkable speed, going to a cupboard from which he took a long-barrelled pistol. He ran with it to the head of the stairs and pointed it down at Sandman. 'No further, Captain, on pain of your life!' he growled.

Sandman glanced at the pistol and kept on climbing. 'Don't be such a bloody fool,' he said tiredly. 'Shoot me, Sir George, and you'll have to shoot Sergeant Berrigan, then you'll have to keep Sally quiet and that means shooting her, so then you'll have three corpses on your hands.' He climbed the last few steps and, without any fuss, took the pistol from the painter's hand. 'It's always best to cock weapons if you want to look really threatening,' he added, then turned and nodded at Berrigan. 'Allow me to introduce Sergeant Berrigan, late of the First Foot Guards, then of the Seraphim Club, but now a volunteer in my army of righteousness.' Sandman saw, with relief, that Sally had received enough warning to pull on a coat. He took off his hat and bowed to her. 'Miss Hood, my respects.'

'You're still limping, then?' Sally asked, then blushed as Sergeant Berrigan arrived.

'He's bleeding hurting me!' Sammy complained.

'I'll bleeding kill you if you don't shut up,' Berrigan growled, then he nodded to Sally. 'Miss Hood,' he said, then he saw the canvas and his eyes widened in admiration and Sally blushed even deeper.

'You can put Sammy down,' Sandman said to Berrigan, 'because he won't go for help.'

'He'll do what I tell him!' Sir George said belligerently.

Sandman crossed to the painting and stared at the central figure of Nelson, and thought that since the admiral's death the painters and engravers had been making the hero ever more frail so that he was now almost a spectral figure. 'If you tell Sammy to go for help, Sir George,' he said, 'then I shall spread it abroad that your studio deceives women, that you paint them clothed and, when they are gone, you turn them into nudes.' He turned and smiled at the painter. 'What will that do to your prices?'

'Double them!' Sir George said defiantly, then he saw that Sandman's threat was real and he seemed to deflate like a pricked bladder. He flapped a paint-stained hand at Sammy. 'You're not going anywhere, Sammy.'

Berrigan put the boy down. 'You can make some tea instead,' Sandman said.

'I'll help you, Sammy,' Sally said, and followed the boy down the stairs. Sandman suspected she was going to get dressed.

Sandman turned to Sir George. 'You're an old man, Sir George, you're fat and you're a drunkard. Your hand

258

shakes. You can still paint, but for how long? You're living off your reputation now, but I can ruin that. I can make quite certain that men like Sir Henry Forrest never hire you again to paint their wives or daughters for fear of you doing to them what you would have done to the Countess of Avebury.'

'I would never do that to . . .' Sir George began.

'Be quiet,' Sandman said. 'And I can put in my report to the Home Secretary that you have deliberately hidden the truth.' That, in reality, was a much lesser threat, but Sir George did not know it. He only feared prosecution, the dock and jail. Or maybe he saw transportation to Australia, for he began to shudder in unfeigned terror. 'I know you lied,' Sandman said, 'so now you will tell me the truth.'

'And if I do?'

'Then Sergeant Berrigan and I will tell no one. Why should we care what happens to you? I know you didn't murder the Countess and that's the only person I'm interested in. So tell us the truth, Sir George, and we shall leave you in peace.'

Sir George sank onto a stool. The apprentices and the two men portraying Nelson and Neptune gazed at him until he snarled at them to go downstairs. Only when they were gone did he look at Sandman. 'The Seraphim Club commissioned the painting.'

'I know that.' Sandman walked to the back of the studio, past the table heaped with rags, brushes and jars. He was looking for Eleanor's portrait, but he could not see it. He turned back. 'What I want to know, Sir George, is who in the club commissioned it.'

'I don't know. Really! I don't know!' He was pleading, his fear almost tangible. 'There were ten or eleven of them, I can't remember.'

'Ten or eleven of them?'

'Sitting at a table,' Sir George said, 'like the Last Supper, only without Christ. They said they were having the painting done for their gallery and they promised me there'd be others.'

'Other paintings?'

'Of titled women, Captain, naked.' Sir George snarled the last word. 'She was their trophy. They explained it to me. If more than three members of the club had swived a woman then she could be hung in their gallery.'

Sandman glanced at Berrigan, who shrugged. 'Sounds likely,' the Sergeant said.

'They have a gallery?'

'Corridor upstairs,' Berrigan said, 'but they've only just started hanging paintings up there.'

'The Marquess of Skavadale was one of the eleven?' Sandman asked Sir George.

'Ten or eleven,' Sir George sounded irritated that he had to correct Sandman, 'and yes, Skavadale was one. Lord Pellmore was another. I remember Sir John Lassiter, but I didn't know most of them.'

'They didn't introduce themselves?'

'No.' Sir George made the denial defiantly because it confirmed that he had been treated by the Seraphim Club as a tradesman, not as a gentleman.

'I think it likely,' Sandman said quietly, 'that one of those ten or eleven men is the murderer of the Countess.' He looked at Sir George quizzically, as though expecting that statement to be confirmed.

'I wouldn't know,' Sir George said.

'But you must have suspected that Charles Corday did not commit the murder?'

'Little Charlie?' For a moment Sir George looked amused, then he saw the anger on Sandman's face and shrugged. 'It seemed unlikely,' he admitted.

'Yet you did not appeal for him? You did not sign his mother's petition? You did nothing to help.'

'He was tried, wasn't he?' Sir George said. 'He received justice.'

'I doubt that,' Sandman said bitterly, 'I doubt that very much.'

Sandman lifted the frizzen of the pistol he had taken from Sir George and saw that it was not primed. 'You have powder and bullets?' he asked, and then, when he saw the fear on the painter's face, he scowled. 'I'm not going to shoot you, you fool! The powder and bullets are for other people, not you.'

'In that cupboard.' Sir George nodded across the room.

Sandman opened the door and discovered a small arsenal, most of it, he supposed, for use in paintings. There were naval and army swords, pistols, muskets and a cartridge box. He tossed a cavalry pistol to Berrigan, then took a handful of the cartridges and pushed them into a pocket before stooping to pick up a knife. 'You've wasted my time,' he told Sir George. 'You've lied to me, you've inconvenienced me.' He carried the knife back across the room and saw the terror on Sir George's face. 'Sally!' Sandman shouted.

'I'm here!' she called up the stairs.

'How much does Sir George owe you?'

'Two pounds and five shillings!'

'Pay her,' Sandman said.

'You can't expect me to carry cash on –'

'Pay her!' Sandman shouted, and Sir George almost fell off the stool.

'I only have three guineas on me,' he whined.

'I think Miss Hood is worth that,' Sandman said. 'Give the three guineas to the Sergeant.'

Sir George handed over the money as Sandman turned to the painting. Britannia was virtually finished, sitting bare-breasted and proud-eyed on her rock in a sunlit sea. The goddess was unmistakeably Sally, though Sir George had changed her usually cheerful expression into one of calm superiority. 'You really have inconvenienced me,' Sandman said to Sir George, 'and worse, you were ready to let an innocent boy die.'

'I've told you everything I can!'

'Now you have, yes, but you lied and I think you need to be inconvenienced too. You need to learn, Sir George, that for every sin there is a payment extracted. In short you must be punished.'

'You insolent . . .' Sir George began, then lurched to his feet and called out a protest. 'No!'

Berrigan held Sir George down while Sandman took the knife to the Apotheosis of Lord Nelson. Sammy had just brought his tray of tea to the stairhead and the boy watched appalled as Sandman cut down the canvas, then across. 'A friend of mine,' Sandman explained as he mutilated the painting, 'is probably going to get married soon. He doesn't know it, and nor does his intended bride, but they plainly like each other and I'll want to give them a present when it happens.' He slashed again, slicing across the top of the painting. The canvas split with a sharp sizzling sound, leaving small threads. He slid the knife downwards again and so excised from the big picture a life-size and half-length portrait of Sally. He tossed the knife onto the floor, rolled up the picture of Britannia and smiled at Sir George. 'This will make a splendid gift, so I shall have it varnished and framed. Thank you so very much for your help. Sergeant? I believe we're finished here.'

'I'm coming with you!' Sally said from the stairs. 'Only someone has to hook me frock up.'

'Duty summons you,' Sandman said to Berrigan. 'Your servant, Sir George.'

Sir George glared at him, but seemed incapable of speaking. Sandman began to smile as he ran down the stairs and he was laughing by the time he reached the street, where he waited for Berrigan and Sally.

They joined him when Sally's dress was fastened. 'Who do you know getting married soon?' Berrigan demanded.

'Just two friends,' Sandman said airily, 'and if they don't? Well. I might keep the picture for myself.'

'Captain!' Sally chided him.

'Married?' Berrigan sounded shocked.

'I am very old-fashioned,' Sandman said, 'and a staunch believer in Christian morality.'

'Speaking of which,' the Sergeant said, 'why have we got pistols?'

'Because our next call, Sergeant, must be the Seraphim Club and I do not like to go there unarmed. I'd also prefer it if they did not know we were on the premises, so when is the best time to make our visit?'

'Why are we going there?' Berrigan wanted to know.

'To talk to the coachmen, of course.'

The Sergeant thought for a second, then nodded. 'Then go after dark,' he said, 'because it'll be easier for us to sneak in, and at least one jervis will be there.'

'Let us hope it's the right coachman,' Sandman said, and snapped open his watch. 'Not till dark? Which means I have an afternoon to while away.' He thought for a moment. 'I shall go and talk to a friend. Shall we meet at nine o'clock, say? Behind the club?'

'Meet me at the carriage house entrance,' the Sergeant suggested, 'which is in an alley off Charles II Street.'

'Unless you want to stay with me?' Sandman suggested. 'I'm only going to pass the time with a friend.'

'No,' Berrigan reddened. 'I feel like a rest.'

'Then be kind enough to place that in my room,' Sandman said, giving the Sergeant the rolled portrait of Sally. 'And you, Miss Hood? I can't think how you might want to pass the afternoon. Would you want to accompany me to see a friend?'

Sally put her arm into the Sergeant's elbow, smiled

264

sweetly at Sandman, so very sweetly, and spoke gently. 'Fake away off, Captain.'

Sandman laughed and did what he was told. He faked away off.

7

'Bunny' Barnwell was reckoned to be the best bowler in the Marylebone Cricket Club, despite having a strange loping run that ended with a double hop before he launched the ball sidearm. The double hop had provided his nickname and he now bowled at Rider Sandman on one of the netted practice wickets at the downhill side of Thomas Lord's new cricket ground in St John's Wood, a pretty suburb to the north of London.

Lord Alexander Pleydell stood beside the net, peering anxiously at every ball. 'Is Bunny moving it off the grass?' he asked.

'Not at all.'

'He's supposed to twist the ball so it moves into your legs. Sharply in. Crossley said the motion was extremely confusing.'

'Crossley's easily confused,' Sandman said, and thumped the ball hard into the net, driving Lord Alexander back in fright.

Barnwell was taking turns with Hughes, Lord Alexander's servant, to bowl to Sandman. Hughes reckoned himself a useful underarm bowler, but he was becoming frustrated at being unable to get anything past Sandman's bat and so he tried too hard and launched a ball that did not bounce at all and Sandman cracked it fast out of the net and over the damp grass so that the ball flicked up a fine silver spray as it shot up the hill where three men were scything the turf. Making a cricket field on such a pronounced slope made no sense to Sandman, but Alexander had a curious attachment to Thomas Lord's new field even though, from one boundary to another, there must have been a fall of at least six or seven feet.

Barnwell tried bowling underarm and was forced to watch his ball follow Hughes's last delivery up the slope. One of the boys who were fielding for the nets tried a fast ball at Sandman's legs and was rewarded with a blow that almost took his head off. 'You're in a savage mood,' Lord Alexander observed.

'Not really. Damp day, ball's slow,' Sandman lied. In truth he was in a savage mood, wondering how he was to keep his promise to Eleanor and why he had even made the promise to elope if her father refused his blessing. No, he understood the answer to the second question. He had made the promise because, as ever, he had been overwhelmed by Eleanor, by the look of her, by the nearness of her and by his own desire for her, but could the promise be kept? He slashed a ball into the net behind with such force that the ball drove the tarred mesh into the back fence, rattling the palings and startling a dozen sparrows into the air. How could he elope, Sandman asked himself. How could he marry a woman when he had no means to support her? And where was the honour in some hole-in-the-wall Scottish wedding that needed neither licence nor banns? The anger surged in him so he skipped down the pitch and drove a ball hard towards the stables where the club members kept their horses during games.

'An exceedingly savage mood,' Lord Alexander said thoughtfully, then took a pencil from the tangled hair behind his ear and a much creased piece of paper from a pocket. 'I thought Hammond could keep wicket, do you agree?'

'This is your team to play Hampshire?'

'No, Rider, it's my proposal for a new Dean and canons of St Paul's Cathedral. What do you think it is?'

'Hammond would be an excellent choice,' Sandman said, going onto his back leg and blocking a sharply rising ball. 'Good one,' he called to Hughes.

'Edward Budd said he'll play for us,' Lord Alexander said.

'Wonderful!' Sandman spoke with genuine warmth, for Edward Budd was the one batsman he acknowledged as his superior and was also thoroughly good company.

'And Simmons is available.'

'Then I won't be,' Sandman said. He collected the last ball with the tip of his bat and knocked it back to Hughes.

'Simmons is an excellent batsman,' Lord Alexander insisted.

'So he is,' Sandman said, 'but he took cash to throw a game in Sussex two years ago.'

'It won't happen again.'

'Not while I'm on the same team, it won't. Make your choice, Alexander, him or me.'

Lord Alexander sighed. 'He really is very good!'

'Then pick him,' Sandman said, taking his stance.

'I shall think about it,' Lord Alexander said in his most lordly manner.

The next delivery came hurtling at Sandman's ankles and he rewarded it with a blow that sent the ball all the way to the tavern by the lower boundary fence where a dozen men watched the nets from the beer garden. Were any of those men Lord Robin Holloway's footpads? Sandman glanced at his coat folded onto the damp grass and was reassured by the sight of the pistol's hilt just protruding from a pocket.

'Maybe you can talk to Simmons?' Lord Alexander suggested. 'Including him will give our side an immense batting force, Rider, a positively immense force. You, Budd and him? We shall set new records!'

'I'll talk to him,' Sandman said, 'I just won't play with him.'

'For God's sake, man!'

Sandman stepped away from the wicket. 'Alexander. I love the game of cricket, but if it's to be bent out of shape by bribery then there will be no sport left. The only way to treat bribery is to punish it absolutely.' He spoke angrily. 'Is it any wonder that the game's dying? This club here used to have a decent field, now they play on a hillside. The game's in decline, Alexander, because it's being corrupted by money.'

'It's all very well for you to say that,' Lord Alexander

said huffily, 'but Simmons has a wife and two children. Don't you understand temptation?'

'I think I do, yes,' Sandman said, 'I was offered twenty thousand guineas yesterday.' He stepped back to the crease and nodded at the next bowler.

'Twenty thousand?' Lord Alexander sounded faint. 'To lose a game of cricket?'

'To let an innocent man hang,' Sandman said, playing a demure defensive stroke. 'It's too easy,' he complained.

'What is?'

'This intellectual bowling.' The sidearm delivery, when the ball was bowled from a straight arm held at shoulder height, was curiously known as the intellectual style. 'It has no accuracy,' Sandman complained.

'But it has force,' Lord Alexander declared energetically, 'far more so than balls bowled under arm.'

'We should bowl over arm.'

'Never! Never! Ruin the game! An utterly ridiculous suggestion, offensive in the extreme!' Lord Alexander paused to suck on his pipe. 'The club isn't certain it will even allow sidearm, let alone over arm. No, if we wish to redress the balance between batsman and bowler, then the answer is obvious. Four stumps. Are you serious?'

'I just think that over arm bowling will combine force with accuracy,' Sandman suggested, 'and might even present a challenge to the batsman.'

'Serious, I mean, about being offered twenty thousand pounds?'

'Guineas, Alexander, guineas. The men who made

270

the offer consider themselves to be gentlemen.' Sandman stepped back and cracked the ball hard into the netting, close to where Lord Alexander was standing.

'Why would they offer you so much?'

'It's cheaper than death on the gallows, isn't it? The only trouble is I don't know for certain which member of the Seraphim Club is the murderer, but I hope to discover that this evening. You wouldn't like to lend me your carriage, would you?'

Lord Alexander looked puzzled. 'My carriage?'

'The thing with four wheels, Alexander, and the horses up front.' Sandman sent another ball scorching up the hill. 'It's in a good cause. Rescuing the innocent.'

'Well, of course,' Lord Alexander said with admirable enthusiasm. 'I shall be honoured to help you. Shall I wait at your lodgings?'

'Keeping Miss Hood company?' Sandman asked. 'Why not?' He laughed at Alexander's blushes, then backed away from the stumps as a young man walked towards the practice wickets from the tavern. There was something purposeful in the man's approach and Sandman was about to fetch his pistol when he recognised Lord Christopher Carne, the heir to the Earl of Avebury. 'Your friend's coming,' he told Lord Alexander.

'My friend? Oh, Kit!'

Lord Christopher waved in response to Lord Alexander's enthusiastic greeting, then noticed Sandman. He blanched, stopped and looked annoyed. For a heartbeat Sandman thought Lord Christopher was about to turn on his heel and walk away, but instead the

271

bespectacled young man strode purposefully towards Sandman. 'You never told me,' he said accusingly, 'that you were visiting my father.'

'Did I need to tell you?' A ball kicked up and Sandman swayed aside to let it thump into the net behind.

'It would have been c-courteous,' Lord Christopher complained.

'If I need lessons in courtesy,' Sandman said sharply, 'then I shall go to those who treat me politely.'

Lord Christopher bridled, but lacked the courage to demand an apology for Sandman's truculence. 'I spoke to you in c-confidence,' he protested, 'and had no idea you would p-pass anything on to my father.'

'I passed on nothing to your father,' Sandman said mildly. 'I did not repeat one word you said. Indeed, I did not even tell him I had seen you.'

'He wrote to me,' Lord Christopher said, 'saying you'd visited and that I wasn't to speak with you again. So it's plain you're lying! You d-did tell him you spoke with me.'

The letter, Sandman thought, must have travelled on the same mail coach that brought him back to London. 'Your father deduced it,' Sandman explained, 'and you should have a care whom you accuse of telling lies, unless you're quite confident you are both a better shot and a better swordsman than the man you accuse.' He did not look to see the effect of his words, but instead danced two quick-steps down the pitch and drove at a delivery with all his strength. He knew the stroke was good even before the bat struck the ball, and then it shot away and the three men scything the playing

272

wicket stared in awe as the ball streaked between them to take its first bounce just short of the uphill boundary and it still seemed to be travelling at the same speed with which it had left the bat when it vanished in the bushes at the top of the hill. It had gone like a six-pounder shot, Sandman thought, and then he heard it crack against the fence and heard a cow mooing in protest from the neighbouring meadow.

'Good God,' Lord Alexander said faintly, staring up the hill, 'good God alive.'

'I spoke hastily,' Lord Christopher said in scant apology, 'but I still don't understand why you should even need to go near Carne Manor.'

'Did you see how hard he struck that?' Lord Alexander asked.

'Why?' Lord Christopher insisted angrily.

'I told you why,' Sandman said. 'To discover whether any of your stepmother's servants had gone there.'

'Of course they wouldn't,' Lord Christopher said.

'Last time you thought it possible.'

'That's because I hadn't thought about it p-properly. Those servants must have known precisely what vile things my stepmother was doing in London and my father would hardly want them spreading such t-tales in Wiltshire.'

'True,' Sandman conceded. 'So I wasted a journey.'

'But the good news, Rider,' Lord Alexander intervened, 'is that Mister William Brown has agreed that you and I should attend on Monday!' He beamed at Sandman. 'Isn't that splendid?'

'Mister Brown?' Sandman asked.

'The Keeper of Newgate. I would have expected a man in your position to have known that.' Lord Alexander turned to a bemused Lord Christopher. 'It occurred to me, Kit, that so long as Rider was the Home Secretary's official Investigator, then he should certainly investigate the gallows. He should know exactly what awful brutality awaits people like Corday. So I wrote to the Keeper and he has very decently invited Rider and myself to breakfast. Devilled kidneys, he promises! I've always rather liked a properly devilled kidney.'

Sandman stepped away from the stumps. 'I have no wish to witness a hanging,' he said.

'It doesn't matter what you wish,' Lord Alexander said airily, 'it is a matter of duty.'

'I have no duty to witness a hanging,' Sandman insisted.

'Of course you do,' Lord Alexander said. 'I confess I am apprehensive. I do not approve of the gallows, but at the same time I discover a curiosity within me. If nothing else, Rider, it will be an educational experience.'

'Educational rubbish!' Sandman stepped back to the wicket and played a straight bat to a well-bowled ball. 'I'm not going, Alexander, and that's that. No! The answer is no!'

'I'd like to go,' Lord Christopher said in a small voice.

'Rider!' Lord Alexander expostulated.

'No!' Sandman said. 'I shall happily send the real killer to the gallows, but I'm not witnessing a Newgate circus.' He waved Hughes away. 'I've batted long enough,' he explained, then ran a hand down the face of his bat. 'You have any linseed oil, Alexander?'

'The real killer?' Lord Christopher asked. 'Do you know who that is?'

'I hope to know by this evening,' Sandman said. 'If I send for your carriage, Alexander, then you'll know I've discovered my witness. If I don't? Alas.'

'Witness?' Lord Christopher asked.

'If Rider's going to be obdurate,' Lord Alexander said to Lord Christopher, 'then perhaps you should join me for the Keeper's devilled kidneys on Monday?' He fumbled with his tinder box as he tried to light a new pipe. 'I was thinking that you really ought to join the club here, Rider. We need members.'

'I can imagine you do. Who'd join a club that plays on an imitation of an alpine meadow?'

'A perfectly good pitch,' Lord Alexander said querulously.

'Witness?' Lord Christopher broke in to ask again.

'I trust you'll send for the carriage!' Lord Alexander boomed. 'I want to see that bloody man Sidmouth confounded. Make him grant a pardon, Rider. I shall await your summons at the Wheatsheaf.'

'I'll wait with you,' Lord Christopher said, and was rewarded by a flicker of annoyance on Lord Alexander's face. Sandman, who saw the same flicker, knew that Lord Alexander did not want a rival for Sally's attention, but Lord Christopher must have taken it as an insult for his face fell.

Lord Alexander gazed at the three groundsmen, who were still leaning on their scythes and discussing

Sandman's ball that had blasted through them like a roundshot. 'I have always thought,' Lord Alexander said, 'that there is a fortune to be made by a man who can invent a device for the cutting of grass.'

'It's called a sheep,' Sandman said, 'vulgarly known as a woolly bird.'

'A device that does not leave dung,' Lord Alexander said acidly, then smiled at Lord Christopher Carne. 'Of course you must spend the evening with me, my dear fellow. Perhaps you can explain this man Kant to me? Someone sent me his last book, have you seen it? I thought you would have. He seems very sound, but he was a Prussian, wasn't he? I suppose that wasn't his fault. Come and have some tea first. Rider? You'll have some tea? Of course you will. And I want you to meet Lord Frederick. You know he's our club secretary now? You really should join us. And you wanted some linseed oil for the bat? They do a very acceptable tea here.'

So Sandman went for a lordly tea.

It was a cloudy evening and the sky over London was made even darker because there was no wind and the coal smoke hung thick and still above the roofs and spires. The streets near St James's Square were quiet, for there were no businesses in these quiet houses and many of their owners were in the country. Sandman saw a watchman noting him and so he crossed to the man and said good evening and asked what regiment he had served in and the two passed the time exchanging memories of Salamanca, which Sandman thought was perhaps the most beautiful town he had ever seen. A lamplighter came round with his ladder and the new gas lights popped on one after the other, burning blue for a time and then turning whiter. 'Some of the houses here are getting gas,' the watchman said, 'indoors.'

'Indoors?'

'No good'll come of it, sir. It ain't natural, is it?' The watchman looked up at the nearest hissing lamp. 'There'll be fire and pillars of smoke, sir, like it says in the good book sir, fire and pillars of smoke. Burning like a fiery furnace, sir.'

Sandman was saved more apocalyptic prophecies when a hackney turned into the street, the sound of its horse's hooves echoing sharply from the shadowed white house fronts. It stopped close to Sandman, the door opened and Sergeant Berrigan stepped down. He tossed a coin up to the driver, then held the door open for Sally.

'You can't . . .' Sandman began.

'I told you he'd say that,' Berrigan boasted to Sally, 'didn't I tell you he'd say you shouldn't come?'

'Sergeant!' Sandman insisted. 'We cannot . . .'

'You're going for Meg, right?' Sally intervened. 'And she ain't going to take kindly to two old swoddies doing her up, is she? She needs a woman's touch.'

'I'm sure two old soldiers can gain her confidence,' Sandman said.

'Sal won't take no for an answer,' the Sergeant warned him.

'Besides,' Sandman continued, 'Meg isn't in the

277

Seraphim Club. We're only going there to find the coachman so he can tell us where he took her.'

'Maybe he'll tell me what he won't tell you,' Sally said to Sandman with a dazzling smile, then she turned on the watchman. 'You got nothing better to do than listen to other folks chatting?'

The man looked startled, but followed the lamp-lighter down the street while Sergeant Berrigan fished in his coat pocket to bring out a key which he showed to Sandman. 'Back way in, Captain,' he said, then looked at Sally. 'Listen, my love, I know . . .'

'Stow it, Sam! I'm coming with you!'

Berrigan led the way, shaking his head. 'I don't know what it is,' he grumbled, 'the ladies tell you that life ain't fair because men get all the privileges, but the mollishers don't half get their own way. You notice that, Captain? It's bitch about this and bitch about that, but who gets to wear the silk, gold and pearls, eh?'

'You talking about me, Sam Berrigan?' Sally asked.

'True love,' Sandman murmured, then Berrigan put a finger to his lips as they approached a wide carriage gate set in a white wall at the end of a short street.

'What it is,' Berrigan said softly, 'is that it's a quiet time of day in the club. We should be able to sneak in.' He approached a small door set to one side of the gates, tried it, found it locked and so used his key. He pushed the door open, looked into the yard and evidently saw nothing to alarm him, for he stepped over the threshold and beckoned Sandman and Sally to follow.

The yard was empty except for a coach, its blue paint trimmed with gold, that had evidently just been washed for it stood gleaming in the dusk with water dripping from its flanks and buckets standing by the wheels. The badge of the golden angel was painted on the door. 'Over here, quick,' Berrigan said, and Sandman and Sally followed the Sergeant to the shadow of the stables. 'One of the lads will be washing it,' Berrigan said, 'but the coachmen will be in the back kitchen there.' He nodded to a lit window in the carriage house, then turned in alarm as a door in the main house was thrown open. 'In here!' Berrigan hissed, and the three of them filed into an alley that led beside the stables. Footsteps sounded in the yard.

'Here?' a voice asked. Sandman did not recognise it.

'A hole twelve feet deep,' another voice answered, 'stone-lined and with a masonry dome over the top.'

'Not much damn room. How wide's the hole?'

'Ten feet?'

'Christ, man, it's where we turn the carriages!'

'Do it in the street.'

Berrigan swayed close to Sandman. 'They're talking about building an ice house,' he breathed in Sandman's ear, 'been discussing it for a year now.'

'What about behind the stables?' the first man asked.

'No room,' the other man answered.

'I mean between the stables and the back wall,' the first man said, and Sandman heard his footsteps getting closer and knew it was only a matter of seconds before they were discovered. But then Berrigan peered out of the alley's far end, saw no one and dashed across a smaller yard to a door that opened into the rear of the house. 'This way!' he hissed.

Sandman and Sally ran after him and found themselves on a servant's stairway that evidently ran from the kitchens in the basement to the upper floors. 'We'll hide upstairs,' Berrigan whispered, 'till the coast's clear.'

'Why not hide here?' Sandman asked.

''Cos the bastards could come back in through this bleeding door,' Berrigan said, then led them up the unlit stairway. Halfway up he edged open a door that led into a corridor that was deeply carpeted and had walls covered in a deep scarlet paper, though it was too dark to see the pattern of the paper or the details of the pictures that hung between the polished doors. Berrigan chose a door at random, opened it and found an empty room. 'We'll be all right in here,' he said.

It was a bedroom; large, lavish and comfortable. The bed itself was high and huge, plump-mattressed and covered with a thick scarlet covering on which the Seraphim's naked angel took flight. A fireplace was there to warm the room in winter. Berrigan crossed to the window and pulled back the curtain so he could gaze down into the yard. Sandman's eyes slowly adjusted to the dim light, then he heard Sally laugh and he turned to see her gazing at a picture above the bedhead. 'Good God,' Sandman said.

'There's a lot of those,' Berrigan commented drily.

The picture showed a happy group of men and women in a circular arcade of white marble pillars. In the foreground a child played a flute and another plucked a harp, both ignoring their naked elders who coupled under the moon that lit the pillared arcade with an unearthly glow. 'Bloody hell,' Sally said respectfully, 'you wouldn't think a girl could do that with her legs.'

Sandman decided no answer was necessary. He moved to the window and stared down, but the yard seemed empty again. 'I think they've gone back inside,' Berrigan said.

'Another one,' Sally said, standing on tiptoe to examine the painting above the empty fireplace.

'D'you think they'll come in here?' Sandman asked.

Berrigan shook his head. 'They only use these back slums in the winter.'

Sally giggled at the picture, then turned on Berrigan. 'You worked in an academy, Sam Berrigan.'

'It's a club!'

'Bleeding academy is what it is,' Sally said scornfully.

'I left it, didn't I?' Berrigan protested. 'Besides, it weren't an academy for us servants. Only for the members.'

'What members?' Sally asked, and laughed at her own jest.

Berrigan hushed her, not because she was being coarse, but because there were footsteps in the corridor outside. They came close to the door, passed on, faded.

'It doesn't really help us being up here,' Sandman said.

'We'll wait for things to quiet down,' Berrigan said, 'and then we'll slip back down to the yard.'

The door handle rattled. Berrigan quickly stepped behind a folding screen that hid a chamberpot and Sandman froze. The footsteps had seemed to pass on down the passage, but the person now trying the handle must have heard the voices and crept back, and suddenly the door was pushed open and a girl walked in. She was tall, slender and her black hair was prettily piled on her head and held in place with long pins with mother of pearl heads. Her shoes had mother of pearl heels, she sported pearl earrings and had a string of pearls strung twice about her elegant, swan-like neck, but otherwise she was quite naked. She took no notice of Sandman, who had half drawn his pistol, but smiled at Sally. 'I didn't know you worked here, Sal!'

'I'm not really working, Flossie,' Sally said.

Sandman recognised the girl then. It was the opera dancer who had called herself Sacharissa Lasorda and who now turned and stared at Sandman and somehow, though she was stark naked and he was fully dressed, she made him feel out of place. She looked him up and down, then smiled at Sally. 'You got the good-looking one, didn't you? But he's taking his time, ain't he?' Then her eyes widened as Berrigan stepped from behind the screen. 'You having a threesome?' she asked, then recognised the sergeant.

'I ain't here, Flossie,' Berrigan growled, 'so close the door when you leave and you ain't seen me. I thought you'd left for higher things?'

'Didn't work out, Sam,' she said, closing the door but staying inside the room.

'What happened to Spofforth?' Sally asked.

'Faked off this morning, didn't he?' She sniffed. 'The bastard! And I need the bleeding rhino, don't I? And this place is always worth a few quid.' She sat on the bed. 'So what the hell are you doing here?' she asked Berrigan.

'What the hell are you doing?' he demanded in return.

'We sneak in here for a rest,' Flossie said, 'on account that no one looks in here in summer.'

'Well just you remember that we ain't here,' Berrigan said fiercely. 'We ain't here, you ain't seen us and don't ask us no questions.'

'Bloody hell!' Flossie gave Berrigan a very level look. 'Pardon me for bloody breathing.'

'And who are you supposed to be with?' Berrigan asked.

'Tollemere. Only he's drunk and snoring.' She sniffed again and looked at Sally. 'You working here?'

'No.'

'Rhino's good,' Flossie said. She eased off a shoe and massaged her foot. 'So what happens if I go downstairs and tell them you're here?' she asked Berrigan.

'Next time I see you,' Berrigan said, 'you get a thorough bloody kicking.'

'Sergeant!' Sandman remonstrated, though he noticed that Flossie seemed remarkably unmoved by the threat.

'She bloody well will get a kicking!' Berrigan said.

'It's all bulge and no bang with you, Sam,' Flossie said, grinning.

'We ain't going to hurt no one,' Sally said earnestly, 'and we're only trying to help someone.

'I won't tell anyone you're here,' Flossie promised. 'Why should I?'

'So who's here tonight?' Berrigan asked.

She rattled off a list of names, none of which was

of interest to Sandman, for neither the Marquess of Skavadale nor Lord Robin Holloway were included. Flossie was certain neither man was in the club. 'I don't mind the Marquess,' she said, ''cos he's a proper gentlemen, but Lord bleeding Robin, he's a bastard.' She pulled her shoe back on, yawned and stood up. 'I'd better go and make sure his lordship ain't missing me. He'll want his supper soon.' She frowned. 'I don't mind working here,' she went on, 'the rhino's good, it's comfortable, but I bloody hate sitting down to supper naked. Makes you feel queer, it does, all the men dressed bang up and us skinned to nothing.' She opened the door and shook her head. 'And I always spill the bloody soup.'

'You will keep mum, Flossie?' Berrigan asked anxiously.

She blew him a kiss. 'For you, Sam, anything,' she said, and was gone.

'For you, Sam, anything?' Sally asked.

'She don't mean nothing,' Berrigan said hastily.

'Mister Spofforth was right,' Sandman interrupted them.

'Right about what?' Sally wanted to know.

'She does have good legs.'

'Captain!' Sally was shocked.

'I've seen better,' Sergeant Berrigan said gallantly, and Sandman was pleased to see Sally blush.

'Out of interest,' Sandman asked as he went to the door, 'what does it cost to be a member here?' He opened the door a crack and peered out, but the corridor was empty.

'Two thousand to join, that's if you're invited, and a hundred a year,' Berrigan said.

The privileges of wealth, Sandman thought, and if the Countess of Avebury had been blackmailing one of the members, or even two or three of the members, then would they not kill her to preserve their place in this hedonistic mansion? He glanced back at the window. It was dark outside now, but it was the luminous dark of a summer night in a gas-lit town. 'Shall we find our coachman?' he asked Berrigan.

They went back down the servants' stairs and crossed the yard. The coach still glistened wetly on the cobbles, though the buckets were gone. Horses stamped in the stables as Berrigan went to the side door of the carriage house. He listened there for a few seconds, then raised two fingers to indicate that he thought there were two men on the door's far side. Sandman pulled the pistol from his coat pocket. He decided not to cock it for he did not want the gun to fire accidentally, but he checked it was primed then he edged Berrigan aside, opened the door and walked inside.

The room was a kitchen, tack room and store. A pot of water bubbled over a fire and a pair of candles burnt on the mantel and more stood on the table where two men, one young and one middle-aged, sat with tankards of ale and plates of bread, cheese and cold beef. They turned and stared when Sandman came in, and the older man, opening his mouth in astonishment, let his clay pipe drop so that its stem broke on the table's edge. Sally followed Sandman into the room, then Berrigan came in and closed the door.

'Introduce me,' Sandman said. He was not pointing the pistol at either man, but it was very obvious and the two could not take their eyes from it.

'The youngster's a stable hand,' Berrigan said, 'and he's called Billy, while the one with the jaw in his lap is Mister Michael Mackeson. He's one of the club's two coachmen. Where's Percy, Mack?'

'Sam?' Mackeson said faintly. He was a burly man, red-faced, with a fine waxed moustache and a shock of black hair that was turning grey at the temples. He was dressed well and could doubtless afford to be, for good drivers were paid extravagantly. Sandman had heard of a driver earning over two hundred pounds a year, and all of them were considered the possessors of an enviable skill, so enviable that every young gentleman wanted to be like them. Lordlings wore the same caped coats as the professionals and learnt to carry the whip in one hand and the bunched reins in the other, and there were so many aristocrats aspiring to be coachmen that no one could be sure whether any particular carriage was driven by a duke or a paid driver. Now, despite his elevated status, Mackeson just gaped at Berrigan who, like Sandman, had a pistol.

'Where's Percy?' Berrigan asked again.

'He's taken Lord Lucy to Weybridge,' Mackeson said.

'Let's hope you're the one we want,' Berrigan said. 'And you're not going anywhere, Billy,' he snapped at the stable hand, who was dressed in a shabby set of the Seraphim Club's yellow and black livery, 'not unless you want a broken skull.' The stable hand, who had been rising from the bench, subsided again.

Sandman was not aware of it, but he was angry suddenly. It was possible that the moustached coachman might have the answer Sandman had been searching for, and the notion that he might get this close and still not discover the truth had sparked his rage. It was a controlled rage, but it was in his voice, harsh and clipped, and Mackeson jumped with alarm when Sandman spoke. 'Some weeks ago,' Sandman said, 'a coachman from this club collected a maid from the Countess of Avebury's house in Mount Street. Was that you?'

Mackeson swallowed, but seemed unable to speak.

'Was that you?' Sandman asked again, louder.

Mackeson nodded very slowly, then glanced at Berrigan as if he did not believe what was happening to him.

'Where did you take her?' Sandman asked. Mackeson swallowed again, then jumped as Sandman rapped the pistol on the table. 'Where did you take her?' Sandman demanded again.

Mackeson turned from Sandman and frowned at Berrigan. 'They'll kill you, Sam Berrigan,' he said, 'kill you stone dead if they find you here.'

'Then they'd better not find me, Mack,' Berrigan said.

The coachman gave another start of alarm when he heard the ratcheting sound of Sandman's pistol being cocked. His eyes widened as he stared into the muzzle and uttered a pathetic moan. 'I'm only going to ask you politely once more,' Sandman said, 'and after that, Mister Mackeson, I shall . . .'

'Nether Cross,' Mackeson said hurriedly.

'Where's Nether Cross?'

'Fair old ways,' the coachman said guardedly. 'Seven hours? Eight hours?'

'Where?' Sandman asked harshly.

'Down near the coast, sir, down Kent way.'

'So who lives there,' Sandman asked, 'in Nether Cross?'

'Lord John de Sully Pearce-Tarrant,' Berrigan answered for the coachman, 'the Viscount Hurstwood, Earl of Keymer, Baron Highbrook, lord of this and lord of God knows what else, heir to the Dukedom of Ripon and also known, Captain, as the Marquess of Ska-vadale.'

And Sandman felt a great surge of relief. Because he had his answer at last.

The carriage rattled through the streets south of the Thames. Its two lamps were lit, but cast a feeble glow that did nothing to light the way so that, once they reached the summit of Shooters Hill where there were few lights and the road across Blackheath stretched impenetrably black before them, they stopped. The horses were unharnessed and picketed on the green and the two prisoners were locked inside the carriage by the simple expedient of fastening the coach doors by looping their handles with the reins that were then strapped tight around the whole vehicle. The windows were jammed shut with slivers of wood, and either Sandman or Berrigan would stand guard all night.

The prisoners were the driver, Mackeson, and Billy,

the stable hand. It had been Berrigan's idea to take the Seraphim Club's newly washed carriage. Sandman had refused at first, saying he had already arranged to borrow Lord Alexander's coach and team and he doubted he had the legal right to commandeer one of the Seraphim Club's carriages, but Berrigan had scoffed at the thought of such scruples. 'You reckon Lord Alexander's coachman knows the way to Nether Cross?' he asked. 'Which means you've got to take Mackeson anyway, so you might as well take a vehicle he knows how to handle. And considering what evils the bastards have done I don't suppose God or man will worry about you borrowing their coach.'

And if the coach and driver were taken then Billy, the stable hand, had to be kept from betraying that Sandman had been asking about Meg, so he too must be taken prisoner. He put up no resistance, but instead helped Mackeson harness the team and then, with his hands and feet tied, he was put into the carriage while Mackeson, accompanied by Berrigan, sat up on the box. The few members of the club, ensconced in their dining room, had no idea that their coach was being commandeered.

Now, stranded on Blackheath, Sandman and his companions had to wait through the dark hours. Berrigan took Sally to a tavern and paid for a room and he stayed with her while Sandman guarded the coach. It was not till after the clocks had struck two that Berrigan loomed out of the dark. 'Quiet night, Captain?'

'Quiet enough,' Sandman said, then smiled. 'Long time since I did picquet duty.'

'Those two behaving themselves?' Berrigan asked, glancing at the carriage.

'Quiet as lambs,' Sandman said.

'You can go to sleep,' Berrigan suggested, 'and I'll stand sentry.'

'In a while,' Sandman said. He was sitting on the grass, his back against a wheel and he tilted his head to look at the stars that were drifting out from behind ragged clouds. 'Remember the Spanish night marches?' he asked. 'The stars were so bright it was as though you could reach up and snuff them out.'

'I remember the camp fires,' Berrigan said, 'hills and valleys of fire.' He twisted and looked west. 'A bit like that.'

Sandman turned his head to see London spread beneath them like a quilt of fire that was blurred by the red-touched smoke. The air up on the heath was clean and chill, yet he could just smell the coal smoke from the great city that spread its hazed lights to the western horizon. 'I do miss Spain,' he admitted.

'It were strange at first,' Berrigan said, 'but I liked it. Did you speak the language?'

'Yes.'

Berrigan laughed. 'And I'll bet you were good at it.'

'I was fluent enough, yes.'

The Sergeant handed Sandman a stone bottle. 'Brandy,' he explained. 'And I was thinking,' he went on, 'that if I go and buy those cigars I'll need someone who speaks the language. You and me? We could go there together, work together.'

'I'd like that,' Sandman said.

'There's got to be money in it,' Berrigan said. 'We paid pennies for those cigars in Spain and here they cost a fortune if you can get them at all.'

'I think you're right,' Sandman said, and smiled at the thought that maybe he did have a job after all. Berrigan and Sandman, Purveyors of Fine Cigars? Eleanor's father liked a good cigar and paid well for them, so well that there might even be enough money in the idea to persuade Sir Henry that his daughter was not marrying a pauper. Lady Forrest might never be convinced that Sandman was a proper husband for Eleanor, but Sandman suspected that Eleanor and her father would prevail. He and Berrigan would need money, and who better than Sir Henry to lend it? They would have to travel around Spain, hire shipping space and rent premises in a fashionable part of London, but it could work. He was sure of it. 'It's a brilliant idea, Sergeant,' he said.

'So shall we do it when this is over?'

'Why not? Yes.' He put out his hand and Berrigan shook it.

'We old soldiers should stick together,' Berrigan said, 'because we were good. We were damned good, Captain. We chased the bloody Crapauds halfway across bloody Europe, and then we came home and none of the bastards here cared, did they?' He paused, thinking. 'They had a rule in the Seraphim Club. No one was ever to talk about the wars. No one.'

'None of the members served?' Sandman guessed.

'Not one. They wouldn't even let you in if you'd been a swoddy or a sailor.'

'They were jealous?'

'Probably.'

Sandman drank from the bottle. 'Yet they employed you?'

'They liked having a guardsman in the hall. I made the bastards feel safe. And they could order me around, which they also liked. Do this, Berrigan, do that.' The Sergeant grunted thanks when Sandman passed him the bottle. 'Most of the time it weren't nothing bad. Run errands for the bastards, but then once in a while they'd want something else.' He fell silent and Sandman also kept quiet. The night was extraordinarily quiet. After a time, as Sandman hoped, Berrigan began talking again. 'Once, there was a fellow who was taking one of the Seraphim to court, so we gave him a lesson. They sent a wagonload of flowers to his grave, they did. And the girls, of course – we paid them off. Not the ones like Flossie, they can look after themselves, but the others? We gave 'em ten pounds, perhaps twelve.'

'What sort of girls?'

'Common girls, Captain, girls that had caught their eye on the street.'

'They were kidnapped?'

'They were kidnapped,' Berrigan said. 'Kidnapped, raped and paid off.'

'And all the members did that?'

'Some were worse than others. There's always a handful that are ready for any mischief, just like in a company of soldiers. And then there are the followers. And one or two of them are more sensible. That's why

I was surprised it was Skavadale that scragged the Countess. He ain't a bad one. He's got a ramrod up his arse and he thinks he smells of violets, but he ain't an unkind man.'

'I rather hoped it would be Lord Robin,' Sandman admitted.

'He's just a mad bastard,' Berrigan said. 'Bloody rich, mad bastard,' he added.

'But Skavadale has more to lose,' Sandman explained.

'Lost most of it already,' Berrigan said. 'He's probably the poorest man there. His father's lost a fortune.'

'But the son,' Sandman explained, 'is betrothed to a very rich girl. Perhaps the wealthiest bride in Britain? I suspect he was ploughing the Countess of Avebury and she had a nasty habit of blackmail.' Sandman thought for a moment. 'Skavadale might be relatively poor, but I'll bet he could still scratch together a thousand pounds if he had to. That's probably the sort of money the Countess asked for if she was not to write a letter to the wealthy and religious bride-to-be.'

'So he killed her?' Berrigan asked.

'So he killed her,' Sandman said.

Berrigan thought for a moment. 'So why did they commission her portrait?'

'In one way,' Sandman said, 'that had nothing to do with the murder. It's simply that several of the Seraphim had rogered the Countess and they wanted her picture as a trophy. So poor Corday was painting away when Skavadale comes to visit. We know he came up the back stairs, the private way, and Corday was hurried off when the Countess realised one of her lovers had arrived.' Sandman was sure that was how it had happened. He imagined the silent awkwardness in the bedroom as Corday painted and the Countess lounged on the bed and made idle conversation with the maid. The charcoal would have scratched on the paper, then there would have been the sound of footsteps on the back service stairs and Corday's ordeal had begun.

Berrigan drank again, then passed the bottle to Sandman. 'So the girl Meg takes the pixie downstairs,' he said, 'and throws him out, then she goes back upstairs and finds what? The Countess dead?'

'Probably. Or dying, and she finds the Marquess of Skavadale there.' Would the Countess have been pleased to see the Marquess, Sandman wondered. Or was their adulterous tangle already at an end? Perhaps Skavadale had come to plead with her to withdraw her demands and the Countess, desperate for money, had probably laughed at him. Perhaps she hinted that he would have to pay even more, but somehow she drove him into a black rage in which he drew a knife. What knife? A man like Skavadale did not wear a knife, but perhaps there had been a knife in the room? Meg would know. Perhaps the Countess had been eating fruit and had had a paring knife which Skavadale seized and plunged into her, and afterwards, when she lay pale and dying on a bed of blood, he had the whimsy to put Corday's palette knife into one of her wounds. And then, or just about then, Meg had returned. Or perhaps Meg had overheard the fight and was waiting outside the room when Skavadale emerged.

'So why didn't he kill Meg as well?' the Sergeant asked.

'Because Meg isn't a threat to him,' Sandman guessed. 'The Countess threatened his betrothal to a girl who could probably pay off the mortgages on all his family's estates – all of them! And the Countess would have ended that engagement and there's no greater tragedy to an aristocrat than to lose his money, for with his money goes his status. They reckon they're born better than the rest of us, but they're not, they're just a lot richer, and they have to stay rich if they're to keep their illusions of superiority. The Countess could have put Skavadale in the gutter, so he hates her and he kills her, but he didn't kill the maid because she wasn't a threat.'

Berrigan thought about that for a moment. 'So he takes the maid off to one of the mortgaged estates instead?'

'That seems to be the size of it,' Sandman said.

'So why is Lord Robin Holloway trying to kill you?'

'Because I'm a danger to his friend, of course,' Sandman replied forcefully. 'The last thing they want is for the truth to be told, so they tried to bribe me and now they'll try to kill me.'

'A big bribe, it was,' Berrigan said.

'Nothing compared to the wealth that Skavadale's bride will bring him,' Sandman said, 'and the Countess put that at risk. So she had to die, and now Corday must die because then everyone will forget the crime.'

'Aye,' Berrigan allowed. 'But I still don't understand

why they didn't just scrag this maid Meg. If they thought she was a danger they wouldn't let her live.'

'Perhaps they have killed her,' Sandman said.

'Then this is a right waste of time,' Berrigan said gloomily.

'But I don't think they'd have taken Meg all the way to Nether Cross just to kill her,' Sandman said.

'So what are they doing with her?'

'Maybe they've given her somewhere to live,' Sandman suggested, 'somewhere comfortable so she doesn't reveal what she knows.'

'So now she's the blackmailer?'

'I don't know,' Sandman said, yet as he thought about it, the Sergeant's notion that Meg was now black-mailing Skavadale made sense. 'Perhaps she is,' he said, 'and if she's sensible she's not asking too much, which is why they're content to let her live.'

'But if she is blackmailing him,' Berrigan suggested, 'then she'll hardly tell us the truth, will she? She's got Skavadale strapped down tight, don't she? She's got the whip on him. Why should she give all that up to save some bloody pixie's life?'

'Because we shall appeal,' Sandman said, 'to her better nature.'

Berrigan laughed sourly. 'Ah well, then,' he said, 'it's all solved!'

'It worked with you, Sergeant,' Sandman pointed out gently.

'That were Sally, that were.' Berrigan paused, then sounded embarrassed. 'At first, you know, in the Wheatsheaf that night? I thought it was you and her.'

296

'Alas no,' Sandman said, 'I am well spoken for and Sally is all yours, Sergeant, and I think you are a most fortunate man. As am I. But I am also a tired one.' He crawled under the carriage, bumping his head painfully on the forward axle. 'After Waterloo,' he said, 'I thought I'd never again sleep in the open.'

The grass was dry under the carriage. The springs creaked as one of the prisoners shifted inside, the picketed horses stamped and the wind sighed in a nearby stand of trees. Sandman thought of the hundreds of other nights he had slept under the stars and then, just as he decided that sleep would never come in this night, it did. And he slept.

8

Early next morning Sally brought them a basket with bacon, hard boiled eggs, bread and a stone jar of cold tea, a breakfast they shared with the two prisoners. Mackeson, the coachman, was phlegmatic about his fate. 'You didn't have much choice, did you?' he said to Berrigan. 'You had to keep us quiet, but it won't do you no good, Sam.'

'Why not?'

'You ever seen a lord hang?'

'Earl Ferrers was hanged,' Sandman intervened, 'for murdering his servant.'

'No!' Sally said in disbelief. 'They hanged an earl? Really?'

'He went to the scaffold in his own carriage,' Sandman told her, 'wearing his wedding suit.'

'Bleeding hell!' She was obviously pleased by this news. 'A lord, eh?'

'But that were a long time ago,' Mackeson said dismissively, 'a very long time ago.' His moustache, which had been waxed so jauntily when Sandman had first seen him, was now fallen and straggling. 'So what happens to us?' he asked gloomily.

'We go to Nether Cross,' Sandman said, 'we fetch the girl and you take us back to London where I shall write a letter to your employers saying your absence from duties was forced.'

'Much bleeding good that will do,' Mackeson grumbled.

'You're a jervis, Mack,' Berrigan said, 'you'll get a job. The rest of the world could be starving, but there's always work for a jervis.'

'Time to get ready,' Sandman said, glancing up at the lightening sky. A small mist drifted over the heath as the four horses were watered at a stone trough, then led back to the carriage where it took a long time to put on the four sets of bridles, belly bands, back bands, martingales, hames, traces, cruppers, driving pads and fillet straps. After Mackeson and Billy had finished harnessing the horses, Sandman made the younger man strip off his shoes and belt. The stable hand had pleaded to be left without bonds on his ankles and wrists and Sandman had agreed, but without shoes and with his breeches falling round his knees the boy would find it hard to escape. Sandman and Sally sat inside with the embarrassed Billy, Mackeson and Berrigan climbed onto the box and then, with a jangle and clanging and a lurching roll, they bounced over the grass and onto the road. They were travelling again.

They went south and east past hop fields, orchards and great estates. By midday Sandman had unwittingly fallen asleep, then woke with a start when the carriage lurched in a rut. He blinked, then saw that Sally had taken the pistol from him and was gazing at a thoroughly cowed Billy. 'You can sleep on, Captain,' she said.

'I'm sorry, Sally.'

'He didn't dare try nothing,' Sally said derisively, 'not once I told him who my brother is.'

Sandman peered through the window to see they were climbing through a beech wood. 'I thought we might meet him last night.'

'He don't like crossing the river,' Sally said, 'so he only works the north and west roads.' She saw he was properly awake and gave him back his pistol. 'Do you think a man can be on the cross and then go straight?' she asked.

Sandman suspected the question was not about her brother, but about Berrigan. Not that the Sergeant was exactly in the cross life, not as the Wheatsheaf understood it, but as a servant of the Seraphim Club he had certainly known his share of crime. 'Of course he can,' Sandman said confidently.

'Not many do,' Sally averred, but not in argument. Rather she wanted reassurance.

'We all have to make a living, Sally,' Sandman said, 'and if we're honest we none of us want to work too hard. That's the appeal of the cross life, isn't it? Your brother can work one night in three and make a living.'

'That's Jack though, isn't it?' She sounded bleak and, rather than meet Sandman's eye, she gazed through the dusty window at an orchard.

'And maybe your brother will settle down when he

meets the right woman,' Sandman suggested. 'A lot of men do that. They start off by being rogues, but then find honest work and as often as not it's after they've met a woman. I can't tell you how many of my soldiers were utter nuisances, complete damn fools, more use to the enemy than to us, and then they'd meet some Spanish girl half their weight and within a week they'd be model soldiers.' She turned to look at him and he smiled at her. 'I don't think you've anything to worry about, Sally.'

She returned his smile. 'Are you a good judge of men, Captain?'

'Yes, Sally, I am.'

She laughed, then looked at Billy. 'Close your bleeding trap before you catch flies,' she said, 'and stop listening to private conversation!'

He blushed and stared at a hedge that crawled past the window. They could not change horses and so Mackeson was pacing the team, which meant they travelled slowly, and the journey was made even slower because the road was in bad condition and they had to pull over whenever a horn announced that a stage or mail coach was behind them. The mail coaches were the most dramatic, their approach heralded by an urgent blast of a horn, then the lightly built and high-sprung vehicles would fly past in a flurry of hooves, rocking like a galloper gun. Sandman envied their speed, and worried about time, then told himself it was only Saturday and, so long as Meg really was hiding at Nether Cross, then they should be back in London by Sunday evening and that left plenty of time to find

Lord Sidmouth and secure Corday's reprieve. The Home Secretary had said he did not want to be disturbed by official business on the Lord's Day, but Sandman did not give a damn about his lordship's prayers. Sandman would keep the whole government from its devotions if that meant justice.

In mid-morning Sandman changed places with Berrigan. Sandman now guarded Mackeson and he lifted his coat to let the driver see the pistol, but Mackeson was cowed and docile. He was taking the carriage down ever narrower roads, beneath trees heavy with summer leaves so that both he and Sandman were constantly ducking beneath boughs. They stopped at a ford to let the horses drink and Sandman watched the blue-green dragonflies flitting between the tall rushes, then Mackeson clicked his tongue and the horses hauled on and the coach splashed through the water and climbed between warm fields where men and women cut the harvest with sickles. Near midday they stopped close to a tavern and Sandman bought ale, bread and cheese which they ate and drank as the carriage creaked the last few miles. They passed a church that had a lych gate wreathed with bridal flowers and then clopped through a village where men played cricket on the green. Sandman watched the game as the coach rattled along the green's edge. This was rural cricket, a long way from the sophistication of the London game. These players still used only two stumps and a wide bail, and they bowled strictly under arm, yet the batsman had a good stance and a better eye and Sandman heard the shouts of approbation as the man punished a bad ball by striking it into a duck pond. A small boy splashed in to retrieve the ball, and then Mackeson, with a careless skill, wheeled the horses between two brick walls and clicked them on past a pair of oast houses and down into a narrow lane that ran steep between thick woods of oak. 'Not far now,' Mackeson said.

'You've done well to remember the way,' Sandman said. His compliment was genuine because the route had been tortuous and he had wondered whether Mackeson was misleading them by trying to get lost in the tangle of small lanes, but at the last turn, beside the oast houses, Sandman had seen a fingerpost pointing to Nether Cross.

'I done this journey a half-dozen times with his lordship,' Mackeson said, then hesitated before glancing at Sandman. 'So what happens if you don't find the woman?'

'We will find her,' Sandman said 'You brought her here, didn't you?' he added.

'Long time back, master,' Mackeson said, 'long time back.'

'How long?'

'Seven weeks near enough,' the coachman said, and Sandman realised that Meg must have been brought down to the country just after the murder and a full month before Corday's trial. 'All of seven weeks ago,' Mackeson went on, 'and anything can happen in seven weeks, can't it?' He gave Sandman a sly look. 'And maybe his lordship's here? That'll cool your porridge, won't it?'

Sandman had fretted that Skavadale might indeed

be at his estate in Nether Cross, but there had been little point in worrying overmuch. He was either there or not, and he would have to be dealt with or not, and Sandman was far more worried that Meg might have vanished. Perhaps she was dead? Or perhaps, if she was blackmailing Skavadale, then she was living in country luxury and would not want to abandon her new life. 'What sort of house is it?' he asked the coachman.

'It ain't like their big ones up north,' Mackeson said. 'They got this one through a marriage in the old days, that's what I heard.'

'Comfortable?'

'Better than anything you or I will ever live in,' Mackeson said, then he clicked his tongue and the horses' ears twitched back as he flicked the leaders' reins and they turned smartly towards a tall pair of gates hung between high flint pillars.

Sandman opened the gates that were latched but not locked, then closed them after the carriage had passed. He climbed back onto the box and Mackeson walked the horses down the long drive that twisted through a deer park and between fine copper beeches until it crossed a small bridge and there, amidst the overgrown box hedges of an untended garden, lay a small and exquisitely beautiful Elizabethan house with black timbers, white plasterwork and red brick chimneys. 'Cross Hall, it's called,' Mackeson said.

'Some marriage portion,' Sandman said jealously, for the house looked so perfect under the afternoon sun.

'All mortgaged now,' Mackeson said, 'or that's what they say. Needs a fortune, this place, and I need to look after these horses. They want water, proper feed, a rubdown and a good rest.'

'All in good time,' Sandman said. He was watching the windows, but could see no movement in any of them. None was open either, and that was a bad sign for it was a warm summer's day, but then he saw there was a smear of smoke coming from one of the tall chimneys at the rear of the house and that restored his optimism. The carriage stopped and he dropped down from the box, wincing as his weight went onto his damaged ankle. Berrigan opened the carriage door and kicked down the steps, but Sandman told him to wait and make sure that Mackeson did not simply whip the horses back down the drive.

Sandman limped to the front door and hammered on its old dark panels. He had no right to be here, he thought. He was probably trespassing, and he felt in his tail pocket for the letter of authorisation from the Home Office. He had not used it once yet, but perhaps it would help him now. He knocked on the door again and stepped back to see if anyone was peering from a window. Ivy grew round the porch and under the leaves above the door he could just see a shield carved into the plasterwork. Five scallop shells were set into the shield. No one showed at any of the windows, so he stepped back into the porch and raised his fist to knock again and just then the door was pulled open and a gaunt old man stared at him, then looked at the carriage with its badge of the Seraphim Club. 'We weren't expecting any visitors today,' the man said in evident puzzlement.

'We have come to fetch Meg,' Sandman replied on an impulse. The man, a servant judging by his clothes, had plainly recognised the carriage and did not think its presence strange. Untimely, perhaps, but not strange, and Sandman hoped the servant would assume it had been sent by the Marquess.

'No one said she was to go anywhere.' The man was suspicious.

'London,' Sandman said.

'So who be you?' The man was tall and had a deeply lined face surrounded by unkempt white hair.

'I told you. We came to fetch Meg. Sergeant Berrigan and I.'

'Sergeant?' The man did not recognise the name, but sounded alarmed. 'You brought a lawyer?'

'He's from the club,' Sandman said, feeling the conversation slide into mutual incomprehensibility.

'His lordship said nothing about her going,' the man said cautiously.

'He wants her in London,' Sandman repeated.

'Then I'll fetch the lass,' the man said and then, before Sandman could react, he slammed the door and shot the bolts and did it so quickly that Sandman was left gaping. He was still staring at the door when he heard a bell ring inside the house and he knew that urgent sound had to be a signal to Meg. He swore.

'That's a good bloody start,' Berrigan said sarcastically.

'But the woman is here,' Sandman answered as he

walked back to the carriage, 'and he says he's fetching her.'

'Is he?'

Sandman shook his head. 'Hiding her, more like. Which means we've got to look for her, but what do we do with these two?' He gestured at Mackeson.

'Shoot the buggers, then bury them,' Berrigan growled, and was rewarded by two of Mackeson's fingers. In the end they took the carriage round to the stables, where they found the stalls and feed racks empty except for a score of broody hens, but they also discovered a brick-built tack room that had a solid door and no windows and Mackeson and the stable boy were imprisoned inside while the horses were left in the yard harnessed to the carriage. 'We'll deal with them later,' Sandman declared.

'Collect some eggs later, too,' Berrigan said with a smile, for the stable yard had been given over to chickens, seemingly hundreds of them, some looking down from the roof ridge, others on the window ledges and most hunting for grain that had been scattered among the weed-strewn, dropping-white cobbles. A cockerel stared sideways at them from the mounting block, then twitched his comb and crowed lustily as Sandman led Berrigan and Sally to the back door of Cross Hall. The door was locked. Every door was locked, but the house was no fortress and Sandman found a window that was inadequately latched and shook it hard until it came open and he could climb into a small parlour with panelled walls, an empty stone fireplace and furniture shrouded in dust sheets. Berrigan followed. 'Stay outside,' Sandman said to Sally and she nodded agreement, but a moment later clambered through the window. 'There could be a fight,' Sandman warned her.

'I'm coming in,' she insisted. 'I hate bloody chickens.'

'The girl could have left the house by now,' Berrigan said.

'She could,' Sandman agreed, yet his first instinct had been that she would hide somewhere inside and he still thought the same, 'but we'll search for her anyway,' he said, and opened the door that led into a long panelled passage. The house was silent. No pictures hung on the walls and no rugs lay on the darkened floorboards that creaked underfoot. Sandman threw open doors to see dust sheets draped over what little furniture remained. A fine staircase with an elaborately carved newel post stood in the hall and Sandman glanced into the upstairs gloom as he passed, then went on towards the back of the house.

'No one lives here,' Sally said as they discovered yet more empty rooms, 'except the chickens!'

Sandman opened a door to see a long dining table draped with sheets. 'Lord Alexander tells me that his father once completely forgot about a house he owned,' he told Sally. 'It was a big house, too. It just mouldered away until they remembered they owned it.'

'A dozy lot,' Sally said scornfully.

'Are you talking about your admirer?' Berrigan asked, amused.

'You watch it, Sam Berrigan,' Sally said. 'I've only

got to lift my little finger and I'll be Lady Whatsername and you'll be bowing and scraping to me.'

'I'll scrape you, girl,' Berrigan said, 'be a pleasure.'

'Children, children,' Sandman chided his companions, then turned sharply as a door opened suddenly at the end of the passage.

The tall, gaunt man with the wild white hair stood in the doorway, a cudgel in his right hand. 'The girl you're looking for,' he said, 'is not here.' He raised the cudgel half-heartedly as Sandman approached him, then let it drop and shuffled aside. Sandman pushed past him into a kitchen that had a big black range, a dresser and a long table. A woman, perhaps the gaunt man's wife, sat mixing pastry in a large china bowl at the table's head. 'Who are you?' Sandman asked the man.

'The steward here,' the man said, then nodded at the woman, 'and my wife is the housekeeper.'

'When did the girl leave?' Sandman asked.

'None of your business!' the woman snapped. 'And you've no business here, either. You're trespassing! So make yourselves scarce before they arrest you.'

Sandman noticed a fowling piece above the mantel. 'Who'll arrest me?' he asked.

'We've sent for aid,' the woman answered defiantly. She had white hair pulled hard back into a bun and a harsh face with a hooked nose curving towards a sharp chin. A nutcracker face, Sandman thought, and one utterly bereft of any signs of human kindness.

'You've sent for help,' Sandman said, 'but I come from the Home Secretary. From the government. I have authority,' he spoke forcefully, 'and if you want to stay out of trouble I suggest you tell me where the girl is.'

The man looked worriedly at his wife, but she was unmoved by Sandman's words. 'You ain't got no right to be in here, mister,' she said, 'so I suggests you leave before I has you locked up for the night!'

Sandman ignored her. He opened a scullery door and looked in a larder, but Meg was not hidden here. Yet still he was sure she was in the house. 'You finish searching down here, Sergeant,' he told Berrigan, 'and I'll look upstairs.'

'You really think she's here?' Berrigan sounded dubious.

Sandman nodded. 'She's here,' he said with a confidence he could not justify, yet he sensed that the steward and his wife were being untruthful. The steward, at least, was fearful. His wife was not, but the tall man was much too nervous. He should have shared his wife's defiance, insisting that Sandman was trespassing, but instead he behaved like a man with something to hide and Sandman hurried up the stairs to find it.

The rooms on the upper floor seemed as deserted and empty as those below, but then, right at the end of the corridor, next to a narrow stairway that climbed to the attics, Sandman found himself in a large bedroom that was clearly inhabited. There were faded oriental rugs on the dark floorboards while the bed, a fine four poster with threadbare tapestry hangings, had a sheet and rumpled blankets. A woman's clothes were draped over a chair and more were carelessly heaped on the two seats below the open windows that looked across a lawn to a brick wall beyond which, surprisingly close, was a church. A ginger cat slept on one of the window seats, its bed a pile of petticoats. Meg's room, Sandman thought, and he sensed she had only just left. He went back to the door and looked down the passage, but he saw nothing except dust motes drifting in the shafts of late afternoon sunlight where he had left doors ajar.

Then, where the sun struck the uneven floorboards, he saw his own footprints in the dust and he walked slowly back down the passage, looking into each room again, and in the biggest bedroom, the one that lay at the head of the fine staircase and had a wide stone fireplace carved with an escutcheon showing six martlets, he saw more scuff marks in the dust. Someone had been in the room recently and their footprints led to the stone hearth, then to the window nearest the fireplace, but did not return to the door and the room was empty and the two windows were shut. Sandman frowned at the marks, wondering if he was seeing nothing more than the errant effects of light and shadows but he could have sworn they really were footprints that ended at the window, yet when he went over he could not open it because the iron frame had rusted itself shut. So Meg had not escaped through the window, even though her footsteps, now obliterated by Sandman's own, ended there. Damn it, he thought, but she was here! He lifted the dust sheet from the bed and opened a cupboard but no one was hiding in the room.

He sat on the end of the bed, another four poster, and stared into the fireplace where a pair of blackened dogs stood on the stone hearth. On a whim he crossed to the fireplace, stooped and stared up the chimney, but the blackened shaft narrowed swiftly and hid no one. Yet Meg had been in here, he was certain of it.

The sounds of footsteps on the stairs made him stand and put a hand on the pistol's hilt, but it was Berrigan and Sally who appeared in the doorway. 'She ain't here,' Berrigan said in disgust.

'Must be a hundred places to hide in the house,' Sandman said.

'She's run off,' Sally suggested.

Sandman sat on the bed again and stared at the fireplace. Six martlets on a shield, three in the top row, two in the second and one underneath, and why would the house display that badge inside and five scallop shells on a shield outside? Five shells. He stared at the martlets and then a tune came to him, a tune and some half-remembered words that he had last heard sung by a camp fire in Spain. 'I'll give you one O,' he said.

'You'll what?' Berrigan asked, while Sally stared at Sandman as though he had gone quite mad.

'Seven for the seven stars in the sky,' Sandman said, 'six for the six proud walkers.'

'Five for the symbols at your door,' Berrigan supplied the next line.

'And there are five scallop shells carved over the front door here,' Sandman said softly, suddenly aware he could be overheard. The song's words were mostly a mystery. Four for the gospel makers was obvious enough, but what the significance of the seven stars was, Sandman did not know, any more than he knew who the six proud walkers were, but he did know what

312

five symbols at the door meant. He had learnt that years before, when he and Lord Alexander had been at school together, and Lord Alexander had excitedly discovered that when five sea-shells were set above a door or were displayed on the gable of a house it was a sign that Catholics lived within. The shells had been placed during the persecutions in Elizabeth's reign, when to be a Catholic priest in England meant risking imprisonment, torture and death, yet some folk could not live without the consolations of their faith and they had marked their houses so that their co-religionists might know a refuge was to be found within. Yet Elizabeth's men knew the meaning of the five shells as well as any Catholic did, so if a priest was in the house there had to be a place where he could be hidden, and so the householder would make a priest's hole, a hiding place so cunningly disguised that it could cheat the Protestant searchers for days.

'You look as if you're thinking,' Berrigan said.

'I want kindling,' Sandman said softly. 'Kindling, firewood, a tinder box and see if there's a big cauldron in the kitchen.'

Berrigan hesitated, wanting to ask what Sandman planned, then decided he would find out soon enough so he and Sally went back downstairs. Sandman crossed the room and ran his fingers along the joints of the linenfold panelling that covered the walls on either side of the fireplace, but so far as he could determine there was no seam in the carvings. He knocked on the panels, but nothing sounded hollow. Yet that was the point of priest's holes; they were almost impossible to detect.

The window wall and the wall by the passage looked too thin, so it had to be the fireplace wall or its opposite where the deep cupboard was – yet Sandman could discover nothing. Yet nor did he expect to find it easily. Elizabeth's searchers had been good, ruthless and well-rewarded for finding priests, yet some hiding places had eluded them despite days of looking.

'Weighs a bloody ton,' Berrigan complained as he staggered into the bedroom and dropped an enormous cauldron onto the floor. Sally was a few steps behind with a bundle of firewood.

'Where's the steward?' Sandman asked.

'Sitting in the kitchen looking as if he's sucking gunpowder,' Berrigan said.

'His wife?'

'Gone.'

'Didn't he want to know what you were doing with that?'

'I told him I'd put a hole in his face if he dared ask,' Berrigan said happily.

'Tact,' Sandman said. 'It always works.'

'So what are you doing?' Sally asked.

'We're going to burn the damn house down,' Sandman said loudly. He shifted the cauldron onto the hearth's apron. 'No one's using the house,' he still spoke loudly enough for someone two rooms away to hear him, 'and the roof needs mending. Cheaper to burn it down than clean it up, don't you think?' He put the kindling in the bottom of the cauldron, struck a spark in the tinder box and blew on the charred linen till he had a flame that he transferred to the kindling. He nursed the flame for a few seconds, then it was crackling and spreading and he put some smaller pieces of firewood on top.

It took a few minutes before the larger pieces caught the flames, but by then the cauldron was belching a thick blue-white smoke and, because the cauldron was on the hearth's apron rather than in the fireplace, almost none of the smoke was being sucked into the chimney. Sandman planned to smoke Meg out, and in case the priest's hole opened to the passage, he had put Berrigan to stand guard outside the bedroom while he and Sally stayed inside with the door shut. The smoke was choking them, so that Sally was crouching by the bed, but she was reluctant to leave in case the ruse worked. Sandman's eyes were streaming and his throat was raw, but he fed another piece of wood onto the flames and he saw the belly of the cauldron begin to glow a dull red. He opened the door a fraction to let some smoke out and fresh air in. 'You want to leave?' he hissed at Sally, and she shook her head.

Sandman stooped down to where the smoke was thinner and he thought of Meg in the priest's hole, a space so dark and black and tight and frightening. He hoped the smell of burning was already adding to her fears and that the smoke was infiltrating the cunning traps and hatches and secret doors that concealed her ancient hiding place. A log crackled, split and a puff of smoke shot out of the cauldron on a lance of flame. Sally had the dust sheet over her mouth and Sandman knew they could not last much longer, but just then there was a creaking sound, a scream and a crash like the impact of a cannon ball, and he saw a whole section of the panelling open like a door – only it was not by the fireplace but along the outer wall, between the windows, where he had thought the wall too thin for a priest's hole. Sandman pulled his sleeves over his hands and, so protected, shoved the cauldron under the chimney as Sally snatched the wrist of the screaming, terrified woman who had thought herself trapped in a burning house and now tried to extricate herself from the narrow, laddered shaft that led down from the dislodged panels.

'It's all right! It's all right!' Sally was saying as she led Meg over to the door.

And Sandman, his coat scorched and blackened, followed the two women onto the wide landing where he gasped cool clean air and stared into Meg's red-rimmed eyes. He thought how good an artist Charles Corday was, for the young woman was truly monstrously ugly, even malevolent-looking, and then he laughed because he had found her and with her he would discover the truth, and she mistook his laughter as mockery and, stepping forward, slapped his face hard.

And just then a gun fired from the hallway.

Sally screamed as Sandman pushed her down and out of the way. Meg, sensing escape, ran towards the stairs, but Berrigan tripped her. Sandman stepped over her as he limped to the balustrade, where he saw that it was the sour-looking housekeeper, much braver than her husband, who had fired the fowling piece up the staircase. But, like many raw recruits, she had shut her eyes when she pulled the trigger and she had fired too high, so that the duck shot had whipped over Sand-man's hair. A half-dozen men were behind her, one with a musket, and Sandman slapped down Berrigan's pistol. 'No shooting!' he shouted. 'No killing!'

'You've no business here!' the housekeeper screamed up at him. She had gone pale, for she had not meant to fire the gun, but when she had snatched it from her husband and aimed it up the stairway as a threat, she had inadvertently jerked the trigger. The men behind her were led by a tall, fair-haired giant armed with a musket. The rest had cudgels and sickles. To Sandman they looked like the peasants come to burn down the big house, whereas in truth they were prob-ably tenants who had come to protect the Duke of Ripon's property.

'We have every right to be here,' Sandman lied. He kept his voice calm as he drew out the Home Secretary's letter which, in truth, granted him no rights whatso-ever. 'We have been asked by the government to inves-tigate a murder,' he spoke gently as he went slowly down the stairs, always keeping his eyes on the man with the gun. He was a hugely tall man, well muscled and perhaps in his early thirties, wearing a grubby white shirt and cream-coloured trousers held up by a strip of green cloth that served as a belt. He looked oddly familiar and Sandman wondered if he had been a sol-dier. His musket was certainly an old army musket, abandoned after Napoleon's last defeat, but it was clean, it was cocked and the tall man held it confidently. 'I have here the Home Secretary's authorisation,' Sand-man said, brandishing the letter with its impressive seal, 'and we have not come to harm anyone, to steal anything or to cause damage. We have only come to ask questions.'

'You've no rights here!' the housekeeper screeched.

'Quiet, woman,' Sandman snapped in his best officer's voice. What she said was correct, absolutely correct, but she had lost her temper and Sandman suspected that these men would rather listen to a reasonable voice than to an hysterical rant. 'Does anyone want to read his lordship's letter?' he asked, holding out the paper and knowing that a mention of 'his lordship' would give them pause. 'And by the way,' he glanced back up the stairs where the smoke was thinning on the landing, 'the house is not on fire and is in no danger. Now, who wants to read his lordship's letter?'

But the man holding the musket ignored the paper. He frowned at Sandman instead and lowered the weapon's muzzle. 'Are you Captain Sandman?'

Sandman nodded. 'I am,' he said.

'By God, but I saw you knock seventy-six runs off us at Tunbridge Wells!' the man said. 'And we had Pearson and Willes bowling to you! Pearson and Willes, no less, and you knocked 'em ten ways crazy and half-way upside down.' He had now uncocked the musket and was beaming at Sandman. 'Last year, it were, and I was playing for Kent. You had us well beat, except the rain came and saved us!'

And, by the grace of God, the big man's name slithered into Sandman's mind. 'It's Mister Wainwright, isn't it?'

'Ben Wainwright it is, sir.' Wainwright, who from

his clothes must have been playing cricket when he had been summoned to the house, pulled his forelock.

'You hit a ball over the haystack, I recall,' Sandman said. 'You nearly beat us on your own!'

'Nothing like you, sir, nothing like you.'

'Benjamin Wainwright!' the housekeeper snapped. 'You ain't here to . . .'

'You be quiet, Doris,' Wainwright said, lowering the flint of the musket. 'Ain't no harm in Captain Sandman!' The men with him growled their assent. It did not matter that Sandman was in the house illegally or that he had filled its upper landing with smoke, he was a cricketer and a famous one and they were all grinning at him now, wanting his approbation. 'I heard you'd given the game up, sir?' Wainwright sounded worried. 'Is that true?'

'Oh no,' Sandman said, 'it's just I only like playing in clean games.'

'Precious few of them,' Wainwright said. 'But I should have had you on our team today, sir. Taking a fair licking, we are, from a side from Hastings. I already had my innings,' he added, explaining his absence from the game.

'There'll be other days,' Sandman consoled him, 'but for now I want to take this young lady into the garden and have a conversation with her. Or maybe there's a tavern where we can talk over an ale?' He added that because he realised it would be sensible to take Meg off the Duke of Ripon's property before someone with a rudimentary legal knowledge accused them of trespass and explained to Meg that she did not have to talk with them.

Wainwright assured them that the Castle and Bell was a fine tavern and the housekeeper, disgusted with his treason, walked away. Sandman let out a breath of relief. 'Meg?' He turned to the girl. 'If there's anything you want to take to London, fetch it now. Sergeant?' Sandman could see the girl wanted to protest, maybe even hit him again, but he gave her no time to argue. 'Sergeant? Make sure the horses are watered. Perhaps the carriage should be brought to the tavern? Sally, my dear, make sure Meg has everything she needs. And Mister Wainwright,' Sandman turned and smiled at the Kent batsman, 'I'd take it as an honour if you'd show me the tavern? Don't I recall that you make bats? I would like to talk to you about that.'

The confrontation was over. Meg, even though she was bitter, was not trying to run away and Sandman dared to hope that all would be well. One conversation now, a dash to London, and justice, that rarest of all the virtues, would be done.

Meg was bitter, sullen and angry. She resented Sandman's incursion into her life, indeed she seemed to resent life itself and for a time, sitting in the back garden of the Castle and Bell, she refused even to talk with him. She stared into the distance, drank a glass of gin, demanded another in a whining voice and then, after Benjamin Wainwright had left to see how his team was faring, she insisted that Sandman take her back to Cross

Hall. 'My chooks need looking after,' she snapped.

'Your chickens?' That surprised Sandman.

'I always liked hens,' she said defiantly.

Sandman, his cheek still stinging from her slap, shook his head in astonishment. 'I'm not taking you back to the house,' he growled, 'and you'll be damned lucky if you're not transported for life. Is that what you want? A voyage to Australia and life in a penal settlement?'

'Piss on you,' she retorted. She was dressed in a white bonnet and a plain brown serge dress that was spotted with chicken feathers. They were ugly clothes, yet they suited her for she was truly ill-favoured, yet also remarkably defiant. Sandman almost found himself admiring her belligerence, but he knew that strength was going to make her difficult to deal with. She was watching him with knowing eyes, and seemed to read his hesitation for she gave a short mocking laugh and turned away to look at the Seraphim Club's carriage, all dusty after its journey, which had just appeared on the village green. Berrigan was watering the horses at a duck pond while Sally, with some of the Sergeant's coins, was buying a jug of ale and another of gin. Pigeons were making a fuss in a newly harvested wheatfield just beyond the Castle and Bell's hedge while scores of swifts were lining the tavern's thatched ridge.

'You liked the Countess, didn't you?' Sandman said to Meg.

She spat at him just as Sally stalked out of the tavern. 'Bastards,' Sally said, 'bloody country bastards! They don't want to serve a woman!'

'I'll go,' Sandman offered.

'There's a potman bringing the jugs,' she said. 'They didn't want to serve me, but they changed their minds when I had words with them.' She flapped a hand at an irritating wasp, driving it towards Meg who gave a small scream and, when the insect would not leave her, began to cry with alarm. 'What are you napping your bib for?' Sally demanded, and Meg, uncomprehending, just stared at her. 'Why are you bleeding crying?' Sally translated. 'You've got no bleeding reason to cry. You've been swanning down here while that poor little pixie's waiting to be scragged.'

The potman, plainly terrified of Sally, brought a tray of tankards, glasses and jugs. Sandman poured ale into a pint tankard that he gave to Sally. 'Why don't you take that to the Sergeant?' he said. 'I'll talk with Meg.'

'Meaning you want me to fake away off,' Sally said.

'Give me a few minutes,' Sandman suggested. Sally took the ale and Sandman offered Meg a glass of gin, which she snatched from him. 'You were fond of the Countess, weren't you?' he asked her again.

'I've got nothing to say to you,' Meg said, 'nothing.' She drained the gin and reached for the jug.

Sandman snatched the jug away from her. 'What's your name?'

'None of your business, and give me some bloody max!' She lunged at the jug, but Sandman held it away from her.

'What's your name?' Sandman asked again, and was rewarded with a kick on his shin. He poured some of the gin onto the grass and Meg immediately went very

322

still and looked wary. 'I'm taking you to London,' Sandman told her, 'and you have two ways of going there. You can behave yourself, in which case it will be comfortable, or you can go on being rude, in which case I'm taking you to prison.'

'You can't do that!' she sneered.

'I can do what I damn well like!' Sandman snapped, astonishing her with his sudden anger. 'I have the Home Secretary's commission, miss, and you are concealing evidence in a murder case! Prison? You'll be damned lucky if it's only prison and not the gallows themselves.'

She glowered at him for a moment, then shrugged. 'My name's Hargood,' she said in a surly voice, 'Margaret Hargood.'

Sandman poured her another glass of gin. 'Where are you from, Miss Hargood?'

'Nowhere you bloody know.'

'What I do know,' Sandman said, 'is that the Home Secretary instructed me to investigate the murder of the Countess of Avebury. He did that, Miss Hargood, because he fears that a great injustice is about to be done.' The day that Viscount Sidmouth worried about an injustice to a member of the lower classes, Sandman reflected, was probably the day the sun rose in the west, but he could not admit that to the lumpen girl who had just sucked down her second gin as though she were dying of thirst. 'The Home Secretary believes, as I do,' Sandman went on, 'that Charles Corday never murdered your mistress. And we think you can confirm that.'

Meg held out her glass, but said nothing.

'You were there, weren't you,' Sandman asked, 'on the day the Countess was murdered?'

She jerked the glass, demanding more gin, but still said nothing.

'And you know,' Sandman went on, 'that Charles Corday did not commit that murder.'

She looked down at a bruised apple, a windfall, that lay on the grass. A wasp crawled on its wrinkled skin and she screamed, dropped the glass and clasped her hands to her face. Sandman stamped on the wasp, crushing the fruit. 'Meg,' he appealed to her.

'I ain't got nothing to say,' she watched the ground fearfully, evidently frightened that the wasp might resurrect itself.

Sandman picked up her glass, filled it and handed it to her. 'If you cooperate, Miss Hargood,' he said formally, 'then I shall ensure that nothing harmful happens to you.'

'I don't know nothing about it,' she said, 'nothing about any murder.' She looked defiantly at Sandman, her eyes as hard as flint.

Sandman sighed. 'Do you want an innocent man to die?' The girl made no answer, but just twisted away from him to stare across the hedge and Sandman felt a rush of indignation. He wanted to hit her and was ashamed of the intensity of that desire, so intense that he stood and began to pace up and down. 'Why are you in the Marquess of Skavadale's house?' he demanded and got no reply. 'Do you think,' he went on, 'that the Marquess will protect you? He wants you there so that the wrong man can hang, and once Corday is

324

dead then what use will you be to him? He'll kill you to stop you testifying against him. I'm just astonished he hasn't murdered you already.' That, at least, got some reaction from the girl, even if it was only to make her turn and stare at him. 'Think, girl!' Sandman said forcefully. 'Why is the Marquess keeping you alive? Why?'

'You don't know a bloody thing, do you?' Meg said scornfully.

'I'll tell you what I know,' Sandman said, his anger very close to violence. 'I know that you can save an innocent man from the gallows, and I know you don't want to, and that makes you an accomplice to murder, miss, and they can hang you for that.' Sandman waited, but she said nothing and he knew he had failed. The loss of his temper was a sign of that failure and he was ashamed of himself, but if the girl would not talk then Corday could not be saved. Meg, just with silence, could defeat him, and now more troubles, niggling and stupid troubles, piled upon him. He wanted to get Meg back to London swiftly, but Mackeson insisted that the horses were too tired to travel another mile and Sandman knew the coachman was right. That meant they would have to stay the night in the village and guard their three prisoners. Guard them, feed them, and keep an eye on the horses. Meg was put into the coach and its doors were tied and windows jammed with wedges and she must have slept, though twice she woke Sandman as she screamed and beat on the windows. She finally broke a window and began to clamber out, then Sandman heard a grunt, a stifled cry and heard her slump back. 'What happened?' he asked.

'Nothing that need trouble you,' Berrigan said. Berrigan, Sandman and Sally slept on the grass, guarding Mackeson and Billy, though there was no fight left in either man for they were confused, frightened and obedient. They reminded Sandman of a French colonel his men had taken captive in the Galician mountains, a bombastic man who had whined and complained about the conditions of his captivity until, in exasperation, Sandman's own colonel had simply freed the man. 'Bugger off,' he had told him in French, 'you're free.' And the Frenchman, so terrified of the Spanish peasants, had begged to be taken captive again. Mackeson and Billy could have walked away from their tired captors, but both were too scared of the strange village and the sheer darkness of the night and the daunting prospect of finding their own way back to London.

'So what happens now?' Berrigan asked Sandman in the short summer night.

'We take her to the Home Secretary,' Sandman said bleakly, 'and let him pick over her bones.'

It would do no good, he thought, but what choice did he have? Somewhere a dog barked in the darkness and then, as Berrigan kept watch, Sandman slept.

9

It was just after dawn when the main door of Newgate Prison was eased open and the first pieces of the scaffold were carried out into Old Bailey. The fence that surrounded the finished scaffold was fetched out first and part of it was placed halfway across the street to divert what small traffic went between Ludgate Hill and Newgate Street this early on a Sunday. William Brown, the Keeper of Newgate, came to the main door where he yawned, scratched his bald head, lit a pipe, then stepped aside as the heavy beams that formed the framework of the scaffold's platform were carried out. 'It's going to be a lovely day, Mister Pickering,' he remarked to the foreman.

'Be a hot one, sir.'

'Plenty of ale over the street.'

'God be thanked for that, sir,' Pickering said, then turned and stared up at the prison's façade. There was a window just above the Debtor's Door and he nodded at it. 'I was thinking, sir, we could save ourselves a deal of trouble by putting a platform under that window. Build it there for all time, see? And put a hinged trap there and a beam over the top and we wouldn't need to make a scaffold every time.'

The Keeper turned and stared upwards. 'You're talking yourself out of a job, Mister Pickering.'

'I'd rather have my Sundays at home, sir, with Mrs Pickering. And if you had a platform up there, sir, it wouldn't obstruct the traffic and it would give the crowd a better view.'

'Too good a view, maybe?' the Keeper suggested. 'I'm not sure the crowd ought to see the death struggles.' The present scaffold, with its screened flanks, meant that only the folk who rented the upper rooms immediately opposite the prison could see down into the pit where the hanged men and women choked to death.

'They see them struggle at Horsemonger Lane,' Pickering pointed out, 'and folk appreciate seeing them die proper. That's why they liked Tyburn! You got a proper view at Tyburn.' In the old century the condemned were taken by cart from Newgate to the wide spaces at Tyburn, where a permanent scaffold of three long beams had stood with embanked seating all around it. It had been a two-hour journey, punctuated by stops where the tavern crowds obstructed the roads, and the authorities had detested the carnival atmosphere that always accompanied a Tyburn hanging and for that reason, and in the belief that executions outside Newgate would be more dignified, they had demolished the old triangular scaffold and with it eliminated the rowdy journey. 'I saw the last hanging at Tyburn,' Pickering said. 'I was just seven, I was, and I've never forgotten it!'

'It's supposed to be memorable,' the Keeper said, 'else it won't deter, will it? So why hide the death throes? I do believe you're right, Mister Pickering, and I shall pass on your suggestion to the Court of Aldermen.'

'Kind of you, sir, kind of you.' Pickering knuckled his forehead. 'So it's a busy day tomorrow, is it, sir?'

'Just the two,' the Keeper said, 'but one of them is the painter, Corday. Remember him? He was the fellow who stabbed the Countess of Avebury.' He sighed. 'Bound to attract a fair crowd.'

'And the weather will encourage them, sir.'

'That it will,' the Keeper agreed, 'that it will, if it stays fine.' He stepped aside as one of his wife's kitchen servants hurried down the steps with a tall china jug to meet a milk-girl carrying two lidded pails on a shoulder yoke. 'Smell it, Betty,' he called after her, 'smell it! We had some sour last week.'

The platform's frame was slotted and pegged into place while the cladding for the sides and the black baize that swathed the whole scaffold were piled on the pavement. The Keeper tapped out his pipe against the door's black knocker, then went inside to change for morning service. Old Bailey had little traffic, though a few idlers vacantly watched the growing scaffold and a half-dozen choirboys, hurrying towards Saint Sepulchre's, stopped to gape as the heavy hanging beam with its dark metal hooks was carried from the prison. A waiter from the Magpie and Stump brought a tray of ale pots to the workmen, a gift from the tavern's landlord who would keep the dozen men well supplied all day. It was traditional to provide the scaffold makers with free ale, and profitable, for the presence of the gallows would mean a glut of customers next morning.

In Wapping, to the east, a chandler unlocked his back door to a single customer. His shop was closed, for it was Sunday, but this customer was special. 'It looks like being a fine day tomorrow, Jemmy,' the chandler said.

'It'll bring out the crowd,' Mister Botting agreed, edging into the shop past hanging swathes of ropes and dead-eyes, 'and I do like a crowd.'

'A skilled man should have an appreciative audience,' the chandler said, leading his guest to a table where two twelve-foot lengths of hemp rope had been laid ready for Botting's inspection. 'One-inch rope, Jemmy, oiled and boiled,' the chandler said.

'Very nice, Leonard, very nice.' Botting lowered his face and sniffed the ropes.

'Like to guess where they're from?' the chandler asked. He was proud of the two ropes that he had boiled clean, then massaged with linseed oil so that they were pliable. Afterwards he had lovingly fashioned two nooses and spliced an eye in each bitter end.

'Looks like Bridport hemp,' Botting said, though he knew it was not. He just said it to please the chandler.

And the chandler chuckled with delight. 'Bain't be a man alive that can tell that ain't Bridport hemp, Jemmy, but it ain't. It's sisal, it is, hawser laid sisal.'

'No!' Botting, his face grimacing from its nervous tic, stooped for a closer look at the rope. He was instructed to buy only the best new Bridport hemp and his bill to the Court of Aldermen would indeed demand repayment for two such expensive ropes, but it had always offended him to waste good rope on gallows scum.

'It came out of the halliard barrel of a Newcastle collier,' the chandler said. 'West African shoddy, at a guess, but boil it, oil it and give it a light coat of boot blacking and no man could tell, eh? A hog apiece to you, Jemmy.'

'A fair price,' Botting agreed. He would pay two shillings and indent nine shillings and ninepence for the two ropes, then slice them after they had served their purpose and sell off the pieces for whatever the market would bear. Neither of the men to be hanged was truly notorious, but curiosity about the Countess of Avebury's murderer might drive the price of Corday's rope up to sixpence an inch. There would be a fat profit, anyway. He tested that the noose of one rope would tighten, then nodded in satisfaction. 'And I'll be wanting some strapping cord,' he went on, 'four lengths.'

'I've a butt of Swedish lanyard all ready for you, Jemmy,' the chandler said. 'So you're still lashing their hands and elbows yourself, are you?'

'Not for long,' Botting said. 'Thank you!' This last was because the chandler had poured two tin mugs of brandy. 'They had a pair of aldermen at the last swinging,' Botting went on, 'pretending they was just there for the entertainment, but I knows better. And Mister Logan was one of them, and he's a good enough fellow. He knows what's necessary. Mind you, the other one wished he'd stayed away. Emptied his belly, he did! Couldn't stand the sight!' He chuckled. 'But Mister

Logan tipped me the wink afterwards and said they'll give me an assistant.'

'A man needs an assistant.'

'He does, he does.' Jemmy Botting drained the brandy, then collected his ropes and followed the chandler to a barrel where the lanyard cording was kept. 'Nice easy job in the morning,' he said, 'just two to top. Maybe I'll see you there?'

'Like as not, Jemmy.'

'We'll have an ale afterwards,' Botting said, 'and a chop for dinner.'

He left ten minutes later, the ropes and cords safe in his bag. He just had to fetch the two cotton bags from a seamstress, then he would be ready. He was England's hangman, and in the next day's dawn he would do his work.

Sandman was in a vile mood that Sunday morning. He had hardly slept, his temper was frayed and taut, and Meg's whining only made his bad temper worse. Berrigan and Sally were hardly more cheerful, but had the sense to keep silent, while Meg complained about being forced to London, then started screeching in protest when Sandman savaged her with accusations of selfishness and stupidity.

Billy, the stable hand, was left behind in the village. He could hardly get back to London ahead of the coach and so he could not warn the Seraphim Club of what was happening and thus it was safe to abandon him. 'But how do I get home?' he enquired plaintively.

'You do what the rest of us did from Lisbon to Toulouse,' Sandman snapped. 'You walk.'

The horses were ragged and tired. They had cropped the grass on the village green, shying away from the intrusive geese that resented their presence, but the animals were used to oats and corn, not thin grass, and they were sluggish in the harness though they responded briskly enough to Mackeson's whip and by the time the sun had climbed above the eastern trees they were going northwards at a fair clip. Church bells jangled a summer sky where high white clouds sailed westwards. 'You a churchgoer, Captain?' Berrigan asked, judging that their progress would have improved Sandman's mood.

'Of course.' Sandman was sharing the box with Berrigan and Mackeson, leaving the carriage's interior for Sally and Meg. It had been Sally's idea to share the coach with Meg. 'She don't frighten me,' Sally had said, 'and besides, maybe she'll talk to another girl?'

'I ain't a church sort of man,' Berrigan said. 'Ain't got time for it, but I do like to hear the bells.' All about them, concealed by the leafy Kent woods, the church towers and spires rang the changes. A dog cart clipped past them, loaded with children in their Sunday best and all carrying their prayer books to morning service. The children waved.

The bells went silent as the services began. The carriage came to a village, its main street deserted. They clopped past the church and Sandman heard a cellist accompanying the old hymn, 'Awake my soul and with the sun thy daily stage of duty run.' They had sung it,

333

he remembered, on the morning of the battle at Salamanca, the mens' voices hard and low beneath a sun climbing into a sky that became pitiless with heat on a day of burning death. Mackeson stopped the team in a ford on the other side of the village and, as the horses drank, Sandman folded down the steps to let Sally and Meg stretch their legs. He looked quizzically at Sally, who shook her head. 'Stubborn,' she murmured to Sandman.

Meg came down and glared at Sandman, then bent to scoop water into her mouth. Afterwards she sat on the bank and just watched the dragonflies. 'I'll kill you,' she said to Sandman, 'if the foxes have eaten my chooks.'

'You care more about your hens than the life of an innocent man?'

'Let him bloody hang,' Meg said. She had lost her bonnet and her hair was lank and tousled.

'You're going to have to talk to other men in London,' Sandman said, 'and they won't be gentle.'

The girl said nothing.

Sandman sighed. 'I know what happened,' he said. 'You were in the room where Corday was painting the Countess and someone came up the back stairs. So you took Corday down the front stairs, didn't you? You left his painting and his brushes in the Countess's bedroom and you hurried him out to the street because one of the Countess's lovers had arrived, and I know who it was. It was the Marquess of Skavadale.' Meg frowned, looked as if she was about to say something, then just stared away into the distance. 'And the Marquess of

Skavadale,' Sandman went on, 'is engaged to marry a very rich heiress, and he needs that marriage because his family is short of money, desperately short. But the girl won't marry him if she knows he was having a liaison with the Countess, and the Countess was blackmailing him. She made money that way, didn't she?'

'Did she?' Meg asked tonelessly.

'You were her procuress, weren't you?'

Meg turned her small, bitter eyes on Sandman. 'I was her protector, culley, and she needed one. Too good for her own good, she was.'

'But you didn't protect her, did you?' Sandman said harshly. 'And the Marquess killed her, and you discovered that. Did you find him there? Maybe you heard the murder? Perhaps you saw it! So he hid you away and he promised you money. But one day, Meg, he'll be tired of paying you. And he's only keeping you alive until Corday is hanged, for after that no one will believe anyone else was guilty.'

Meg half smiled. 'Why didn't he kill me there and then, eh?' She stared defiantly at Sandman. 'If he killed the Countess, why wouldn't he kill the maid? Tell me that, go on!'

Sandman could not. It was, indeed, the one thing he could not explain, though everything else made sense and he believed that, in time, even that mystery would unravel. 'Perhaps he likes you?' he suggested.

Meg stared at him incredulously for a few seconds, then gave a short bark of raucous laughter. 'The likes of him?' she asked. 'Liking me? No.' She brushed an insect off her skirt. 'He let me look after the chooks, that's all. I like chooks. I've always liked chooks.'

'Captain!' Berrigan, sitting up on the coach's box, was staring north. 'Captain!' he called again. Sandman stood and walked to the carriage and stared northwards across some fields and up a low, thickly wooded hill and there, on the crest where the London road crossed the skyline and made a gash in the trees, was a group of horsemen. 'They've been looking down here,' Berrigan said, 'like they was dragoons and they was trying to work out how many redcoats they could see.'

Sandman had no telescope and the horsemen were too far away to see clearly. There were six or seven of them and Sandman had the impression, no more, that they were gazing towards the coach and that at least one of them had a telescope. 'Could be anyone,' he said.

'Could be,' Berrigan agreed, 'only Lord Robin Holloway likes to wear a white riding coat and he's got a great black horse.'

The man at the centre of the group had a white coat and was mounted on a big black horse. 'Damn,' Sandman said mildly. Had Flossie talked in the Seraphim Club? Had she revealed that Sandman had trespassed there? In which case they would surely have connected him with the missing carriage and then started to worry about Meg in Kent, and then they would send a rescue party to make sure that Sandman did not bring the girl to London, and even as he thought that so he saw the group of horsemen spur forward and disappear into the trees. 'Whip 'em on,' he told

336

Mackeson. 'Sergeant! Get Meg into the carriage! Hurry!'

How long before the horsemen arrived? Ten minutes? Probably less. Sandman thought of turning the coach and going back to the village where there had been a crossroads, but there was no room to turn the vehicle and so, when Meg was safely bundled aboard, Mackeson urged the horses on and Sandman told him to take the first turning off the road. Any lane or farm track would do, but perversely there was none, and as the coach lurched on Sandman expected to see the horsemen appear at any second. He stared ahead, watching for the dust to show above the trees. At least the countryside was heavily wooded here, which meant that the coach would be hidden almost until they encountered the riders, and then, just as Sandman was despairing of ever finding an escape route, a narrow lane fell off to the right and he ordered Mackeson to take it.

'Rough old road, that,' Mackeson warned him.

'Just take it!'

The vehicle swung into the lane, narrowly missing the gnarled bole of an oak tree as it negotiated the sharp bend. 'I hope this goes somewhere,' Mackeson sounded amused, 'or else we're stuck to buggery.'

The coach lurched and swayed alarmingly, for the lane was nothing but deep old cart ruts that had solidified in the dry mud, but it ran between thick hedges and wide orchards and every yard took them farther from the London road. Sandman made Mackeson stop after a couple of hundred yards and then stood on the carriage roof and stared back, but he could see no horsemen on the road. Had he let his fears make him too cautious? Then Meg screamed, screamed again, and Sandman, scrambling down off the roof, heard a slap. The scream stopped and he jumped down to the road. Berrigan dropped the unbroken window. 'Only a bleeding wasp,' he said, flicking the dead insect into the hedge. 'You'd think it was a bleeding crocodile the fuss she bleeding makes!'

'I thought she was murdering you,' Sandman said, then he started to climb back up onto the coach, only to be checked by Berrigan's raised hand. He stopped, listened and heard the sound of hoofbeats.

The sound passed. The group of horsemen was on the main road, but they were not coming down this narrow lane. Sandman touched the hilt of the pistol stuck into his belt and he remembered a day up in the Pyrenees when, with a small forage party, he had been hunted by a score of dragoons. He had lost three men that day, all cut down by the straight French swords and he had only escaped because a Greenjacket officer had chanced by with a dozen men who had used their rifles to drive the horsemen away. There was no chance of a friendly rifle officer today. Would the horsemen search the lane? The hoofbeats had faded, but Sandman was reluctant to order the coach on for the vehicle was noisy, but he reflected that Meg's scream had been noisier still and that had brought no pursuers, so he hauled himself up to the box and nodded to Mackeson. 'Gently now,' he said, 'just ease her on.'

'Can't do nothing else,' Mackeson said, nodding ahead to where the lane bent sharply to the left. 'I'll have to take her on the verge, Captain, and it's a tight turn.'

'Just go slowly.' Sandman stood and looked back, but no horsemen were in sight.

'So what are we going to do?' Mackeson asked.

'There'll be a farm down here somewhere,' Sandman said, 'and if the worst comes to the worst we'll unhitch the horses, manhandle the coach round, and harness up again.'

'She ain't a vehicle built for rough roads,' Mackeson said reprovingly, but he clicked his tongue and gave an almost imperceptible tremor to the reins. The lane was narrow and the turn was excruciatingly tight, but the horses took it slowly. The carriage lurched as the wheels mounted the verge and the horses, sensing the resistance, slackened their pull so that Mackeson cracked the whip above their heads and twitched the reins again and just then the leading left wheel slid down a bank obscured by grass and dock leaves and the whole carriage tilted and Mackeson flailed for balance as Sandman gripped the handrail on the roof. The horses neighed in protest, Meg screamed in alarm, then the spokes of the wheel, taking the weight of the whole carriage in the hidden ditch, snapped one after the other and, inevitably, the wheel rim shattered and the coach lurched hard down. Mackeson had somehow managed to stay on his seat. 'I told you she ain't built for the country,' he said resentfully, 'it's a town vehicle.'

'It ain't any kind of bloody vehicle now,' Berrigan said. He had scrambled out of the canted passenger compartment and helped the two women down to the road.

'Now what will you do?' Mackeson demanded of Sandman.

Sandman teetered on the top of the coach. He was watching the road behind and listening. The wheel had broken loudly and the body of the carriage had thumped noisily onto the ditch's bank, and he thought he could hear hoofbeats again.

He drew the pistol. 'Everyone!' he snapped. 'Be quiet!'

Now he was sure he could hear the hooves, and he was certain the sound was getting closer. He cocked the pistol, jumped down to the road and waited.

The Reverend Horace Cotton, Ordinary of Newgate, seemed to crouch in his pulpit, eyes closed, as though he gathered all his forces, physical and mental, for some supreme effort. He took a breath, clenched his fists, then gave an anguished cry that echoed from the high beams of the Newgate chapel. 'Fire!' he wailed. 'Fire and pain and flames and agony! All the bestial torments of the devil await you. Fire everlasting and pain unimaginable and unassuaged weeping and the gnashing of teeth and when the pain will seem to you to be unbearable, when it will seem that no soul, not even one as rotten as yours, can endure such inflictions for a moment longer, then you will learn that it is but the beginning!' He let that last word ring about the chapel for a few seconds, then lowered his voice to a tone of sweet reason that was scarce above a whisper. 'It is but the beginning of your anguish. It is but the commencement of your punishment which will torment you through eternity. Even as the stars die and new firmaments are born, so you will scream in the fire which will rend your flesh like the tearing of a hook and like the searing of a brand.' He leant from the pulpit, his eyes wide, and stared down into the Black Pew where the two condemned men sat beside the black-painted coffin. 'You will be the playthings of demons,' he promised them, 'racked and burnt and beaten and torn. It will be pain without end. Agony without surcease. Torment without mercy.'

The silence in the chapel was broken by the sound of mallets erecting the scaffold beyond the high windows and by Charles Corday's weeping. The Reverend Cotton straightened, pleased that he had broken one of the wretches. He looked at the pews where the other prisoners sat, some waiting for their own turn in the Black Pew and others biding their time before they were taken to the ships that would carry them to Australia and oblivion. He looked higher up at the public gallery, crowded as it ever was on the day before a hanging. The worshippers in that gallery paid for the privilege of watching condemned felons listen to their burial service. It was a warm day and earlier in the service some of the women in the gallery had tried to cool themselves with fans, but no painted cardboard fluttered now. Everyone was still, everyone was silent, everyone was caught up in the terrible words that the Ordinary span like a web of doom above the heads of the two condemned men.

'It is not I who promises you this fate,' the Reverend

Cotton said in warning, 'it is not I who foresees your soul's torment, but God! God has promised you this fate! Through all eternity, when the saints are gathered beside the crystal river to sing God's praises, you will scream in pain.' Charles Corday sobbed, his thin shoulders heaving and his head lowered. His leg irons, joined to an iron band about his waist, chinked slightly as he shuddered with each sob. The Keeper, in his own family pew just behind the Black Pew, frowned. He was not sure these famous sermons were of much help in keeping order within the prison, for they reduced men and women to quivering terror or else prompted an impious defiance. The Keeper would have much preferred a quiet and dignified service, mumbled and sedate, but London expected the Ordinary to put on a display and Cotton knew how to live up to those expectations.

'Tomorrow,' Cotton thundered, 'you will be taken out to the street and you will look up and see God's bright sky for the very last time, and then the hood will be placed over your eyes and the noose will be looped about your necks and you will hear the great beating of the devil's wings as he hovers in waiting for your soul. Save me, Lord, you will cry, save me!' He fluttered his hands towards the ceiling beams as if signalling to God. 'But it will be too late, too late! Your sins, your wilful sins, your own wickednesses, will have brought you to that dread scaffold where you will fall to the rope's end and there you will choke and you will twitch and you will struggle for breath, and the struggle will avail you nothing and the pain will fill you! And then the darkness will come and your souls will rise from this earthly pain to the great seat of judgement where God awaits you. God!' Cotton raised his plump hands again, this time in supplication as he repeated the word. 'God! God will be waiting for you in all His mercy and majesty, and He will examine you! He will judge you! And He will find you wanting! Tomorrow! Yes, tomorrow!' He pointed at Corday, who still had his head lowered. 'You will see God. The two of you, as clearly as I see you now, will see the dread God, the Father of us all, and He will shake His head in disappointment and He will command that you be taken from His presence, for you have sinned. You have offended Him who has never offended us. You have betrayed your maker who sent His only begotten son to be our salvation, and you will be taken from before His great throne of mercy and you will be cast down into the uttermost depths of hell. Into the flames. Into the fire. Into the everlasting pain!' He drew the sounds out into a quavering moan, and then, when he heard a gasp from a frightened woman in the public gallery, he repeated the phrase. 'Into the everlasting pain!' He shrieked the last word, paused so that the whole chapel could hear the woman sobbing in the gallery, then leant towards the Black Pew and dropped his voice into a hoarse whisper. 'And you will suffer, oh, how you will suffer, and your suffering, your torment, will commence tomorrow.' His eyes widened as his voice rose. 'Think of it! Tomorrow! When we who are left on this earth are having our breakfast you will be in agony. When the rest of us are closing our eyes and clasping our prayerful hands to say a grace of thanks to a benevolent God for providing us with our porridge, with our bacon and eggs, with toast and chops, with braised liver or even,' and here the Reverend Cotton smiled, for he liked to introduce homely touches into his sermons, 'perhaps even a dish of devilled kidneys, at that very moment you will be screaming with the first dreadful pains of eternity! And, through all eternity, those torments will become ever more dreadful, ever more agonising and ever more terrible! There will be no end to your pains, and their beginning is tomorrow.' He was leaning out from the canopied pulpit now, leaning so that his voice fell like a spear into the Black Pew. 'Tomorrow you will meet the devil. You will meet him face to face and I shall weep for you. I shall tremble for you. Yet above all I shall thank my Lord and Saviour, Jesus Christ, that I shall be spared your pain, and that instead I shall be given a crown of righteousness for I have been saved.' He straightened and clutched his hands to his chest. 'I have been saved! Redeemed! I have been washed in the blood of the Lamb and I have been blessed by the grace of Him who alone can take away our pain.'

The Reverend Horace Cotton paused. He was forty-five minutes into the sermon and had as long again to go. He took a sip of water as he stared down at the two prisoners. One was weeping and the other was resisting, so he would try harder.

He took a breath, summoned his powers, and preached on.

*   *   *

No horsemen came down the lane. The sound of their hooves sounded loud on the London road for a while, then they faded and at last vanished in the heat of the day. Somewhere, very far off, church bells began ringing the changes after matins.

'So what are you going to do?' Mackeson asked again, this time with an undisguised note of triumph. He sensed that the wreck of the coach had ruined Sandman's chances and his pleasure in that gave him a kind of revenge for the humiliations that had been heaped on him over the last day and two nights.

'What I'm going to do,' Sandman retorted, 'is none of your damn business, but what you're going to do is stay here with the carriage. Sergeant? Cut the horses out of the traces.'

'I can't stay here!' Mackeson protested.

'Then start bloody walking,' Sandman snarled, then turned on Meg and Sally. 'You two are riding bareback,' he said.

'I can't ride,' Meg protested.

'Then you'll bloody well walk to London!' Sandman said, his temper slipping dangerously. 'And I'll make damn sure you do!' He snatched the whip from Mackeson.

'She'll ride, Captain,' Sally said laconically, and sure enough, when the team was cut from the traces, Meg obediently scrambled up the unfolded carriage steps to sit on a horse's broad back with her legs dangling down one flank and with her hands gripping the fillet strap that ran along the mare's spine. She looked terrified while Sally, even without a saddle, appeared graceful.

'What now?' Berrigan asked.

'Main road,' Sandman said, and he and the Sergeant led all four horses back along the lane. It was a risk using the London road, but the horsemen, if they were indeed looking for the missing carriage, had taken their search southwards. Sandman walked cautiously, but they met no one until they came to a village where a dog chased after the horses and Meg screamed for fear when her mare skittered sideways. A woman came out of a cottage and slapped at the dog with a broom.

A milestone just beyond the village said that London was forty-two miles away. 'A long day ahead,' Berrigan said.

'Day and night,' Sandman said gloomily.

'I ain't staying up here all day and night,' Meg complained.

'You'll do as you're told,' Sandman said, but at the next village Meg began to scream that she had been snatched from her home and a small indignant crowd followed the plodding horses until the village rector, a napkin tucked into his neck because he had been plucked from his dinner table, came to investigate the noise.

'She's mad,' Sandman told the priest.

'Mad?' The rector looked up at Meg and shuddered at the malevolence in her face.

'I've been kidnapped!' she screamed.

'We're taking her to London,' Sandman explained, 'to see the doctors.'

'They're stealing me!' Meg shouted.

'She's got bats in her belfry,' Sally said helpfully.

'I've done nothing!' Meg shouted, then she dropped to the ground and tried to run away, but Sandman ran after her, tripped her, and then knelt beside her. 'I'll break your bloody neck, girl,' he hissed at her.

The rector, a plump man with a shock of white hair, tried to pull Sandman away. 'I'd like to talk with the girl,' he said. 'I insist on talking to her.'

'Read this first,' Sandman said, remembering the Home Secretary's letter and handing it to the rector. Meg, sensing trouble in the letter, tried to snatch it away and the rector, impressed by the Home Office seal, stepped away from her to read the crumpled paper. 'But if she's mad,' he said to Sandman when he had finished reading, 'why is Viscount Sidmouth involved?'

'I'm not mad!' Meg protested.

'In truth,' Sandman spoke to the rector in a low voice, 'she's wanted for a murder, but I don't want to frighten your parishioners. Better for them to think that she's ill, yes?'

'Quite right, quite right.' The priest looked alarmed and thrust the letter back at Sandman as though it were contagious. 'But maybe you should tie her hands?'

'You hear that?' Sandman turned on Meg. 'He says I should tie your hands, and I will if you make more noise.'

She recognised defeat and began to swear viciously, which only made the rector believe Sandman's claim. He began using his napkin like a fly-swatter to drive his parishioners away from the cursing girl who, seeing that her bid for freedom had failed, and fearing that Sandman would pinion her if she did not cooperate, used a stone watering trough as a mounting block to get back onto her horse. She was still swearing as they left the village.

They trudged on. They were all tired, all irritable, and the heat and the long road sapped Sandman's strength. His clothes felt sticky and filthy, and he could feel a blister growing on his right heel. He was still limping because of the damage he had done to his ankle jumping onto the stage of the Covent Garden theatre, but like all infantryman he believed the best way to cure a sprain was to walk it out. Even so it had been a long time since he had walked this far. Sally encouraged him to ride, but he wanted to keep a spare horse fresh and so he shook his head and then fell into the mindless trudge of the soldier's march, scarce noticing the landscape as his thoughts skittered back to the long dusty roads of Spain and the scuff of his company's boots and the wheat growing on the verges where the seeds had fallen from the commissary carts. Even then he had rarely ridden his horse, preferring to keep the animal fresh.

'What happens when we get to London?' Berrigan broke the silence after they had passed through yet another village.

Sandman blinked as though he had just woken up. The sun was sinking, he saw, and the church bells were calling for evensong. 'Meg is going to tell the truth,' he answered after a while. She snorted in derision and Sandman held his temper in check. 'Meg,' he said gently, 'you want to go back to the Marquess's house, is that it? You want to go back to your chickens?'

348

'You know I do,' she said.

'Then you can,' he said, 'but first you're going to tell part of the truth.'

'Part of?' Sally asked, intrigued.

'Part of the truth,' Sandman insisted. He had, without realising it, been thinking about his dilemma and suddenly the answer seemed clear. He had not been hired to discover the Countess's murderer, but rather to determine whether or not Corday was guilty. So that was all he would tell the Home Secretary. 'It doesn't matter,' he told Meg, 'who killed the Countess. All that matters is that you know Corday did not. You took him out of her bedroom while she was still alive, and that's all I want you to tell the Home Secretary.'

She just stared at him.

'That is the truth, isn't it?' Sandman asked. She still said nothing, and he sighed. 'Meg, you can go back to the Marquess's house. You can do whatever you want with the rest of your life, but first you have to tell that one small part of the truth. You know Corday is innocent, don't you?'

And, at last, at long last, she nodded. 'I saw him out the street door,' she said softly.

'And the Countess was still alive?'

'Of course she was,' Meg said. 'She told him to come back the next afternoon, but by then he was arrested.'

'And you'll tell that to the Home Secretary?'

She hesitated, then nodded. 'I'll tell him that,' she said, 'and that's all I'll tell him.'

'Thank you,' Sandman said.

A milestone told him that Charing Cross lay eighteen

349

miles ahead. The city's smoke filled the sky like a brown fog while to his right, glimpsed through the folds of darkening hills, the shining Thames lay flat as a blade. Sandman's tiredness vanished. Part of the truth, he thought, would be enough and his job, thank God, would be done.

Jemmy Botting, hangman of England, came to Old Bailey in the early evening to inspect the finished scaffold. One or two passers-by, recognising him, called out ironic greetings, but Botting ignored them.

He had little to inspect. He took it on trust that the beams were properly bolted together, the planks nailed down and the baize properly secured. The platform did sway a little, but it always had and the motion was no worse than being on the deck of a ship in a very slight swell. He pulled the peg that held the trapdoor's support beam in place, then went down below into the gloom beneath the platform where he seized the rope that tugged the beam free. It gave way with a judder, then the trapdoor swung down to let in a wash of evening sunlight.

Botting did not like that judder. No one had been standing on the trapdoor, yet still the beam had been reluctant to move, so he opened his bag and took out a small jar of tallow that had been a gift from the chandler. He climbed the wooden framework and greased the beam until its surface felt slippery, then he raised the trapdoor and clumsily pushed the beam back into place. Two rats watched him and he growled at them. He clambered down to the Old Bailey's cobbles and pulled the rope again and this time the beam slid easily and the trapdoor thumped down to bang against two of the upright supports. 'Bloody works, eh?' Botting said to the rats that were quite unafraid of his presence.

He replaced the trapdoor and beam, put the tallow back in his bag and climbed to the top of the scaffold where he first replaced the locking peg, then gingerly tested the firmness of the trapdoor by putting one foot on its planks and slowly easing his weight onto that leg. He knew it was secure, knew it would not give way beneath him, yet still he tested it. He did not want to become London's laughing stock by pushing a prisoner onto a trap that gave way before the rope was round the man's neck. He grinned at the thought, then, confident that all was ready, he went to the Debtor's Door and knocked loudly. He would be given dinner in the prison, then provided with a small bedroom above the Lodge. 'Got any rat poison?' he asked the turnkey who opened the door. 'Only there's rats the size of bleeding foxes under the scaffold. That platform can't have been up more than two hours yet there's already rats there.'

'Rats everywhere,' the turnkey said, then locked the door.

Beneath them, even though it was a warm evening, the cellars of Newgate Prison held a chill and so, before Charles Corday and the other condemned man were put into the death cell, a coal fire was lit in the small hearth. The chimney did not draw well at first and the cell filled with smoke, but then the flue heated and the air cleared, though the stench of coal smoke stayed. A metal chamber pot was put in a corner of the cell, though no screen was provided for privacy. Two iron cots with straw palliasses and thin blankets were put by the wall and a table and chairs were provided for the turnkeys who would watch the prisoners through the night. Lamps were hung from iron hooks. At dusk the two men who would die in the morning were brought to the cell and given a meal of pease pottage, pork chops and boiled cabbage. The Keeper came to see them during their supper and he thought, as he waited for them to finish their meal, that the two men were so utterly dissimilar. Charles Corday was slight, pale and nervous while Reginald Venables was a hulking brute with a lavish dark beard and a grimly hard face, yet it was Corday who had committed murder while Venables was being hanged for the theft of a watch.

Corday merely picked at his food then, his leg irons clanking, went to his cot where he lay down and gazed wide-eyed at the damp stones of the vaulted ceiling. 'Tomorrow . . .' the Keeper began as Venables finished his meal.

'I hope that damn preacher won't be there,' Venables interrupted.

'Silence while the Keeper's talking,' the senior turnkey growled.

'The preacher will be there,' the Keeper said, 'to offer what spiritual comfort he can.' He waited as the turnkey removed the spoons from the table. 'Tomorrow,' he started again, 'you will be taken from here to the Association Room where your irons will be struck and your arms pinioned. You will already have

352

been given breakfast, but there will be brandy for you in the Association Room and I advise you to drink it. After that we walk to the street.' He paused. Venables watched him with a resentful eye while Corday seemed oblivious. 'It is customary,' the Keeper went on, 'to slip the hangman a coin because he can make your passage to the next world less painful. Such an emolument is not something of which I can approve, but he is an officer of the city, not of the jail, and so I can do nothing to end the practice. But even without such an emolument you will find that your punishment is not painful and is soon done.'

'Bloody liar,' Venables snarled.

'Silence!'

'It's all right, Mister Carlisle,' the Keeper said to the offended turnkey. 'Some men,' he continued, 'go unwilling to the scaffold and attempt to hinder the necessary work. They do not succeed. If you resist, if you struggle, if you try to inconvenience us, then you will still be hanged, but you will be hanged painfully. It is best to cooperate. It is easier for you and easier for your loved ones who might be watching.'

'Easier for you, you mean,' Venables observed.

'No duties are easy,' the Keeper said sanctimoniously, 'not if they are done with proper assiduity.' He moved to the door. 'The turnkeys will stay here all night. If you require spiritual comfort then they can summon the Ordinary. I wish you a good night.'

Corday spoke for the first time. 'I'm innocent,' he said, his voice close to breaking.

'Yes,' the Keeper said, embarrassed, 'yes indeed.' He

found he had nothing more to say on the subject so he just nodded to the turnkeys. 'Good night, gentlemen.'

'Good night, sir,' Mister Carlisle, the senior turnkey, responded, then stood to attention until the Keeper's footsteps had faded down the passage. Then he relaxed and turned to look at the two prisoners. 'You want spiritual bloody comfort,' he growled, 'then you don't disturb me and you don't disturb the Reverend Cotton, but you get down on your bloody knees and disturb Him up there by asking Him for bloody forgiveness. Right, George,' he turned to his companion, 'spades are trumps, is that right?'

In the Birdcage Walk, which was the underground passage that led from the prison to the courtrooms of the Session House, two felons were working with pick-axes and spades. Lanterns had been hung from the passage ceiling and the flagstones, great slabs of granite, had been pried up and stacked to one side. A stench now filled the passageway; a noxious stink of gas, lime and rotted flesh.

'Christ!' one of the felons said, recoiling from the smell.

'You won't find Him down there,' a turnkey said, backing away from the space that had been cleared of its flagstones. When the Birdcage Walk had been built the paving slabs had been laid direct on the London clay, but this clay had a mottled, dark look in the uncertain light of the guttering lanterns.

'When was this bit of the passage last used?' one of the prisoners asked.

'Got to be two years ago,' the turnkey said, but sounded dubious, 'at least two years.'

'Two years?' the prisoner said scornfully. 'They're still bloody breathing down there.'

'Just get it over with, Tom,' the turnkey encouraged him, 'then you get this.' He held up a bottle of brandy.

'God bloody help us,' Tom said gloomily, then took a deep breath and struck down with his spade.

He and his companion were digging the graves for the two men who would be executed in the morning. Some of the bodies were taken for dissection, but hungry as the anatomists were for bodies they could not take them all and so most were brought here and put into unmarked graves. Although the passage was short and the prison buried the corpses in quicklime to hasten their decomposition, and though they dug up the floor in a strict rotation so that no part of it was excavated too soon after a burial, still the picks and spades struck down into bones and rotting, deliquescent clay. The whole floor was buckled, looking as though it had been deformed by an earthquake, but in truth it was merely the flagstones settling as the bodies decomposed beneath. Yet, though the passage stank and the clay was choked with unrotted flesh, still more corpses were brought and thrust down into the filth.

Tom, ankle-deep in the hole, brought out a yellow skull that he rolled down the passageway. 'He looks in the pink, don't he?' he said, and the two turnkeys and the second prisoner began to laugh and somehow could not stop.

Mister Botting ate lamb chops, boiled potatoes, and

turnips. The Keeper's kitchen provided a syrup pudding to follow, then a tin mug of strong tea and a beaker of brandy. Afterwards Mister Botting slept.

Two watchmen stood guard on the scaffold. Just after midnight the skies clouded over and a brief shower blew chill from Ludgate Hill. A handful of folk, eager for the best positions by the railings that fenced off the gallows, were sleeping on the cobbles and were woken by the rain. They grumbled, shrugged deeper into their blankets and tried to sleep again.

Dawn came early. The clouds shredded, leaving a pearl-white sky laced with the frayed brown streaks of coal smoke. London stirred.

And in Newgate there would be devilled kidneys for breakfast.

10

Sally's horse, a gelding, had fallen lame just after Sunday's nightfall, then Berrigan's right boot had lost its sole, so they tied the gelding to a tree, Berrigan scrambled onto the back of the third horse and Sandman, whose boots were just holding together, led the two girls' horses. 'If we don't return all the horses to the Seraphim Club,' Sandman remarked, worrying about the beast they had simply abandoned, 'they could accuse us of horse thieving.'

'They could hang us for that,' Berrigan retorted, then grinned, 'but I wouldn't worry about it, Captain. With what I know about the Seraphim Club they ain't going to accuse us of anything.'

The remaining three horses were so bone tired that Sandman reckoned they would probably have made faster progress by leaving them behind, but Meg had resigned herself to telling the partial truth and he did not want to disturb her by suggesting she walk, especially after she began complaining again, saying her chickens would be eaten by the foxes, but then Sally had begun singing and that stopped the whining. Sally's first song was a soldier's favourite, 'The Drum Major', that told of a girl so in love with her redcoat that she followed him into the regiment where she became the drum major and escaped detection till she took a bath in a stream and was almost raped by another soldier. She escaped him, the officers discovered her identity and insisted she marry her lover. 'I like stories that end happily,' Berrigan had remarked, then laughed when Sally began her second song, which was also a soldier's favourite, but this one was about a girl who did not escape and Sandman was somewhat shocked, but not too surprised, that Sally knew all the words, and Berrigan sang along and Meg actually laughed when the Colonel took his turn and failed to perform, and Sally had still been singing when the robin redbreast pounced on them from behind a hollow tree beside the road.

The patrolling horseman suspected that the four bedraggled travellers had stolen the three carriage horses, in which he was not far wrong, and he faced them with one of his pistols drawn. The gun's muzzle and the steel buttons on his uniform blue coat and red waistcoat shone in the moonlight. 'In the name of the King,' he said, not wanting to be mistaken for a highwayman, 'stand! Who are you? And where are you travelling?'

'Your name?' Sandman had snapped the question back. 'Your name, rank? What regiment did you serve in?' The redbreasts were all men who had served in the cavalry. None was young, for it was reckoned that a young man would be too amenable to temptation, and so steadier, older and well-recommended cavalrymen were hired to try to keep the thieves off the King's highways.

'I ask the questions here,' the redbreast had retorted, but tentatively because there was an undeniable authority in Sandman's voice. Sandman might be in dusty, crumpled clothes, but he had plainly been an officer.

'Put the gun up! Quickly, man!' Sandman said, deliberately talking to the redbreast as though he was still in the army. 'I'm on official business, authorised by Viscount Sidmouth, the Home Secretary, and this paper bears his seal and signature, and if you cannot read then you had better take us right now to your magistrate.'

The redbreast carefully lowered the flint of the pistol, then slid the weapon into its saddle holster. 'Lost your coach, sir?'

'Broke a wheel thirty miles back,' Sandman said. 'Now, are you going to read this letter or would you rather take us to your magistrate?'

'I'm sure everything's in order, sir.' The patrolling redbreast did not want to admit that he could not read and certainly did not want to disturb his supervising magistrate who would, by now, have sat down to a lavish supper, and so he just moved his horse aside to let Sandman and his three companions pass. Sandman supposed he could have insisted on being taken to the magistrate and used his letter from the Home Office to arrange another carriage or, at the very least, four fresh saddle horses, but that would all have taken time, a lot of time, and it would have disturbed Meg's fragile equanimity, and so they walked on until, well after midnight, they trailed across London Bridge and so to the Wheatsheaf where Sally took Meg to her own room and Sandman let Berrigan use his room while he collapsed in the back parlour, not in one of the big chairs, but on the wooden floor so that he would wake frequently, and it was when the bells of Saint Giles were ringing six in the morning that he dragged himself upstairs, woke Berrigan and told him to stir the girls from their beds. Then he shaved, found his cleanest shirt, brushed his coat and washed the dirt from his disintegrating boots before, at half past six, with Berrigan, Sally and a very reluctant Meg in tow, he set out for Great George Street and the end, he hoped, of his investigation.

Lord Alexander Pleydell and his friend, Lord Christopher Carne, almost gagged when they entered the Press Yard for the smell was terrible, worse than the reek of the sewer outflows where the Fleet Ditch joined the Thames. The turnkey who was escorting them chuckled. 'I don't notice the smell no more, my lords,' he said, 'but I do suppose it's mortal bad in its way, mortal bad. Mind the steps here, my lords, do mind 'em.'

Lord Alexander gingerly took the handkerchief away from his nose. 'Why is it called the Press Yard?'

'In days gone by, my lord, this is where the prisoners was pressed. They was squashed, my lord. Weighted down by stones, my lord, to persuade them to tell the truth. We don't do it any longer, more's the pity, and as a consequence they lies like India rugs.'

'You squeezed them to death?' Lord Alexander asked, shocked.

'Oh no, my lord, not to death. Not to death, not unless they made a mistake and piled too many rocks on!' He chuckled, finding the notion amusing. 'No, my lord, they just got squashed till they told the truth. It's a fair persuader to a man or woman to tell the truth, my lord, if they're carrying half a ton of rocks on their chests!' The turnkey chuckled again. He was a fat man with leather breeches, a stained coat, and a stout billy club. 'Hard to breathe,' he said, still amused, 'very hard to breathe.'

Lord Christopher Carne shuddered at the terrible stench. 'Are there no drains?' he enquired testily.

'The prison is very up to date, my lord,' the turnkey hastened to assure him, 'very up to date, it is, with the proper drains and proper close stools. Truth is, my lord, we spoils them, we does, we spoils them, but they is filthy animals. They fouls their own nest what we give them clean and tidy.' He put down his billy club as he closed and bolted the barred gate by which they had entered the yard that was long, high and narrow. The stones of the yard seemed damp, even on this dry day, as though the misery and fear of centuries had soaked into the granite and could not be wrung out.

'If you no longer press the prisoners,' Lord Alexander enquired, 'what is the yard used for instead?'

'The condemned have the freedom of the Press Yard, sir, during the daylight hours,' the turnkey said, 'which is an example, my lords, of how kindly disposed towards

361

'em we are. We spoils them, we do. There was a time when a prison was a prison, not a glorified tavern.'

'Liquor is sold here?' Lord Alexander enquired acidly.

'Not any longer, my lord. Mister Brown, that's the Keeper, my lord, closed down the grog shop on account that the scum was getting lushed and disorderly, my lord, but not that it makes any difference 'cos now they just have their liquor sent in from the Lamb or the Magpie and Stump.' He cocked an ear to the sound of a church bell tolling the quarter hour. 'Bless me! Saint Sepulchre's telling us it's a quarter to seven already! If you turn to your left, my lords, you can join Mister Brown and the other gentlemen in the Association Room.'

'The Association Room?' Lord Alexander enquired.

'Where the condemned associate, my lord, during the daylight hours,' the turnkey explained, 'except on high days and holidays like today, and those windows to your left, my lord, those are the salt boxes.'

Lord Alexander, despite his opposition to the hanging of criminals, found himself curiously fascinated by everything he saw and now gazed at the fifteen barred windows. 'That name,' he said, 'salt boxes. You know its derivation?'

'Nor its inclination, my lord,' the turnkey laughed, 'only I suspects that they're called salt boxes on account of being stacked up like boxes.'

'The salt b-boxes are what?' Lord Christopher, who was very pallid this morning, asked.

'Really, Kit,' Lord Alexander said with uncalled-for

asperity, 'everyone knows they're where the condemned spend their last days.'

'The devil's waiting rooms, my lord,' the turnkey said, then pulled open the Association Room door and ostentatiously held out his hand, palm upward.

Lord Alexander, who took pride in his notions of equality, was about to force himself to shake the turnkey's hand, then realised the significance of the palm. 'Ah,' he said, taken aback, but hurriedly fished in his pocket and brought out the first coin he found. 'Thank you, my good man,' he said.

'Thank you, your lordship, thank you,' the turnkey said and then, to his astonishment, saw he had been tipped a whole sovereign and hastily pulled off his hat and tugged his forelock. 'God bless you, my lord, God bless.'

William Brown, the Keeper, hurried to meet his two new guests. He had met neither man before, but recognised Lord Alexander by his clubbed foot and so took off his hat and bowed respectfully. 'Your lordship is most welcome.'

'Brown, is it?' Lord Alexander asked.

'William Brown, my lord, yes. Keeper of Newgate, my lord.'

'Lord Christopher Carne,' Lord Alexander introduced his friend with a rather vague wave of the hand. 'His stepmother's murderer is being hanged today.'

The Keeper bowed again, this time to Lord Christopher. 'I do trust your lordship finds the experience both a revenge and a comfort, and will you now permit me to name the Ordinary of Newgate?' He led them to

363

where a stout man in an old-fashioned wig, a cassock, surplice and Geneva bands was waiting with a smile on his plump face. 'The Reverend Doctor Horace Cotton,' the Keeper said.

'Your lordship is most welcome,' Cotton bowed to Lord Alexander. 'I believe your lordship is, like me, in holy orders?'

'I am,' Lord Alexander said, 'and this is my particular friend, Lord Christopher Carne, who also hopes to take orders one day.'

'Ah!' Cotton clasped his hands prayerfully and momentarily raised his eyes to the rafters. 'I deem it a blessing,' he said, 'when our nobility, the true leaders of our society, are seen to be Christians. It is a shining example for the common ruck, don't you agree? And you, my lord,' he turned to Lord Christopher, 'I understand that this morning you will see justice done for the grave insult committed against your family?'

'I hope to,' Lord Christopher said.

'Oh, really, Kit!' Lord Alexander expostulated. 'The revenge your family seeks will be provided in eternity by the fires of hell . . .'

'Praise Him!' the Ordinary interjected.

'And it is neither seemly nor civilised of us to hurry men to that condign fate,' Lord Alexander finished.

The Keeper looked astonished. 'You would surely not abolish the punishment of hanging, my lord?'

'Hang a man,' Lord Alexander said, 'and you deny him the chance of repentance. You deny him the chance of being pricked, day and night, by his conscience. It should be sufficient, I would have thought, to simply transport all felons to Australia. I am reliably informed it is a living hell.'

'They will suffer from their consciences in the real hell,' Cotton put in.

'So they will, sir,' Lord Alexander said, 'so they will, but I would rather a man came to repentance in this world, for he surely has no chance of salvation in the next. By execution we deny men their chance of God's grace.'

'It's a novel argument,' Cotton allowed, though dubiously.

Lord Christopher had been listening to this conversation with a harried look and now blurted out an intervention. 'Are you,' he stared at the Ordinary, 'related to Henry Cotton?'

The conversation died momentarily, killed by Lord Christopher's sudden change of tack. 'To whom, my lord?' the Ordinary enquired.

'Henry Cotton,' Lord Christopher said. He seemed to be in the grip of some very powerful emotion, as if he found being inside Newgate Prison almost unbearable. He was pale, there was sweat on his brow, and his hands were trembling. 'He was G-Greek reader at Christ Church,' he explained, 'and is now the sub librarian at the Bodleian.'

The Ordinary took a step away from Lord Christopher, who looked as if he was about to be ill. 'I had thought, my lord,' the Ordinary said, 'to be connected instead with the Viscount Combermere. Distantly.'

'Henry Cotton is a g-good fellow,' Lord Christopher said, 'a very good fellow. A sound scholar.'

'He's a pedant,' Lord Alexander growled. 'Related to Combermere, are you, Sir Stapleton Cotton as was? He almost lost his right arm at the battle of Salamanca and what a tragic loss that would have been.'

'Oh indeed,' the Ordinary agreed piously.

'You are not usually tender about soldiers,' Lord Christopher observed to his friend.

'Combermere can be a very astute batsman,' Lord Alexander said, 'especially against twisting balls. Do you play cricket, Cotton?'

'No, my lord.'

'It's good for the wind,' Lord Alexander declared mysteriously, then turned to offer a lordly inspection of the Association Room, staring up at the ceiling beams, rapping one of the tables, then peering at the cooking pots and cauldrons stacked by the embers of the fire. 'I see our felons live in some comfort,' he remarked, then frowned at his friend. 'Are you quite well, Kit?'

'Oh yes, indeed, yes,' Lord Christopher said hastily, but he looked anything but well. There were beads of sweat on his brow and his skin was paler than usual. He took off his spectacles and polished them with a handkerchief. 'It is just that the apprehension of seeing a man launched into eternity is conducive to reflection,' he explained, 'very conducive. It is not an experience to be taken lightly.'

'I should think not indeed,' Lord Alexander said, then turned an imperious eye on the other breakfast guests who seemed to be looking forward to the morning's events with an unholy glee. Three of them, standing close to the door, laughed at a jest and Lord

Alexander scowled at them. 'Poor Corday,' he said.

'Why do you pity the man, my lord?' the Reverend Cotton asked.

'It seems likely he is innocent,' Lord Alexander said, 'but it seems proof of that innocence has not been found.'

'If he was innocent, my lord,' the Ordinary observed with a patronising smile, 'then I am confident that the Lord God would have revealed that to us.'

'You're saying you have never hanged an innocent man or woman?' Lord Alexander demanded.

'God would not allow it,' the Reverend Cotton averred.

'Then God had better get his boots on this morning,' Lord Alexander said, then turned as a barred door at the other end of the room opened with a sudden and harsh squeal. For a heartbeat no one appeared in the doorway and it seemed as though all the guests held their breath, but then, to an audible gasp, a short and burly man carrying a stout leather bag stumped into sight. The man was red-faced and dressed in brown gaiters, black breeches and a black coat that was buttoned too tightly over his protuberant belly. He respectfully pulled off a shabby brown hat when he saw the waiting gentry, but he offered no greeting and no one in the Association Room acknowledged his arrival.

'That's the man Botting,' the Ordinary whispered.

'Ponderous sort of name for a hangman,' Lord Alexander observed in a tactlessly loud voice. 'Ketch, now, that's a proper hangman's name. But Botting? Sounds like a disease of cattle.'

367

Botting shot a hostile glance at the tall, red-haired Lord Alexander who was quite unmoved by the animosity, though Lord Christopher recoiled a step, perhaps in horror at the hangman's beef-like face that was disfigured by warts, wens and scars and subject to involuntary grimaces every few seconds. Botting gave the other guests a sardonic look, then heaved a bench aside so he could drop his leather bag onto a table. He unbuckled the bag and, conscious of being watched, brought out four coils of thin white cord. He placed the coils on the table and then took from the bag two heavy ropes, each with a noose at one end and a spliced eye at the other. He placed the two ropes on the table, added two white cotton bags, then stepped smartly back a pace. 'Good morning, sir,' he said to the Keeper.

'Oh, Botting!' The Keeper's surprised tone suggested he had only just noticed the hangman's presence. 'And a very good morning to you, too.'

'And a nice one it is, sir,' Botting said. 'Hardly a cloud up aloft, hardly one. Still just the two clients today, sir?'

'Just the two, Botting.'

'There's a fair crowd for them,' Botting said, 'not over large, but fair enough.'

'Good, good,' the Keeper said vaguely.

'Botting!' Lord Alexander intervened, pacing forward with his crippled foot clumping heavily on the scarred floorboards. 'Tell me, Botting, is it true that you hang members of the aristocracy with a silken rope?' Botting looked astonished at being addressed by one of the Keeper's guests, and even more by such an extraordinary figure as the Reverend Lord Alexander Pleydell

368

with his shock of red hair, hawklike nose and gangly figure. 'Well?' Lord Alexander demanded peremptorily. 'Is it so? I have heard it is, but on matters concerning hanging then you, surely, are the *fons et origo* of reliable information. Would you not concur?'

'A silken rope, sir?' Botting asked weakly.

'My lord,' the Ordinary corrected him.

'My lord! Ha!' Botting said, recovering his equanimity and amused at the thought that perhaps Lord Alexander was contemplating being executed. 'I hates to disappoint you, my lord,' he said, 'but I wouldn't know where to lay hands on a silken rope. Not a silken one. Now this,' Botting caressed one of the nooses on the table, 'is the best Bridport hemp, my lord, fine as you could discover anywhere, and I can always lay hands on quality Bridport hemp. But silk? That's a horse of a different colour, my lord, and I wouldn't even know where to look. No, my lord. If ever I has the high privilege of hanging a nobleman I'll be doing it with Bridport hemp, same as I would for anyone else.'

'And quite right too, my good man.' Lord Alexander beamed approval at the hangman's levelling instincts. 'Well done! Thank you.'

'You will forgive me, my lord?' The Keeper gestured that Lord Alexander should step away from the wide central aisle between the tables.

'I'm in the way?' Lord Alexander sounded surprised.

'Only momentarily, my lord,' the Keeper said, and just then Lord Alexander heard the clank of irons and the shuffle of feet. The other guests drew themselves up and made their faces solemn. Lord Christopher

Carne took a step back, his face even paler than before, then turned to face the door that led from the Press Yard.

A turnkey came in first. He knuckled his forehead to the Keeper, then stood beside a low slab of timber that squatted on the floor. The turnkey held a stout hammer and a metal punch and Lord Alexander wondered what their purpose was, but he did not like to ask, and then the guests closest to the door hauled off their hats because the Sheriff and Under-Sheriff were ushering the two prisoners into the Association Room.

'Brandy, sir?' One of the Keeper's servants appeared beside Lord Christopher Carne.

'Thank you.' Lord Christopher could not take his eyes from the slender, pale young man who had come first through the door with legs weighed down by the heavy irons. 'That,' he said to the servant, 'that is Corday?'

'It is, my lord, yes.'

Lord Christopher gulped down the brandy and reached for another.

And the two bells, the prison tocsin and the bell of Saint Sepulchre's, began to toll for those about to die.

Sandman expected the door of the Great George Street house to be opened by a servant, but instead it was Sebastian Witherspoon, Viscount Sidmouth's private secretary, who raised his eyebrows in astonishment. 'An unseemly hour, Captain?' Witherspoon observed, then frowned at Sandman's dishevelled state and the ragged looks of his three companions. 'I do trust you have not all come expecting breakfast?' he said in a voice dripping with contempt.

'This woman,' Sandman did not bother with the niceties of a greeting, 'can testify that Charles Corday is not the murderer of the Countess of Avebury.'

Witherspoon dabbed at his lips with a napkin stained with egg yolk. He glanced at Meg, then shrugged as if to suggest that her testimony was worthless. 'How very inconvenient,' he murmured.

'Viscount Sidmouth is here?' Sandman demanded.

'We are at work, Sandman,' Witherspoon said severely. 'His lordship, as you doubtless know, is a widower and since his sad loss he has sought consolation in hard work. He begins early and works late and does not brook disturbance.'

'This is work,' Sandman said.

Witherspoon looked again at Meg and this time he seemed to notice her looks. 'Must I remind you,' he said, 'that the boy has been found guilty and the law is due to take its course in one hour? I really cannot see what can be done at this late juncture.'

Sandman stepped back from the door. 'My compliments to Lord Sidmouth,' he said, 'and tell him we are going to seek an audience with the Queen.' He had no idea whether the Queen would receive him, but he was quite sure Witherspoon and the Home Secretary did not want the animosity of the royal family, not when there were honours and pensions to be had from the crown. 'Her Majesty, I believe' Sandman went on, 'has taken an interest in this case and will doubtless be intrigued to hear of your cavalier attitude. Good day, Wither-spoon.'

'Captain!' Witherspoon pulled the door wide open. 'Captain! You had better come in.'

They were shown into an empty parlour. The house, though it was in an expensive street close to the Houses of Parliament, had a makeshift air. It was not perma-nently lived in, but was plainly let on short leases to politicians like Lord Sidmouth who needed a temporary refuge. The only furniture in the parlour was a pair of stuffed armchairs, both with faded covers, and a heavy desk with a throne-like chair behind. A beautifully bound prayer book lay on the desk next to an untidy pile of regional newspapers which all had articles ringed in ink. Sandman, when they were left alone in the drab parlour, saw that the marked articles were accounts of riots. Folk up and down Britain were taking to the streets to protest against the price of corn or the intro-duction of machinery to the mills. 'I sometimes think,' Sandman said, 'that the modern world is a very sad place.'

'Has its consolations, Captain,' Berrigan said care-lessly, glancing at Sally.

'Riots, rick burning,' Sandman said. 'It never used to be like this! The damned French let anarchy into the world.'

Berrigan smiled. 'Things used to be better in the old days, eh? Nothing but cricket and cream?'

'When we weren't fighting the Frogs? Yes, it did seem like that.'

'No, Captain,' the Sergeant shook his head, 'you just

had money then. Everything's easier when you've got cash.'

'Amen to that,' Sally said fervently, then turned as the door opened and Witherspoon ushered in the Home Secretary.

Viscount Sidmouth was wearing a patterned silk dressing gown over his shirt and trousers. He was newly shaven and his white skin had a sheen as though it had been stretched and polished. His eyes, as ever, were cold and disapproving. 'It seems, Captain Sandman,' he said acidly, 'that you choose to inconvenience us?'

'I choose nothing of the sort, my lord,' Sandman said belligerently.

Sidmouth frowned at the tone, then looked at Berrigan and the two women. The sound of crockery being cleared came from deeper in the house and made Sandman realise how hungry he was. 'So,' the Home Secretary said with distaste in his voice, 'who do you bring me?'

'My associates, Sergeant Berrigan and Miss Hood . . .'

'Associates?' Sidmouth was amused.

'I must acknowledge their assistance, my lord, as no doubt Her Majesty will when she learns the outcome of our enquiries.'

That not so subtle hint made the Home Secretary grimace. He looked at Meg and almost recoiled from the force of her small eyes and the sight of her mangled teeth and pocked skin. 'And you, madam?' he asked coldly.

'Miss Margaret Hargood,' Sandman introduced her,

'who was a maid to the Countess of Avebury and was present in the Countess's bedroom on the day of her murder. She personally escorted Charles Corday from the bedroom before the murder, she saw him out of the house and can testify he did not return. In short, my lord, she can witness that Corday is innocent.' Sandman spoke with a deal of pride and satisfaction. He was tired, he was hungry, his ankle hurt and his boots and clothes showed the effects of walking from Kent to London, but by God he had discovered the truth.

Sidmouth's lips, already thin, compressed into a bloodless line as he looked at Meg. 'Is it true, woman?'

Meg drew herself up. She was not in the least awed by his lordship, but instead looked him up and down, then sniffed. 'I don't know nothing,' she said.

'I beg your pardon?' The Home Secretary blanched at the insolence in her voice.

'He comes and kidnaps me!' Meg shrieked, pointing at Sandman. 'Which he got no bleeding right to do! Takes me away from my chooks. He can fake away off where he came from, and what do I care who killed her? Or who dies for her?'

'Meg,' Sandman tried to plead with her.

'Get your bleeding paws off me!'

'Dear God,' Viscount Sidmouth said in a pained voice, and backed towards the door. 'Witherspoon,' he said, 'we are wasting our time.'

'Got ever such big wasps in Australia,' Sally said, 'begging your lordship's pardon.'

Even Viscount Sidmouth with his thin, barren lawyer's mind was not oblivious of Sally's charms. In the dark room she was like a ray of sunlight and he actually smiled at her, even though he did not understand her meaning. 'I beg your pardon?' he said to her.

'Ever such big wasps in Australia,' Sally said, 'and that's where this mollisher's going on account that she didn't give her testimony at Charlie's trial. She should have done, but she didn't. Protecting her man, see? And you're going to transport her, aren't you, my lord?' Sally reinforced this rhetorical question with a graceful curtsey.

The Home Secretary frowned. 'Transportation? It is for the courts, my dear, not me to decide on who should be . . .' His voice suddenly tailed away for he was staring with astonishment at Meg, who was shivering with fear.

'Very large wasps in Australia,' Sandman said, 'famously so.'

'*Aculeata Giganta*,' Witherspoon contributed rather impressively.

'No!' Meg cried.

'Big ones,' Sally said with extraordinary relish, 'with stingers like hatpins.'

'He didn't do it!' Meg said, 'and I don't want to go to Australia!'

Sidmouth was looking at her much as the audience must have gazed on the pig-faced lady at the Lyceum. 'Are you saying,' he asked in a very cold voice, 'that Charles Corday did not commit the murder?'

'The Marquess didn't! He didn't!'

'The Marquess didn't?' Sidmouth asked, utterly mystified now.

'The Marquess of Skavadale, my lord,' Sandman explained, 'in whose house she was given shelter.'

'He came after the murder,' Meg, terrified of the mythical wasps, was desperate to explain now. 'The Marquess came after she was dead. He often called on the house. And he was still there!'

'Who was still there?' Sidmouth enquired.

'He was there!'

'Corday was?'

'No!' Meg said, frowning. 'Him!' She paused, looked at Sandman then back to the Home Secretary whose face still showed puzzlement. 'Her stepson,' she said, 'him what had been ploughing his father's field for half a year.'

Sidmouth grimaced with distaste. 'Her stepson?'

'Lord Christopher Carne, my lord,' Sandman explained, 'stepson to the Countess and heir to the Earldom.'

'I saw him with the knife,' Meg snarled, 'and so did the Marquess. He was crying, he was. Lord Christopher! He hated her, see, but he couldn't keep his scrawny paws off her neither. Oh, he killed her! It wasn't that feeble painter!'

There was a second's pause in which a score of questions came to Sandman's mind, but then Lord Sidmouth snapped at Witherspoon. 'My compliments to the police office in Queen Square,' that office was only a short walk away, 'and I shall be obliged if they will provide four officers and six saddle horses instantly. But give me a pen first, Witherspoon, a pen and paper and wax and seal.' He turned and looked at a clock on the mantel.

'And let us hurry, man.' His voice was sour as though he resented this extra work, but Sandman could not fault him. He was doing the right thing and doing it quickly. 'Let us hurry,' the Home Secretary said again.

And hurry they did.

'Foot on the block, boy! Don't dally!' the turnkey snapped at Charles Corday who gave a gulp, then put his right foot on the wooden block. The turnkey put the punch over the first rivet then hammered it out. Corday gasped with each blow, then whimpered when the manacle dropped away. Lord Alexander saw that the boy's ankle was a welt of sores.

'Other foot, boy,' the turnkey ordered.

The two bells tolled on and neither would stop now until both bodies were cut down. The Keeper's guests were silent, just watching the prisoners' faces as though some clue to the secrets of eternity might lie in those eyes that so soon would be seeing the other side.

'Right, lad, go and see the hangman!' the turnkey said, and Charles Corday gave a small cry of surprise as he took his first steps without leg irons. He stumbled, but managed to catch himself on a table.

'I do not know,' Lord Christopher Carne said, then stopped abruptly.

'What, Kit?' Lord Alexander asked considerately.

Lord Christopher gave a start, unaware that he had even spoken, but then collected himself. 'You say there are doubts about his guilt?' he asked.

'Oh indeed, yes, indeed.' Lord Alexander paused to

light a pipe. 'Sandman was quite sure of the boy's innocence, but I suppose it can't be proven. Alas, alas.'

'But if the real k-killer were to be found,' Lord Christopher asked, his eyes fixed on Corday who was quivering as he stood before the hangman, 'could that man then be convicted of the crime if Corday has already been found g-guilty of it and been hanged?'

'A very nice question!' Lord Alexander said enthusiastically. 'And one to which I confess I do not know the answer. But I should imagine, would you not agree, that if the real killer is apprehended then a posthumous pardon must be granted to Corday and one can only hope that such a pardon will be recognised in heaven and the poor boy will be fetched up from the nether regions.'

'Stand still, boy,' Jemmy Botting growled at Corday. 'Drink that if you want to. It helps.' He pointed to a mug of brandy, but Corday shook his head. 'Your choice, lad, your choice,' Botting said, then he took one of the four cords and used it to lash Corday's elbows, pulling them hard behind his back so that Corday was forced to throw out his chest.

'Not too tight, Botting,' the Keeper remonstrated.

'In the old days,' Botting grumbled, 'the hangman had an assistant to do this. There was the Yeoman of the Halter and pinioning was his job. It ain't mine.' He had not been tipped anything by Corday, hence had made the first pinion so painful, but now he relaxed the cord's tension a little before lashing Corday's wrists in front of his body.

'That's for both of us,' Reginald Venables, the second

prisoner, big and bearded, slapped a coin on the table. 'So slacken my friend's lashings.'

Botting looked at the coin, was impressed by the generosity, and so loosened Corday's two cords before placing one of the noosed ropes round his neck. Corday flinched from the sisal's touch and the Reverend Cotton stepped forward and placed a hand on his shoulder. 'God is our refuge and strength, young man,' the Ordinary said, 'and a very present help in times of trouble. Call on the Lord and He will hear you. Do you repent of your foul sins, boy?'

'I did nothing!' Corday wailed.

'Quiet, my son, quiet,' Cotton urged him, 'and reflect on your sins in decent silence.'

'I did nothing!' Corday screamed.

'Charlie! Don't give 'em the pleasure,' Venables said. 'Remember what I told you, go like a man!' Venables sank a mug of brandy, then turned his back so that Botting could lash his elbows.

'But surely,' Lord Christopher said to Lord Alexander, 'the very fact that a man already stands c-convicted and has been p-punished, would make the authorities most reluctant to reopen the case?'

'Justice must be served,' Lord Alexander said vaguely, 'but I suppose you make a valid point. No one likes to admit that they were mistaken, least of all a politician, so doubtless the real murderer can feel a good deal safer once Corday is dead. Poor boy, poor boy. He is a sacrifice to our judicial incompetence, eh?'

Botting placed the second rope about Venables's

shoulders, then the Reverend Cotton took a step back from the prisoners and let his prayer book fall open at the burial service. ' "I am the resurrection and the life," ' he intoned, ' "he that believeth in me, though he were dead, yet shall he live." '

'I did nothing!' Corday shouted, and turned left and right as though he could see some way of escape.

'Quiet, Charlie,' Venables said softly, 'quiet.'

The Sheriff and Under-Sheriff, both in robes and both wearing chains of office and both carrying silver-tipped staves, and both evidently satisfied that the prisoners were properly prepared, went to the Keeper, who formally bowed to them before presenting the Sheriff with a sheet of paper. The Sheriff glanced at the paper, nodded in satisfaction and thrust it into a pocket of his fur-trimmed robe. Until now the two prisoners had been in the care of the Keeper of Newgate, but now they belonged to the Sheriff and he, in turn, would deliver them into the keeping of the devil. The Sheriff pulled aside his robe to find the watch in his fob pocket. He snapped open the lid and peered at the face. 'It lacks a quarter of eight,' he said, then turned to Botting. 'Are you ready?'

'Quite ready, your honour, and at your service,' Botting said. He pulled on his hat, scooped up the two white cotton bags and thrust them into a pocket.

The Sheriff closed his watch, let his robe fall and headed for the Press Yard. 'We have an appointment at eight, gentlemen,' he announced, 'so let us go.'

'Devilled kidneys!' Lord Alexander said. 'Dear God, I can smell them. Come, Kit!'

They joined the procession.

And the bells tolled on.

It was not far. A quarter-mile up Whitehall, right into the Strand and three quarters of a mile to Temple Bar, and after that it was scarcely a third of a mile down Fleet Street, across the ditch and up Ludgate Hill before the left turn into Old Bailey. No distance at all, really, and certainly not after the police office in Queen Square had brought some patrol officers' horses. Sandman and Berrigan were both mounted, the Sergeant on a mare that a constable swore was placid and Sandman on a wall-eyed gelding that had more spirit. Witherspoon brought the reprieve out of the house and handed it up to Sandman. The wax of the seal was still warm. 'God speed you, Captain,' Witherspoon said.

'See you in the 'sheaf, Sal!' Berrigan shouted, then lurched back as his mare followed Sandman's gelding towards Whitehall. Three patrolmen rode ahead, one blowing a whistle and the other two with drawn truncheons to clear a path through the carts, wagons and carriages. A crossing sweeper leapt out of the way with a shrill curse. Sandman thrust the precious document into his pocket and turned to see Berrigan making heavy weather of his mare. 'Heels down, Sergeant! Heels down! Don't snatch on the reins, just let her run! She'll look after you!'

They passed the royal stables, then took to the pavement in the Strand. They rode past Kidman's the Apothecary, driving two pedestrians into its deep doorway, then past Carrington's, a cutlery store where Sandman had purchased his first sword. It had broken, he remembered, in the assault on Badajoz. It had been nothing heroic, merely frustration at the army's apparent failure to get into the French fortress and in his anger he had slashed the sword at a marooned ammunition cart and snapped the blade off at the hilt. Then they galloped past Sans Pareil, the theatre where Celia Collet, actress, had entranced the Earl of Avebury. An old fool marrying a sharp young greed and, when their undying love proved to be no more than unmatched lust, and after they had fallen out, she moved back to London where, to keep herself in the luxury she felt her due, she took back her old theatre servant, Margaret Hargood, to be her procuress. Thus had the Countess snared her men, she had blackmailed them and she had thrived, but then the fattest fly of all came to her web. Lord Christopher Carne, innocent and naive, fell for his stepmother and she had seduced him and amazed him, she had made him moan and shudder, and then she had threatened to tell the trustees of the entailed estate, his father and the whole world if he did not pay her still more money from his generous allowance, and Lord Christopher, knowing that when he inherited the estate his stepmother would demand more and more until there would be nothing left but a husk, had killed her.

All this Sandman had learnt as the Viscount Sidmouth scribbled the reprieve in his own handwriting. 'The proper thing,' the Home Secretary had said, 'is for the Privy Council to issue this document.'

'Hardly time, my lord,' Sandman had pointed out.

'I am aware of that, Captain,' Sidmouth said acidly. The steel nib scratched and spattered tiny droplets of ink as he scrawled his signature. 'You will present this,' he said, sprinkling sand on the wet ink, 'with my compliments, to the Sheriff of London or to one of his Under-Sheriffs, one of whom will certainly be upon the scaffold. They may enquire why such an order was not signed in council and then forwarded to them by the Recorder of London and you will explain that there was no time for the proper procedures to be followed. You will also be so kind as to pass me that candle and the stick of sealing wax?'

Now Sandman and Berrigan rode, the seal on the reprieve still warm, and Sandman thought what guilt Lord Christopher must have endured, and how killing his stepmother would have brought him no relief for the Marquess of Skavadale had discovered him almost in the act of the murder and the Marquess, whose family was near penury, had seen his life's problems solved at a stroke. Meg was the witness who could identify Lord Christopher as the murderer, and so long as Meg lived, and so long as she was under the Marquess's protection, so long would Lord Christopher pay to keep her silent. And when Lord Christopher became Earl, and so gained the fortune of his grandfather, he would have been forced to pay all he had inherited. It would all have gone to Skavadale, while Meg, the lever by which that wealth would have been prised from the Avebury estate, would have been bribed with chickens.

Sidmouth had sent messengers to the channel ports, and to Harwich and to Bristol, warning officials there to keep a watch for Lord Christopher Carne. 'And what of Skavadale?' Sandman had asked.

'We do not know if he has yet taken any monies by threat,' Sidmouth said primly, 'and if the girl speaks the truth then they did not plan to begin their depredations until after Lord Christopher had inherited the earldom. We might disapprove of their intentions, Captain, but we cannot punish them for a crime that is yet to be committed.'

'Skavadale concealed the truth!' Sandman said indignantly. 'He sent for the constables and told them he didn't recognise the murderer. He would have let an innocent man go to his death!'

'And how do you prove that?' Sidmouth asked curtly. 'Just be content that you have identified the real killer.'

'And earned the forty pound reward,' Berrigan put in happily, earning a very dirty look from his lordship.

As they rode, their horses' shoes echoing from the walls of Saint Clement's Church, Sandman saw a dozen reflections of himself distorted in the roundel panes of Clifton's Chop House and he thought how good a pork chop and kidney would taste now. The Temple Bar was immediately ahead and the space under the arch was crowded with carts and pedestrians. The constables shouted for the carts to move, bullied their horses into the press and yelled at the drivers to use their whips. A wagon loaded with cut flowers was filling most of the archway and one of the constables started beating at it with his truncheon, scattering petals and leaves onto the cobbles. 'Leave it!' Sandman bellowed. 'Leave it!' He had seen a gap on the pavement and he drove his horse for it, knocking down a thin man in a tall hat. Berrigan followed him, then they were past the arch, Sandman was standing in the stirrups and his horse was plunging towards the Fleet Ditch, sparks flying where its shoes struck the cobbles.

The first church bells began to strike eight and it seemed to Sandman that the whole city was filled with a cacophony of bells, hoofbeats, alarm and doom.

He settled back in the saddle, slapped the horse's rump, and rode like the wind.

Lord Alexander, as he passed through the towering arch of the high Debtor's Door, saw in front of him the dark hollow interior of the scaffold and he thought how much it resembled the underside of a theatre's stage. From outside, where the audience gathered in the street, the gallows looked heavy, permanent and sombre with its black baize drapery, but from here Lord Alexander could see it was an illusion sustained by raw wooden beams. It was a stage set for a tragedy ending in death. Wooden stairs climbed to his right, going up into the shadows before turning sharply left to emerge in a roofed pavilion that formed the rear of the scaffold. The roofed pavilion was like the privileged stage boxes, offering the important guests the best view of the drama.

Lord Alexander was first up the steps and a huge cheer greeted his appearance. No one cared who he was, but his arrival presaged the coming of the two doomed men and the crowd was bored with waiting. Lord Alexander, blinking in the sudden sunlight, took off his hat and bowed to the mob who, appreciative of the gesture, laughed and applauded. The crowd was not large, but it filled the street for a hundred yards southwards and quite blocked the junction with New-gate Street immediately to the north. Every window in the Magpie and Stump was taken and there was even a scatter of spectators on the tavern's roof.

'We were asked to take chairs at the back,' Lord Christopher pointed out when Lord Alexander sat him-self in the very front row.

'We were requested to leave two front row places for the Sheriff,' Lord Alexander corrected him, 'and there they are. Sit down, Kit, do. What a delightful day! Do you think the weather will last? Budd on Saturday, eh?'

'Budd on Saturday?' Lord Christopher was jostled as the other guests pushed past to the rearmost chairs.

'Cricket, dear boy! I've actually persuaded Budd to play a single wicket match against Jack Lambert, and Lambert, good fellow that he is, has agreed to stand down if Rider Sandman will take his place! He told me so yesterday, after church. Now that's a match to dream of, eh? Budd against Sandman. You will come, won't you?'

A cheer drowned conversation on the scaffold as the sheriffs appeared in their breeches, silk stockings, silver-buckled shoes and fur-trimmed robes. Lord Chris-topher seemed oblivious of their arrival, gazing instead at the beam from which the prisoners would hang. He seemed disappointed that it was not bloodstained, then he looked down and flinched at the sight of the two unplaned coffins waiting for their burdens. 'She was an evil woman,' he said softly.

'Of course you'll come,' Lord Alexander said, then frowned. 'What did you say, my dear fellow?'

'My stepmother. She was evil.' Lord Christopher seemed to shiver, though it was not cold. 'She and that maid of hers, they were like witches!'

'Are you justifying her murder?'

'She was evil,' Lord Christopher said more emphatically, apparently not hearing his friend's question. 'She said she would make a claim on the estate, on the trustees, because I wrote her some letters. She lied, Alexander, she lied!' He winced, remembering the long letters in which he had poured out his devotion to his stepmother. He had known no women until he had been taken to her bed and he had become besotted by her. He had begged her to run away to Paris with him and she had encouraged his madness until, one day, mocking him, she had snapped the trap closed. Give her money, she had insisted, or else she would make him the laughing stock of Paris, London and every other European capital. She threatened to have the letters copied and the copies distributed so everyone would see his shame, and so he had paid her money and she demanded more and he knew the blackmail would never end. And so he killed her.

He had not believed himself capable of murder, but in her bedroom, begging her a final time to return him the letters, she had mocked him, called him puny, said he was a fumbling and stupid boy. He had pulled the knife from his belt. It was hardly a weapon, it was little more than an old blade he used to slit the pages of uncut books, but in his mad anger it sufficed. He had stabbed her, then hacked and slashed at her loathsome and beautiful skin, and afterwards he had rushed onto the landing and seen the Countess's maid and a man staring up at him from the downstairs hall and he had recoiled back to the bedroom where he had whimpered in panic. He expected to hear feet on the stairs, but no one came, and he forced himself to be calm and to think. He had been on the landing for only a split second, hardly time to be recognised! He snatched a knife from the painter's table and tossed it onto the red-laced body, then searched the dead woman's bureau to find his letters that he had carried away down the back stairs and burnt at home. He had crouched in his lodgings, fearing arrest, then next day heard that the painter had been taken by the constables.

Lord Christopher had prayed for Corday. It was not right, of course, that the painter should die, but nor could Lord Christopher be persuaded that he himself deserved death for his stepmother's murder. He would do good with his inheritance! He would be charitable. He would pay for the murder and for Corday's innocence a thousand times over. Sandman had threatened that exercise of repentance and so Lord Christopher had consulted his manservant and, claiming that Rider Sandman had a grudge against him and planned to sue the trustees and thus tie up the Avebury fortune in the Court of Chancery, he had promised a thousand guineas to the man who could rid the estate of that threat. The manservant had hired other men and Lord Christopher had rewarded them richly for even making the attempt on Sandman's life. Now, it seemed, further payment would be unnecessary for Sandman had evidently failed. Corday would die and no one would then want to admit that an innocent man had been sent to dance on Botting's stage.

'But your stepmother, surely, had no claim on the estate,' Lord Alexander had been thinking about his friend's words, 'unless the entail specifically provides for your father's widow. Does it?'

Lord Christopher looked confused, but then made a great effort to concentrate on what his friend had just said. 'No,' he said, 'the whole estate is entailed on the heir. Onto m-me alone.'

'Then you will be a prodigiously rich man, Kit,' Lord Alexander said, 'and I shall wish you well of your great fortune.' He turned from his friend as a huge cheer, the loudest of the morning, greeted the hangman's arrival on the scaffold.

' "I will keep my mouth as it were with a bridle," ' the Reverend Cotton's voice grew louder as he climbed the stairs behind the first prisoner, ' "while the ungodly is in my sight." '

A turnkey appeared first, then Corday, who was still walking awkwardly because his legs were not used to being without irons. He tripped on the top step and stumbled into Lord Alexander who gripped his elbow. 'Steady, there's a good fellow,' Lord Alexander said.

'Hats off!' the crowd bellowed at those who stood

in the front ranks. 'Hats off!' The roar of the crowd was massive as they surged forward to crush against the low wooden rail that surrounded the scaffold. The City Marshal's men, arrayed just behind the rail, raised their staves and spears.

Lord Alexander felt assaulted by the noise that echoed back from the prison's granite façade. This was England at play, he thought, the mob given its taste of blood in the hope that, given this much, they would not demand more. A child, sitting on his father's shoulders, was screaming obscenities at Corday, who was weeping openly. The crowd liked a man or woman to go to their deaths bravely and Corday's tears were earning him nothing but scorn. Lord Alexander had a sudden urge to go to the young man and comfort him, to pray with him, but he stayed seated because the Reverend Cotton was already close beside Corday. '"O teach us to number our days,"' the Ordinary read in a singsong voice, '"that we may apply our hearts unto wisdom."'

Then the crowd roared in mocking laughter because Corday had collapsed. Botting had half climbed the ladder and was just lifting the rope from the prisoner's shoulders ready to attach it to one of the hooks of the beam, when Corday's legs turned to jelly. The Reverend Cotton leapt back, the turnkey ran forward, but Corday could not stand. He was shaking and sobbing.

'Shoot the bugger, Jemmy!' a man shouted from the crowd.

'I need an assistant,' Botting growled at the Sheriff, 'and a chair.'

One of the guests volunteered to stand and his chair

was brought into the sunlight and placed on the trap-door. The crowd, realising this was going to be an unusual execution, applauded the sight. Botting and a turnkey hoisted Corday onto the seat and the hangman deftly undid the line holding Corday's elbows and retied it so that it bound the prisoner to the chair. Now he could be hanged, and Botting clambered up the ladder, attached the rope, then came down and rammed the noose hard over Corday's head. 'Snivelling little bastard,' he whispered as he jerked the rope tight, 'die like a man.' He took one of the white cotton bags from his pocket and pulled it over Corday's head. Lord Alexander, silent now, saw the cotton pulsing in and out with Corday's breathing. The boy's head had dropped onto his chest so that, if it had not been for the flicker of cotton at his mouth, he might already have been dead.

'"Show Thy servants Thy work,"' the Reverend Cotton read, '"and their children Thy glory."'

Venables came up the steps and received only a perfunctory cheer from a crowd that had exhausted itself at Corday's expense. The big man nevertheless bowed to his audience, then walked calmly to the trapdoor and waited for rope and blindfold. The scaffold creaked beneath his weight. 'Do it quick, Jemmy,' he said loudly, 'and do it well.'

'I'll look after you,' the hangman promised, 'I'll look after you.' He took the white hood from his pocket and pulled it over Venables's head.

'"The Lord gave and the Lord hath taken away,"' the Reverend Cotton said.

Lord Alexander, who had found himself appalled by the last few moments, became dimly aware of some disturbance at the southern, narrow end of Old Bailey.

'"Blessed be the name of the Lord,"' intoned the Ordinary.

'God damn it!' Sandman found himself blocked by the press of traffic at the junction of Farringdon Street and Ludgate Hill. Off to his right the Fleet Ditch stank in the early morning sun. A coal wagon was turning into Fleet Street and it had jammed on the corner and a dozen men were offering advice while a lawyer in a hackney was telling his driver to whip the coal heaver's horses even though there was no room for it to move because an even larger wagon, loaded with a score of oak beams, was scraping past. The mounted constables, whistles blowing and truncheons drawn, clattered into the junction behind Sandman, who kicked a pedestrian out of his way, wrenched his horse to the left, swore at the lawyer whose coach blocked him, then had his bridle seized by a well-meaning citizen who thought Sandman was fleeing the constables.

'Get your bloody hands off me!' Sandman shouted, then Berrigan rode alongside and thumped the man on the head, crushing his hat, and Sandman's horse was suddenly free and he kicked it alongside the wagon with the huge oak beams.

'No point in hurrying!' the driver called. 'Not if you're going to the hanging. The culleys will be dangling by now!' All the bells of the city had rung the hour, the ones that always chimed early and even the laggards had struck eight, but the funeral bell of Saint Sepulchre still tolled and Sandman dared to hope that Corday was still alive as he burst out of the tangled traffic and kicked the horse up towards Saint Paul's Cathedral, which filled the crest of Ludgate Hill with its steps, pillars and dome.

Halfway up the hill he turned into Old Bailey and for the first few yards, as he passed the law courts in the Session House, the road was blessedly empty, but then it widened as he passed the big yard of Newgate Prison and suddenly the seething crowd stretched across the whole street, blocking him, and he could see the beam of the gallows reaching across the sky and the black scaffold platform beneath, and then he just drove the horse at the crowd. He was standing in the stirrups, shouting, just as the Royals, the Scots Greys and the Inniskillings had stood and shouted as they drove their big horses into the French corps they had destroyed at Waterloo.

'Make way!' Sandman bellowed. 'Make way!' He saw the men on the scaffold and noticed that one seemed to be sitting, which was strange, and he saw a priest there, and a knot of spectators or officials at the scaffold's rear, and the crowd protested at his savagery, resisted him, and he wished he had a weapon to thrash at them, but then the constables drove alongside him and thrust at the press of people with their long truncheons.

Then a sigh seemed to pass through the crowd,

and Sandman could see no one but the priest on the scaffold's black stage that stretched halfway across the widest part of the street.

Which meant the trapdoor had opened.

And Saint Sepulchre's bell tolled on for the dying.

Venables swore at the Ordinary and cursed the Keeper, but gave no insults to Jemmy Bolting for he knew well enough that the hangman could hasten his end. 'Stop weeping,' he told Corday.

'I did nothing!' Corday protested.

'You think you're the first innocent person to die up here?' Venables asked. 'Or the hundredth? It's a scaffold, Charlie, and it knows no difference between the guilty and the innocent. Are you there, Jemmy?' Venables had the white hood over his eyes, so he could not see that the hangman had shuffled to the corner of the platform to pull the safety peg. 'Are you there, Jemmy?'

'Not long now, boys,' Botting said, 'have patience.' He vanished down the back stairs.

'It's Rider!' Lord Alexander was standing now, to the annoyance of the guests seated behind him. 'It's Rider!'

The crowd had at last sensed that something untoward was happening. Their first inkling was when Lord Alexander, tall and striking, stood by the pavilion and pointed towards Ludgate Hill, then they turned and saw the horsemen who were trying to force their way through the crowd.

'Let them through!' some of the people shouted.

'What's happening?' Venables roared from the trapdoor. 'What's happening?'

'Sit down, my lord,' the Sheriff said to Lord Alexander, who ignored him.

'Rider!' he shouted across the crowd, his voice drowned by their commotion.

Jemmy Botting cursed because he had pulled the rope and the tallow-greased beam had juddered, but not moved. 'God damn you to bloody hell!' he cursed the beam, then took hold of the rope a second time and gave it a monstrous tug and this time the beam moved so swiftly that Botting was thrown backwards as the sky opened above him. The trap fell with a thump and the two bodies fell into the scaffold's pit. Venables was dancing and throttling, while Corday's legs were thrashing against the chair.

'Sheriff! Sheriff!' Sandman was nearing the scaffold. 'Sheriff!'

'Is it a reprieve?' Lord Alexander roared. 'Is it a reprieve?'

'Yes!'

'Kit! Help me!' Lord Alexander limped on his club foot to where Corday hung, twitched and gagged. 'Help me haul him up!'

'Let go of him!' the Sheriff bellowed, as Lord Alexander reached for the rope.

'Let go, my lord!' the Reverend Cotton demanded. 'This is not seemly!'

'Get off me, you damned bloody fool!' Lord Alexander snarled as he pushed Cotton away. He then seized the rope and tried to haul Corday back up to the platform, but he did not possess nearly enough strength. The white cotton bag over Corday's mouth shivered.

Sandman thrust aside the last few folk and rammed his horse against the barrier. He fumbled in his pockets for the reprieve, thought for a dreadful instant that it was lost, then found the paper and held it up towards the scaffold, but the Sheriff would not come to receive it. 'It's a reprieve!' Sandman shouted.

'Kit, help me!' Lord Alexander tugged feebly at Corday's rope and could not raise the dying man by even an inch, and so he turned to Lord Christopher. 'Kit! Help me!' Lord Christopher, eyes huge behind his thick spectacles, held both hands to his mouth. He did not move.

'What the bloody hell are you doing?' Jemmy Botting shouted at Lord Alexander from beneath the scaffold and then, to make sure he was not cheated of a death, he scrambled over the supporting beams to haul downwards on Corday's legs. 'You'll not have him!' he screamed up at Lord Alexander. 'You'll not have him! He's mine! He's mine!'

'Take it!' Sandman shouted at the Sheriff, who still refused to lean down and accept the reprieve, but just then a black-dressed man pushed his way to Sandman's side.

'Give it to me,' the newcomer said. He did not wait for Sandman to obey, but instead snatched the paper, hoisted himself onto the railing that protected the scaffold and then, with one prodigious leap, jumped to catch hold of the scaffold's edge. For an instant his black boots scrabbled on the baize for a lodgment, then he managed to grip the exposed edge left by the fallen trapdoor and heaved himself onto the platform. It was Sally's brother, dressed all in black and with a black ribbon tying his black hair, and the regulars in the crowd cheered for they recognised and admired him. He was Jack Hood, Robin Hood – the man that every magistrate and constable in London wanted to see caper on Jem Botting's stage, and Jack Hood mocked their ambition by flaunting himself at every Newgate hanging. Now, on the scaffold at last, he thrust Corday's reprieve towards the Sheriff. 'Take it, God damn you!' Hood snarled, and the Sheriff, astonished by the young man's confidence, at last took the paper.

Hood strode to Lord Alexander's side and took hold of the rope, but Jemmy Botting, fearing that his victim would be snatched at the last minute, had scrambled onto Corday's lap so that his weight was added to the choking noose. 'He's mine!' he shouted up at Lord Alexander and Hood. 'He's mine!' Corday's wheezing breath was drowned in the morning's din. Hood heaved, but could not raise the combined weight of Corday and Botting. 'He's mine! Mine!' Botting screamed.

'You!' Sandman snapped at one of the City Marshal's javelin men. 'Give me your hanger! Now!'

The man, bemused, but cowed by Sandman's snap of command, nervously drew the short curved sword that was more decorative than useful. Sandman snatched the blade from him, then was assaulted by another of the scaffold guards who thought Sandman planned an assault on the Sheriff. 'Bugger off!'

Sandman snarled at the man, then Berrigan thumped his fist on the crown of the man's head.

'Wait!' the Sheriff shouted. 'There must be order. There must be order!' The crowd was shrieking, its noise filling the street like a great roar. 'Marshal!' the Sheriff called. 'Marshal!'

'Give up the sword!' the Marshal bellowed at Sandman.

'Hood!' Sandman shouted as he stood in the stirrups. 'Hood!' Hands reached up to haul him out of the saddle, but Sandman had the highwayman's attention now and he tossed him the hanger. 'Cut him down, Hood! Cut him down!'

Hood deftly caught the blade. The constables who had escorted Sandman and Berrigan from Whitehall now pushed away the Marshal's men. Lord Christopher Carne, eyes still wide and mouth agape, was staring in horror at Rider Sandman, who at last noticed his lordship. 'Constable,' Sandman spoke to the horseman nearest him, 'that's the man you arrest. That man there.' Sandman pointed and Lord Christopher turned as if to escape, but the stairs from the pavilion led only down to the prison itself.

Jemmy Botting had his arms about Corday's neck, embracing him like a lover as he heaved his weight up and down on the hanging man's lap. 'Mine,' he crooned, 'mine,' and he heard the scraping in the boy's throat, then Jack Hood was sawing the hanger blade at the rope. 'No!' Botting screamed. 'No!' But the rope, though it was supposed to be the best Bridport hemp, cut like rush string and suddenly Corday and Botting, still locked in their embrace, were falling and the legs of the chair splintered on the cobbles as the rope's cut end flicked empty in the London wind.

'We must cut him down,' the Sheriff said, having at last read the reprieve.

The crowd, fickle as ever, now cheered because the victim they had despised had cheated the hangman. He would live, he would go free, he would paint.

Sandman slid from his horse and gave the reins to a constable. Other constables had used the ladder that waited for any member of the crowd who wanted to be touched by a hanged man's hand and those men now took hold of Lord Christopher Carne. Sandman saw his lordship weeping and felt no pity. Worse, he could hear Venables's choking noises and see the dying man's rope quivering above the black-draped platform. He turned away, trying and failing to discover some consolation that even one soul had been stolen from the gallows. 'Thank you, Sergeant,' he said.

'It's over then,' Berrigan said, dismounting.

'It's over,' Sandman said.

'Rider!' Lord Alexander shouted from the scaffold. 'Rider!'

Sandman turned back.

Lord Alexander limped about the hole made by the fallen trapdoor. 'Rider! Would you play a single wicket match? This Saturday?'

Sandman stared in momentary astonishment at his friend, then looked at Hood. 'Thank you,' he shouted, but the words were lost in the crowd's howling. Sandman bowed. 'Thank you,' he called again.

Hood returned the bow, but then held up a single finger. 'Just one, Captain,' he called, 'just one, and they'll hang a thousand before you snatch another back.'

'It's against Budd!' Lord Alexander shouted. 'Rider, can you hear me? Rider! Where are you going?'

Sandman had turned away again and now had his arm round Berrigan's shoulder. 'If you want breakfast at the 'sheaf,' he told the Sergeant, 'then you'd best hurry before the crowd fills the taproom. And thank Sally for me, will you? We would have failed without her.'

'We would, too,' Berrigan said. 'And you? Where are you going?'

Sandman limped away from the gallows, ignored by the crowd who demanded that Corday, their new hero, be brought to the scaffold's platform. 'Me, Sam?' Sandman answered. 'I'm going to see a man about a loan so that you and I can go to Spain and buy some cigars.'

'You're going to ask for a loan,' Berrigan said, 'in those boots?'

Sandman looked down to see that both boot soles were gaping away from the uppers. 'I'm going to ask for a loan,' he said, 'and for his daughter's hand in marriage as well, and though I'm not a betting man, I'll wager you the price of a new pair of boots that he'll say yes to both. He's not getting a rich son-in-law, Sam, he's just getting me.'

'Lucky him,' Berrigan said.

'Lucky you,' Sandman said, 'and Sally, too.' He smiled and they walked on down Old Bailey. Behind them Venables slowly choked as, above him, Corday blinked in the new day's sunlight. Sandman looked back once from the corner of Ludgate Hill and he saw the gallows black as any devil's heart, and then he turned the corner and was gone.

Historical Note

I have tried to keep the facts of the tale as accurate as may be. There was, indeed, an occasional Investigator appointed to enquire into the circumstances of capital cases, and he was selected by the Home Secretary who, in 1817, was Henry Addington, first Viscount Sidmouth.

This was one of the busiest periods for the gallows of England and Wales (Scottish law was, and remains, different). There was a belief that savage and extreme punishment would curb crime and so 'the bloody code' was forged and, by 1820, there were over 200 capital crimes on the statute books. Most of these were property crimes (theft, arson or forgery), but murder, attempted murder and rape were also punishable by death as, indeed, was sodomy (between 1805 and 1832 there were 102 executions for rape in England and Wales and 50 for sodomy). Most executions were for robbery (938 between 1805 and 1832), with murder the second most common capital offence (395 cases). In all there were 2028 executions in England and Wales between 1805 and 1832, and the victims included women and at least one child as young as fourteen. This averages about 75 executions a year, of which about one fifth took place outside Newgate, while the rest were in assize towns or at Horsemonger Lane, but some years the gallows were much busier and the period between 1816 and 1820 was among the busiest, averaging over 100 executions a year. Yet, and this is a crucial point, only about ten per cent of those condemned to death were actually executed. The vast majority had their sentences commuted (almost invariably to transportation to Australia). Thus, between 1816 and 1820, when 518 executions took place in England and Wales, there were actually 5853 sentences of death passed.

What accounts for this enormous discrepancy? Mercy? It was not a merciful age. Instead the figures betray a cynical exercise of social control. The friends and relatives of a person condemned to death would invariably petition the crown (which meant the Home Secretary) and they would do their utmost to secure the signatures of prominent members of society, such as aristocrats, politicians or senior churchmen, knowing that having such names on a petition made it more likely to be granted. Thus were bonds of subservient gratitude forged. This was never made explicit, but the process of condemnation, petition and reprieve was so well understood and established that it cannot have another explanation.

Many felons were unlucky and had their petitions rejected, or else made no petition, and their deaths became public spectacles. In London the executions used to be at Tyburn's famous gallows, 'the triple tree', which stood at what is now Marble Arch, but in the late eighteenth century the scaffold was moved to Old Bailey. I have tried, in the first and last chapters, to describe the process of a Newgate execution as accurately as it may be depicted after a lapse of two hundred years, and I have used the real names of many of the participants; thus the Keeper of Newgate was William Brown (and he did indeed serve devilled kidneys to the guests who came to watch the hangings), the Ordinary was Horace Cotton and the hangman was James ('Jemmy') Botting, who lacked an assistant in 1817. Charles Corday, of course, is fictional, but he could well have survived his hanging. A number of folk survived, usually because they were cut down too soon, and it would be some years before the 'long drop' was adopted which killed more or less instantaneously. I owe a great debt of gratitude to Donald Rumbelow, author of, among many other good books, *The Triple Tree*, for his great help in disentangling some of the more confusing details of Newgate procedure during the Regency period. I am also most grateful to Elizabeth Cartmale-Freedman, who helped with the research, and to James Hardy Vaux who, in 1812, during his involuntary exile in Australia, compiled his *Vocabulary of the Flash Language*.

The original inspiration for *Gallows Thief* came from V. A. C. Gatrell's book *The Hanging Tree* (Oxford, 1994), a book that combines a scholarly account of the English and Welsh experience of execution between 1770 and 1868 with a fine and controlled anger against capital punishment. *The Hanging Tree*'s cover picture alone, which is Gericault's sketch of an English public hanging in 1820, is a stunning indictment of a barbaric punishment. To Professor Gatrell I offer thanks and the assurance that any mistakes in *Gallows Thief* come not from him, nor from any other source, but are entirely of my own making.